THE ONCE AND FUTURE, NOW

M F Mathias

Text copyright © M F Mathias 2023
Design copyright © M F Mathias 2023
All rights reserved.

M F Mathias has asserted his right under the Copyright, Designs and Patents Act 1988 to be identified as the author of this work.

No part of this book may be reprinted or reproduced or utilised in any form or by electronic, mechanical or any other means, now known or hereafter invented, including photocopying or recording, or in any information storage or retrieval system, without the permission in writing from the Publisher and Author.

This title is intended for the enjoyment of adults, and is not recommended for children due to the mature content (swearing, violence) it contains.

First published 2023

Formatting services carried out by Rowanvale Books.

A CIP catalogue record for this book is available from the British Library.
Paperback ISBN: 9798373047807

To Mam, Monty and all of us moulded by Millbrook.

CHAPTER ONE

A BEGINNING

12 years ago

It was called 'Bloody Thursday'.
Something happened in the world for 12 seconds on that day.
It was bad.
Like really, really bad.
It was a wave of complete hate, and it touched every single inch of the world.

In a café quite close to Baggot Street Bridge in Dublin, Grainne Leary sat reading the paper that had been left by a previous customer, waiting for her poached eggs to arrive. She'd just been for a check-up at the dentist and thought she'd pop in before heading home. She loved this cafe. Since her retirement, two years before, she'd made a weekly visit into the city from where she lived on the outskirts, and she always started with a bit of food and a cup of tea. The place was light, never too packed and she liked the waitresses. She especially loved 'that young eastern European girl' as she called her. The girl had told Grainne her name and it was on her name badge, but Grainne didn't feel she'd pronounce it properly, so she just called her 'dear'. They always enjoyed a chat, she always asked how Grainne was and how her son over in London was doing, especially since the arrival of his baby daughter. Grainne liked that and liked her.

Her order hadn't arrived yet and Grainne took a sip of tea. She looked up at the clock hanging above the counter. Ten past two.

She stood up violently from her chair, letting it crash to the floor before telling the waitress to piss off back to where she came from and die. She picked up the small jug of milk that was on the table and, screaming, threw it hard against the wall. The waitress, Mila – who, incidentally, was Polish – wasn't paying any attention. She was on the far side of the room smashing old Pat Hurley's face repeatedly into the remains of his ham and tomato panini.

Outside the café people had either gotten out of their cars to attack strangers or had used their cars to ram anybody they could.

It was a sunny Texas morning and Ted Stryffeler jr, 22, had just tapped 'send' on an email arranging a meeting. A local youth soccer team were looking for a bit of sponsorship and Ted, who had just taken over the family business, Stryffleler Blinds, wanted to help out. I say just, but Ted Junior had managed west San Antonio's leading blinds provider for about 10 months, and he loved it. He sat back on his new ergonomic office chair and thought he would offer Gloria a cup of coffee. He'd only just stopped calling Gloria 'Aunt Gloria'. She'd been office manager since the business started in '92 and, although she could have retired five years ago, he was so glad she'd stayed on. When it came to Stryffeler Blinds for all of west San Antonio's darkening needs, Gloria had been there and done that.

On the dot of ten past eight, he opened the bottom draw of his desk, pulled out his pistol and shot her eighteen times just as she was picking up his monitor to crush his head.

Ho Choi Jung was really enjoying his cruise in the east China sea. They'd just visited Shanghai, his second time there and his wife Choi Jung Mi's first. A wonderful day had been followed by a lovely dinner on board. He felt calm pleasure in retirement and barely thought of his old life as a postman in a small village north of Seoul. They'd both gotten into the routine of having a walk around the ship after dinner and before bed. She asked him what he was thinking but he didn't want to answer, he wanted to punch her in her face which is what he was about to do when she grabbed him and threw him overboard.

They called it Bloody Thursday because it was easy, but it only lasted seconds and for people in Australia, New Zealand and all the way to Apia in Samoa it happened on the Friday and the fact that it was the middle of night saved many of them from the chaos. Twelve seconds and a death rate in the millions; stabbings, shootings, strangulations, loving gentle pets attacking their owners and vice versa, and literal family feuds. When the madness ended, nearly eight billion people vomited as one, as if they needed to expel the evil that had gotten into them.

I like beginnings. Lovely word, full of hope, full of anticipation or it could be one of fear if you let it in. You don't have to, it's all up to you, it is your decision, so why not choose hope?

Most people don't.

Beginnings is where we are at and where there are beginnings you will find me, or someone like me. Why? Because we tell stories. The beginning and the end and every point in between. To the creatures who can see us – and there aren't many – we are known by a multitude of names. Watchers and Tellers are common. Witnesses amongst certain Magick races. Guardian Angels I have heard from 'This' world but never in 'That' one. We aren't though. No wings and we never ever get involved in the story, so no guarding. But we are witnesses or watchers and we are tellers. Our purpose, one we have had from the real, actual, beginning and will have at the very, very end is to witness stories and then tell them to those that will listen. You see, stories feed the spirit of the Worlds. Those moments of hope, of despair, of joy, of struggle, of love and everything above, below and alongside is sustenance to life.

I call myself Garan. A conceit, because my people don't have names but, in the year you know as 580AD, I decided I wanted a name and the name Garan made me happy. So, if you are listening to this or reading it or if it's been downloaded into your brain cloud then you are now at the beginning with me.

It had been a few decades since my last story, and I spent the following years travelling the Worlds telling that and other stories I have. I then spent a delicious four years sitting in a tree in a church yard in Wales, just thinking and watching and occasionally annoying the squirrels. You don't need to know that. Or maybe you do? Yes, of course you do, because that's where I was when I felt the urge of a new story. One minute I was watching a sad man walk his dachshund past my tree, the world of worry on his shoulders, but for his hound complete love in his heart, and the next I was in neither of the Worlds but in between. A place of balance, a place of deities.

I was in the palace of the Morrigu and I knew right there and then that my story was to be one of importance. The palace hall was of white marble, with grand columns and statues of gods and goddesses, both those who had been and those who were yet to come. The hall stretched for as far as my eyes could see but, in the middle, stood a television, a red mat in front and on it, a small table with a clean ashtray. There was a couch and an armchair facing the television and, sitting on them, the Morrigu. It was as if they had lifted a living room from the 1980s and placed it in the centre of a mile-long hall.

As soon as I appeared their eyes quickly glanced up at me before returning to the programme they were watching. It was Badb, dark eyed, dark haired and dark humoured Badb, that spoke first. Whilst we had seen each other over the centuries I had not seen her in this form for millennia. Dressed in a smock of feathers, she was draped across the one armchair, her legs hanging over the armrests. She smiled but didn't take her eyes from the television.

'So, we can start then?' she said in a broad Glaswegian accent. She looked up again at me briefly. 'Morning fathead.'

It was my turn to smile; she was a potty mouth in any form. I bowed. 'A very good morning Badb Catha.'

To her left was the couch and, sitting closest to Badb, a wizened old woman, hunched up with a thick woollen blanket covering her legs. She continued to watch the television but answered Badb, in the thick Welsh accent of the northern mountains 'Yes sister, we can, but only after this is finished. The story starts when we do...' She looked up at me and smiled a toothless smile, her eyes alight like a fire. 'Apologies, Tale-teller, I am well aware the story starts when you arrive but if you'll indulge an old woman. You are the one who has given yourself a name, are you not?'

I bowed again, a little surprised that she knew that detail of my life 'Yes Ceridwen of Macha, I have given myself the name Garan.'

'Strong name,' she said, almost to herself, as she turned her attention back to the screen.

'A wonderful name...' purred the woman on the other side of the couch.

Dannan was the maiden of the Morrigu, and her beauty made men's legs turn to jelly. She was dressed in underwear and a t-shirt, her red hair tousled as she changed position to make herself more comfortable. She looked directly at me and though I am unaffected by such things as lust and desire, I could recognise the dangerous but wonderful power that exploded from her. 'Come, Garan the Watcher, and do some watching with us. We have one more episode of the Coronation Street to enjoy and then we are all yours.' Her accent was of the south west of the green island called Ireland, a place she loved very much.

I bowed to her 'A lovely offer, Dannan of the Flowers, I thank you.'

She shifted towards the armrest of the couch and patted the seat next to her. Half an hour later the credits rose up the screen and, as one, they put out the cigarettes they had been smoking. Just outside this mock-up of a living room, a stool appeared.

Badb blew out the last remaining smoke 'Garan, time to piss off and do your job. We have given you a stool to make you more comfortable.' I needed no stool, nor did I ever feel uncomfortable, but the gesture was well meant, and I appreciated it.

'Mistress Badb,' I said, simply, in thanks.

'So?' asked Dannan 'This is it?'

'We can't talk about this here!' said Badb.

Ceridwen snapped her fingers, the hall that held the sitting room disappeared and now we were in a cramped cottage, the only light was from an open wood fire beneath a large black bubbling cauldron. The Morrigu stood around it, their faces lit in orange while I sat on my stool at the back of the room.

'End of the Worlds?' asked Badb.

'Could be,' shrugged Ceridwen.

'What do we want? What do we need?' Dannan was not asking her sisters, she was reciting, she was asking the universe and she knew the answer.

'A big story,' they said in unison. 'Sacrifice.'

'Yes, it is starting with sacrifice and all will lead from there.' said Ceridwen.

'Time for me to change, sisters,' said Badb, almost sadly. 'Glad I managed a quick fag before…' and, with a sucking noise, she was gone and where she had been, she was again, this time as a crow. She didn't mind being a crow, she minded changing into one just like she minded changing back. 'I bloody hate that,' she cawed, flapping her wings and landing on Ceridwen's shoulder, gently tapping the side of her head with her beak as a mark of affection.

'So, the Dark rises? Will we help?' Dannan asked.

Ceridwen looked up from the cauldron, 'We won't take sides this time, sister but we will push and pull a little.' She smiled.

'Battle! I want battle,' cawed Badb.

'Yes, let's do some meddling…let us feed off this story. Let us send prophecies,' laughed Dannan.

They looked up at me. 'Bye Garan,' said Ceridwen 'Enjoy.' And I was somewhere else for …**another beginning.**

I was in a blood spattered cavern, deep under the ground in Herefordshire, with three equally blood covered individuals, two men and a woman. Cloaked and on their knees, they took down their hoods, looked at each other and smiled. Now I could see them clearly, I could see that not one of them was more than a teenager. The young woman held up a scythe and wiped it on one of the numerous bodies that lay, mutilated, before them.

The power they felt was exquisite. The sacrifices had worked, and the gateway had opened. They sensed him before they saw him, even for people as dark as they, the evil slithering in through the rip in reality they'd created made them feel revulsion. The three had lived many lives, his return their sole purpose. Unlike other long-lived peoples, they were kept alive by evil, their souls transplanted into the bodies of sacrificial humans especially selected by the three as their next vehicle through life. The fate of the souls they ripped out? They didn't know and they didn't care.

The one now called Cate was the first to steady herself into action. 'Quickly, move the body into the rip.'

The body was another that the soul had just departed, torn screaming in terror from something into nothing. The breeding farms of the Dark produced good stock which were physically perfected from birth. The form on the floor, stark as the only carcass in that ancient cave not covered in blood, was one of a physical giant. The two men, both strong, struggled to lift the body.

'Swing it.' Cate said.

'You are not in charge, sister!' the one called Killian snapped.

'Just do it,' she answered.

He was about to shout again but the one called Shane interrupted. 'Can't we just get an acolyte in here and do this? We aren't slaves!'

You can change your body every forty years for millennia, make it bigger, faster, taller, better, but if you were an idiot in your first life you were more than likely an idiot for eternity. That's what Cate thought before she responded. 'Are you serious? We have waited since the time when Magick started to seep from This world – thousands of years! We've overseen the coming together and training of millions of warriors of darkness and chaos. We've changed our lives and our bodies. I've put up with you two bastards waiting for this moment – and now, after everything, you want Simon, an HR manager from Shrewsbury, to join us for the return of a god just because you *don't want to lift something?*'

'*Do it now.*' This from the gate, not in the language they had been speaking; this was ancient and though they didn't recognise the words, they understood them. The only pumping blood in the place drained from their faces, Cate dropped to one knee, eyes down, while the two men quickened towards the bright lights of the gate. The last collective effort saw them swing the body into the gate and...

...nothing.

The men joined the woman on their knees and then...

...nothing.

After about two minutes, they started to look up at each other, slivers of doubt sliding in. They had been close before, they had failed before or been thwarted by Arthur or by the three king bastards, but they'd never heard the voice until now. Surely, this was it?

They heard laughing then, slow starting with manic rising. It sounded like war. Their eyes fixed on the floor.

'Look up, my loyal children.' The voice was deep and sonorous, beautiful even, and they did as they were bid.

A god stood naked before them. They had chosen this body well. He was physical perfection, six foot four inches, with a strong, handsome face. It was only now that Cate saw the irony: they had chosen a kind face. It terrified her even more.

He looked down at his hands and flexed his fingers. Still smiling, he shook his feet, getting used to his new shell. For a moment he glowed, and they felt power. He laughed again.

Killian heard movement behind him and turned to see the mutilated bodies of the sixty-six people they had recently tortured and killed rise and stand, pupil-less eyes fixated on nothing.

The god stopped laughing. 'So? What now?' he asked, the smile still on his handsome face.

Cromh du, Foul One, the destroyer of souls, the horned god, had returned and those mad people who hold banners that say 'the end of the world is nigh' had never been closer to being right in their lives.

***

A hundred miles or so west of this blood-soaked cave was another cavern. It existed between Worlds but, at the same time, didn't exist at all. Twelve bodies awoke after more than three quarters of a century asleep. One was Arthur ap Uther, the once and future King, who slept until the world needed him most.

He rubbed his eyes and had an enormous stretch. The others were in various states of awakening, groaning and yawning and looking to their leader who, oblivious to their stares, was gazing at toes he hadn't seen since 1943. He looked up, rolled his eyes at them and shouted, a huge gutsy 'TEA!'

CHAPTER TWO

THE PROPHECY OF GERTRUDE OLIVER

Now. Whenever now is.

Gertrude Oliver lay on her hospital bed, propped upright by a tower of pillows. She had the smiling, serene face of a woman who'd spent most of her life on her feet and was just glad to have a proper reason to be in bed at midday. The reason she was able to lie down unselfishly was that she needed an operation. She was also smiling because she was sedated. Not heavily but enough to smile while her family crammed themselves into a small but private hospital room.

Gertrude was the centre of their lives at home, and she was the same here. Two grandkids sat on the end of the bed, mesmerized by whatever was on their tablet screens, with Gertrude's youngest girls, the grandkids' mothers, sitting in chairs nearby, also oblivious to the world around them as they looked at their phones. Her eldest, Shirley, and second daughter, Judy, were sat at her bedside talking over each other and at their mother. At that very moment Gertrude thought back to a programme she'd seen on the Vietnam war where she'd heard that, though injured soldiers had been given morphine, it didn't actually remove the pain, they knew it was there, but it had taken the edge away. She looked over at her girls, smiling and nodding and thought that maybe the hospital had given her 'pain in the arse' morphine where she could see her daughters moaning, knew they were moaning but really didn't care. Jonathan, her husband, sat next to her just staring into space, holding her hand. He had a great talent for blocking out the white noise that was his family.

'Yes love,' she answered a moan from Shirley, probably something to do with her charmed life that Gertrude could only have dreamed of at that age.

Something changed.

No one in the room but Gertrude felt it. The drugs stopped working but the pain disappeared. Everything became crystal clear as if, for the first time in years, someone had fiddled inside her head and made her eyes come back into focus. There was fear but it was dampened for a moment by a deep longing for what her eyesight had once been and a sadness for something that was lost.

'Shut up.' she said suddenly to Shirley, interrupting another monologue. The grandkids looked up as did her three other daughters, mouths open.

'Mum!' Shirley exclaimed, utterly hurt and shocked, having not been told to do anything by her mother since 1983.

'Shut up.' This time Gertrude pointed her finger at Shirley, and it worked. 'Get out! Everybody, leave the room. I love you but get out. Move!'

Jonathan stood up, concern etched on his face. 'Not you love,' she said. 'Stay, I'm fine. Get my phone. No questions. Hurry,' she added firmly.

The girls were shaken now. 'Mum, we're worried. What's the matter? Shall I get a nurse?' Melanie asked as they all gathered by the door.

'Last time, Melanie Oliver, out!'

Once the door had closed, she took the phone from Jonathan and was about to fish in the bag for her reading glasses before realising she didn't need them. She scrolled down the phone's address book and pressed the screen when she'd found the number she was looking for.

'Good morning…' The person on the other end of the phone stopped, looked at the clock and realised it was five minutes past midday, so she chuckled and carried on in her light Cardiff accent. 'Sorry. Good afternoon, thank you for calling 'All

Our Futures' prophecy line. I am Pria, how can we help you or how can you help us? Pria had been saying the same thing for about 17 months but still managed to imbue the set script with a newness which not many amongst the 'zombies', as the first contact prophecy takers were nicknamed, could manage. She waited with a smile while there was a tiny pause. A booming northern English voice broke the silence.

'It's Dave from Fylde! It's going to piss down with rain in Yorkshire next Thursday.' Then, before she could ask for his designated prophecy ID and password, the line went dead.

'Idiot,' she whispered to herself, her smile breaking for a second. 'All Our Futures' had been around, in one shape or another for tens of thousands of years. For the first tens of thousands of those years, give or take a week, people had just shouted prophecies into nothingness unless there was an audience or enough gossips to make sure other people heard it. There had always been various musings, shoutings and announcements by Magickers, seers, prophets, soothsayers and drunks walking home after a big night, but it was only, say, at the birth of royalty where anyone got to hear them.

By the early eighteenth century Magickers were employed to roam the country catching second-hand prophecies or spending time near the people who made them. It was very haphazard. With this in mind, by the nineteenth century, the Magick community, heavily influenced by the British Empire of the time, did what the British Empire did best, well not best because that was invading and conquering countries that were quite happy messing up their own lives, but bringing order out of chaos. And that meant creating a huge prophetic bureaucracy.

Departments were set up all over the isles, and prophets who were part of the Magicker community organised themselves into 'orders' or 'societies'. It was all very Victorian. Seers would write down their prophecies and send them off by post to be looked at by their betters and, if they were any good, they even got a bit of money for them.

Fast forward to our time and here we see Tŷ Aneurin – Aneurin House if you prefer English – 8 floors of office space that everybody in Cardiff thinks is the HQ of a utility company... that's if they think of it at all. It's there, it's big, but come on, how often do you think about what goes on in a building?

I don't know what the rest of Tŷ Aneurin is for but the second and third floor is a dedicated call centre for receiving prophecies. Fourth and fifth floors analyse the ninety-nine percent humdrum prophecies and pass on difficult ones to those who can deal with them. Sixth floor has the inhouse seers and soothsayers who are really no better than the phone zombies on 2 and 3. Eighth floor deals with the 1%, the very rare and very important. Seventh floor? Management and HR, someone has to work out wages, sickness and leave. Even two headed Kraals from the terror caves of the Soothadeen ranges want to know how much holiday they have left before April.

You probably know this because you live there but your world can be an awful, nasty place. It's not just the eternal battle between good and evil but also the non-stop bickering. If it's not nations or religions, it's some other group. Those humans don't like some other humans, the orcs don't like anyone, not even themselves, while the elves love themselves a little too much and are too stuck up to dislike anybody else, otherwise they would. It's tiring and a waste. With so much conflict, information becomes important, prophecy even more so. It's worth a lot of money and in 1983 it was monetised by Margaret Thatcher (your third ever Magick-adept Prime Minister) who privatised the prophecy industry.

To be fair, nobody could have done it but her. Privatising prophecy was akin to privatising punk. Most types with 'The Gift' who became prophets or seers were unlikely to have become engineers or scientists. They were so far out there they made hippies look like extremely anal statisticians or people who'd been in the army for 22 years. But, with a lot of stick and absolutely no carrot whatsoever Mrs Thatcher succeeded and now we have call centres like this one; prophecy, professionalism and capitalism combined. Timed loo breaks, funny jumper Fridays and phone zombies on minimum pay with minimal training for maximised targets.

It was a great first job for a young person from a Magick family who just wanted some money; and that brings us back to Pria. She started at Tŷ Aneurin as a stop gap, thought it was easy and stayed and here she is, about to take another call, having just listened to Eve from Redcar telling her that someone's Uncle Phil somewhere in California was going to stub his toe. Pria typed it up and sent it upstairs. She hated the days when all she had was what the zombies called space wasters. But her day – and the course of human history – was about to change.

She pressed the button to accept another call.

'Good afternoon, thank you for calling 'All Our Futures' prophecy line, I'm Pria. How can we help you or how can you help us?'

'Hello love, Gertrude Oliver, here. My ID is FM227,' said the voice of Mrs Oliver from her hospital bed.

'Hello, Mrs Oliver, I'm just putting in your details. Password please?'

'Yes, of course, it's 'Jonathan 1971,' and I'm not being rude, but this is coming very soon, and I have the same feeling as last time,' said Gertrude.

Pria smiled. 'Of course Mrs Oliver…' Pria saw Gertrude Oliver's prophecy record onscreen and stopped smiling. In the 17 months she'd been working at Tŷ Aneurin, Pria had only had a priority two call once. Mrs Oliver was a priority one. She had prophesized twice in the last forty years, and both had been big, and both had been bang on. Pria paused for a second. 'Hold please, I'm putting you through.'

She pressed two buttons on her keyboard. Then she stood up and shouted to Carla Lewis, the shift manager who sat at the main desk in front of all the phone desks, like the invigilator's table in a school sports hall during exam time. In front of her was the kind of light normally seen on the top of police cars. It started flashing red.

'Ma'am, priority one, I've put it through,' Pria sat down. Carla looked at the big screen behind her to see who was not on a call.

'Ok,' she turned back to the room, 'pay attention! I want desk 5 and 17, as well as Pria, transcribing the priority one. Up you go!'

Up on the 8th floor, everything went bananas.

Kiyohisa Taguchi, Yvonne Fenner and Kristy Bell were the Magickers on duty. They all stopped what they were doing and dashed to the 'Priority room'. Outside, people ran everywhere, shouting. They needed to be ready but at least in Taguchi, Fenner and Bell they had the best so at least there was no panic there.

The priority room was glass walled on three sides with the fourth taken up by a huge window looking out on the Welsh capital. In the centre was a table in the shape of a hexagon, a seat at each of the six sides and what looked like a crystal on a plinth in the middle. The three Magickers sat, equally spaced, around the table, a segment separating each from the others. In front of them a sunken tray containing a turquoise gel was built into the table.

The gel was the latest thing, developed in Taguchi's native Japan, and purchased recently by 'All Our Futures'. It amplified the meanings of a prophecy; words could only tell you so much. The three transcribers placed their hands into the blue gel.

The call came through. The crystal glowed, the gel glowed, they glowed.

Silence hit; a sense of awe grew until…

'HELLO LOVE, are you still there?' It was Gertrude. She continued 'It's here, I can't hold it in, I have to let it…'

The prophecy came in Gertrude Oliver's voice but amplified in sound and texture; it went on for about two minutes, her voice booming while panicked people transcribed and analysed.

Silence. And then…Gertrude. 'Did you get that loveys? It's a big one so I hope you got it all.' And then, as if to herself,

'Well, well, well, the end of the world is on its way…' Another silence then, 'OK, lovely to speak to you all, ta ta, toodleoo.' And Gertrude ended the call.

Kiyohisa, Yvonne and Kristy stared at each other. Their faces showed the seriousness of the situation: if all that Gertrude had prophesied came to pass, everything was going to change.

As with all prophecies of this import, the people who had listened and transcribed brought the recordings to the priority room and waited outside.

Kristy Bell waved them in. There was panic there, none of them had heard a prophecy this big before. They were brought inside and invited to sit at the board table with Kristy, Yvonne and Kiyohisa.

Kristy smiled and broke the tension. Everybody liked her, she'd been at the firm for more years than anyone could remember. Organiser of Secret Santas and of do's – leaving, Christmas and summer – and rememberer of birthdays and special occasions. Everybody liked Kristy so you can imagine the surprise on everybody's faces when, still smiling, she pulled a pistol from her small handbag and, calmly and with one shot per person, started firing at everybody around the table.

Pria. Bang. Gone.

Panic.

People got up, screaming, two ran for the door.

Bang, then bang. Gone.

Yvonne Fenner, Kristy's friend of ten years, bang, gone. The pistol aimed at Kiyohisa Taguchi. The young Japanese man had been recruited recently so Kristy didn't know that he wasn't just a Magicker of prophecy but one of battle and, when she squeezed off another shot, he mouthed, summoned and threw a blazing wave of heat at her. The round hit him in the chest, knocking him to the ground. His shock at these developments were mixed with anger knowing that this prophecy was being stolen. Why not pay for it? It would be theirs and theirs alone albeit for a time. There was honour in that, honour in business, there was no honour in this slaughter.

He was bleeding out from the wound but also weakening by use of such violent, powerful magick. He had no idea if Kristy was dead or if she had people coming to finish them all off. He needed to get the message out, to democratise it, and he knew it would take the last vestiges of his life force to do it. He didn't know her name, but Pria's dead eyes stared at him from the floor and, through his anger, he saw that she still clutched her prophecy recording device. He needed to get to it, he had to get it in his hand, and he needed to release his life Magick so it could be broadcast out amongst the soundwaves. And maybe, just maybe, someone would be listening. It might not work but he had no other option. Bleeding, and breathing heavily, he crawled over.

Meanwhile, on the other side of the table Kristy lived. Just.

The blast had hit her, burning her skin raw. She'd screamed, dropping to her scorched knees but still leaning on the table.

'BASTARDS', she screamed. It was the first swear word that had passed her lips since she had started working for the company thirty years before. Since she had left the training pens. Since she'd become Kristy Bell.

She'd thought she'd been forgotten. She hadn't been contacted for decades. Kristy had a husband, a real one, one she loved. She had two daughters.

Why now?

It didn't matter. While she had loved being Kristy, it was time to be a Dark Mistress again.

Her prophecy recording device had been destroyed in the blast alongside her laptop. She managed to crawl to the central recording device, typed in what she needed and sent it. The agony was unbearable, she wanted to cry but there were no tear ducts undamaged from the wave of heat. She destroyed all evidence of Gertrude's prophecy from all systems and crushed out of existence the PRD tubes that the others had left before their last living seconds on earth.

Then she heard a grunt and realised that she wasn't the only one alive in the room.

'Shit.' Her second swear word in thirty years came from gritted teeth as she saw her dropped pistol metres away. She managed to crawl over the corpse of her friend Yvonne and gingerly pick it up just in time to see Kiyohisa's hand clutch the PRD of Pria, the nice girl who was in Kristy's monthly book club.

'No!' she screamed struggling to lift the pistol up.

'No!' he heard as his fingertips touched the PRD.

She fired. Missed.

His hand reached it.

She aimed again and fired.

He held it now, clutching it tightly. He grimaced and released his life force. The prophecy was released into the world.

The bullet hit him.

He was already dead.

Kristy thought she had done it, but she didn't feel satisfaction at completing her mission, she felt cheated. Why hadn't they just left her alone? She could smell her burning flesh as the alarms rang throughout the building. The pain was so great that she fell to the floor, screaming again at the impact. She thought of Ron, Jemma and Jessica and then pressed the gun into her forehead and pulled the trigger.

Bang. Gone.

CHAPTER THREE

HOW DO YOU SOLVE A PROBLEM LIKE KING ARTHUR?

Cromh Du looked over the city from his office near the top of the building. His building. Was it his building though? It wasn't his by might or guile, he hadn't commanded armies to take or destroy it. It was another one of the 'portfolios' his disciples had acquired in his name.

He was brooding.

He stared at the little lights that shone from the thousands of windows of London. 'Little lights, little people, little lives,' he muttered.

Cromh Du walked back to his desk and sat, his huge, muscular frame physically forcing the chair down. He had not enjoyed himself since his return. Had it really been twelve years since that day? The Glorious Return, his people called it. The mortals – the ants – called it Bloody Thursday, but they barely mentioned it now, fearing that speaking of it might cause it to happen again. The repercussions of that day were still felt; malevolence spewed forth from chimney, weapon, keyboard or mouth and it made its way around the world, weakening mankind, making the human race ripe for the rule of a dark god.

Continents, nations, cultures, peoples, races, religions, sects and groups concentrated so much on the miniscule things that made them different that they were blinded to what united them. It had always been so but since that Thursday, disunity and mistrust had grown. Hope was dying and the apathy, despondency and hate that grew to take its place, meant that the world provided him with more power than he could ever remember. But the waiting was also so very, very boring.

From the moment Cromh Du had returned to the Worlds of the Living, his desire was to get out there, get his armies together, and slaughter, destroy and conquer. But his people had counselled patience. They had stayed his instinctive move to gather the Dark and tear this so-called civilisation to shreds. He closed his eyes in pleasure at the exquisite prospect of genocide. He shivered as he remembered the ecstasy of the World Wars that he had fed off and exulted in, even in exile, building his strength ready for his return.

'Why not do it again?' It wasn't the first time the thought had come, and he knew why. A mortal once said that the definition of madness was to do the same thing over and over again and expect a different outcome. Funny that an ant should come up with something so interesting.

He had been more than dubious when his children had explained their plan. It had seemed wrong, counter intuitive. In This World his forces had been defeated 80 years ago, the disciples of the Dark who had infiltrated the Nazis had been crushed, some of his best prospects destroyed forever. They could have rebuilt quickly and fought soon after, but his people had learned a valuable lesson and now they hid in plain sight. They lay low in the higher echelons of life while they built and plotted.

They had also lost the grand fight in That World but, being a place without too much governance, it carried on much as before. The races that followed the Dark just went back to their own and enjoyed being bastards. The orcs returned to their lands in the east, fought amongst themselves or went on raids, and the goblins did likewise. The elves remained in isolation and the other myriad races just got on with things: no extinction, no grand plans, no big battles, just eating, shitting, sleeping, and rutting.

Cromh Du sneered at the petty lives of the Dark races and rose from his desk to stare out of the window once again. It was in This World where the plans were being made, but the patience needed for effective planning made him angry. Cromh Du was battle, carnage, and bowel-loosening fear, not politics, economics, or climate change. Frustrated, he clenched his fists. But patience meant that they had not showed their hands; if they had, it would have meant the rise of Arthur. Best, his children had told him, to bide their time, to destroy people's lives, create anger, fear, and chaos with stealth, and feed off what was to come.

He had listened and he admitted that it was working. The world was at a tipping point but now it was their time to listen. They had waited long enough and the prophecy they had received pointed to action. That's why he had his murderous children here. They needed to move on Arthur. Now.

***

Cromh Du's children were not used to waiting but wait they did. Shane Oriole sat back on the sofa while Cate Crowley and Killian Penhalligan stood and prowled. He was the future of politics, she was darling of the 'airwaves', and the other was head of a business empire...with torture.

The body of Cate Crowley had changed little. Soon after the return of Cromh Du she'd started as a newsreader or 'anchor' as Americans call them. For ten years she'd been the face of the news, telling people what was happening in the world. Stern face for bad news, smile of sunshine for the good. Cate Crowley made them think that everything was going to be OK, despite the fact that she was telling them about war, murder, hijacks, suicide bombings and other evils.

Cate, beautiful, confident, caring Cate was really, malicious, dangerous, evil Cate. She was adored as the nation's 'voice' and the love was made even stronger when she came first on the hit Saturday night show 'Celebrity Military Bootcamp Disco Off'. She no longer read the news; she didn't need to as she now had her own shows. Yes 'shows' plural. Tuesday morning was DNA tests, fighting, toothless mouths shouting, and Cate in the middle, judging and caring. Thursday night was celebs, name dropping, chummy, knee touching while laughing, pushing books, films and shows, with Cate in the middle as everybody's friend.

Just at that moment she wanted to explode in anger, but she didn't dare. If the Dark One wanted them all out here for a month, she'd be phoning out for four weeks' worth of supplies.

Killian Penhalligon was equally angry but hid it better. When near Cate, they were like twins of perfection, both striking in looks, sharp in intellect and full of darkness. Penhalligon was the current darling of British politics. Celebrity looks and connections to match, champion of the common man but in reality, establishment front and centre. Much to Crowley's chagrin he was as popular as her and that was never meant to be the plan. In fact, he'd moved up faster than her, faster than any of them had expected. From candidate to MP, head of the party and Leader of Her Majesty's opposition in 8 years, and the new party was only a year older.

Sprawled on the sofa, Shane Oriole was utterly relaxed and unfazed by the wait. He was a thug, plain and simple. Businessman, criminal and double-hard bastard. Every forty or so years these three selected their next bodies to take over. They had a choice in all things but, unlike his brother and sister, Shane didn't go for looks. He wanted a body suited to stamina and violence, and he revelled in it. His part of the grand plan was business. His intelligence hadn't come through books or BBC 4, it came from deep inside. It was cunning, it was evolutionary. He was the first fish who crawled from the primordial gloop and encouraged those behind him to follow so that he could control them while he watched those left behind slowly die. He loved business – not the selling part or making anything, not for him creating something, nor even making money – no, all Shane Oriole wanted was to win, to crush, to dominate. Making a profit was a side-benefit while destroying other people. He spoke.

'I'm hungry.'

'You always bloody are,' Cate said, rolling her eyes,

Shane looked at her, 'It's ok for you, little miss starve myself body.'

Ignoring him, not letting him get on her nerves as usual, Cate went over to the drinks cabinet and poured herself one. She was the whisky drinker, that had never changed, whatever body she inhabited. 'Scotch' the ants called it. How derivative. She could just about handle a 12-year-old malt when there was nothing else to drink but here, she knew she could expect good stuff, special stuff, 50 years old.

She took a sip and closed her eyes with pleasure.

The distillery was in a Scottish valley she knew well. In the old language, the place had been called the Valley of Slaughter but that had been forgotten – at least by the ants – thousands of years ago. The slaughter had been such that the blood they had spilled that day had tainted both land and water, making the whisky even more special. She sipped it again, feeling it travelling down her throat.

'Drink?' She asked her brothers.

They both thanked her as she handed them over.

'Fifty-year-old? Not shy of 500 pounds?' Killian ventured as she handed him a glass.

'Five hundred and nine,' she replied.

Killian smiled. He liked knowing the cost of things. He knew the most expensive wines, art, food, cars and clothes but he didn't know the true worth of anything. And he didn't care. He bought a bottle of wine because it was expensive not because he liked the taste. A high-performance car was status, not an appreciation of engineering, design or speed. He only cared that it made him look good or that it would make people jealous.

The double doors to the main office clicked and slowly swung open, summoning them.

Oriole sprung to his feet, glad the waiting was over and walked straight in. Cate and Killian looked at each other. He shrugged, and they followed.

The moment they passed through the doors they felt Cromh Du's dark power. Though they were born of darkness it hit them. They all tried to mask their reaction, but Cromh Du could tell they were affected and it made him happy. Oriole sat in one of the chairs opposite the Dark God's desk while Killian stood directly behind him, using the back of the chair as a crutch until the nausea passed. Her Magick the most powerful of the three, Cate stood to one side, almost untouched except for the paleness of her skin as the blood retreated from it. She finished off the whisky in a final gulp.

'My children. I would tell you to get comfortable, but we haven't the time. It's fortunate that you have called so many of our people together in one place, as I have news and instructions for you.' As he spoke, he dampened his own Magick. However pleasant it was to toy with them, this was not a time for games.

'Firstly, daughter, after all of your work, have you found the one they call the Messenger?'

Cate nodded 'We have Dark-Father. As per the prophecy that was revealed to all, the high priests of our enemies intend to send her to Arthur. They believe the Messenger's meeting with him will be the starting point of our defeat. It seems that Arthur is unaware of their plans, but it matters not because the Messenger will not reach him. I have sent someone to stop her.'

Cromh Du nodded in acknowledgement, taking some satisfaction in the jealousy and suspicion on the faces of her brothers. 'It seems we are at a point of culmination, my children. Prophecies pour out like water from a broken cup, stars align and there are portents everywhere. The time has come for us to act.'

He moved to his desk and sat down, 'Prophecies have shouted out our glory, our victories and our demise in equal measure. We must ensure that we do not fail. For the first time since my arrival in this form, Arthur's warriors have been specifically named as the ones who will thwart the Dark.'

Cate and Killian looked at each other again, concern etched on their deceptively beautiful faces. Shane looked away uncomfortably.

Cromh Du frowned. 'Speak,' he ordered quietly, looking directly at Oriole.

Shane sat up straight. 'But Father, Arthur and his men are no longer a fighting force. Most of them have disappeared, others rot in reality, while we hear that Arthur has given up, a broken man. They cannot stop us. It's the Three Kings that should concern us!'

Cromh Du sprang to his feet, Oriole physically shrank while his siblings stepped back. They had felt their father's anger many times before.

'I have followed your plans of patience through to their conclusion. I was dubious, but you were correct. We are in almost total control in This World and our armies are amassed at the borders of every southern Kingdom in That World. These prophecies tell us that the time to act is now!'

Oriole turned to Cate and Killian, waiting for them to respond. Cate moved back towards the desk.

'Father, with panic spreading through Britain, the fear of war, of food shortages, we are only weeks away from control of the country. Killian could be the Prime Minister soon.'

Cromh Du stared at them for precisely three calm seconds. Then, with one powerful hand, he flipped his desk over their cowering heads. They all fell to the floor, prostrated before his anger.

'YOU THINK THIS IS A DISCUSSION? NO MORE WAITING!' Cromh Du's voice screamed inside their minds, the pressure threatening to explode their skulls. 'Don't you understand that all your plans will be for nothing if Arthur meets the messenger? Or if even one of his warriors is left alive? That would mean the end for us!'

His children continued to cower, but he said no more and, when they looked up, he was smiling as if nothing had happened.

They rose from the floor. 'The messenger will be dead soon Father,' Cate said nervously, 'and we will kill Arthur and his warriors, but it will take time to hunt them all down. They could be anywhere. And we do not know where Arthur is.'

Cromh Du smiled and walked slowly up to her. He grabbed her chin and brought his face close to hers. Then he sniffed. Her evil, combined with her Magick and the scent she was wearing made him want her, but he wouldn't take her. Not his only daughter. She was petrified and he could smell it, but her face showed nothing. He let go. 'Don't worry, I have been approached by someone who has told me everything. We have Arthur.'

They listened intently as he told them all he knew and discussed with them what was to happen.

Finally, he addressed Shane 'Your hatred of the Three Kings is well known, my son. I understand you have had Adda Mynyddmawr in your sights for weeks. The deed will be done tomorrow. What of the other two?'

Shane grunted 'Tommaltach is too well defended but that will soon change, and we have not seen the Druid for months.' He paused, smiled and clapped his hands 'But Mynyddmawr dies tomorrow.'

Slowly Cromh Du unbuttoned his shirt, taking it off and dropping it to the floor. His muscles rippled with movement, his skin turning black as coal, his eyes glowing red.

'Meeting is over my children,' he growled. Both sides of his skull began to bulge and horns protruded. 'Time to be a little more myself, I think,' he said as the horns became antlers. He turned to look out at the little lights again.

'Go and find Arthur and his men,' he ordered.

They turned and walked out but before they left the room, he shouted.

'And kill them all!'

CHAPTER FOUR
THE FIRST KILLING

'Kelly?' The barista shouted. They were at full tilt; an impatient queue of coffee addicts was getting bigger. 'I Would Cocoa' was actually a hot chocolate cafe or a Drinking Chocolate Emporium as the owner insisted on calling it, but at five minutes to eight in the morning it was taken over by people craving a hit of caffeine. Chocolate – hot, drinking or giving you a lovely massage – was not going to cut it.

'Kelly?' This time the shout was louder, more urgent because the barista had to move on.

A pinch faced woman with a face like thunder appeared. 'Is it a large cappuccino, extra shot with a hazelnut sprinkling?' She snapped. He took a quick glance down at the drinks before him. 'It's the only cappuccino here,' he answered with a smile.

Thunder Face rolled her eyes, 'Well, I SUPPOSE that's me. My name is Kerry not Kelly. KE-R-EE.' He passed over the large cappuccino, extra shot with a hazelnut sprinkling with 'Kelly' scrawled on the side, never changing his smiling expression.

'Thank you, Kerry. Have a lovely day,' he said.

Not getting the conflict she so clearly sought, she stormed off grumbling loudly. He'd been in since six and that was only the second arsehole so far, so on the whole not too bad.

The 'he' I'm talking about has 'Barry' on his name badge, but it's not his real name. His name is Bedwyr Bedrydant and he was a warrior of Arthur. Bedrydant was Old Welsh for 'perfect sinews', so he was 'Bedwyr of the Perfect Sinews' but you'll have heard of him as Bedivere because those fools that wrote about Arthur in the Middle Ages couldn't pronounce any of his warriors' names. So, Bedwyr became Bedivere and Peredur became Percival which he really hates, and then they invented people like Lancelot because they wanted it more 'modern'. Don't even get me started on 'Queen Guinevere…'

After moving to London, Bedwyr changed his name to Barry because even Bedivere was weird. He'd left Arthur and headed to London to disappear, and if anywhere helped you do that, it was that place. He called himself Barry Morgan; he'd met a load of Barrys since his return this time and he used Morgan as a reminder of the place in which he had been born so many centuries before.

He remembered the day he had left Arthur, and it still made his heart ache thinking about it. The ones that remained had all gathered downstairs. Bright winter morning sun had been shining through the pub windows as the last of the warriors took their seats at the tables. All except Galahad who leaned on the high bar he'd installed himself, and Owain who, oblivious to the seriousness of the coming conversation, dozed in a comfy seat next to the fire. Cai, close to anger as always, was next to him, poking and prodding at the fire though it was burning perfectly well. For a while, the only noise had been the mumbled chat occasionally interrupted by the booming laughter of bright-eyed Tristan and mountainous Adda Mynyddmawr.

Cai sighed loudly, 'Where is the old man? Let's get started. I've things to do.'

'What things?' Bedwyr asked with humour. He was always the calm yin to Cai's explosive yang.

'Playing with yourself!' called Adda, laughing, and there was a ripple of laughter as others joined in.

'Go to hell fat man,' Cai answered.

Adda laughed again which enraged Cai even more. 'Piss off!' he shouted.

'Be calm,' said Bedwyr to his sword brother, indicating the empty seat beside him. Cai slumped angrily and as he did so, the door opened and Arthur walked in.

He shone. Not literally, but his presence made the room lighter, more alive. Arthur, the once and future king, still dressed in the woven wool trousers and shirt he wore every time he had returned, whether decades or a thousand years ago. His face was always expressive whether it was conveying happiness, gloom, or deep thought and right now, his countenance was serious. But before the king could speak, the door he'd just come in through crashed open again and a body sprawled, full length on the floor. Everybody turned to see a young man in armour furiously trying to overcome his steel burden and get up which he eventually did with all the elegance of a baby giraffe's first attempt at standing. He smiled sheepishly; his face was all his Jamaican mother's but his smile? That looked familiar to anyone who cared to look.

Arthur gave the boy a sympathetic look, then, hearing Adda and Tristan laughing, turned a warning gaze on them. In thousands of years roaming the earth, there were only three people who could make Adda quiet with a stare and Arthur was one.

'This is Neil,' Arthur said. 'He is new, and he is one of my Fir C'nu.' Neil, still embarrassed, waved as Arthur continued. 'Actually, he is the only one that will be staying with me from now on. I've sent the others away. I don't need them anymore.'

There were gasps around the room. The Fir C'nu had been a constant in their long lives. Arthur had never been celibate, more horse manure from the fake news of antiquity but he'd lived many lives, and would it be so strange that he'd had a few dalliances with women over the years? He even married a few.

Since the beginning, Arthur and his warriors had been called back into This World when they were needed most, when evil was strong, when the end was near. I don't know who decided that. It just happened. They always awoke in the same cave, situated between This World and That, sometimes after a generation, sometimes after hundreds of years; back in the world after deep, dreamless, deathlike sleep. They had awoken at the same age every time, all of them, from 16-year-old Tristan to Arthur in his mid-thirties. They woke, they lived, loved and aged, albeit a tiny bit more slowly than you mortals. The C'nu was a cult that had grown up around the story of Arthur, taking the name of the goddess of the place where the cave was situated. In time, the men of C'nu, the 'Fir' came to be drawn from the descendants of Arthur, the sons, grandsons and the great-multiplied-many-times grandsons of the King. There were always twenty, and their roles changed with the situation at hand. During the times when Arthur was gone, it was their job to guard the cave to ensure that he and his warriors were safe. When he returned, the Fir C'nu became his personal retinue, pledged to fight alongside him and to give him advice about the new world he had awoken into. They were required to serve ten years before returning to the world with enough riches to live well and a package that involved a lovely pension, private healthcare and an annual magazine telling people what the old gang was up to. It was unthinkable that Arthur would send any of them away, still less that he would keep only one.

All the warriors had known that this meeting was serious but now it seemed even more so.

Arthur looked at the gathered crowd. 'We have skirted this issue for far too long. I know how miserable some of you are. I know that some of you are confused and some of you are angry.' He paused, looking at each one of them in turn. 'No one is more miserable, confused, or angry than me. We came back nine years ago, and though we've travelled and searched and opposed the Dark wherever and whenever we have found it, we still don't know why we've been called back. The world is a cesspit, and it's getting worse. But it isn't the Dark's doing, it's just...' he threw his hands up in disgust and raised his voice. 'It's just bloody awful.'

He sat down wearily and rested his elbows on his knees. 'I think that what Merlin told us before he left is correct. I think this is our last life.'

As the grumbling began, Tristan put his hand up. Arthur smiled and nodded for him to speak. 'So, if we die this time, that's it, it's over? We actually die?'

Arthur nodded again. 'Yes. We've done what we were meant to. It's time to live a full life. Those who've left have already gone to do just that but now it's time for you to make a decision. Me and Gal have decided to stay in This World, in this place, and you are all welcome to stay.'

Adda Mynyddmawr, Adda *the big mountain*, one of the Three Kings, who was making one of his many visits growled, 'You still have to fight the Dark, Lord. They've gone nowhere!'

'Don't you think we've given enough already, Adda King? Don't you think we've done our bit? Isn't twenty, thirty lives and painful deaths enough for the universe? Enough for the Light?' Arthur didn't shout, he rarely did, but his anger was clear. Even fearless Adda lowered his eyes and held his palms up placatingly. 'Fair point.'

Bedwyr stood 'Adda?' he asked. Adda looked at him. 'You said you were heading off today? Can I come with you?'

'Of course you can, boy. But after I meet up with Piogerix and Tommaltach in London I don't know where I'm headed,' Adda replied.

Bedwyr smiled. 'London is where I want to be. I have a mind to go to University.'

'University!' exclaimed Cai, standing. 'What are you going to do there? That's ridiculous. You aren't a student. You're a warrior. Come on, Bed this is stupid. We don't have to stay here, we can join Peredur and Gwalch abroad!' Cai was angry and that was because he was scared. Bedwyr was clever enough to go to any university, but Cai knew he wasn't and that would be the end of them. This just proved what he'd always believed; that he needed Bedwyr more than Bedwyr needed him.

'Come on Cai, come with me!'

'Where? London? What the hell am I going to do there?'

'Anything you wanted to do,' said Arthur, moving over and putting an arm around Cai's shoulder.

Cai angrily shook the arm off him. 'I'm not going to London! I'm a warrior not a bloody student! No one really knows that this is our last life, do they?' He turned to Bedwyr. 'We should wait!' Then, before Bedwyr could answer, Cai stormed out.

Bedwyr made to follow but Arthur put a hand out to stop him. 'Leave him to settle, Bed, you know you can't talk to him when he's like this.'

Bedwyr stopped and bowed his head in surrender. Arthur put his hand behind Bedwyr's head and smiled his wonderful open smile 'So you're going to be a student? Good for you.'

'I... I don't know. It's something I've thought about in the past few years, a chance to learn. And now, after today, there's nothing stopping me.'

'What are you going to study, Bed?' Tristan asked.

'I don't know yet, Cub,' Bedwyr replied using Tristan's nickname. 'I reckon I might be great at history.' He smiled, and everybody chuckled.

Now, sprinkling powdered chocolate on a large cappuccino, he smiled at the memory. That day he had left with Adda and, soon after, Bedwyr of the perfect sinews, warrior of the Light, was living in a shared house, working two jobs, and studying International Relations at university. And he was happy.

As for Adda, he had left London pretty sharply. 'Too many bloody rules in this country,' he had told Bedwyr. 'I'm headed back to America, land of the free, where I can shoot people when they do something stupid. Enjoy tupping young, impressionable students, Bed, don't waste those boyish good looks and Adonis-like body on bloody books!' And off he'd gone.

Bedwyr stayed, rent free, in one of the many properties owned by Tommaltach, one of Adda's fellow Kings. He didn't need to live rent free and neither did he need to work, Galahad had set up bank accounts for everybody when they arrived back in This World and he had enough money to pay for a house two times over – even in London. He couldn't get over the price of things, what people were willing to pay for everyday stuff. This was his first time back since the war and, before that, the War to End Wars. In 1943 he'd done nothing but fight though he'd managed to socialise in 1914. This time was richer, safer and healthier but everything was far more expensive. A pint in a pub was beyond ridiculous, he couldn't understand how they could afford it. And coffee? It really was the emperor's new clothes.

'Dras?' he shouted. 'Dras?'

'Yep.' A young man came to the counter.

'Faerie?' Bedwyr asked, in the Faerish tongue.

'I am!' the Faerie smiled, surprised. 'Man?' he asked.

Bedwyr smiled and nodded, 'This world or That?' asked the Faerie.

'This...I'm very refined.'

The faerie laughed, thanked him and walked away answering his mobile. The name Dras would have given his heritage away, but Bedwyr had felt a tiny shudder, the shudder that creatures blessed with Magick, or 'World crossers', feel in the presence of another.

'BARRY!' Despite the years of using the name Bedwyr still didn't always respond to it and given the tone of the shout, he'd just missed it, again. He looked up to see Sabrina, his boss.

'Sorry! I was miles away.'

'Isn't this your day off?' she asked.

He shrugged. 'Yes, but I knew you were a team member down, so I thought I'd help out,' he replied as he took his apron off.

'I'm not paying for that time,' she said, hands on her hips.

Showing off one of his huge smiles, Bedwyr bowed his head a little. 'Then you can have that gift on me, Sabrina. Have a lovely day.' And, with that, he walked into the staff area, folded his apron into his kit bag and put his coat on, shuddering for a second time that day, this time with a little bit more force. It wasn't that unusual – it happened most days as customers went in and out, so he ignored it and opened the fire escape, stepping out into the rancid smell of a London back alley, a land of bins and smoke breaks. For a moment, the smell forced a counter-memory of the hills of his childhood. He'd had many lives but only one childhood and he smiled as he thought of the hill behind his family's home.

That smile was his last as a giant hammer smashed into his face, killing him instantly.

As Bedwyr Bedrydant died in that back alley, clouds formed, and it began to rain as if the universe was mourning his leaving. I must admit I shed a few tears myself.

Two forms stood over his body. The man, and he was a man, who had wielded the hammer whispered a word and it disappeared. In a fair fight, he would have towered over Bedwyr. He bowed his head, his honest face sad. His shorter companion wasn't so sombre and didn't see the single tear fall down the other's cheek.

'Boom!' The shorter man laughed loudly. 'Yes! We did it. Boom, boom, boom.' With every boom he punched the air in front of him. His fourth boom was interrupted by a fist to the face, knocking him down. Despite the power of the punch, the smaller man rolled and stood immediately, growling a word of power, his eyes alight with fury. A spear appeared in his right hand and he twirled it expertly before taking up a fighting stance in front of the big man.

'What was that for, you bastard?' said Jiakall of the Spins, blood gushing from his newly misshapen nose. The big man, Red Viper, made no response. He simply stared down at Bedwyr's body.

Seeing his companion weaponless, Jiakall of the Spins thought for one second that this was his chance to make his name. Kill Red Viper! He looked at the other man's face but while he was momentarily confused by the tear running down it, good sense prevailed.

'A kill is a kill, you arsehole!' he barked, to save face.

'Have you no honour, you snivelling little man?' Red Viper demanded. 'Isn't it bad enough that we're involved in this mess, that we had to kill this hero in such a dishonourable manner?'

'To hell with honour. We're getting paid big time and we'll be known as the assassins that killed Bedwyr of Arthur…' he laughed '…and did it easily…' He spat at the body.

Red Viper leaned down and used his gloved hand to wipe away the spittle. Standing, he whispered a word and in his hand a sword appeared. He paused for a second before, with blinding speed, he closed the distance between himself and Jiakall, cutting his throat with one slash then plunging the weapon into his stomach. The smaller man fell to his knees, his eyes wide with shock. The assassin's code from all colours and levels stated that when two worked together each was protected from violence at the hands of the other. It had always been that way. Jiakall's face changed from shock to anger then fear as blood bubbled up from his mouth. He fell to the ground next to the body of Bedwyr and died.

Red Viper whispered a word and his sword disappeared. He looked down and spoke to Arthur's dead warrior. 'I am sorry, Bedwyr Bedrydant, not to have faced one such as you as warriors should. It is a shame I will carry all my life, but I will also carry the honour of sending you to the Hall and, when it is my time to go there, we will drink together.'

Then he looked at the body of Jiakall of the Spins. 'I ended your life through treachery, yet I feel no guilt.' He paused and allowed the fallen assassin a final, begrudging tribute. 'You were excellent with a spear.'

He stayed motionless for a second more then spoke another word of Magick. A large turquoise sheet appeared which he laid on the floor next to Bedwyr. He rolled the body onto it and, as he folded the sheet, both it and the body it wrapped became smaller and smaller until all that remained was a small flat patch, the size of a stamp, which Red Viper stuck onto the part of the trousers that covered his calf.

He repeated the process with his former colleague and, once the small square was pressed down, he whispered a spell and moved both his hands up and down his body. his warrior garb was transformed into a graphite-coloured suit, a style that, sadly, conflicted with the white trainers he wore.

Then, Red Viper walked off to find a pub. He needed a drink.

CHAPTER FIVE
TOMMALTACH HEARS THE PROPHECY

'Yep?' Tommy McKracken shouted a careless response to the gentle tapping on his door. He put down his mobile phone and looked at the door in expectation. It was clear that the knocker hadn't heard because the silence was followed by a few more light knocks.

'Yep?' Tommy repeated in the same tone.

The door opened a fraction and the large green head of an ogre tentatively peaked through the gap.

'Drod! For the love of gods!' Tommy's accent – Northern Irish, or 'Norn' Irish as he might have said himself – did exasperation well. 'You aren't spying on your older sister in the shower, open the door properly. Jasus, you've been with me for what now?'

Drod knew this. 'Sixty years boss.'

'Sixty years boss.' Tommy repeated. 'And how many times have I told you about coming in here properly?'

Drod of the Scratched Arse clan just stared. Tommy knew he was thinking but it looked as if someone had pulled the plug on Drod and he'd shut down.

It was a while. Well, it felt like one before finally 'Lots of times?'

'A lot of times son,' Tommy replied, quietly. 'A lot of bloody times.'

He had to admit, they weren't the brightest, but Tommy liked hiring ogres as muscle. They were cheap, they didn't ask many questions and they fitted in. Despite their size, ogres had been hunted in This World and That since before they could remember. Evolution had given ogres two pushes. The first gave them enormous strength so they could twat people who were trying to kill them, and the second gave them a particular Magick that allowed them to change their appearance to suit their surroundings. In the same way that giants or gawr as we call them in these parts (more on that later) disguise themselves by becoming topographical, ogres can change their appearance to that of any species they need to blend in with. I don't mean they can become an otter or a griffon, but any two-legged species is possible. Human, for instance, orc, elf or lawyer. It meant that Tommy could walk around with bodyguards who were cheap, docile and weren't green, with black tufty hair and large yellow tusks that protruded from their bottom jaw.

'What you after?' asked Tommy. His question was rewarded by more Drod buffering. After half a minute of what felt like waiting behind a stupid person on the self-service tills in a supermarket, Tommy sternly prodded, 'Drod!'

It was as if the ogre had been paused then un-paused. 'Tell Tale Tit here,' he rapped out. 'Says urgent.'

They called every snitch 'Tell Tale Tit', but Tommy had never heard 'urgent' before. 'Who is it?' he asked.

'Tell Tale Tit, shaky, smelly.'

Tommy nodded. That could only be one person. 'Send Ants in.'

'I stay?' Drod asked.

'You stay.'

They called him Ants, but it wasn't his real name; nobody used his real name probably because he was the only one left who knew it. Prophet he was, and drug addict to boot. Always shaking, moving, and fidgeting, you know? 'Ants in his pants', hence the name.

Ants fizzed in, eyes darting like prey, searching the room for danger. He scratched his greasy hair, then his nose, then wiped his dirty hands on his food-stained jeans.

Before he could start on the routine again, Tommy leaned forward; he didn't like Ants. 'What d'you want?'

'Ok Boss?' Ants sniffed hard to clear his blocked nose and swallowed what he had unblocked. 'I think I should sit.' He said this quickly, then stepped back knowing he was pushing his luck with hard man Tommy McKracken but pushing it anyway. Tommy didn't show it, but that bit of balls surprised him. This junkie was scared of his own shadow so whatever he had to say was not only legit, it was big. He pointed to one of the two seats reserved for guests opposite his grand oak desk.

'Sit.'

This overjoyed Ants. Respect for his prophetic gifts at last! It made him confident. Overly so. He licked his lips. 'Drink would be nice.'

'Leaving this room without two broken arms would also be nice.' Tommy replied.

Ants sat back in his seat, making a small buzzing noise, wiping his dripping nose with the palm of his hand and, in the same movement, running it through his hair. 'This is going to cost.' He zipped out the words hoping that he wasn't going too far again.

'I'll pay if it's worth paying for. Now cut the shit, you little turd, and out with it. My patience is disappearing fast.'

Head scratch, sniff. 'A prophecy was broadcast, blasted, into the air...Zip!' he shouted. 'Into the air. From one of the companies...bang! Not meant to, not meant for us. Big. Bits, big bits...' he scratched his crotch as if he was sandpapering an old bench... 'Bits you'll want, Big Boss. Fifty thousand.'

Though Ants would never have known it, Tommy McKracken was flabbergasted. For this wee druggie to ask for that much when people were getting no more than a hundred quid for quick prophecies! Tommy had heard that something had happened in Cardiff at one of the call centres, something big, but nobody knew any details. How the hell somebody like Ants had got hold of it was beyond him. 'Tell me,' he said, with a stone-cold calm, 'and you'll get paid.'

That was enough for Ants, he needed money. He broke into a stream of words telling the old King as much as he'd heard which wasn't everything but it was enough. Ants smiled after mentioning the Once and Future King, sniffed, hawked, spat in his hands and wiped them on the seat of his jeans. 'Already heard the Dark were moving against Arthur and his men.' He laughed, then stopped immediately. That wasn't part of what he wanted to say. Tommy stood up suddenly and Ants did the same, shrieking and pushing the chair back so hard he almost fell over with it.

'Right, bog off,' Tommy told him. Then, looking at the ogre who was waiting patiently at the back of the room, he said, 'Drod go and tell Teacher to give this wee bastard two grand and a bag of whatever takes his fancy, Ok?'

'Boss,' Drod replied.

It wasn't fifty grand but two was beyond the imagination of someone like Ants. He was bowing himself out of the room as quickly as he could, high on the prospect of money and drugs, when Tommy shouted, 'Ants!'

This time it was the snitch-prophet's turn to peep fearfully around the door.

'When did you get this?'

'L... last week,' Ants stammered.

'Last week!' Tommy stormed, his calm breaking at last. 'Why the hell did you wait until now?' he shouted.

'I'm sorry! I felt it coming up y'know, when I was with Buckley in his gaff. We've been up for a while, but I came to see you as soon as I saw straight, honest...'

As soon as you needed some more poison to put in your veins Tommy thought. 'Piss off,' he said, turning away from the junkie and sitting down. Now it was his turn to stare, to buffer.

Tommy McKracken had been born Tommaltach and most of his friends still called him that. He and the other two Kings had been born mortal but had been given the terrible gift of long-life millennia ago. Strangely, not once had any of them regretted it. Having lived a few thousand years, they found that you tended not to sweat the small stuff and Tommy rarely sweated anything; he had built a life and was happy with where he was. He hadn't had a drink since 1999 and he hadn't wanted one, but he wanted a quick one now, a whiskey from home. Like I said, he didn't sweat the small stuff, but he was sweating now. He moved to sit on the edge of the desk and picked up the landline to get things started but as quickly as he picked the receiver up, he put it down again, his brain furiously trying to organise. He needed to talk to those he trusted, and he needed that talk to be face to face, But that didn't necessarily mean the face had to be his.

'Drod!' he shouted and the ogre appeared immediately. 'Get my bosses in here, toot sweet. Tell them to drop everything and be here in an hour.'

For the first time in sixty years of employment, Drod didn't hesitate. There was obviously something up with his normally calm boss. He turned back at the door. 'Proper fighting?' he asked.

'Not yet, big boy, but probably yes, proper fighting.'

**

The four of Tommy's five lieutenants in attendance looked worried. They rarely met like this. Yes, they had team meetings once a month, but an emergency meeting was rarely called. Tommy trusted them all and they him, any one of them would die for him. All five had come from tough backgrounds and all five had gone through the best universities in the world, organised and paid for by Tommy.

He spent the next ten minutes explaining what he'd heard and what he thought it meant. If the Dark were going to act, they'd do it soon.

He slid loose sheaves of paper over the table. 'We can't contact these people in the normal ways – we can't risk it. You know we're always bugged. Send out your best finishers and find the people I've given you.'

The door opened wide, and the missing lieutenant stood as if about to deliver an agonised monologue in some west end theatre on opening night. He looked terrified.

'What?' asked Tommy quietly.

'I'm so sorry, Boss. It's just come through.'

'What? Come on lad spit it out.'

'Bedwyr was killed this morning. Owain, Gwalchmai, Geraint and Peredur yesterday. No details yet,' he said.

Tommy swore under his breath. 'They must know where everybody is! What about Tristan? Culhwch? Anybody else?'

The Lieutenant shook his head. Nobody needed any more instructions. They all knew they had to move.

As always, Tommy left his headquarters through the back. Drod – now looking extremely human-being like – went before him and opened the door to the car. His other bit of muscle, Glarv, also of the Scratched Arse clan, followed behind.

A shout rang out. Hey!'

They'd had a bad few hours and, expecting the worst, Glarv and Drod moved in front of Tommy, semi-automatics pulled from their holsters. Tommy whispered his words of Magick and a narrow-bladed sword appeared in his right hand. He crouched in a defensive fighting posture until he saw who was shouting and stumbling down the alleyway towards them. Ants. He was all over the place and he fell, twice, hard. 'Boss,' he managed with a groan.

'Off face,' said Drod.

Tommy sighed. 'Yep. Boys pick him up and see what he wants.'

They did as they were bid and Ants stood between them, his eyes trying hard not to roll back into his head as he swayed. Tommy held onto his chin. 'Speak son, have you remembered something else?'

'No…No I had my own prophecy. I had it ages ago but I have a lot of 'em. It's only now – after seeing you – I've got this weird feeling it's for you. I was off my chops but Buckley wrote it down.' He pulled out a scrap of paper and thrust it forward, almost falling over.

'Caratacus, Son of No-one, goes west.' it said in barely legible scrawl.

'Oh gods, no,' Tommy murmured as Ants lost consciousness and slipped to the floor. 'Glarv pick this wee shite up, look after him. Drod get in.' He opened the car door himself, got in, leaned forward and put his hand on the driver's shoulder.

'Twickenham.'

CHAPTER SIX

WAKE UP CARATACUS LEWIS!

The alarm started going off. Not the 'RAH RAH get out of bed or you'll die' kind of alarm, but the delicate strumming of a harp that came from a phone. From under a huge duvet came a hand trying and failing to find the said phone. The hand continued groping blindly about until it pushed the phone off the bedside stand. A groan came from under the duvet as the harps became less soothing and more annoying.

The lump under the duvet stuck its head out. The head belonged to the star of the next few paragraphs (or more depending on what he intends to do) Caratacus Lewis.

Caratacus Lewis's messy brown hair was sticking up with level 10 bedhead, while his face was covered in about 4 days' worth of similarly-coloured stubble. He had an eye mask on, which he pulled off to find the phone on the floor. The room was pitch dark but, he managed to see the outline of his phone that was flashing, face down.

'Sod. Off,' he said as he pressed the correct button to stop the noise. He put the phone back on the bed stand and flopped his head back on to his pillow.

It was 8 o'clock. That was when his alarm went off during the week and it usually started an hour of snoozing before Caratacus was ready to prepare for the day ahead. His next alarm was scheduled to go off at 08.20hrs with the next one at 08.40 hrs which was when he usually took off his mask and checked social media before heading down for breakfast. The phone on floor debacle had ruined everything. He tried to snooze, but it was too late, he was awake.

''Sake…' he mumbled, taking off his mask and letting the hand holding it flop to the bed.

Even without the mask, the room was in pitch darkness. He leaned over and pressed a small switch by his bed which made the curtains open slowly. He then pressed the next switch over, and the blinds went up with a light whirr. The early morning sunshine flooded in to show a large room of pale yellows and whites.

Caratacus got up and put his pyjama bottoms on. He did it just in time as he heard a light knocking on the door.

'Morning Mam,' he said.

'Are you decent, darling?' asked a voice with a Welsh accent,

'Yep.'

His mother popped her head around the door and smiled. '*Bore da*, my love. Morning. I heard you were awake and thought you might want your cup of tea now.'

Still a bit sleep addled, he smiled and put his thumbs up.

A shit, shower, and no shave later, he was back in his bedroom and waiting for him on one of the bed stands was a mug of tea. He took a sip before putting it back down and getting dressed. On his bed, as usual, his mother had left clean socks, pants, and a T-shirt folded as if a drill sergeant was due for an inspection. He dressed, with intermittent sips of tea, getting a clean pair of jeans out of his dedicated jeans drawer before selecting and putting on an expensive pair of shoes from his footwear closet.

He ambled downstairs and walked into the open plan kitchen.

The three-storey house was in Twickenham, south-west London, famous for posh types, thesps and rugby. Caratacus had lived in this house all his life. Even if he'd had an ambitious strand in his DNA, which he didn't, he would have had no need to move away. The house was spacious and modern. Left to his mother in the year he was born; he had grown up here and, when he was 21 and had finished scraping through a university degree, his Mam had moved out to make sure her precious angel had space to do whatever he wanted. As long as her boy was happy, she would've been happy living in the garden shed. She adored him, bloody hell, she came to his house every morning of the working week to make his breakfast and tidy his house before she started her own cleaning jobs.

In the kitchen, his mother stood at the large wooden dining table in the middle of the room.

A small woman of about 5 foot nothing was Mrs Lewis; 5 foot nothing of condensed energy fuelled by motherly worry and gossip. As Welsh as coal, as Welsh as drizzle. She bustled towards Caratacus, who leant down in anticipation, put a hand on each of his cheeks and dragged him down for a kiss as if she hadn't seen him for ages when, in fact, they'd been in this very room together yesterday morning.

'Eggs on toast? Beans on toast? Sausage sandwich? Eggs, beans and sausage on toast?' she offered.

'It's ok Mam, I'm so early I'm thinking of stopping off in Branco's. I'll have a bit of toast there.'

She tutted as she headed back to the sink. 'Bit of toast indeed? Make sure you have something proper, now. You can't go to work on an empty stomach, love.'

Caratacus watched her and, smiling, mouthed the words, 'Most important meal of the day…' as Mrs Lewis said, 'Most important meal of the day.'

In the hall, he was two seconds into putting his coat on when his mother called, 'Put your coat on, now, and your scarf. It's a lovely day out there but there's still a nip, mind.'

He smiled. 'I'll see you Monday yeah?'

She appeared in the kitchen doorway. 'No problem, love. Don't forget to get a proper lunch, I've put a lasagne in the freezer. No skimping meals. Here's an apple.'

Caratacus rolled his eyes. 'Mam, I'm thirty-eight, I'm fine, I can buy my own fruit.'

'But will you though? If I wasn't here to look after you, you'd waste away to nothing.'

Caratacus smiled again. 'I'd be lost Mam.' And, with a wave over his shoulder, he left the house.

It was a glorious day. He couldn't feel the nip in the air his mother had warned about but it was cool enough that, once he had put his earphones in, he put his hands back in the pockets of his long winter coat. 'The preacher's coat' his friends called it, and he loved it as much as his shoes. Nearly.

Caratacus arrived at Branco's café at quarter to ten every weekday morning before work without fail. If he arrived early, his schedule was completely thrown.

Today, he was an hour early. He didn't like it.

'Morning, my love,' his godmother Maria shouted as she sped past him with two mugs of tea.

'Morning, Aunty Maria,' Caratacus called to her disappearing back. The café was constant motion and commotion. Maria's husband, Giulio, turned away from the till to see the newcomer. Caratacus called him 'Zio', Italian for uncle.

When Zio saw who it was, he rolled his eyes and a wry smile appeared on his face. 'Here he *bladdy* is, *bladdy* Peter Pan!' he exclaimed. It was the same every day, Caratacus would come in and Zio would lambast him, blaming the boy for all his ills, real or imaginary. And while it all seemed like a bit of fun, sometimes, Caratacus couldn't help but think that Zio actually meant it.

'I *don* know whether to call you *bladdy* Peter Pan or *bladdy* Riley!' the former name was his daily one and one he'd had since he was sixteen, the latter was a new one for Caratacus.

'Riley?' he asked.

'Yeah! The *bladdy* life of Riley! What is your poor *mather* doing today for you eh? Building a new house for her poor boy or out looking for new clothes for him?'

Bladdy was really bloody and when he said mather he meant mother because like Mrs Lewis, Giuliano and Maria still had the accents they had grown up with. They had come over from a small town in the hills of Italy to find a fortune that never turned up and start a family that did.

'Why you so early Cati? Wet the bed?' he asked.

Caratacus wasn't all that keen on being teased at his usual time. An hour earlier? Even less so. 'Is Franco in?' he asked quickly.

Zio rolled his eyes. 'Francesco!' he shouted.

'Pap?' came the response from the kitchen.

'Your useless friend, that stopped you becoming a doctor and looking after your father in his old age is here for free drinks,' Zio replied, still shouting.

'Dad, leave him alone,' said Livia, the youngest daughter. Then, with a smile that could stop traffic, she looked over at Caratacus. 'Morning Cati,' she purred.

Caratacus's friend Franco had two brothers and five sisters, and he loved them all. The family featured heavily in most of his earliest memories which always involved being in and out of each other's houses. He jealously guarded the solitude and safety of his and his mother's life together, but he loved this family.

'I'm taking five,' Franco shouted, coming around the counter to Caratacus.

'It's never *bladdy* five though is it?' retorted his father.

Franco ignored him and hugged Caratacus. 'OK mate?'

'No probs here.'

Franco picked up the two cappuccinos that his mother had placed on the counter and nodded towards a booth by the front window. They chatted amiably about nothing for five minutes until Franco asked, 'So, pint tonight?'

Caratacus shook his head. 'Nah, I've got a few things on this weekend.'

Franco laughed. 'Oh get lost, Cati. What have you got on? Come out for a pint!'

'I just fancy chilling, to be honest.'

'That's all you do. You haven't been out in months. Why not come and watch Quins with me tomorrow?'

When younger, Caratacus, Franco and their friends would sometimes spend their Saturday afternoons watching Harlequins, their local rugby side. But, in recent years, Caratacus's interest in rugby and socialising had shrunk. As far as he could see, the less cluttered his life was, the easier it got, the lazier he got, the happier he was.

'I really am busy, Franco. Maybe the next game?' he said.

His friend shrugged and moved out of the seat. 'Yeah Ok. But you really need to sort your life out mate. See you Monday then. Message me during the weekend if you fancy.'

''Course I will.'

The conversation had made Caratacus uncomfortable, so he stood as well. He and Franco hugged and Zio came over, clamped Caratacus' cheeks in both hands and planted a kiss on his nose. 'Go and do something with your life, Cati, eh?'

A few minutes after leaving the cafe Caratacus heard the screech of tyres and – like everybody around him - turned towards the noise in time to see a body hitting a car windscreen and flying over the roof. It took all of two seconds, but Caratacus felt as if an hour and a half had passed and he just stared at the body lying on the road in front of him. A shocked crowd had gathered to stare down at what looked like a woman's body lying under a pile of old clothes.

Caratacus looked around for somebody to deal with the situation because he was quite certain that person wasn't going to be him. Then he recognised the woman on the ground. She was the local mad lady. Everybody had always called her Aunt Fanny, because it sounded funny, and because 'fanny' was rude. She always wore a ragged top hat, was always dressed in seemingly hundreds of layers of clothing and was always pushing a shopping trolley around the streets of Twickenham. When they were kids, they'd made fun of her, and she'd always told them to bog off. Now, looking down at her, that made Caratacus feel guilty and responsible. He looked around and started to panic.

She was still alive. She wasn't moving much but he could see that she was crying. Again, he looked around him. 'Somebody do something!' he pleaded. One of the spectators, a man he didn't know, stared at him. 'Why don't *you* do something?' he asked.

It was like a magical command, hypnotism, because though he didn't want to, Caratacus went to Aunt Fanny. He sat down and cradled her head in his lap. She fell quiet and in a moment of horror, he thought she'd died.

Then, Aunt Fanny opened her eyes and whimpered and, instead of compassion, Caratacus Lewis felt anger. He was angry because she'd made him step forward and get involved and he was angry because he was terrified. He heard someone say that they'd called an ambulance and all he could do was repeat the sentence to her in a whisper. She opened her eyes again and, this time, her bright blue eyes focused on him, and she smiled a painful smile. 'Ah it's you,' she said.

Caratacus heard a noise in his head. 'Cuckoo.' It was like a calm centre to all this chaos. She's mad, he thought. She's cuckoo.

'Hello,' he said, lamely. She doesn't know me, he thought.

'Caratacus,' she said quietly.

Bloody hell, she does know me, he thought.

'Caratacus ap Neb,' she said.

Ah, he thought, it must be another Caratacus. Then common sense caught up and knocked on the inside of his skull. 'Yeah sure you idiot, there are two people called Caratacus living in Twickenham.'

'No,' he replied, looking down at her. 'My name's Lewis – Caratacus Lewis, Aunt….' he stopped himself just in time.

'Fanny?' she said.

He smiled, weakly. 'Sorry.'

'It doesn't matter, I even call myself that, now. Have done since I moved here in the Twenties.'

A Hundred years ago? Cuckoo, he thought.

She carried on, her voice no more than a croaking whisper. 'I didn't think they'd care enough to bump me off.' She coughed then, and blood seeped from the side of her mouth.

'Ambulance is coming,' he said. Idiot, he thought, say something better. But all he could do was hug her closer.

She smells, he thought, which made him feel guilty, and that made him angry again. She was fading, he didn't know how he knew, but he knew, and he wanted to be somewhere else. Anywhere else.

He grimaced as she reached up to his face. He could see the smooth thin translucent skin of her hand and felt the smoothness of her fingers as they touched his cheek. He felt revulsion and then came the guilt, and the anger. She spoke – a whisper but her voice was still clear.

'Listen, my name is Buddug ferch Branwen, I am long lived and, for you, Caratacus, I have a gift…'

Cuckoo, he thought.

'…and I am not cuckoo you little arse…' She grabbed his arm in a vice like grip as she began to shine with a bright light. Caratacus tried to pull away again but she held on to him as the light moved over him as well. His body began to tingle and it felt as though he was burning from the inside out, or as if he was being filled with power like a tap pouring water into a kettle. His breathing quickened as the sensation increased but, still, he was unable to get out of the old woman's grip.

He heard a sound and looked up just in time to see paramedics moving people out the way. He heard them say, 'Let us through!' And then he fainted.

When Caratacus came around, he was sitting on the ground, his back against a wall with a blanket around him. His vision focused just in time to see Aunt Fanny's— Buddug's face being covered by a blanket. For a moment he felt sadness, but it was overwhelmed by a wave of unidentified emotion rushing through him. He blew out, trying to force whatever he was feeling out. It felt a lot like he'd taken an Ecstasy pill. He was glad the blanket was around him, not just because of the comfort but because it was hiding an involuntary erection. He lifted his knees, panicked at the thought that he felt turned on by somebody dying, that this was a new kink of his.

A paramedic bent towards him. 'Let's help you up.'

Caratacus stood hesitantly, the paramedic steadying him, presumably thinking his stoop was due to an injury rather than involuntary penis growth. 'You ok?' she asked, 'Did you hurt anything when you fell?'

'I'm going to sit down again if that's ok with you,' Caratacus said, carefully. It wasn't just the erection, he felt as if he was going to explode.

'Of course,' she said. 'Take a few moments lovey ok? I'll be back in a second.'

He smiled at her kindness and exhaled again. He had this strange feeling that everything was about to change.

CHAPTER SEVEN

OUR HERO GOES TO WORK

It wasn't long before a police officer came to check on Caratacus, to see if he was ok and up for questions. He still wasn't all there and blurted out 'Nobody bloody helped her!'

The police officer patted his back and left him, sitting on the pavement staring into space. He still felt very odd. Along with wanting to re-faint and still feeling as if he'd taken a very powerful Class A drug, he also felt as if he'd added a load of magic mushrooms, the drug spice and a viagra to the mix. He wanted to scream, and cry and laugh. Instead, he just sat there, staring into space. One of the other coppers, a young woman, came and asked him if he wanted to sit down on a bench nearby.

'Yeah,' he said, and she escorted him as if he was elderly. As he sat down, he looked up to thank her and let out a little shriek. For that moment, he could have sworn she was pale, like white pale, or green...maybe green and her eyes were red… he wiped his face.

She looked at him puzzled and then smiled. She leaned in close. 'Magicker eh? Never seen an orc before?' she said sarcastically. Coppers of all races are great at sarcasm.

'*What*?' He couldn't have heard her properly.

She snapped back into police mode. 'Magicker sir? Where from?'

He couldn't make out what she was saying. 'A *what*? What do you mean? I'm from here!'

She looked around, making sure no-one could hear her. 'It's ok sir, I'm not one of your usual orcs...well I suppose that's obvious really seeing that I'm a police officer.' She laughed at her own little joke. He looked up and saw a... a face, the normal face of a young girl in a police officer's uniform and then – flash, horrible, green – then flash, young girl.

'I feel strange.' He tried to get up but flopped down again feeling as weak as a kitten.

'Do you want to go in the ambulance?' she asked.

The thought of going in the same ambulance as Aunt Fanny's body was like a dose of smelling salts. Clarity rushed through his brain, and he knew immediately that all he wanted was to go back to normality. No hit and runs, no dead old smelly ladies, no drugs, no green- faced law enforcers. He wanted to go to his shop, drink tea and watch his assistant do all the work. He wasn't going home to change because that didn't happen on a Friday. He would work for a few hours, he would buy lunch, then work for an hour or two more. And then he would go home, have a curry and watch boxsets. That's what happened every Friday and that's what would happen today.

'Can I head off? I need to get to work.' The police officer nodded. Caratacus handed her his business card at full stretch as if proximity to her might suck him back in to the green weirdness.

'I'll be in touch,' she said. 'Are you sure you're OK, sir?

Caratacus forced a smile, then started walking off, gradually getting faster to put some distance between him and things that he considered shit.

He stopped 19 times on the small walk to work, once to be sick, twice to sit in bus stops and the other times just to stand, wavering like a zombie. People avoided him because they thought he was talking to himself, but he wasn't, he was answering the crows. The weirdness didn't even stop when he reached work. On the ground floor, beneath his shop, was a newsagents owned by Paddy Kingrani an Irish-Pakistani or Pakistani-Irishman. Paddy waved as usual, but Caratacus didn't because Paddy seemed to be on fire and had glowing red eyes and sharp teeth.

Paddy looked puzzled, 'Are you OK, Caratacus?

'No!' Caratacus answered, hurrying through the door and into what he hoped was non-weird safety.

He clumped up the threadbare seventies style carpeted stairs. Mail for tenants long since moved out, was piled on every step. Every day Caratacus thought about getting it sorted and every day he decided it would definitely be a job for 'tomorrow'.

Doing things 'tomorrow' was a permanent diary marker for him. Another one was 'Get Mam to <<insert task>>' and, at that very moment, he wanted to text his mother and get her over with a change of clothes and a flannel for his forehead. He opened the door to the shop, walked in and a rugby ball smashed into his face knocking him to the floor.

I know Caratacus, I have known him since he was born. Before this day, he had never experienced losing consciousness and this was his second time in an hour. His eyes opened and his faculties started to return. He blinked a few times and noticed a pound coin under his sofa. It had rolled there last week, and he had not been that bothered about picking it up.

Freezing cold liquid slapped into his face. 'BALLS!' he shouted and sat upright before seeing who the culprit was and slumping back to the floor. Standing before him, holding a mug – his mug – was his assistant, Marged. Before we go on, the 'g' in Marged is a hard one, like in Margo. I try not to sweat the small things but getting people's names right...well it's important.

I love Marged but I don't know if she is going to be important in Caratacus's story yet. She had been brought up in the very west of Wales, near where Caratacus' mother was born. She had lived with her parents and five older brothers on a dairy farm at the foot of the Preseli Mountains. The boys were rugby mad and so was Marged. Sadly for the boys, Marged was the only one of the six siblings who was any good. Growing up on a farm meant there was no time for playing chase or Pooh sticks like the other kids in Cwm Llechau. Marged was driving a tractor from the age of eight and helping out in every aspect of the farm. She worked like her brothers, and she was built like her brothers, and even though there was no girls' side in Cwm Llechau she trained every Tuesday and Thursday night, and she was good. The coaching team were often heard lamenting Marged's gender and, even more bitterly, her tendency to damage the match-fit male players in training. It took only two months and a few phone calls before she'd been selected to play for Harlequins and travelled to London to begin a new life as a semi-professional rugby player.

Mrs Lewis had received a call from Tudor Lewis-Jones from the Welsh in London Society and while Mrs Lewis was trying not to lose her posh phone voice, Mr Lewis-Jones had told her about a young girl from the old country, not much English, who had been selected to play for Harlequins and needed a place to live and if she could think of anywhere. Mrs Lewis had a small house, with a small spare bedroom, next door to her son whose house had four spare bedrooms; so naturally Mrs Lewis told Mr Lewis-Jones that she would gladly put the young girl up in her own home for as long as she needed. They soon became like mother and daughter. They enjoyed having the opportunity to speak Welsh together, they knew the same places and people from Pembrokeshire, and they shared a work ethic found in less than 0.00001% of the population. Marged trained like a machine but, while her teammates appreciated their down time, Marged couldn't handle it and it wasn't long before Mrs Lewis begged her son to let Marged work in the shop when she wasn't playing. I was going to say that she didn't ask for much, but she had literally never asked Caratacus for anything, ever, before.

It was probably shock that made him say yes and while Marged was a pain in the arse, Caratacus had to admit that she never stopped, and the shop looked a lot tidier.

He didn't care about tidiness at this moment though.

'Ow!' he shouted as Marged prodded his nose. He was lying on the floor facing up and over him sitting on his chest and looming over him was the face of his assistant.

'Hurts there then?' Marged asked innocently.

'Yes!' Caratacus stared at her. 'It's the reason I shouted 'Ow'!'

She leaned in, concentrating as if she was about to draw him. 'Shall I snap it back in?'

'What?'

'Your nose.'

'Why? Is it broken?'

'No, it's just something I've heard on the telly.'

A look of horror spread across his face 'No! No, I do not want you to 'Snap' it back in!' His sarcasm was lost on Marged.

'Can you get off me please?' he asked weakly.

'Alright then. Cup of tea?' she asked as she got up, glancing down at his jeans.

Caratacus remembered that he'd wet himself and got up, turning away as he stood, hoping she hadn't noticed. 'Yes please.'

As she moved into the makeshift kitchen, he collapsed with a grunt onto the sofa. The shop wasn't actually aimed at selling anything but modelled on what Caratacus wanted to do during the day which is why there was an area just inside the door with a large comfy sofa, an equally comfortable armchair, a low coffee table and a widescreen television.

Caratacus slumped in the middle of the sofa checking to see if the wet patch on his jeans was obvious. It wasn't and with one less thing to worry about he leaned his head back and closed his eyes.

'Pissed your pants, have you?'

Caratacus's eyes snapped open to see Marged putting a mug of tea down in front of him.

He grabbed a cushion and thrust it over his lap 'N...no!' he spluttered, 'I just had an accident with a cup of coffee,' he added, quickly.

'Well, truth be told, it looks like you have pissed yourself,' Marged said.

Trying to maintain his dignity while holding the cushion over his nether regions, Caratacus got up and went to the small staff toilet. He liked his days to be uneventful. He didn't like events, especially ones that required any sort of effort from him. He wanted this Friday to be the same as the last one. As much as Caratacus Lewis worked at anything, he did work quite hard to achieve uniformity in his life. This was not a usual Friday; it wasn't a usual any day and he did not like it one bit. And, right now, he was about to get reacquainted with his arch enemy 'the tap in the toilet.' He despised it. It behaved as if it was sentient and, having become sentient, was searching for a personality somewhere between mildly annoying and (wrongly) finding itself funny. It had two handles and one spout, which meant you had to have the manual dexterity of someone who handled nerve gas for a living to reach the correct temperature. Caratacus failed and, instead of a steady trickle of tepid water that he could direct over the wet patch, a fountain of magma-esque water sprayed into his hands drenching the entire front part of his jeans.

'OH, PISS OFF!' he shouted at the universe.

He kicked off his shoes, peeled his wet jeans off his legs and hung his shirt on the toilet door handle. Looking at the offending jeans, he decided to scrub the stained section and put them on the cistern to dry. He stood there looking at himself in the mirror, shaking his head at the tired man in a T-shirt, boxers and socks. In situations like this, he thought, the only way is up.

'Boss! There's some foreign man here to see you,' Marged shouted from the shop.

Caratacus rolled his eyes. People from Carmarthen – about 30 miles away from her parents' farm – were considered foreign by Marged.

'Can you please apologise and tell him I'm indisposed at the moment?' he shouted back.

'Wha?!' came the shouted reply from Marged.

Caratacus swore under his breath and shouted again, knowing that the 'foreign man' would be listening as well. 'Please tell the gentleman that I'm in the middle of something and, if he leaves his name and number, I'll get back to him as soon as I can.'

There was a pause before and almost aggressive 'Eh!?!' from the shop.

If Caratacus had been born David Banner and become a physicist or something and then been changed by gamma rays in an experiment gone wrong, this was the time that he would have gone green and ape shit. Instead, he just gripped the side of the sink with two hands and breathed deeply.

He then opened the door slightly and, through clenched teeth, hissed, 'Marged!'

As if by magic – and I mean magic that moves heavy machinery fast – Marged appeared.

'Boss?'

'Tell him I can't come out.'

'You having a poo?'

'What? NO!'

'You've got a red face.'

'I wasn't having a poo.'

'A pee then was it?'

'No, I was just....' he stopped and hissed even more quietly '...it doesn't matter what I'm doing. I don't understand why you want to know all the time?' he stopped, realising she'd made him go off on a tangent again. He closed the door, leant his head on it and then opened it again immediately.

'Marged.'

'Yes Boss.' It was as if they had just started the conversation from scratch. 'Tell the foreign gentleman that I am indisposed, get his name and number and then tell him that I'll give him a ring either this afternoon or Monday morning. Do you understand?'

She nodded. 'Tell Tommy McKracken you're possessed, and you'll ring him back.' She turned to leave.

'Wait! Wait!' he hissed again. She stopped and turned, staring at the half face peeking around the toilet door.

'I didn't say *possessed*. Why would I say I'm possessed? What I said...' he blinked. 'Tommy McKracken?' he whispered.

'The foreign man,' she said blankly.

'Tommy McKracken?' he asked again. She nodded.

That's hilarious, Caratacus thought. Marged had said that Tommy McKracken was here in his shop to see him. That couldn't be correct because he didn't know any Tommy McKracken and he certainly didn't know Tommy McKracken who ran the premium crime cartel of south and west London. The Tommy McKracken who dished out hurty kneecaps and concrete swimming shoes, who made people disappear and was responsible for all kinds of undesirable activity.

He opened the door a little wider, forgetting that he was in his underwear and socks and whispered sharply. 'Listen, Marged. Are you telling me that, in my shop, there is a man called Tommy McKracken who's asking for me?'

Before she could answer, Caratacus heard a shout. 'Bloody hell, are you dense son? She is telling you that, yes! Tommy McKracken is asking for you. Get your arse out here toot sweet.'

Caratacus closed the door and again leant his head against it. At that moment what he wanted more than anything else was his mother. He sighed, put on his jeans and opened the door to go and meet Tommy Mckracken.

CHAPTER EIGHT
MEET OUR CASSIE

Still not fully awake Cassie Newton knew the alarm would be going off soon. That, or Olivia would start crying. She was exhausted and wished she could return, once again, to the deep, dark, velvety sleep of a few minutes before but she knew that it was too late for that. She had to wake up properly, so she did what she did every morning to jolt herself out of bed. She opened the box she kept in her mind, the one that held her worries and problems. They tumbled out. Rent, money, food, money, Olivia, money, money, bloody money.

Enough.

Awake.

She threw off the duvet, swung her legs off the bed and sat, rubbing the remnants of the sleep from her eyes.

The alarm chose that moment to go off. Cassie turned her head and stared at it. She whispered a word, just one word of power, and the alarm stopped. It wasn't much, just one of the few she was allowed to use in the hell of exile. Small words but she loved them. The feeling of the words, letters and syllables on her tongue, the little spark in her stomach and the minuscule amount of pleasure that travelled through her entire body made switching off the alarm clock or lighting a cigarette an absolute blessing.

She opened a packet of twenty Marlboro lights, took one out and put it between her lips. She mumbled a word around it and the cigarette lit. Cassie inhaled deeply and sat there staring into space, smoking until the cigarette was finished before stubbing it out in the full ashtray beside her bed. She looked around her floor for something to wear, eventually deciding on the grey, pink-lined hoody and grey tracksuit bottoms she had worn the day before and the day before that. She finished the ensemble with cheap slippers, so worn that she might as well have walked around the house barefoot.

'Mum!' Olivia shouted from the other room.

Cassie bowed her head and closed her eyes. Her daughter had woken half an hour earlier than usual so there would be no morning telly, no quiet second cigarette and no 30 minutes of peace.

'Mum!'

'I'm coming!'

She walked out of her room and opened her daughter's door. The room depressed her almost as much as hers did and a little less than her living room/kitchen. Dreary dark cream walls had mould edging up two sides and the oak brown curtains, slightly ajar, shed light onto a once white carpet. Without realising she was doing so, Cassie brightened as she saw her daughter's face. Olivia struggled up using the side of the cot and held out her hands with a whiny 'Mum?'

That one syllable wiped the pleasant moment away. Grabbing arms wanting more, taking Cassie's life away. This pissing, shitting, never satisfied, needy parasite. This…this thing, the reason she was stuck in this shit hole and reduced to…this! Angrily she picked up her daughter, took her through to the living room/kitchen and put her down on the couch. Olivia was oblivious to the change in her mother's mood because it wasn't a change; it was just her mother's mood.

Half an hour later, Cassie threw the plastic bowl that held remnants of Olivia's supermarket own brand porridge and her toast-crumb strewn plate into the washing up bowl. She gave them a brief blast from the tap before deciding, as she did every day, that she'd do them later. She sipped her tepid, tasteless tea then threw what was left down the sink.

KNOCK KNOCK.

She peered around the door, always worried about unexpected callers. A nondescript, well dressed gentleman smiled stiffly.

'Yeah?' She sighed.

Still smiling, he handed her an envelope. 'Mistress,' he said simply.

Her eyes opened wide in shock and darted around the dank stairway to ensure he was alone. 'What do you want?'

His expression didn't change, he just stood there, offering her the envelope. He said nothing. She snatched it, opened and read the letter. She looked into the man's eyes.

'No,' she said.

He held out a box, one that might usually hold a ring.

'No,' Cassie repeated. He didn't move. She closed her eyes for a moment before opening them and snatching the box.

'When do I get payment?'

He ignored her and walked slowly away from her, down the stairs.

She closed the door. I think she would like to have slumped to the floor then, sitting with her back against the door trying to process what the letter had told her. But she didn't because she couldn't; she now had, as she would have called it herself 'a complete shit of a day' ahead. She marched over to the sofa, picked up Olivia and took her to her bedroom to prepare her for nursery. Olivia knew her mother wasn't in the mood for messing around most mornings but had the good sense to realise that this one was doubly so, so made a minimum of fuss.

On the ten minute walk to Growing Buds Nursery, Olivia kept up a stream of inane comments and questions which Cassie ignored. She was too busy thinking of the day ahead. Olivia's chatter was nothing but white noise to her until a persistent 'Mum!' tripped the tiny, maternal switch in her head. 'WHAT?' she flared.

Olivia knew her mother was angry, but she carried on regardless. Anger was nothing new. She dealt with it as she always did, with a tiny cutesy voice while looking down and suddenly becoming shy, the same tactic she used when being complimented by adults.

'Did you always want to be a mummy, or did you want to be something important?' she asked.

It stopped Cassie in her tracks, and she turned to face her daughter. 'What do you mean by that?'

Olivia shuffled her feet and looked down. 'Why don't you work? Cain Thomas said that people who don't work are all scroungers.'

Usually, Cassie would have shrugged this off but today wasn't usual. She crouched down to be at eye level with Olivia. 'Being a mummy,' she said, 'is a very important job. Without my mummy work you would have no clean clothes and nothing to eat. What does Cain Thomas know anyway....?' She was about to leave it there but thinking of the day ahead, she paused for a moment, closed her eyes, and gently touched her forehead to her daughters. 'Hey kidda, don't forget that I love you the world, ok?' Olivia leaned back to look at her mother and smiled her smile 'I love you the world too Mummy,' and with that Cassie stood up, took Olivia's hand and continued their journey.

The usual gang were waiting outside Growing Buds. Were they her friends? She'd never had friends growing up, just competitors.

She thought about the box back at the flat. There would be a competitor today. Something in Cassie Newton flared. Fear? Excitement? Both, I suspect.

'Hiya love!' Dianne was the first to speak. Even that sounded sarcastic because Dianne was a massive cow. Dianne made out she was everybody's friend, while actually pitting her so-called 'mates' against each other. She was the only one of the nursery mother's gang who had any money. Her husband, Dean, was a builder and worked every hour the gods sent. Cassie thought it was because Dianne was a massive cow and he wanted to keep away from her, her passive-aggressive quips and their mewling, badly behaved kids. Cassie hated her but Dianne was the power in their group and, trained to be a Dark Mistress or not, Cassie could not escape her influence. Dianne could make Cassie's awful life even worse so she played her games.

'Hiya Dianne,' she smiled, imagining the things she could do to Dianne if she was allowed to. She tingled as the image brought to mind the box that waited for her at home.

The others were all dressed more or less like Cassie, but Dianne was always kitted out as if she was about to compete in a dressage competition. Before her exile, if Cassie had noticed them at all, she would have looked at them with utter disdain as beings in urgent need of being put down like a sick pet. But now, she had been here for three years, and these women were... were what? With the exception of Dianne, she had stopped wanting to murder them a while go. Did she like them? Cassie wasn't sure what 'like' meant. She had been brought up in constant competition, taught to trust nobody but herself, to associate with others only in order to get something done or to survive. A life of mistrust and hate.

Another mother, Katie, called over. 'Hiya mate!' Cassie didn't hate Katie. In fact, in the second shock of her day she realised that she actually liked Katie.

'Hi,' she replied.

Again, she thought about the box back home. There would be no room for liking later.

Once the kids had rushed in through the opened nursery door, the mothers headed off for a few hours of freedom. It was Thursday, the day when they went to the café for drinks and a natter. Now, when the task she had been given meant that she might never see the café again, Cassie realised that she liked Thursdays; a chance to relax and talk to an adult.

'Right girls, time for Allesandro's.' Dianne didn't need to say it, they went there every Thursday. It was just another example of her taking over. Back in the training pens, Cassie would've ripped her tongue out, left her for a few weeks then fed it back to her. She smiled at the thought. 'I'm sorry, I can't today,' she said.

Moans and questions all came at the same time. Everybody liked Cassie, though it had taken them a while to warm to her when she had first arrived. She was quiet and, at first, when she looked at them, the mothers felt uncomfortable. It was as if she was reading them, totting up every single thing they had ever said or done and finding them wanting. It was only later, when they realised that she was just quiet and had no angle whatsoever that she had been welcomed into the group. She occasionally went on nights out with them, and she was always there for babysitting. The girls had asked about her past but Cassie would tell them nothing, not even about Olivia's father, and because they liked her, they stopped asking. All except Dianne. She didn't like Cassie. Cassie knew that and she was pretty sure that Dianne knew she knew. Cassie was too quiet by half and wouldn't play her games, but at least she was quiet enough not to get in Dianne's way and that was enough.

Cassie's mind went back to the box and a shiver went through her. 'I've got solicitors stuff to sort out,' she told them.

'Nothing bad, love?' Dianne asked, fake-smiling.

'Nothing bad,' Cassie smiled back. What a massive cow she thought and pictured herself hammering a nail into the top of Dianne's head...really slowly...while Dianne screamed and she laughed.

They all said goodbye and Katie gave her a hug. Hugs still freaked her out but now, she had learned not to go rigid or to pat the hugger's back as if she was violently winding them.

The walk back home was a strange one. Cassie had spent every day hating this new life. She had exchanged a life of hardship, pain and solitude but one of power for one of exile in this dreadful world. She had found different forms of hardship and pain here but, all of a sudden, she realised that because of those mothers, those had eased a little and maybe she wasn't so alone. She still hated This world, still spent her time wanting to cut people's heads off but now, for the first time, she realised that it wasn't...*really* awful, just awful.

And now, just when she was getting used to her new life, her past had come to spoil things.

Cassie closed her front door, walked into the living room and took the box out of the drawer where she'd put it. She could feel the power emanating from it and her heart hammered in her chest. It was buzzing, she was buzzing.

She put the box on the low table between the telly and the sofa and sat down. She stared at it for a while, then took a cigarette out and, lighting it with a murmured a word of power, took a long slow drag. She thought of the instructions she'd been given. She had perfect recall and remembered every word. A memory that forgot nothing had helped in the training pens but now it provided a constant reminder of how she'd messed up her life.

In the time it took her to smoke her cigarette she had analysed every aspect of the task ahead. Once clear in her mind, she went along to the bathroom, took off her clothes and got into the shower. She looked at the pile of clothes she'd left on the floor. They needed a wash. Or maybe she should get some new ones. The thought surprised her. New clothes were a luxury, she may as well have thought about buying a new yacht. New clothes? Stupid thought. She'd just have to stick to washing.

As she stepped out of the shower and dried herself, the pressure in her stomach was building.

She picked the box up and carried it through to the bedroom. Still naked, she stood and opened the box slowly, ceremoniously, gazing at the stone inside.

She reached in, tentatively, and touched the stone. Her entire body shuddered as power jolted through her. A feeling of ecstasy spread to every part of her. When it reached between her legs, her knees buckled a little and she leaned forward to steady herself on the bed frame. She clenched her teeth, lips tight as she tried to stifle a moan of orgasm.

Cassie put the stone back in the box. It was too much. She breathed in deeply sat down on the bed and took the stone in her hand once more. She was better prepared this time but still the power hit her hard. Her hand glowed red and the energy pulsated through her, only stopping when all the stone's dark power had poured into her. She dropped it to the floor.

It took all she had not to weep for the memory of the power she had once had, and how it had been stripped from her. She had wanted to cry so many times since it happened, but she had never allowed herself such weakness and would not now. No tears from Cassie. There was no time for emotion. This new power was temporary, limited to the task in hand, and it needed to be used as wisely and as quickly as possible.

Cassie looked for the mirror that was leaning against the wall. It wasn't big enough, so she extended her left hand, palm out, and spoke three words of power. The entire wall became a mirror. Despite the feeling of such exquisite power the reflection depressed her. Her small frame had not changed, but her face was grey and lifeless. For three years she hadn't really looked at her reflection and, now that she saw herself again, she felt ashamed.

She looked around her, wanting distraction. The stone had released her power, blocked for so long, and she could tear down this house if she wished. But no. She had to move. Focus. The right stance and the right movement followed by the right words in the right order with the right stresses on the right syllables, all combined with her newly released power and natural talent, made clothes take shape on her body.

Cassie hadn't consciously thought about what she should wear for the task she had been set, she had simply let the spell work its Magick. Now, her eyebrows rose appreciatively. Crepe jersey jacket and matching pencil skirt and Manolo Blahnik shoes. She felt different. She looked at her shoes. She loved them. All she had worn since exile were slippers, trainers or her best heels (twenty-eight pounds from Primark, used for forced christenings, rare nights out and the times she had been forced to go to 'tea' at Dianne's house and eat sandwiches with the crusts cut off).

But, despite the expensive shoes and power suit, she still looked like a washed-up teenager in her mother's clothes. She put her right hand in front of her face and whispered words of power, a rare smile appearing on her face. Then she lowered her hand, the face that stared back at her was still her own, but now she was Cassandra Newton transfigured. The face in the mirror was radiant, fully made-up, hair in a new, shining business-like bob. Her reflection exuded power, guile, intelligence and obvious sexuality. Cassie studied herself in the mirror-wall, standing to attention and lifting her chin before nodding, dismissing the image with a click of her finger and heading for the door.

She knew this power was temporary. Even now she felt it ebbing, like tiny grains of sand in a timer, slowly falling away from her body. But she had one thing to do for herself before she did as she had been bid.

She walked downstairs to the bottom floor and rang the bell of the flat where her landlord lived. The door flew open. 'What do you want?' Mr Popplewell demanded.

Compared to Popplewell, Cassie loved Dianne.

His face was angry. It always was. 'If your boiler is on the blink again then tough shit, I'm fed up of throwing money at you and that bastard kid. I'm doing this to make money not be a bloody charity.'

This had been the only place she could afford when she arrived in This World with little money and no power. She hadn't known anything, then, and this...this creature had taken advantage. She looked at him now. In his forties, bald and fat, he had a pair of old shorts on and a food-stained t-shirt that rode up, showing the bottom half of his bulging belly. When she'd turned up, he hadn't seen a desperate young mother in need, he'd seen money and a victim. A flash of memory – rough flabby hands pawing at her body when she couldn't afford the rent, the pressure of his body on top of her when she needed money for Christmas, that slavering mouth on her neck when he demanded to know, again, why he should carry on renting the flat to her.

As if he could read her mind, he smiled lavasciously at her. 'Short of money love?'

In her imagination, she used her thumbs to push those bloodshot, yellowing eyes back into his head as he screamed to his knees. But she couldn't kill him. Instead, she calmly touched him on the forehead. A slight look of surprise and angry impatience just about reached Popplewell's face before it went numb. His arms dropped to his sides and he stood there, as if somebody'd switched him off.

Cassie said one word. 'Terror.'

His face changed while his body remained motionless. It twisted into fear. Cassie knew he was more scared than he had ever been or ever would be – at least until she had escaped this hell hole and returned to torture and kill him. She was pleasantly surprised, if a little revolted, to see that he had pissed himself. She carried on.

'This morning you received my rent for the next 12 months. You will never, ever, ever come to my flat again and when I slip a note through the door requesting that you fix something, you will do it within three hours.'

Though the desire to kill him was almost overwhelming, this power was temporary, and she and Olivia needed this place. 'You will go back in your shithole and you will feel terror for the next hour, then you will go to the fire stairs at the back of this building, walk halfway up then throw yourself off.' It wouldn't kill him, but he'd be in pain for months.

She took her hand away. 'Now, piss off.'

He closed the door as if there was no one there.

Luckily, the pub she needed – the Oak – was close by. Cassie walked there quickly and with purpose.

She'd been in the Oak a few times. Once or twice on a small crawl before heading into 'town'. These nights out didn't happen often and incredibly for someone who was brought up to feel no fear, in the beginning they terrified her. At the time she wanted to kill all the girls in her group, not just that massive cow Dianne. Her childhood, her training was all about the need to survive and her gut told her that sticking with these women would ensure she did. In time she found herself looking forward to the nights out. Time away from that flat, from bills, from lists of what to buy and what she couldn't afford and time away from Olivia.

She hoped that, at half past ten in the morning, there'd be nobody in the pub because the way she dressed would draw attention. Actually, anybody under seventy-five would draw attention in the Oak. It was the pub that opened the earliest and took all the 10:30 until 12 trade before the alcoholics moved onto the Barley Mow for the racing.

She immediately recognised the three old gents to the right. Anybody who'd been in the Oak more than once would have. All in their seventies, they were basically the pub's human furniture. They clapped, whistled, and cheered on seeing a young girl.

'Morning,' she muttered.

'Court or courting?' One shouted as the other two laughed.

'Very funny.' she replied without breaking step on the way to the bar.

Behind that bar was Gordon Owens, the landlord. He always worked the day shift to save on wages.

'Rum and coke please,' Cassie said.

Gordon smiled. 'No probs.'

Cassie touched Gordon's hand daintily with a finger. 'Keep the change and I'm just popping to the toilet.'

Gordon nodded and put Cassie's fictitious ten pounds into the till.

Cassie had never worked out why the humble pub toilet furnished the Magickal portals of This World, the places where you started somewhere and arrived somewhere else. When she was first exiled, she wanted to cry every time she saw a pub toilet which if you thought about it was weird but if you had no Magick you could not use them. Without Magick they were just places you could wee and poo in.

The portals meant that it was possible to travel *from* any pub, but not *to* any pub. OK, let me explain. All pubs within, let's say two or three miles were connected. If you had Magick within you and knew the right words, you could have a pint in one village pub, nip to the toilet and come out of the toilet in another for the next one. You could have a massive all-day drinking session in the pubs of that place, having a drink in every one and your pedometer would not get over a thousand steps. Problems: the further the travel the more Magick it takes from you, and you can't travel over huge tracts of water, so no trips to the continent and no taking a wee and ending up Christmas shopping in New York. The big water stops you but travelling that distance? If you could? The blokes in Mick's Bar in the big apple would find a desiccated corpse in the one cubicle in the place.

I digress. From every pub near you, you can travel to about 20 pubs on this island. From the Oak, you could travel to only ten pubs in Britain, and they had been mapped by Robert Roberts, a local druid in 1925. One of them was the Bear and Staff, in London, where Cassie needed to go. There is no sense to it, no logic because Magick doesn't make sense, it's not logical. Cassie thought of none of this stuff. She thought of the right words and while she did that, she worried a little about the energy and the Magick she was about to use.

Careful to waste not an ounce of magical energy, Cassie entered a stall, locked the door, said the necessary Magickal words and found she had travelled to some much nicer toilets. She gave herself a last check over in the mirror then made her way out through the bar into the noise of the city.

It wasn't sunny but, after the pub, the light was blinding. Cassie shielded her eyes while she turned around to check that she had come out of the right pub. Yes, there was the sign. The Bear and Staff. After three years in a flat on an estate, the sound and bustle of the people and traffic assaulted her. This was her first time in London, and she could feel the Magick of the place underneath her feet. History on history, culture on culture, happenings on happenings, squashing, pressing, creating and recreating. It wasn't just the old places, the holy wells, the standing stones, the forests and caves that held, breathed and nurtured Magick, cities like this did the same.

Within ten minutes Cassie had reached her destination. An office block stood before her but standing there, she realised the people who had tasked her had messed up. This wasn't right.

She was meant to gain access to this building which was why she was dressed to the nines but all of it, the suit, the heels, the lot, was all for nothing. Someone with her Dark power had no chance of getting in here; she could feel the protective Magick. This wasn't a normal building; this was a Fort Knox of the Light. That made Cassie worried. Her masters never messed up.

There was nothing to do but wait. She walked to the other side of the road, and stood, watching, smoking and waiting.

It wasn't long before her victim walked out the front.

She'd expected a girl, but this was a woman in her mid-thirties, and Cassie recognised an opponent not a target. It was that ability to analyse her competitors that had allowed her not only to survive but to dominate in the training pens.

To her surprise her opponent made a beeline towards her and surprised her again, as she walked past, saying: 'I haven't got long for lunch so let's work out the rules and go from there.'

Cassie followed her into a café. The woman she'd come to kill sat down and indicated that Cassie should take the seat opposite. Cassie didn't like that.

Her name was Lexie Diomedes, Cassie knew that much. Brown eyes and hair to match. Lexie looked straight into Cassie's eyes and smiled, sarcastically. 'I'm slightly insulted. They've sent a child.'

'A child who is going to end you,' Cassie retorted but, inside, she cursed herself. This world had influenced her too much. Talking? At the top of her powers after release from the pens, she would never have talked. She'd have grabbed the butter knife from the table and stabbed it straight through the bitch's eye. Done. Get job, do job, finish job, prepare for next job, that's how she'd been trained.

But, the thought wormed its way in, maybe it wasn't This World that had changed her, maybe it was HIM. For the second time in under five seconds she cursed herself. She had to sort this, get a hold of herself, and get the upper hand. But Lexie spoke first.

'So, little girl, you think I wasn't expecting you? I've been preparing for you scum *all my life*, not just because of some bloody prophecy your lot recently found. I smelt you as soon as you landed.' Cassie's silence just prompted Lexie to carry on talking.

'Well, this is nice. So, who are you? Anyone I've heard of? It's always nice to know who you are about to destroy. Aren't you going to tell me what Set you belong to?' she asked with the lightness of a date.

'I don't belong to any of them,' Cassie spat. Then anger flared again. Why the hell were they *talking*? Anger increased even further when Lexie smiled again.

'My God, you're the exile, aren't you?' She paused, a confused look on her face, 'I thought you were dead,' before breaking into a smile. 'Oh, how exciting— they've sent a celebrity for me to kill.' Lexie's laugh was like the sound of glass breaking. She hadn't finished though. Putting on an exaggerated American accent, her voice mimicked that of a teenager. 'So, tell me, how is the boyfriend? Are you still together? Do you still luuuurve him? What about the little one you had together *against the rules*? Did you keep it?' she laughed again.

Cassie's hand shot out as fast as lightning, fingers straight, aiming for Lexie's throat. But they stopped an inch from their target, halted by an invisible barrier. The air fizzed where finger touched shield. Cassie pulled her hand away as quickly as she had attacked, face calm but blood boiling. It had happened so fast that not one of the diners had noticed.

Lexie wasn't smiling any more. 'Sensitive little one, aren't you?'

'I'm keeping your heart for myself you bitch,' whispered Cassie before realising the waiter was coming over. They both sat up straight, smiling as if they were old friends.

'Can I get you anything?' he asked, dead behind the eyes.

Cassie beamed. 'No thank you, I'm here to see my older sister. She's dying.'

Dead behind the eyes registered nothing, 'Just drinks?'

Lexie's gaze didn't move from Cassie's face. 'No thanks, we need to go. Something's come up and it needs to be sorted.'

As the waiter wondered away, Lexie stood 'Let's get this done, I need to get back to work. I've got a pile of admin to do.'

'Last twenty minutes of your life,' Cassie said as if she was talking about the weather.

Lexie smiled again. 'The car park behind the building opposite is a place between Worlds, fancy that? Car parks seem like your sort of scene?'

Lexie was correct, the car park was in both Worlds. They both shuddered when they stepped through. No matter how much you travelled through the worlds, when you passed between, the shudder always hit.

Another woman was there sitting on a wall, legs swinging. Fifty-something, she would not have looked out of place in the company of the former Aunt Fanny of Twickenham. Her greying mousy hair was all over the place, as if she had washed it and left it to dry in a humid environment and she was dressed a floral print dress and old wellington boots.

'My name is Nu-Camadd,' she shouted, 'and I am goddess of this dreadful little car park. You are welcome but if you are here to fuck or fight you must dedicate that violence and passion to me.'

The women looked at each other, Lexie shrugged and Cassie nodded in agreement. A god, even one of a 'dreadful little car park' had power and could cause mischief so it was best not to get on her wrong side. They looked at her and bowed deeply.

Cassie clicked her fingers and held out her right hand. A Japanese Wakizashi sword appeared, and the feeling of its grip felt like home. She swiped it through the air two or three times before settling into her stance.

Lexie produced a similar sword and settled into her stance eyes on Cassie.

Cassie nodded first, 'Alexis Diomedes, I see you,' she said.

Still in stance Lexie's eyes narrowed. 'Come on then, exile – name? It's Cassie isn't it? Cassie…?'

'Newton,' Cassie said.

Lexie frowned, 'Really?'

Cassie nodded.

Lexie nodded. 'Cassie Newton, I see you.'

Most fights take a while to start. Opponents face each other and circle, testing strengths, weaknesses, looking for openings. The start is usually like a game of chess. This one wasn't. Cassie had used Magick getting here and hadn't fought anybody since way before Olivia was born. She didn't have time or patience for chess, strategy or thinking three or four moves ahead. She just attacked, fire and fury. Literal fire – flames shot out of Cassie's hand and when Lexie sidestepped, Cassie had already made up the twenty feet between them, slashing at her opponent's throat. Lexie was lucky to escape just a nick below the left shoulder.

Lexie screamed – in frustration rather than pain – and started to throw blasts of Magick back. Cassie avoided them with ease and went back on the attack, this time relying on her sword rather than her Magick. The goddess and I had witnessed many fights over the millennia, but we knew we were watching two fighters of rare skill. But this was a battle to the death and both were desperate. Lexie was desperate because she had never come under such continued attack from such uncontrolled fury. Cassie was desperate because she knew she was running out of Magick and was starting to physically weaken; but her desperation came not from a fear that she wouldn't win but from a fear that she would not have enough Magick left to travel home afterwards. Olivia needed picking up that afternoon.

She leapt high, slashing down, and as expected, Lexie's sword came up to meet it. The clash was loud but as soon as they connected Cassie hawked and, with all the spittle she could muster, spat into Lexie's mouth. The Chosen One of the Light had been trained to fight, to survive since she was two years old. That life of service meant that after the slightest pause she brought up her sword to where she thought the next attack would come. A slight pause was all Cassie needed. She rammed her rigid left hand into Lexie's throat then dropped to her knees, spinning and cutting with a backslash through the tendons of Lexie's legs. Her opponent fell to the ground with a grunt, clutching throat and legs, her sword falling at her side. She managed to look up in fury. 'So, what's nex…'

The sentence was cut off at the same time as her head.

Cassie stayed in stance for several seconds, panting, knowing that it was over. As she dropped her stance and as she stood up straight, she heard Nu-Camadd slow-clapping behind her.

Cassie ignored the ironic applause and dropped to her knees next to the headless body. Staring down at her dead opponent, she punched through the ribcage and ripped out the heart. Now, she had taken head and heart, and the power surged through her; dark intoxicating power, old blood Magick. She was already glowing red, now, her eyes and aura pulsated with the same violent colour. Without a seconds thought she put the blood covered heart to her mouth and, her eyes dead, she took a bite. Cassie Newton slowly chewed on her vanquished foe's heart then swallowed. Her head dropped for a moment then she threw it back and screamed a scream of victory. A scream of pain, of joy and of anguish.

Eventually, she opened her eyes and stood up. She stared at the heart in her hands as if noticing it for the first time before throwing it carelessly to the floor. The movement made her stumble. She had taken power from the victory, but the fight had weakened her physically and her unexercised leg muscles were cramping. She looked at Lexie's lifeless eyes staring at her and, against her will, she thought of her Olivia, and of *him* and felt anger and guilt. She realised in that moment that she didn't hate Lexie, hadn't hated her even as they were fighting.

Why? Hate was her default setting, her training demanded it, she had clung to it. Why had it abandoned her now?

Applause brought her back to reality; she looked around and saw that Nu-Camadd had started her slow hand-clap again. The goddess had changed. The mischievous eyes were still there but they were bright. Gone were the thinning grey wisps of hair and, instead, bright copper hair framed the powerful face of a woman in her twenties, a face no mortal had seen since the Catuvellauni tribe sacrificed malefactors to her by drowning them in the waterhole that had used to exist below the carpark over two thousand years before.

She stopped clapping and stood. 'Oh girl, I thought I would get a bit of a thrill from a bitch fight, maybe a little bit of relief from the arthritis in my hands but this...' She looked at her youthful hands and laughed. 'Who was she?' she asked.

Cassie ignored her and wiped the sword on Alexis Diomedes' shirt before a word of power made it disappear. She reached into her inside pocket and pulled out a cloth 'bag for life' and forced the decapitated head into it, blood already staining the bottom.

Cassie Newton stared over at me, but she got no reaction. I have seen fights before and I will see them again, my face showed nothing. She nodded in acknowledgement of me as a witness and I smiled and nodded back. Then she turned to Nu-Camadd and bowed.

Nu-Camadd wasn't smiling now, no mischief, she was serious and full of power. Her voice was strong, and she floated about three feet off the ground, eyes glowing green.

'Cassie Newton, I see you and I thank you for this gift. This death marks your heart, but it is only the beginning.'

Her feet touched ground once more and she nodded at Cassie.

Without further acknowledgement Cassie turned away, holding out the bag and whispering it away before walking back to the pub.

It was still empty of customers but this time there was someone behind the bar. The young girl behind the bar was busying herself doing nothing and smiled when she saw Cassie. But the smile disappeared when she saw the blood smeared across Cassie's face and spattered quite liberally over her clothing.

'Do you need an ambulance?' she asked.

Cassie looked down. She hadn't realised the state she was in, which was why she'd had some pretty weird stares on the walk back to the pub.

'No... I'm fine, nosebleed. I get them, just need a bit of a rest. Can I have a double whisky, straight? No ice?' She smiled.

The barmaid did a double push on the whiskey optic and put the glass down on the bar in front of her. Cassie quickly touched the barmaid's hand. 'Here's a tenner, keep the change.'

The barmaid smiled but the transaction featuring an invisible tenner reminded Cassie that, very soon, this Magick power would be gone and exile − bleak, empty exile − would mean she'd have to pay for things with real money. She took a sip, placed the drink down and left the pub.

Outside she waited and looked from person to person as they passed her by until... Bingo. Man, fifties, well dressed, walking somewhere in a hurry. She set off, walking quickly to keep up. As soon as she was side by side with him Cassie touched his hand. 'Excuse me?'

He stopped suddenly and faced her, looking utterly confused. She looked at him straight in the eye. 'There's a cashpoint around the corner, go there and get £250 and bring it back to me now.'

He didn't acknowledge her, his expression never changed. He went. He came back. He gave her the money. She didn't count the money; she didn't have to. 'Go away and forget this ever happened,' she said and watched him go.

Two hundred and fifty pounds! Having this much money was nearly as intoxicating as the first brimming of Magick she'd felt a few hours before. She felt something then, something very, very rare, so rare that she nearly didn't recognise it. Happiness. It came when she thought of having some actual money and remembering that she wouldn't be paying rent to that sex-pest downstairs.

But the happiness disappeared as she thought about how quickly the money would slip through her fingers. She'd need school shoes for Olivia, or next year's school uniform, she was growing so fast. What about Christmas club? Or the leccy or gas bill or even some much-needed new knickers for herself? Despair returned and instead of thinking of new underwear she wondered about how much a bottle of cheap whiskey and a pile of painkillers would cost her.

She went back into the bar and downed the double whisky in one.

Toilet, touch, words, Magick, Oak.

In the toilet at the Oak, she scrubbed the blood off her face and hands before going to the bar and downing the rum and coke, now watered down with melted ice cubes before leaving, with an absentminded wave to the three old men.

She had to change. Damn, she should have done it in the pub. Instead, she ran towards the concrete shell of a bus stop, muttering words of power as she got there. The change took seconds, leaching away the last remnants of her power, and she left the bus stop at speed, arriving at the nursery school's gates just in time to see the stream of excited children leaving the building, bursting with the need to tell their grown-ups, everything about their day.

In the distance she saw Olivia pelting out of school and that weird feeling happened again, the one she thought was happiness. It grew even more when Olivia noticed her and ran towards her, a huge smile on her face. As she got closer, Cassie's tummy clenched as it so often did. Olivia had her father's smile and it caused more damage than killing a daughter of prophecy with a sword in a car park. Olivia hugged her mother's leg and Cassie ruffled her hair with as much love as she could muster.

'Wow Mummy you look really pretty.' Her daughter said reminding her that while she might have magicked away her business clothes, she hadn't changed her make-up. She smiled a thank you.

The walk home involved saying 'that's nice' and 'yes' a lot to Olivia's continual chatter. Cassie wasn't listening. Her old life had crashed into her new one. Both were awful and full of struggle. She thought of happiness again and remembered with pain the short time spent with Olivia's father; she wanted to scream. She opened the flat door and hung up the coat and bag that Olivia had thrown to the ground before running into the living room/kitchen. She needed a cigarette.

But something was wrong. Olivia had stopped talking but the telly wasn't on.

'Mum!'

Cassie ran to the living room and there sitting on her tiny, old, salvaged sofa was a man. He was handsome, wore a dark suit, expensive shoes and was utterly coiffured. She recognised him.

He smiled, a reptilian smile 'Hello darling,' he said to Olivia 'I've come to see your Mummy, she's been a very good girl.'

CHAPTER NINE

DEATH IN NAWLINS

It wasn't quiet in the place he was in, but it was a lot quieter than outside. The bar was small but also colourful and bright; flags and signed T shirts adorned the walls and ceiling. The girl behind the actual bar was replenishing its shelves with newly washed glasses ready for the late afternoon surge that was soon to be upon them. She looked like she'd just stepped out from a roller derby track but without the protection and skates.

He realised he'd acclimatised to the place and the bar wasn't that quiet after all. You could hear the noise from the Quarter outside, people talking or hollering, music blaring from other bars, the cars working out the one-way system or the clip clopping of the horses that showed visitors the madness and grandeur of the place. In the background he heard the twin sounds of New Orleans. The first, the brass instruments, flocked together like magic, dragging their owners with them to make get-up-and-dance, bombastic, arms-waving-in-the-air music. The second, the forlorn calling of the large ship horns, was just as much the music of this part of the Mississippi as anything you would hear on the routes of the streetcars, whatever their names, or in the French quarter, garden district, or anywhere where the native beats of the Mardi gras grow.

Other than him there were two older guys in the bar, one black, one white, same age, laughing so hard at exactly the same thing they had laughed at when they were young so many years ago.

He must have slipped back into daydreaming because he hadn't heard the black friend slip into the space at the bar beside him. His job meant that he only startled internally when he heard 'First time in Nawlins?' The question was asked in a friendly manner from a deep voice shaped by a 40 a day lifetime habit. The man placed down his two empty glasses on the bar in front of him.

'First time for more years than I can remember friend but not my first time. I was born further on up the river,' he said.

'Well, you're local then,' the man laughed.

'Guess I am,' he laughed, and then again. 'Guess I am.' And, hearing the booming laughter from the person with him, he laughed more, turned and offered his hand. 'Louis Ranier Endicott.' Louis said.

The man, still smiling, took it and shook it. 'Michael Merle Dowden but you can call me Mickey.'

'Mickey,' said Louis in affirmation.

Mickey continued '...and that reprobate over there is my good friend Robert Vincent, but y'all can call him what we all do, ain't that right Bobby? Bobby!'

The final 'Bobby' was in a raised voice and when Bobby heard it, he put his hand up in acknowledgement.

'You home for bidniz or pleasure?' asked Mickey.

Louis turned back to the bar and took a sip of his julep. 'Business,' he replied, a darkness changing his demeanour.

Mickey shook his head slowly. 'Hmm, I'm sorry for intruding friend, it seems like this bidniz in't the fun type. I'll leave you in peace. Danielle?' This was to roller derby girl. 'Same again and whatever my friend here wants.'

'Hey Mickey, you don't have to do that.' Louis argued lightly.

Mickey smiled his broad smile. 'I know I don't have to, but I want to and by the looks on your face when we just talked, I think you need one.'

Louis put out his hand to shake in gratitude, but he didn't want to. He wanted to take this man, this smiling, friendly man in his arms and hug him; hug him and cry. Then he could really tell him why he was home, tell him everything. Louis Ranier

Endicott had joined the army at 17 because there was nothing else for him. Service was the antidote to comfort and decay and so he served. He had a deep knowledge of Motown, of the Saints and soon after his first tour he realised he had an aptitude for death. He was also a great gambler. No, I am wrong. Once in a very long while he was a great gambler where he'd make serious money. The rest of the time he was gods awful. After eight years the balance between amazing soldier and debt-ridden liability tipped too far in the latter's favour and the Army got rid of him.

At first an old army buddy got him a job utilising his skills as someone who could get rid of obstacles for a few hundred dollars. Yeah, big men have goons but sometimes you needed to look for tradesmen to do a proper job. Did he want to do it? Hell no! But the debts meant he had to. Get contract, stalk, kill, get paid, gamble, need money, get contract, stalk, kill, get paid, gamble, you get the idea. Then stop. Three years ago, in an Italian restaurant in Boston run by an Irish bookie, where they also did karaoke, he met Francine Futrowsky and that was it. It seems cupid was an even faster shot than him. They talked and drank for hours and for the first time since leaving home he felt relaxed. They carried on drinking, then they kissed, cabbed and spent the night together, and when he woke up she was there, and he couldn't imagine life without her again. Fortunately for him she felt the same way. They married soon after. He did some driving work but found his true calling when two Endicotts became three and Ellie Mae Endicott joined them to change their lives forever.

Contentment is what you should aim for in life. Balance, or the search for balance is a constant and too much joy will, after a spell, lead to a tip the other way. Three years of joy with Francine, two with Ellie Mae meant that the scales were on the move and the tip was in the form of a loud knock on the door when Louis was reading to his daughter. The loud knock was from his gambling past. The gentleman reminded him of his debts, told him the who and when and added what would happen once it was done and in no uncertain terms what would happen to Ellie Mae, then Francine if it wasn't.

After the man left, Louis cradled his daughter until Francine came home three hours later. She knew his past, he had told her the morning after the karaoke. She hadn't cared and it wasn't mentioned again as this man before her, her best friend, had never been that person. However now, for all their sakes, they needed him to be that man again, so she stayed strong and gave him their blessings. The next day his tickets, hotel booking and information on the mark was hand delivered to the mailbox and a week later he was here for the stalk. New Orleans it's written, Nawlins it's said. He had been here two weeks watching the mark, getting to learn about them, know them, their patterns, their manners. This man that they had sent him to kill was not going to die easy if he was to die at all. Louis soon believed that if this job was to be successful, to ensure his wife and daughter were going to live, then it would end with his end.

He'd had the message that it had to be done today. He'd phoned to say goodbye to the girls, no tears for Ellie Mae but hours of crying with Francine before 'Goodbye I will love you two forever.' And then there was a calmness in acceptance. Breakfast at Brennans followed by a leisurely walk through the quarter, gift buying for the girls that he Fed-exed with a last letter to both and then here for a julep. It was almost time.

He looked at Mickey who looked like he knew what he was thinking, knew that what was happening in Louis' life was big. Mickey delicately clapped Louis' shoulder. Everything was going to be ok it meant and for that second Louis really did feel it.

Danielle had handed over the three drinks to Mickey and he slid one to Louis. His broad smile had become a rueful one.

'Hey Louis, you stay strong now y'hear and come back and see us tomorrow?'

Louis smiled 'Thank you Mickey, I will, thank you for the drink.'

Mickey's full on smile returned and suddenly Louis slipped himself off the stool and they hugged. A big, nice hug. Sometimes you people aren't complete wastes of time. Neither would have done it usually, neither of them knew why they did it now, but both understood it needed to be done and both felt the better for it.

For the next ten minutes he nursed the bought drink and during that time a foursome, two couples, came in and ordered some mojitos from an expressionless Danielle, but other than that, it remained music and talk intermingling from the radio and laughter exploding from Mickey and Bobby. He finished the drink and indicated to Danielle that he needed to speak to her.

'Same again?' she asked like a beautiful, bored robot.

'No thanks, I was hoping to buy a drink for Mickey and his friend.' he replied.

'There's no need, they never accept drinks. They own the place.'

Louis let out a light laugh and turned to leave.

'Y'all come back here tomorrow, Louis Ranier Endicott,' shouted Mickey.

'I hope I can,' Louis replied as he left the bar.

For the last week at this very time his mark, Adam Moneymore left his hotel on Royal Street and drank his way around the quarter, his pattern was pretty constant broken only by where he ate. He ate alone but never drank alone, he seemed to be a man who people gravitated to, a man made for parties. A thought kept aggravating Louis, the man who gave him this job said that once done $2 million would be given to Francine. That is so much money that any killer in North America would do this job, hell if they had asked, maybe he would have done the job without the threatening. That last bit, he knew was not true, he loved his life, and two or twenty million dollars wouldn't have changed that. Moneymore must have either done something so big that it could not be ignored, or he was one of the most dangerous people walking around the world at this moment. The strange thing was Louis couldn't guess which. The man was not tall, but he was built like a bull, shoulders to carry things on, he wore his grey hair in a top knot and had a beard that had hidden his face for a long, long time. He was closer to 60 than 50 years old which made Louis wonder what sort of machine he'd been in his heyday. But while the man was dangerous and walked like a warrior aware of his talent, he made friends wherever he went, and Louis couldn't help but like him.

If this wasn't what it was, he knew that he'd have walked away from this job or he thought with a surprise, gone drinking with the old goat. He checked his phone for the time and realised he'd been there for half an hour and hadn't seen him. Had he left earlier or had his plans changed? Not a man for panic, Louis headed into the hotel. It was all or bust, it had to happen tonight.

The woman behind reception smiled 'How can we help you today?'

Lightly he said, 'Oh hi there, I'm a close friend of Mr Moneymore who I believe is staying here. We were meant to meet here before going for drinks, but he seems to be late.'

The woman beamed. 'A friend of Mr Moneymore? Lucky man! And may I say a friend of Mr Moneymore is a friend of ours, isn't that right Reynell?' she said to a colleague who came out of the back office.

Reynell squealed 'You a friend of Mr Moneymore? He is one of my most favouritist guests we've ever had. How can we help you honey?'

'He was meant to meet Mr Moneymore here,' and then to Louis, 'I just come on duty sorry.'

'Well, I'm sorry, but he left about an hour ago and I doubt he'd have come back in, not without saying hello to Reynell,' the receptionist said with enough sass to fuel a city generator. She laughed, full and loud, and yet a-bloody-gain he smiled. For a man close to murder and then a bloody death he sure was laughing and smiling a lot…

Louis thanked them and started to leave when Reynell looked up from her paper. 'Well don't drink in any of the bars 'til you catch up with him you hear? With the drinking you two got ahead of you the last thing you need is to be turning up to him all liquored-up.'

He'd tried three of the usual bars and nothing. It wasn't panic setting in, but it didn't exactly feel like calm either. The good news was Moneymore had been in the last one. The barman smiled wistfully as if remembering a lost love not a hairy arsed old man and suggested a bar just along the street.

That bar had a live band playing and was starting to fill up with the early evening party crowd. He went in and looked around but no Moneymore. He headed towards the toilet and then in the next instant found himself about eight feet away from his original position and lying on the floor. The reason for this instant transportation had absolutely nothing to do with the Magick you have witnessed in earlier chapters and all to do with Louis not looking where he was going and walking in at the same time that the massive frame of the man he was looking for was coming out.

The bar instantly felt drama and kerfuffle, and while the music didn't stop, the early revellers did and looked towards the sudden noise.

Louis lay on the floor, feeling like he'd run into a bus. He struggled to suck in air, having had the wind knocked out of him. The bus was the man he was sent to kill. Adam Moneymore to him, but to us? We know him as Adda Mynyddmawr. 'Adam Big Mountain'. After a few hundred years of correcting the pronunciation of his name, Adda had decided to make life easier by giving himself an anglicized one when amongst English speakers. Alas, my friends, this is a tale full of killing but equally tragic is the oft murdering of the Welsh language by people who don't want to try and say words properly.

'GODS!' came the voice. 'I'm sorry, I didn't see you.' Then Louis was flying. Wait, it's still not magic, Adda Mynyddmawr had picked him up off the floor like he was a rag doll. 'Are you ok?' he asked.

Louis tapped Adda's hand gently to release the grip. There was no malice, but Louis' mind was in overdrive. He'd never messed up a job like this and now he was face to face with the man he was meant to kill. He looked into the concerned, blue eyes and was even more certain that he did not want to kill this man. The man's eyes flickered from concern to something else and Louis' thought was followed quickly by another one, this time 'I don't think this man can *be* killed, anyway.'

In an instant the eyes resorted to normal and then to humour.

'You ok?'

Louis needed to get out of there. 'Yeah, I'm fine...thank you sir...' he said as he made to leave. Adda didn't stop him, just walked alongside him as they both left the bar.

'I'm not being rude, but I'm fine.' Louis insisted.

'I'm also not being rude, so you'll accept a drink off me as an apology.' Adda replied and just as he saw Louis about to protest, put his arm around his shoulders like a friend and steered him across the street. 'I don't want any arguments young 'un, I am getting you a drink. Adda Moneymore.' He introduced himself.

'Adam?' Louis asked. This man was called Adam. He winced thinking he'd given away the fact he knew the man.

'Did I say that?' Adda continued conversationally. 'I tell people my name is Adam because foreigners can't get their head around Adda. Don't get me started on Moneymore, also not my name but that's another story and one for a bar, so let's get to one and I'll tell you.'

Still a tad dazed and being directed by a man with an arm like a hairy tree trunk, Louis found it hard to argue and before he knew it, they were at a door. Not a bar door, just a run of the mill door to someone's house. All the way there Moneymore had talked, and Louis wasn't sure if he'd been talking to him.

Adda now addressed Louis directly, his granite hard face with its thick beard looming only two inches from Louis' which wasn't needed as the man had one volume level and that was 'speaking to someone in the other room.' 'Hey Boyo, I need you to listen. I need to buy you a drink, but I also have some business to attend to, so you are going to have to come into this one with me and the thing is, it's a bit different. Everything will be fine so stick next to your Uncle Adda OK?'

They walked through the door, Louis nodded,

'O...

There was no 'K', there was just Louis throwing up. It came from nowhere; it was a shudder and an explosion from his stomach.

Adda laughed his booming laugh. 'Sorry I forgot about the shudder and forgot it maybe your first time. It's ok, you'll get over it in a few minutes.'

It was like the place was expecting people who entered to be sick because the floor of the small entry room they were standing on was a huge iron grate with running water below it.

Adda lurched beyond the entry room and into the bar holding up his large hand to get someone's attention.

Louis looked up. The bar was large, open and busy, especially at one end when at – he looked at his watch – at around five-thirty about twenty people were crowded around a small stage with two people murdering 'Summer Loving' on karaoke. She sure looked like a young, even blonder Olivia Newton-John, but she couldn't sing to save her life. His voice was better than Travolta's but, unfortunately, he looked like he'd eaten Travolta recently. Regardless, the crowd was loving it. Louis thought it must be some sort of underground bar for a youth culture he hadn't heard of. A large cross section, although far from all, had extremely bright hair colouring, bright blondes, deep reds and even vibrant blues. The other person that stood out was the karaoke MC. Louis thought he was a dwarf but then remembered his wife had told him that wasn't allowed anymore, adding that he should say 'short person'. He sure looked like a dwarf though. It wasn't his size that marked him out anyway, it was his bright blue beard and his hair that could have only been gelled using red, extra strong, industrial concrete, shaped up into huge foot long spikes.

'BOY!' Louis knew Adda was bawling at him. Adda was sat on the stool, grinning like a Cheshire cat holding what looked like two posh buckets of exotic drinks in his two massive hands.

'MOJITOS!' he shouted even though Louis was at his side by then.

Louis took the drink and listened as Adda talked about New Orleans, the South in general, and why he loved it so much. The big man spoke about the place like he was the local, and for a moment Louis wished Francine and Ellie Mae were here so they could meet this funny, friendly man he was meant to kill.

If he was to kill him and save his family, he had to do it now and that 'now' was the very 'now' when Adda backhanded Louis on to the floor. It was the second time in two hours he had been put on his backside and he looked up to see why. They came out of nowhere. There were four of them and all attacked at the same time trying to punch and kick Adda. They landed a few but it was like they were trying to harm an elephant by throwing cotton wool balls at it. The old man grabbed the closest man by the hair with his huge hand and punched him with his spare. Adda grabbed the second assailant by the front of his shirt and slapped him back and forth a few times and he hadn't even gotten off his stool. The two remaining attackers came on carefully, understanding what this fat old man could do now.

'Wait!' Adda shouted, laughing like a lunatic holding his hands out, palms facing towards them placatingly.

They looked like they were going to charge again but stopped suddenly when Adda stopped smiling.

'My turn to speak. You,' he pointed at the closest. 'Go help your wee friends come around and I can knock all four of you out when I get back.' He looked over at the woman behind the bar. 'We can carry on the fight can't we Aunty Tina?'

Aunty Tina nodded. 'Stay in this part away from the Karaoke, and you paying for breakages.'

Adda nodded back. 'Got it.'

The two men still looked confused and so did Louis as he picked himself up off the floor.

Adda didn't wait for the agreement, he walked past Louis and through his would-be assailants towards the Karaoke stage and its accompanying throng.

'It's six of the clock and it's Friday,' the Karaoke MC announced, 'and you know what that means?'

A huge cheer went up from the beautiful, literally bright, young things with non-regulars cheering because they liked to cheer or were drunk.

'Ladies and Gentlemen, Men and Women of Mer, denizens of This and That.' It felt like the start of a world heavyweight boxing bout. The crowd around the tiny karaoke stage had increased and the bar had definitely gotten busier. 'It's six, it's Friday and iiiiiiiiiiiiiit's Happy Hour!' Another cheer and this time the throng started chanting 'Heeby' over and over again with shouts of 'We love you Heeby!' cutting through.

Heeby, who Heeby Jeebies, the bar we are now in was named for, shushed the crowd and, after a short while, they obeyed.

He smiled. 'Welcome to you. Happy hour begins once we hear a song from our friend, shrinking violet, defeater of the Gawr, Kenigan Bonesucker, known to the Mer..' a big cheer erupted from the bright young things, 'as Wreck-sender but known to us by his given name, I, Heeby Jeeby, we, Heeby Jeebies give you: Adda y Mynyddmawr!'

The whine of a song came on. It was the introduction of 'Wicked Game' by Chris Isaacs. Adda went at it like he was preaching a sermon at a funeral and everyone there listened like it mattered. Adda sang it three levels lower than bass, people could feel it in the bottom of their stomach, changing key from three levels below bass to two levels below bass for the line repeated three times.

'And IIIIIIIIIIIIIIIIIIIIIIIIIIIIIIIIIIII will never fall in love again.'

It was weirdly mesmerising, and the bar just watched, in silence.

Silence; pause and...

'Nobody loves no one....' the last line... Adda with the performance of a twice a night Vegas lounge singer closed his eyes and bowed his head, casting a spell of further silence over the entire place.

With the solemnity of an honour guard Heeby walked over to Adda, taking the microphone off him like he was taking an untouched bottle of scotch from an alcoholic about to fall off the wagon and then they embraced. It was theatre....

Adda slowly put one of his arms in the air and eyes still closed, smiled.

The crowd in the bar exploded. People were on their feet applauding, cheering and Louis was even surprised to see a couple of the bright haired people crying. Even the conscious assailants started clapping.

'What is going on?' he said to no one in particular.

One of the four attackers thought he was talking to him and mumbled that he didn't know and then gave a small apologetic smile.

The smile turned to shock as Adda ruffled the man's hair like a child's as he resumed his stool by the bar. 'Right boys, want to give me another go?' Adda smiled his big open smile. The men stepped back; they weren't the brightest but even they saw which way this was going. From nowhere, a newcomer, a bigger man, stepped between them, tall and broad shouldered. He reached into the inside pocket of his worn leather jacket and pulled out a pistol. His frustration with what had happened with the four men written clearly on his face. He pointed it at the middle of Adda's face.

'Enough of this crap. Die fat-man.' he said.

Without a thought, there wasn't time, Louis reacted. There was no way Adda could avoid this, but Louis was closer, and he drove himself at the would-be assassin's hand, knocking it as the shot was fired. The gun clattered to the floor and Louis with it.

The man snarled and to Louis' shock seemed to pull out what he recognised as a Claymore sword from thin air. Louis didn't know but I do and I'm telling this story and it was a Claymore sword, a big one with a basket hilt. It was lovely. With the panache of a dancer, the man pulled into a beautiful fighting stance, legs apart, sword above his head, point towards Adda's throat at the same time as a horn like a unicorn's protruded from the centre of his head, his eyes glowing red. He snarled, his face full of hatred.

Adda stood still and smiled, lifted both of his arms, his hands just apart and shouted.

'MINCEMAKER!'

A bigger sword appeared in his hands. If the claymore was a beast, then this was its bigger, meaner brother. In a flash, he parried his opponent's sword aside. Leather jacket stepped back a few paces and returned to his previous fighting stance.

Adda looked lovingly at his sword blade, now held close to his chest. He nuzzled his bearded chin against its blade.

'Mincemaker,' he said as if talking to a faithful dog.

'Come on, fat man, and let's get on with this. I don't know why there is so much money on such an old has been,' said leather jacket.

You are expecting a tale of battle, of attack and defence, of to and fro and banter, big old banter. Yeah? Sorry to disappoint. There were two swings by Adda, massive arcs, full of power, met by Leather Jacket's sword, then a third, equally fast and powerful. This one was met by the top of Leather Jacket's head and the sword stopped below his collar bone.

Adda wiped off bits of Leather Jacket on Leather Jacket's leather jacket, kissed the blade and threw it towards the corner of the room. It disappeared. The big man held out his hand to Louis. The people in Heeby's, for those thirty seconds were transfixed by what was happening at the bar before returning their attention back to a girl singing Crystal Gayle's 'Don't it make your brown eyes blue'. The two other conscious assassins, showing an extreme but not seen before this time, excellent knack for survival, dragged their two colleagues away, apologising repeatedly.

Louis had known death and war and through all that, he hadn't seen anything so clinically brutal as the ending of that man... with a horn. Adda fixed him with a stare. 'Now tell me boy. Why is a man meaning to kill me now deciding to save my life?'

Louis' mouth opened and closed a few times as he struggled to comprehend what was happening 'You...you knew?'

'I never forget a face and I've seen yours around the Quarter this last week. I know the call for my head went out. You don't think you or the bozo attempts today were the first. So?'

'They are going to kill my family if I don't kill you. They are as good as dead now so you may as well kill me. I couldn't go on and if you don't I will.'

'Woah, woah, woah,' Adda replied. 'Let's not get ahead of ourselves. Your wife and your little girl, Ellie Mae isn't it? They are fine. It's done, everything is going to be ok. Your family are safe. There are people I trust with them now and will stay with them until you are home.'

Louis believed him. Stress and tension left his body like air from a lock in space and he cried. He cried on Adda, huge sobs of relief. 'It's ok matey,' said Adda, softly, which made Louis cry even more. After a small while, Louis wiped the tears away from his face with the palm of his hand and, embarrassed with crying, turned away and wiped his hand on his trousers.

'How did you know?' he asked quietly.

'Like I said I saw you and had you followed, they did their research and found everything out,' Adda replied.

'But I was going to kill you tonight, I didn't plan to save you,' said Louis.

Adda's smile was never far away, and it was back now. 'I was told by a mutual friend about the truth of your heart and took the decision. No matter what happened, I was going to save your wife and child. I keep being told I'm one of the Goodies and there's some sort of code and stuff.'

'Who is our mutual friend?' asked Louis utterly confused.

'Mickey Dowden. He owns a bar 3 streets down. He has the wonderful talent for reading people's souls with a touch and seeing yours, seeing you didn't really want it to happen, he had to tell me.'

'By mind magic?'

'What? What the hell is that? No! by text.'

This time Louis laughed. He sat on the stool, not trusting his legs to support him. 'What now?' he asked.

'We drink my friend. Also, we sing, we dance, we eat good food, and we sleep. Tomorrow you can go home to your girls.'

'And you?'

Louis thought that Adda was pausing for an answer, but he wasn't. He was watching someone who had come into the bar and was standing on the newly washed sick grate. His face became serious. 'Forget tomorrow, I think everything is about to change for me in the next five minutes.' Louis turned to see a young man walk through the bar. He walked towards them but there was no menace in him.

'Adda, King, I see you.'

'Speak.'

'It's a message from Tommaltach King. It's time for you to come home, it's the Darkness, the end.'

Lines of concern tightened around Adda's face. 'When am I needed?'

'I have a ticket for you to fly tomorrow.'

Adda smiled and turned to the bar. 'Aunty Tina, 3 mojitos, 3 tequila chasers. Keep them coming until we fall down.'

The tequilas arrived. Adda held up his drink in toast and Louis and a confused messenger joined him.

'Tomorrow,' Adda said.

'Tomorrow,' the others answered.

A beautiful girl with bright blue hair sat on the karaoke stage with her fish tail flopped over the side, singing 'It's the end of the world as we know it' by REM not knowing she was right.

Everybody cheered.

CHAPTER TEN
TOMMY SENDS CARATACUS WEST

'Have you pissed yourself?' asked Tommy. Before he allowed Caratacus to answer he continued speaking 'Doesn't matter, sit yourself down, son.' He indicated the middle seat of the sofa opposite the television.

Caratacus sat down and immediately worried about what the hell he had done to get a visit from Tommy McKracken.

He looked at the all-powerful crime lord. Tommy's tightly bearded face looked as if it had been there and done that which is probably because it had. That face looked sixty but also expressed about ten thousand years. His eyes, though, were the burning, shining eyes of youth and power. They were blue crystal and looked like they powered the little menace. Caratacus' thoughts stayed on 'little' and realised that the Tommy in front of him was only 5 foot 8 inches, but whenever he or anybody else talked about the Ulsterman they thought of someone much taller.

His eyes shifted swiftly from Tommy to the massive bloke who stood just behind him.

Flash.

It wasn't a bloke; it was a huge green thing in a suit with yellow tusks growing from its mouth.

'What the…?' he shouted as he got up sharp and sudden. He stepped back in fear to be met by the sofa he'd just gotten up from, his backside was re-acquainted with the seat within a second. He looked to Tommy and then back to the green muscle only to find it was just a normal looking man albeit a man who didn't so much look like a brick shit house as like one who had eaten one.

Tommy's face changed from mild disinterest to concern. He sat forward. 'Drom? Head off to the car, go and get yourself a bite to eat and I'll ring you when I need you.' Without a word, probably because he couldn't think of one, Drom left.

'You can go too sweetheart,' Tommy said to Marged while still looking at Caratacus. Marged folded her arms in a silent and a most definite *piss off*.

The sinking feeling that had been with Caratacus since seeing the crime lord in his shop prepared to slip further as Marged tried to stare the visitor out.

'Please Marged,' he said.

She scrunched up her eyes and in Welsh said, '*Touch a hair on his head and I will find you.*'

Tommy didn't look at her but almost off-handedly replied in the same language. '*I'm not here to hurt him. I'm here to see him safe. Off you go before I change my mind with you.*

Arms still folded and a face like she was sucking a lemon, Marged sauntered backwards never taking her eyes off Tommy, even when she was opening then closing the door to the shop.

Caratacus had quickly put his clothes back on and, while still getting waves of ecstasy and nausea and still soaking wet from the belly button down, leant forward to introduce himself.

'Caratacus Lewis,' he said.

Tommy's voice stayed level 'For the love of gods son, I know who you are. I should do. I am your godfather!'

'What?' asked Caratacus, forgetting who he was talking to.

'I'm your godfather. I thought you knew?' Tommy said.

'No, I didn't…'

'Well, you do now. Anyway, there is no need to get all misty eyed, your Uncle Tommy hasn't had a hug off you for a few decades and doesn't want one off you now.' He sat forward with a stare that would have turned Medusa to stone.

'I take it something happened to you today. I take it you're feeling different. Am I right? Oit with it son, you're sweating like a pig and look like you're going to keel over. I have an idea what's happening, but do you?'

Caratacus told Tommy about his morning, about the old woman, and about how he was feeling. '...and I didn't piss myself....' he added at the end.

'Has she gone? Poor, poor wee girl. Are you sure it was hit and run?'

Caratacus nodded, 'I saw it.' Tommy took his phone out and, in a moment, just said 'Fanny Hill, find out what's happened.' Then straight to Caratacus, 'What you are feeling and what you have been feeling is a release of Magick.' Caratacus just stared, he probably would have been a little less surprised if Tommy McKracken had broken into song.

'Magic?' he said hesitantly.

'No. Magick. OK son, listen to me because this is going to be a lot to take in and it doesn't help that you're shitting yourself there because I'm Tommy McKracken. As of today, your life has changed. Things you didn't know about and wouldn't believe are a fact and I'll start off with a few right now. Magick exists, you have a load of it and today some ancient Goddess released it which is why you can feel it and…'

'And…?' interrupted Caratacus.

'At a very basic level son, I need you to do something for me. In a few hours' time you are going on a trip to Wales, and you'll find a bloke called Arthur and you need to convince him to go with you to see the Lady of the lake and get his sword back.'

It didn't feel like amazing ecstasy anymore it felt like a lot of horse tranquiliser.

'You're my godfather?' Caratacus' mind started to catch up.

'Jasus! This is going to take longer than I thought. Move past that. I know your mother and have known her family for years. Sorry if I haven't been putting a pound coin in your birthday card but hey maybe you appreciate the house you live in and this shop as not bad compensation, eh?' Realising that this bombshell would make explaining the important things even tougher Tommy back tracked.

'Ignore that,' he clicked his fingers as he saw Caratacus' eyes go glazed. Caratacus jumped and stared, slack jawed at his newly found godfather.

'Now listen to me. We haven't got time for you to piss about. Firstly, Magick exists...no... listen forget that for a moment, there are two worlds...erm dimensions maybe, but worlds, they exist together but are different, they are side by side but….JASUS…' Tommy annoyed himself trying to find the right words and the outburst shook Caratacus out of any sort of zombification.

'It's hard to explain but there always have been two worlds and here, 'This' world is full of wee shitbags like you, and politics and...and money and science and all that nonsense. Magick exists here but it's virtually disappeared. Now the other world...That World is one full of Magick, and different species like elves and orcs you know from books and….' he was speaking so fast he was getting stuck 'Drom! You saw Drom and he's an ogre, so yeah Magick, wizards, ogres and no mobile phones. Lots of things you think as fairy tales are true. Are you feeling me son?'

'I am feeling you Tommy McKracken,' Caratacus said, leadenly.

'This is what you are going to do. Go home, take off your pissed jeans…'

'I haven't pissed myself…'

'...pack a bag. I've put a few grand in your account. Get a train down to Fishguard Harbour, get yourself to Cwm Llechau and get yourself into the Triple T pub where I've booked a room for you. Then, find the 'Once and Future' pub, tell Galahad, big fella, lovely guy, that I sent you, get Arthur and make your way north to find the Lady of the Lake, get the sword and wait for my instructions. Happy?'

'Instructions…'

Tommy checked his watch and nodded. Caratacus phone chirped about 5 times, one after the other.

'That should be the confirmation of where you are staying, the money in your account and the tickets down there. Here…'

He lifted himself a bit and then took a piece of folded paper from his back pocket. This is more information than you need. Look at it, remember it and then destroy and when I say destroy, I mean rip it into tiny pieces, eat some of them, flush some of it and burn the rest, ok?'

'Burn instructions.'

Tommy got up and sat next to Caratacus. 'Listen Caratacus.' His voice for the first time was conciliatory 'I know you are a lazy wee shite who relies on his mother far too much, but this is serious, it couldn't get any more serious and you have to step up.'

Caratacus sat back, right back, on the sofa and blew in exasperation as if trying to expel the day.

'I'm sorry...Mr McKracken...'

'Tommy...'

'Tommy...I just want to be honest so please forgive me if I ask this again because this is pretty tough to get my head around.'

'I can understand that. It was pretty tough for me to explain but go ahead,' replied his godfather.

'OK, can I ask what the hell is happening to me. I feel like...'

'You are going to explode?' interrupted Tommy.

Caratacus pointed at Tommy. 'Yes!'

'That's the Magick growing and your body reacting to it son. I'm not really a Magicker, it's never really been part of me. It seems like when Fanny Hill died you being so close must have affected you in some way. In what way I do not know. Now, when you are thousands of years old like your Uncle Tommy here, you don't believe in coincidences.'

'Thousands of years?' asked Caratacus.

'Let's not get ahead of ourselves. I was coming to you today anyway. I needed someone unconnected to anyone I know, or any of my world to go back west and pick up the King. I had picked you, but I had no knowledge about all this or your Magick. You're forty years old for Gods' sake, surely, it's too late for you to play a part.'

'Thirty-eight...'

'Whatever.'

'You said King, I thought I was going to an Arthur? Is his name Arthur King?'

Tommy sat back and crossed his legs 'Youse call him King Arthur, many call him Arthur King. It doesn't matter, you haven't time for this. Whatever is happening you need to go. I certainly don't understand what is going on.' Tommy said the last line to himself, got up and straightened his jacket. Caratacus had neither the inclination, brain space nor the courage to ask about whether this King Arthur was anyone other than an eccentric man but what he did have all those three for was a last chance to get out of all this mess.

'Err...Tommy...this magic stuff is all well and good, but couldn't you find someone else for this. I mean I'm very busy with the shop and looking after Marged...'

Tommy leant close, his face inches from Caratacus, his voice low, almost a growl. 'Shop my hairy arse. You barely get here by ten on any day of the week. Tomorrow, you're only here for an hour. If it's any longer it's because of the film you are watching. Your Saturday record is selling 2 books so don't be trying your *'I'm busy'* bullshit with me, son. Are you hearing me?'

Tommy was right, Caratacus knew he was right, and Tommy knew that Caratacus knew he was right. He paused for a second because he didn't know what to say. Rather than explain himself, make excuses with tiny denials where he knew he was on solid ground like the fact he'd sold 3 books once, he thought that the best response to someone who ordered 'disappearings' was to nod and say 'ok, sorry, go on.'

It was like a switch was flipped and Tommy smiled. It felt like the whole world smiled as well and became a teensy-weensy less threatening.

The switch flipped again, and a serious look came over Tommy. Caratacus' head was all over the place.

'Time to get home and pack aye?' said Tommy as he headed to the door. 'You can come in now Marged,' he added.

He opened the door to find Marged, arms still folded glaring at him.

I don't think he meant to, but he smiled and the faintest suggestion of a laugh escaped. Not a laugh, a chuckle and those ancient eyes glistened with humour. 'Maybe I should be sending her. She really does scare the hell out of me.'

She stamped in while Tommy held the door open, then he stopped and looked back at Caratacus. 'Don't dawdle. Time is a ticking.' And Tommy left.

'Shall I follow him and lamp him?'

'What? Good God no!' Caratacus exclaimed. 'That's Tommy bloody McKracken!' she shrugged as if nothing had happened. 'Tea?' she asked.

Every part of his fibre wanted to say yes, send her out for biscuits and put on a film. Anything just to get back to real life but he felt the paper in his hand, weighing down not only his hand but his life, as if it was made of lead.

'Marged, let's close the shop for the weekend and can you look after it next week? In between training?' he asked, weak voiced and utterly drained.

'Yup,' she said.

Magic, Arthur, London's premium Northern Irish gangster, a dead magic-giving woman.

He was about to leave but instead, he sat.

'I'll have a cup of tea now Marged. And can I have an extra sugar please?'

CHAPTER ELEVEN

KNIGHTS OF MYTH ANONYMOUS

'Hi, my name is Terry,' Terry smiled an open smile. 'Firstly, can I say it's nice to see so many of us here this evening with the rain and everything,' he said in a lilting Rhondda accent. He paused, making time to look at each of the people sitting before him. 'Welcome, welcome all.'

He shifted on his chair and, as it scraped the floor, the noise was made louder by the old but solid wooden floorboards underneath and the spacious empty room they were in. The chairs the six men were sitting on had seen better days, as had the hall, as had the entire building.

It was known as the 'Worky's' and, in its heyday, it had been the centre of the community and of the lives of the people who lived there. The chairs had changed over time but the hall and the building it was part of had changed little since the day they'd been completed. Designed, built, and paid for by the contributions of the men who had toiled underground a century and a half ago. The subjects of King Coal digging once again, but this time into their paltry earnings to have something for themselves. These men of the Dark had a vision and in this Workingman's club they saw potential for a life better than they had for their children and their children's children. This place was intended as an escape from the harshness of work and the cramped conditions of home. It was to be a refuge from one life and the centre of another, a place of meeting for those firebrands who demanded more, a place of books and learning for those who wanted to know more. Pub, entertainment hall, library, meeting place, a centre to a world and a beating heart of a community. The bodies of those pioneers who had the idea and had built it, and the generations that followed, had returned underground, but this time permanently. The last decades of the twentieth century had taken their toll on the club as they had on the village and every village in the valley and the valleys surrounding.

Poverty and apathy saw the Worky's move away from the centre to the periphery of memory, only kept alive there by a generation that wanted to do more together. They recalled the final days of splendour, the Friday night bingo for the women, the men in the bar, both dressed up to the nines, the dos, the comedian...the filthy bugger, and then nothing. The bar died when the last of the volunteers and regulars did.

Death. Flatline.

Beep. Pause. Beep. Pause. Beep.

Life, a flicker, just.

A toddler group moved into the Worky's. Bloody expensive is childcare, bloody extortionate, but 'Seren's' wasn't, so it boomed. The council were gutted when those mothers got in touch. They had become reluctant landlords, ones who would have knocked the old shed to the earth in a flash but were worried about the backlash at the ballot box they'd have from nostalgia, a very powerful nemesis in the world of one's perception of progress. When mothers come together, they are more powerful than a nation with nuclear missiles and as scary as a nation with nuclear missiles who has an idiot in charge.

They'd already managed to get the hall hire for next to nothing but within a month they'd forced the council to cough up money for improvements. The council only bloody went and did them. Within three months the place was bouncing. Ruth's Zumba was the place to be, while Pilates by Andrew Evans? well... Pilates wasn't posh but when it was 'by' someone and by someone as well spoken and dishy as Andrew Evans then it was like a starred restaurant. The people flocked there to see sexy Andrew Evans. Sorry, women flocked there to see his routine, his scissors, his side-kick-kneeling, and his gorgeous cheeky smile. Next came the bar opening. On a Saturday at first, then Sunday lunch time started, followed by all day and then Friday night. The council shut up as soon as they started to break even. And so, at half seven on a Wednesday evening after Diet Club, a support group had started and that's where we are, in the hall, a closed bar at one side and on the other, a stage, curtains closed over stacked chairs and in the middle a circle of people.

Terry, still smiling, closed his eyes and inhaled deeply and exhaled equally so. He looked around as if noticing people for the first time and then clapped to give himself energy. The six, in their sixties or over, all looking as grey as the weather outside, looked at him expectantly.

'OK, who is going to start us off?' Terry asked.

Silence, accompanied by a lot of sheepish looking down on the floor, was the response.

Suddenly the door banged open and just like the chair scrape earlier it was made louder by the almost empty hall.

The seven men sat in a circle at the centre looked towards the noise and were all surprised to see a tall, blonde, young man bustle in, shaking a wet umbrella and taking off his coat. He was smiling and his whole demeanour made it feel like the sun had walked in. He strolled in as if he owned the place, but it wasn't with arrogance, just as if he'd been coming here as long as they had. He shook the remnants of Welsh weather off his coat and hung it up, balancing the big umbrella against the wall and then strode over.

He reached the circle, smiling and nodding to the men who couldn't help but smile and nod in return. There were even a few 'arite butt's, butt not meaning arse but friend in the valleys of southern Wales. He stopped when he realised he hadn't got a chair and rushed with repeated 'sorrys' towards the stage and a loose chair below it.

He picked it up and brought it back towards the circle. The men had already made space for the glowing, wide shouldered boy. He sat down, a big grin on his face and he shook hands warmly with the two men who had moved apart, clapping one on the shoulder as if they had been in school together.

He leant forward in his chair and looked at Terry who was easily recognisable as the man in charge with the clipboard he held.

'Sorry,' the man said.

'No problem...err?' the err was Terry's way of asking the newcomer's name.

'Tristan.' He got up then, took two steps and extended his hand to Terry who took it.

'Terry,' Terry replied.

'Terry? Terry.' Tristan said it as if he had never heard anything so exotic in his life, it was like he was tasting it.

'Have I missed anything? I took the portal from the Tavistock off City Road and it took me to Treorchy instead of here and so I had to take two other pubs to get myself up the road.' He laughed at his silliness.

Terry and the men just nodded, not knowing what the hell he was talking about. All except Clive who said, 'I've been in the Tavistock, twenty years ago, nice place.'

'It's near my house,' said Tristan which only seemed to puzzle the circle more. He continued, completely undeterred, 'So glad I'm not late. Shall I start?'

Terry's experience and facilitator training wanted to bring the session back to some order but there was something about the man that he wanted to know about, so he let him carry on.

'Hi everybody, my name is Tristan, I am from the line of Eudaf Hen, of the Kings of Cernow and I am of Arthur. I don't know how this works, but I'll give it a go. The reason I am here is because I'm feeling lost and a bit confused.' He stopped speaking and he stopped smiling and it was as if the sun was lost. Every man in that circle sat up and perched forward in their chairs.

'I am not of Arthur any more,' Tristan continued, a serious look on his face as he took time to look around the circle. 'I left and I don't know if I'm sorry. I couldn't handle it any more. All of us stuck in that pub, him crying or angry or…or nothing, just sitting there doing nothing. He's got depression but he won't accept the fact. We were all depressed though! I had to go, I had to do something, we all did, but all I feel is guilt. So instead of anger and being depressed at being stuck, all I feel is guilt which brings on depression, it's all so bloody bleak.'

The silence was deafening, even the rain stopped as if it wanted to listen as well.

'What if this is our last life? We've been called back for thousands of years. Thousands! Every time these people get into trouble or those bastards…sorry…the Dark start to meddle. Why can't they just leave things be? It must be exhausting thinking of new ways to take over the world or enslave it or destroy it. What a waste! And then as soon as it's bad, we wake up in that cave…yes, a cave, after sleeping for sometimes hundreds of years. Sometimes you don't fall asleep, sometimes you are killed. Actually killed! It's not normal because when you wake up, you wake up the second after that final sword stroke, the stab, the fall, the fight, the pain, the fear, and it's with you as soon as you wake up. The moment you wake up!'

He paused as if he'd interrupted his inner self.

'Don't get me started on the changes when you wake. A lot of it's great but it takes time. Saddles! Iron! Flying! Porn! You sleep for 60 years and wake into a world of online porn…Jesus, the porn…sorry. I had to leave that pub….'

He smiled briefly, and jokingly said, 'Not because of the porn…' The men mesmerised by the story, stopped and blinked at the break and they all laughed a little. He carried on.

'I really couldn't stay. Especially when some of the boys left. No one has heard from Geraint. Gwalch and Owain were off shooting people in the middle east. I don't want to fight; I've had a gutsful of it. At least the last time, that was 1943, we had machine guns, no more face to face. It makes things easier, but do you know what? I still don't like large bangs and I get so bloody anxious you know? Do you know what else pisses you off? Sorry…the stories. People believe anything.'

He sat back exasperated and continued. 'Sir? Sir…. bloody sir, Sir Tristan? Do you know what? If any of us could go back in time we would go back and punch Chretien de Troyes and that arse…. sorry, Mallory straight in the face. We allowed the two little arseholes...sorry...a little bit of access and they reward us with...with that crap.... sorry... We were all fuming. One of the older stories puts the old man committing incest and if you think we were, are, angry then she was absolutely tamping. All that romance crap...sorry. My story! My life! Iseult? It was Esyllt. My Esyllt. It's starting to make my blood boil now! Those King Arthur films? Round bloody table? Where the hell did they get this stuff from? Lancelot? Who the hell is Lancelot?'

Tristan leaned back in his chair and the rest of the group copied his exact movement but unlike him, they soon sat forward in expectation for the next part.

'Gal knows that I'm in Cardiff. I bet the old man doesn't care. I just think he needs help with his depression y'know, a group like this maybe and drugs, a shed load of drugs. I don't know why we are here, not in an existential way although that would be nice. Last time, we were here to fight Nazis. Now they were proper baddies, with baddies uniforms y'know? But this time? We woke up in that bloody cave and nothing, no one to fight, no one to rescue.'

He paused, briefly.

'Actually, I'm wrong. The whole world was in trouble. We had so many horrid people to fight that we didn't know who we were meant to. We still don't! If the world is going mental without the Dark causing it, if we don't know why we are here then maybe they are right. This is our last life, our real life and when we die, that's it, the end! If not, why are we here? What are we for?'

Deafening silence.

Terry frowned 'Erm Tristan? Are you meant to be here?' he asked tentatively.

Tristan looked directly at Terry and smiled his wonderful smile. 'That is exactly what I'm getting at Terry, my friend. I'm not sure I'm meant to be here…'

Terry interrupted quietly 'No butt, I don't mean in general, I mean here, in this meeting?'

Tristan looked confused 'Well, Cerranna. She's a half-elf, one of the IT lecturers at my uni told me there was a support group up here because there isn't one in Cardiff. Which seems daft when you think about how many of us live there.'

'What sort of support group?' Terry asked simply. The other six men gawped on as if they were watching television.

'Um, y'know? Us!' He pointed at the men around the room 'People from the Worlds, or the ones from That World communities who live here or ones like me... you know? Us!' he laughed starting to look confused 'I don't get it...us!'

The floor screeched loudly as Terry moved his chair an infinitesimal way forward towards Tristan. 'Are you looking for Am Dram or storytelling? Because you are very good and…'

Tristan looked around the circle 'I'm here to talk because I want to meet other...other, Other people and this support group for Other people, I was told would help me.'

'Tristan. This is a support group for ex-miners.'

'Miners?'

'Miners. People who worked underground. This is a support group; loneliness, mental health, support, you know? We all worked in the village pit before it closed in the 80s. That is, all except for Selwyn who was a miner two valleys over but moved here a few years ago.'

Despite the confusion both Tristan and Selwyn both smiled at each other, Tristan mouthing the word 'Alright?' and Selwyn nodding and putting his thumb up in response.

'There is a support group on a Thursday evening at the same time. I've always wondered about it, but it makes sense now. It says it's a support group for others, but you mean it's for what you call Others.'

Tristan laughed then 'Bloody hell! I'm so sorry. So, you must have no idea what the hell I'm on about then?' he stood

then and started walking out, the loud echoes from each step until…
'Hey butt…'
It was Selwyn.
Tristan stopped.
'We can't help with caves, swords and all that carry on…'
Tristan turned.
'But we all know depression.'
Tristan, paused for a moment, smiled, walked back and sat down.

They are going to stay for the whole two hours, they all get their turn, there is laughter and tears and they all feel better for it. Tristan asks if he can come back, and they all want that. They all give him their mobile numbers, and Selwyn and Trevor give him their names so they can link up on their socials. They all have a pint together at the pub that Tristan arrived in, a journey which they all get now. The night has made Tristan feel great and while he will not admit it, it better prepares him for the visitor that awaits him sitting next to his door in the corridor of his student hall giving him the news that he needs to prepare for the worst and meet with the three Kings for what could be the end, but let's leave this bit here.

I will take you back a few hours to when Tristan sits back down after he hears Selwyn for the first time.

Trevor Hargreaves puts his hand up. Terry prompts him to speak with a nod. He looks over at Tristan and asks.

'Is Gwenyvere hot?'

'Piss off.' laughs Tristan and then '…not sorry…'

CHAPTER TWELVE
THE DARK ARRIVE IN LLANDUDNO

We are in a conference hall in the Glenbridge hotel in Llandudno. Llandudno for those of you who do not know is a seaside town on the north coast of Wales, a place with a promenade for promenades. It has a pier, a cable car up to the great Orme where wild goats roam and it has busloads of tourists, things for them to do and places for them to stay. It has venues and it has conferences and that's why I am here and because I am, you are. We are attending a conference.

The theme of the morning sessions was 'The plight of the refugee.' And they'd had some wonderful speakers.

Ted Elphick based out of El Paso talked about his delivery service for dark Magick sacrifices. Ted had realised the earning power of the Hispanic, but not in terms of shitty jobs that Americans didn't want to do. Their worth was in sacrifice. 10 years ago, Ted had one truck that he used to transport economic migrants across the Mexican border into the United States and from there distribute to his customers. It was a bespoke service. If some man from LA wanted an actress for a snuff movie, no questions asked, Ted provided. He name-dropped Dark Lord Quentin A'queriere, pointing into the audience to where he thought he sat. Lord A'quieriere was one of his first and best customers, five Hispanics a month and had he ever been late? No way Jose...Jose being his little joke. Now he had 50 trucks, 2 giant holding pens either side of the border and a cutting edge (his second little joke) distribution centre outside San Antonio.

The next speaker was a small-time politician from southern Italy who was recruiting and forcing African immigrants to rob, rape and disrupt in towns throughout her electoral region. The atmosphere of populism and blame didn't need to be fed much to grow poisonous, but this certainly moved things along. First, she moved desperate immigrants to the town, making money by providing them with barely seaworthy dinghies to risk their lives travelling over the Mediterranean.

Once arrived, her overseers would not allow them to mix which in turn created mistrust amongst the local population. Her gangs were then sent in to make the immigrants even more hated. One immigrant kills a local in a fight therefore they are all murderers.

You humans are very easy to incite, you want easy solutions to complex problems. She stood at the election on a platform as the only person to talk about immigration even though all her political opponents talked about the issue. They just did it in a thoughtful way but who wants to hear thoughtful? She won by a landslide.

The crowd in the conference cheered themselves hoarse. They would do though. They were from the higher echelons of the Dark. They were its Lords, Ladies and neither, but these immortals, these sinister chosen, these lost, these jealous, these angry weren't usually ones to gather. They weren't really the conference going kind, but they came. They came because it was time.

Back in London the doors of a lift opened. There stood a bellhop. This one was a tall, sombre looking 93-year-old. He was dressed in a gold buttoned, maroon uniform. A bellhop's cap perched neatly on his head, and he stood with a placid expression on his face. In his liver spotted, life-lived hands he held a choke leash like the ones cruelly used on dogs that could be taught to behave a better way. A leash that says more about the person than it does the dog.

In that leash, a man around the same age as the one who held him. The old man was naked except for a pair of worn white underpants. He was on his knees and by the swelling of his eyes had been crying for some time but was too tired to continue. Through swollen eyes he noticed the three newcomers to his life and his pain. A high-pitched keening noise emanated from deep inside of his stomach. He tipped forward, his forehead touching the floor the same time as his hands that had been tied together firmly in front of him. In a swift jerking movement, he was yanked upright. The quick movement seemed alien when considering the slow, calming man who did it.

The men said nothing as they entered the lift. Only Cate acknowledged the captor.

'Good evening, Kelvin,' she said formally.

Kelvin nodded. The only noise other than the sniffling of the captive was the lift music in the background. Thunderstruck, by AC/DC, played on panpipes made the scene seem as dark as it was.

Cate lifted the captive's chin but before she could say anything, he jerked it away. It was action through terror rather than defiance. She went down on one knee and grabbed it again, this time holding the chin tighter, and the leashed man whimpered pitifully.

'Shh,' she said tenderly and then whispered something into his ear. His face relaxed instantly, his eyes dulling, his jaw going slack. A touch of contentment made his lips curl ever so slightly. Cate had gotten up but had continued muttering, forming a spell with the words, and using the Magick that swirled so powerfully within her. She held out her beautifully groomed right hand and the spell brought forth a dagger. In a flash she slashed it through the man's throat, it slid through like a hot knife through butter and after a moment blood streamed.

Kelvin stood, unimpacted by the violence and straining only slightly due to holding up a nearly decapitated body. The other three held each other's hands, forming a circle and quietly chanted using the blood Magick and its darkness that they needed. That blood, that violence, that lust, that fear connecting with their inherent Magick and the Magick of the words, so ancient, shifted the lift not up, not down but to where it needed to go. They needed to go 200 miles, which they did, in less than a second. They felt the lurch and knew they had travelled. They had arrived in Llandudno.

The doors slid open. Shane, almost as an afterthought, stepped towards the body and dipped his little finger on his right hand into the wound, brought it to his mouth and licked the tip.

'Hmmmm. Been a while,' he said smiling.

'Animal,' Cate said in disgust.

'Snob,' was his response.

Without another word to Kelvin, they exited the lift. They had entered a large, modern and rather plush lift and now left a very cramped one that had probably been put in during this hotel's refurbishment during the autumn of 1967. It had that fifty-year musky smell which was only challenged by the whiff of newly congealing blood mixed with fear-induced piss.

As the three arrived in the foyer they were immediately met by their Major-domo. The winged, pale skinned woman bowed low as they walked towards her.

'All is well and all who were summoned are in attendance,' Kaslika said.

'As they should be,' grunted Shane.

'What news on our little wasp? When will we hear?' asked Cate.

'Hear about what? Is this what the Dark Lord was talking about Cate?' said Killian looking concerned.

Kaslika answered, her voice hopeful with good news. 'It has been done in the last five minutes my Mistress.'

Cate stared at Kaslika and then she barked a laugh and put her hands on her cheeks in genuine surprise. She turned to Killian and Shane.

'Brothers. The Messenger of prophecy is dead. Killed as Kaslika said in the last five minutes. We are yet another step forward to our goal.'

Shane smiled but Killian was furious. 'Why the hell was I not informed of this?' he snapped.

Cate answered 'Father asked, and I made a decision. You didn't need to know. We lost too many of our good people attempting to kill Arthur's men. We still haven't killed all of them and the Three Kings live. And of course there is still Arthur. We needed this done so I decided to send one of the best and one who would not be missed,' explained Cate.

'And who is the best...?' asked Killian.

'The Banished.' Cate smiled, expecting the angry reaction that followed.

Kaslika felt the anger and immediately dropped to one knee, head facing down.

'The girl! The Exile?' growled Shane.

Killian angrily grabbed Cate by the shoulder and spun her to face him. She immediately struck his arm away and with an open hand pushed him back. For an instant his instinct was to attack before common sense and the realisation that no matter how powerful he was, his sister was at least his equal took over.

'She was banished until we needed her. We! Not you. How dare you go behind our backs! What if the Messenger had destroyed her? She was meant to be a sacrifice when we needed more power. What about her Magick? How the hell could you have returned it to her?' he shouted.

'Oh, do calm down brother. Something needed to be done. She was the best before being impregnated. If she had failed then we'd lost nothing, but she was the best and we cannot afford not to use all the power at hand especially when we are so close.'

She stepped forward, pouting, flirting, moving into his space placatingly.

'Come on brother we are so close to winning this, to ending them for millennia. I've done the right thing and I think you know that. Maybe I was hasty in planning it so quickly, but she did it!'

Killian was still angry, but his pragmatism took over. Cate was right but it wasn't the plan that angered him, it was that she and their Dark Lord had taken the decision without him. What else was she hiding?

He calmed and tried to take control of the situation. 'How can the exile be able to do this? No Magick, living with the ants and hasn't she got a brat? How good can she be?' he asked.

'A shot, a few hours of Magick and detailed instructions. That's it.' Cate answered.

'Why did she do it? What did you promise?' Shane asked.

Cate smiled. 'The note said that doing this may help her situation in the future, maybe a couple of blocks on her Magick removed. She doesn't have it for long. I did it myself and no blood Magick was involved.'

'Give me her address and I'll see her after this. If she is there to be used, then I have need of her.'

'What for?' Cate's eyes narrowed.

Killian smiled, pleased with his sister's annoyance 'You are not the only person with secrets sister. Our source has delivered again, and we have the location of another of Arthur's men.'

'Which one?' asked Shane excitedly.

'We have not been told and I have my suspicions but let's wait to see if the little bitch is as good as she's meant to be.'

'She has, only this morning, killed the prophesized so-called Messenger of the Light,' Cate snapped.

'One of Arthur's men will be a different matter but why not find out? I'll see her myself; I've never met her, and it will give me a nice break before I am forced back to the tedium of Parliament,' Killian said.

Kaslika stood up gracefully. 7-foot-tall usually gets a reaction, this time it was expectancy. 'Your audience awaits you, Masters,' she nodded to the two men and then to Cate. 'Mistress,' she added.

'Indeed, they do,' Killian responded and all three walked through.

I have loved so many things you people have invented over the years. They are too numerous to mention here when I have a tale to tell, but for a storyteller as old as time, the smell of a book is something quite divine. Another is that moment of silent, blackness before a film is about to begin in the cinema. That anticipation at the start of a journey is a place of trepidation and of safety.

The reason I mention it is that we are at the start of a small film at the Glenbridge. We just had the blackness and now colour has flooded the screen. After nothing, even the stark yellows and creams of Kurdistan shone through and lit the people watching.

You don't know the three protagonists, but they were introduced to the members of the audience through the title of the film, it read: The death of Peredur, Gwalchmai and Owain.

Applause and cheers broke out from the audience, some even stood but order and silence soon returned so they could watch properly.

There was a man on a cross. He was dead. Peredur had admitted defeat a few moments before the cameras rolled and his last words were to tell his friends he loved them. Off screen the audience could hear noises. The noise of hammering coupled with screaming from two soldiers whose wrists and feet were being nailed to crosses. The hammering stopped and the cries of pain increased when the crosses that bore their weight were erected either side of their dead friend.

The crowd started clapping as Cate Crowley walked into shot. She smiled at the camera before turning to the man suffering on the cross to her left.

'Anything witty to say Gwalchmai?' Cate asked. 'You Owain?' she continued.

Both mouths of the warriors moved but no words came out. For a brief moment Cate's smile disappeared before she brought her emotions back under control. The camera angle changed. A beaming Cate Crowley stood below, a spear in her hand. It was obvious that the voices of the warriors had been muted because while you couldn't hear them you could see them remonstrating with her. She moved herself to directly below the dead warrior, placed the spear tip at his throat and thrust up once. Blood streamed down the body, covering Cate's hair, face and pristine suit.

A groan of delight came from the audience in the full conference room. Some clapped, one got up and shouted 'Yes' which was met with some laughter. They watched enraptured as Cate did the same again to Owain then she was below Gwalchmai. She looked at the camera, her face covered in blood, her eyes shining with power. She licked her lips and smiled. 'Three down Arthur ap Uther. We know where you and your friends are. You are next...' and thrust the spear into the throat of a screaming Gwalchmai of the Hawks.

The lights of the conference room came on to signify the end of the film. They all started cheering at the demise of three of Arthur's men, but that cheer turned into a roar when the lights revealed their leaders on stage.

Killian Penhalligan, Shane Oriole and Cate Crowley took the applause like royalty because to this audience they were. Yes, they were the politician, the businessman and the TV personality but some of the audience had known them for thousands of years and knew them as the gods they were.

They walked the stage, waving and smiling at the throng, sometimes accepting the hands of people who had moved to the front just wanting to make contact. When the people were moved back by security, all three acknowledged the front rows. They took their time to meet the leaders amongst their people.

It's a lazy supposition that there is no loyalty amongst the Dark. There are some selfish creatures amongst the Light too. Once you believe completely in what you are doing and that you can do no wrong in what you want to achieve, you are all ending on the same side. It is the black and whiters who bring This world to too much chaos or too much order, and no one benefits from that.

Killian stepped forward and smiled, polished as always and used to crowds. 'Brothers, sisters, others of freedom. We greet you and we see you. Our time is here.'

The audience erupted again before Killian held his hands up as if begging to continue. 'We thought that when faced with being talked at by one of Britain's best loved politicians or the sweetheart of the airwaves, you might want to listen to Shane address you first...'

Shane held up his hand smiling, happy to be the target of the little joke. It showed his character as the old rogue and one of them. He stood. 'Last week we received a prophecy, one that may not have been released but one, let's say, that we acquired,' He said acquired and used 'air speech' marks, smiled conspiratorially then continued. 'The time for us to act is now, the time for chaos is coming and what we have fought for, for millennia and more, specifically over the past eighty years, is here.' It wasn't only the other two that could hold a crowd. This Dark god had led thousands to slaughter, had brought down empires and had built a criminal one of his own. He knew how to lead.

'When we started to change tack – no pitched battles, no showing ourselves, no short termism – I know many of you were sceptical. We aren't great at staying friends,' a ripple of laughter came from the crowd, 'but it's worked. We are sowing discord; we are the ones who are winning. We are controlling people's lives without bringing the weight of those righteous bastards down upon us. Them.' He pointed out into the darkness of the hall, 'They don't care about the Light, they are exactly like us, they don't care about the ants really. They are the liars.'

'Liars!' Came a shout followed by a few claps and soft laughter.

Killian pointed in the general direction of the voice and turned and nodded to his brother indicating that he was taking over. 'Yes. Liars. They want power as much as we do. They think they are saving the Worlds, saving the Ants from us but all they do is keep them in slavery without calling it that. They are liars and hypocrites.'

He paused, the crowd in the palm of his hand.

'The prophecy stated that Arthur and his warriors are still a danger to us. They have to be destroyed if we are to succeed.'

Boos and cries of 'bastard' and worse flew from the audience. The once and future and his followers had been a thorn in their side for as long as they remembered. They despised him.

Killian put his finger to his lips to quiet them.

'Our plan to keep the return of our Dark Lord secret all those years ago worked and that is down to the people in this room. Arthur has floundered with nobody for him to defeat. Most of his so call circle of warriors have deserted him, they are doing nothing, just wandering, lost, around a world that has forgotten them. Except of course,' and he pointed to the large empty screen, reminding them of what had come before. 'Except of course,' he repeated. 'Gwalchmai, Owain and Peredur.'

He laughed and clapped his hands, joined by the people in the conference hall. The cheer of 'Three down,' was repeated but died down when they saw him shaking his head.

He paused, playing the ones watching like a piano. He lifted his hand, thumb down showing four fingers. 'Four down. Bedwyr joined them this morning.' He said simply and more cheers rang out.

'We still cannot find some of the warriors which is a concern and therefore we ask those of you who've been tasked with their deaths to double your efforts, empty the coffers if need be, but you cannot fail.' He paused slightly, 'But what of Arthur? What of the bastard? Well, we've heard news that he decays visibly. With no one to fight and no one to lecture, just like we planned he is lost; fat, broken and…' Killian raised his arms waiting for the renewed cheers of the crowd to recede.

'We know where he is! We have death squads ready, and he dies in days,' he shouted and again the crowd went into raptures.

The three looked at each other, feeding on the adulation. They enjoyed the moment because they knew that rivalry and envy and thirst for power would return. They also knew that they hadn't had it their own way. They had failed to find some of the warriors who had left Arthur, failed to kill even one of the Three Kings especially having found Mynyddmawr hiding in New Orleans. The prophecy was clear. Until Arthur was dead then Cromh Du would continue to weaken.

Cate stepped forward, hands out to silence. 'We have often been burdened by complacency. We are born to rule so that is bound to happen, but we have prepared this time. We knew the Light wouldn't roll over, and even when we vanquish Arthur once and for all, they still won't be a pushover. Only this week we found out that they had been preparing a warrior of prophecy from thirty-eight years ago. The prophecy stated that a Messenger would come from the blood of Merlin and they would begin our end. But just like Arthur, we have found her!'

She strolled to the front of the stage, whispered words of Magick and the head of Lexie Diomedes appeared in her hand. Cate tossed it carelessly to the ground 'And here she is. Like I said. We took it very seriously.' She smiled her sass and the crowd roared again.

It was Shane's turn again. 'Now to business. You all know your tasks. Our armies in That World are ready to move and take over the Kingdoms of men and some of the Elven Queendoms. There will be little fighting as we already have the children of every king, queen, chieftain, clan leader or leader south of the Horixon Mountains. My brother here now has control of the British army as well as a Dark army which has been in hiding in the north for some time. In This World and That we have the biggest army ever assembled.'

Cate cut in quickly to make sure there was no more cheering. This was the business end of the meeting and there were things that needed to happen. 'We have That world in our power, and we'll cause such chaos in This. Once we subjugate this island and the prophecy is ended then our Dark Lord and master will bring the Worlds to their knees, and we will rule forever in freedom and chaos.

'All military commanders go back to your posts. All others, when you have heard that the army has landed over the bridge at Cantre'r Gwaelod, cause chaos. In a month's time Cromh Du will rule.'

For the final time that day, the audience stood, applauded, and cheered. The Dark Three left, and while they did, manacled human slaves were led into the conference room by the hotel staff all holding sacrificial daggers. The conference goers were all going back to where they were needed, and they weren't going to travel by public transport.

CHAPTER THIRTEEN

THE TRAIN TO WALES

He reached Paddington in no time at all. He had gone through things with Marged, swearing her to secrecy, and afterwards had messaged his mother telling her he was off to a book sale in Cardiff.

She replied 'OK LOVE WILL POP IN HOUSE TO WASH LOVE YOU THE WORLD MAM XXX'

She always messaged as if she was shouting at him because she never used punctuation and always wrote in capitals.

He deffo wasn't lying. He was indeed going to Wales, just a hundred miles past where she thought. She'd be suspicious because he hardly ever went further than five miles from the house, but he wanted to give the impression that he couldn't be reached. Case packed on the fifth go because he didn't have a clue what he needed for a weekend delivering a letter to a mythological king, who now lived in a pub in the middle of nowhere, he pulled a box from the top of his wardrobe and sat on his bed with it on his lap. He looked at it the way a very handsome and unlikely archaeologist would look at a golden idol before stealing it, avoiding traps, losing it to his French nemesis and then avoiding arrows from an indigenous tribe and escaping on a plane which had a snake on. These were French, these were designer, these were expensive, and these were sneakers. Not footwear or trainers or shoes, the designer called them sneakers and, at hundreds of pounds, they deserved to be called whatever they wanted. Caratacus was in love. He stroked them, held them up to gaze at them, and then put them on. 'Beautiful,' he said looking down.

Still sitting, he stopped for a moment. He felt tired and confused and he also felt peeved that his weekend was being taken away from him and for what? Weirdness, that's what. Whatever he had felt – and not for one moment did he entertain the thought that it was magic – whatever he'd felt had gone now. All that remained was annoyance.

The thing is, what you, my dear reader, know now and what he didn't was that things had changed, he just wasn't paying attention. He arrived in Paddington, looking around for information. He thought the trip was uneventful, but this is what he had missed getting there.

He left home and Mrs Pangbourne, his neighbour, said 'Good morning' to him. He looked back and replied with the same. I say looked back, but he didn't really look back, he just pointed his face in her direction. So, he looked but didn't see. He didn't see that Mrs Pangbourne was a lime shade of green and I am not saying that her face was painted like it was Halloween; her skin was green. He also didn't notice that all her teeth were really sharp. Mrs Pangbourne, who he'd known all his life was a demon from the 3rd circle. Pretty standard.

When Caratacus was on the tube to Paddington, his head was down, reading tweets from excessively optimistic people, world leaders who were idiots, and various people calling other people racist. He didn't look up, but if he had he would have noticed strangely dressed people. He wouldn't have known this, but he would have seen: two Magick users, a three- eyed warrior of the Rhu-raj, two demons, two priestesses and the god of the Bakerloo line. But he didn't look up, so he didn't notice anything and the saddest thing about this, is the God of the Bakerloo line did look awesome in his gold cloak.

It's a good lesson for you. Sometimes all you need to do is lift your head and look.

And now we are at Paddington, and on the train. As soon as he took his seat, Caratacus stuck in his headphones, tapped play and dozed off.

He woke up when someone fell into the seat beside him. I could have written 'sat' but it wasn't any sort of civilised sit. The person flopped; they fell. Despite the sunny weather the – Caratacus glanced very quickly out the corner of his eye – the man was wearing a huge jacket and a hat that had flaps over his ears. Caratacus looked out the window to ignore him. He shifted his body weight towards it to give Captain Shambles the room he needed. Not long after coming into Reading station, Caratacus realised that the bloke had been talking to him. He accidently glanced over, and the man was facing him and talking. Caratacus took out one of the headphones.

'...and, thing is ,yes, I am well aware that honey badgers are hard animals, but you know, a snake could bite it yeah?'

No response from Caratacus.

'Or an elephant could just stamp on it, like, on its head and that would defeat it. An eagle could swoop down and keep flying down and ripping it with its talons and then take off again. A honey badger can't fly, the eagle could take all day and then win that fight. Do you know what I mean?'

Caratacus just stared, frowning. He didn't.

'Thumb wars,' the bloke said.

'What'? Caratacus replied. It was the first thing he'd said since sitting down, and it came out as a noise. It sounded like the 'what' of a sullen teenager.

'Do you play thumb wars? I'm really quite good, and it'll make the journey go quicker.'

'Thumb wars?'

'Thumb wars.' The man nodded.

'Thumb wars?'

'Thumb wars.'

The man stuck his hand out, gripped like an Action man toy from the seventies, thumb up, stretched back. Classic move.

For a split second Caratacus was going to grip hands. He didn't want to, he just felt obliged. But his inner self, the one that was so annoyed with having his Friday and life completely messed about took over.

'No thanks mate, got a lot of thinking to do if you don't mind,' he said, tapping his head to emphasis thinking.

The bloke just smiled, totally unperturbed. 'Thinking, eh? Well, you know where I am if you need a game.'

Caratacus smiled uncomfortably and then grimaced as the man shouted at a woman who was standing at the other side of the carriage putting a small bag on the luggage rack above her seat. 'HEY LOVE, FANCY A GAME OF THUMB WARS?'

Caratacus sank down into his seat. Even if it wasn't an utterly weird request to make, the human laundry basket also made it sound like thumb wars was a euphemism, and the girl he'd shouted at was lovely. A ten out of ten lovely. He stared out the window so hard he thought it would crack.

'Ok then,' Caratacus heard and peeked up.

That lovely girl from the other side of the carriage started walking over.

The man just said 'Great', as if he'd expected it.

Caratacus continued to stare out the window as the man beat the lovely woman three-two in a best of five. She giggled throughout and, crushingly, Caratacus realised that she was flirting with HIM and the man either didn't notice or didn't care.

Five minutes later.

Caratacus tried not to look but now the man was playing thumb wars with the guard. A group of about six or seven people were standing nearby or kneeling on their seats watching and cheering, and the lovely girl was playing her mate, who was also lovely, just a few seats ahead.

Seven minutes later.

The whole carriage was singing 'Yellow submarine' by the Beatles. New people got on and immediately joined in on the singing. It's important to tell you that the carriage was not full of hen or stag parties, they were mostly people going home to Newport or Cardiff or Bridgend or Swansea except for Mr and Mrs Morris who were going to visit her sister in Pembrokeshire so were going all the way. They were nearly all on their feet and all of them were singing. Soon, they had moved on to 'Caught in a trap' by the King. By the way reader, that's Elvis not Arthur.

Caratacus found himself tapping his feet.

He was relieved to remember that he was getting off and changing trains in Newport. The train stopped, he stood up apologetically to indicate he was getting off. Even though he hadn't really taken part in any of the fun, everybody, including the man, cheerfully said goodbye.

The new train looked exactly the same as the first and, by coincidence, he found himself sitting in the exact seat he was in on the other one. The carriage was pretty empty, although he did recognise the Morrises who sat at the far end. Mrs Morris waved in recognition and Caratacus waved back, sort of smiling. After putting his bag up, he sat down, headphones in and tapped play. Cardiff soon passed by, Bridgend too, and before long they pulled in to Swansea.

The man formerly identified and now reidentified as Captain Shambles got on and sat next to him.

'Hi there,' he said, no recognition whatsoever. Caratacus' eyes narrowed but he still replied with a hello of his own. Should he say anything or was the man taking the piss and wanted him to say something? He looked into the man's face and in turn, and still smiling innocently, the man stared at his. Caratacus' thinking process assumed the man was an idiot with no master plan who had nothing to do with him, and turned away intending to listen to some music when...

'I agree with your mother. 'Love actually' is better than 'Notting Hill'.'

Caratacus opened his mouth to speak but couldn't. Once every few months in what he considered payment to his mother for what he also considered doing little bits of stuff in his life, Caratacus invited her around and they watched a film of her choice. Mrs Lewis loved 'film night'. She counted down to it, crossing the days off on her 'Dogs of the World' calendar. It was a time when, rather than seeing him leave or arrive, they spent time together. She treasured it, but it was a random Thursday night to him. She even picked the films. A night that his mother still remembers as one of the best of her life was the night, they watched two Richard Curtis films back-to-back. He had commented that 'Love actually' was rubbish and, for the first time ever, she disagreed. Caratacus found it funny that she had such strong feelings and kept pushing that 'Notting Hill' was better, gently ribbing her. It didn't take long for Mrs Lewis to realise he was, but it soon became their thing. Only a few people close to them knew about it. This cheerful man dressed as a jumble sale was not one of them.

Caratacus looked at him, even shifting position in his seat so he was facing him a little more.

'OK, enough of this nonsense. Why are you following me and what do you want?' He said.

The smile on the man's face didn't change, well, neither did every other part of his face.

Caratacus broke. 'Look! What's the big deal, man? Why the hell are you following me? Why act so bloody weird? Why not just talk to me if that's what you are here for?'

The man laughed but like a mickey-taking child. 'Wowee, you really do think it's all about you, eh?' he replied.

He made an over exaggeratedly serious face and impersonated Caratacus in a childish voice: 'What do you want? I am really important. The world revolves around me. If I was chocolate, I would eat myself.' He jumped up a little and shuffled his bum back on his seat while laughing.

'Oh, do one will you!' Caratacus had had enough.

The man looked at him, as if a spell had broken, no more humour shone from that face.

'That's enough, boy,' he said. Caratacus opened his mouth to reply but the man held up his finger and continued. 'No, I said that's enough. Grown up speaking.'

Caratacus hadn't really been spoken to like that since school and he had never reacted to it well then.

'Who the f…' he started to say.

'Oh, shut up you spoilt child. Manawydan's balls, you really are a grumpy little sod, aren't you? Listen, I am Piogerix, former King and current druid. Tell me, Caratacus ap Neb—'

'That's not my name,' interrupted Caratacus.

'What did Tommaltach tell you?' Piogerix said.

'Who?'

'Tommaltach?' Piogerix asked before he corrected himself, 'Tommy.'

Ah so he knew Tommy thought Caratacus. That made sense.

'He told me I was to go to the middle of nowhere, stay in a pub for a weekend and deliver a letter to someone claiming to be King Arthur, then take him to a place called Lady in the Lake.'

'It *is* King Arthur,' said Piogerix.

'Whatever,' replied Caratacus.

Piogerix laughed again but this time sadly. 'You really have no idea how important what you are doing is do you?'

Caratacus bristled. 'No. You listen to me. It's not important. I'm just doing this small thing for Mr McKracken who, as you know, is not a person you, me or anybody says no to. That's it! What do you want? Why are you following me?'

Piogerix still smiled 'How do you know I wasn't travelling anyway? That's what I do…at present anyway. I travel. A druid is always learning his art, travel develops it. Tommaltach suggested I check in on you if I was about. I am, so I am. Anyway, I remember your mother. Good looking girl.'

Caratacus made a disgusted face as Piogerix continued, 'He also tells me that you are a massive waste of potential and worse, she has wasted hers by waiting on you hand and foot.'

'Hey, you don't know me, and she likes to help. I work bloody hard!' Caratacus started back up the sliding scale of being pissed off.

He fumed, the harsh truth heard out loud increasing his anger. He poked a finger at Piogerix and, as it touched the man/king/druid whatever, something happened, the world went deeply silent as if God had paused it to make a cup of tea or check his socials. Piogerix flew from his seat over to the two empty ones on the other side of the train's aisle. Caratacus' hands crackled with energy, and he looked at them, puzzled, then over at Piogerix who, he noticed, was trying to get up despite all his clothes actively attempting to stop him. Piogerix was laughing, and hearing it, Caratacus stopped being puzzled and returned to anger.

'Stop bloody laughing!' he said as he lifted his lightning-infused hands.

For just a moment, Piogerix showed fear and then, just like Caratacus, his eyes flashed blue. He mouthed a single word, put his hand out; palm facing away and said, 'No.'

This time it was Caratacus on pause, crackling hands included, stuck, motionless. Piogerix stood up, straightened his ton of clothes, and took off his hat. He then sat and stared at Caratacus like a magic eye picture.

'Well, well, spoilt boy really has got some power eh?' he said before tweaking Caratacus' nose between two fingers making a noise like a horn.

He shuffled, as if trying to move all his clothing into a more comfortable state, then leaned forward again and, for a moment, just stared at Caratacus before saying matter-of-factly, 'I don't think that we've got off to a very good start.' He laughed, feeling a bit embarrassed. 'Tell you what, let's forget this bit, let's forget everything from Swansea on?'

He stood holding his hat in one hand and placing his other on Caratacus' head. He whispered a few words of Magick, eyes glowing as he did so. Caratacus' world went black.

'...yeah Four Weddings and a Funeral was great, I agree with you.'

Caratacus looked around as if he had just landed from outer space. He looked at the weird sack of clothes with the rubbish hat who had sat next to him in Swansea and was still talking to him, and he didn't have a clue what this man was on about. Had he fallen asleep?

Had the bloke been so boring that he'd switched off?

'What?' he managed, utterly confused.

'Ah well. It doesn't matter now as this is my stop. Piogerix,' he offered his hand.

Still confused, Caratacus took it. 'Caratacus,' he answered.

'Nice name, old British. Thanks for the chat and the game of thumb wars, you aren't bad,' Piogerix said and then he was gone.

The train pulled off and Caratacus, still confused, registered that the station was Carmarthen and then watched the man...Piogerix... saunter past the window smiling.

'Weirdo,' Caratacus whispered. He sat back in his seat and listened to music until Fishguard Harbour.

***

The car ride had taken no more than twenty minutes. For the entire journey the driver had been on her phone talking to one of her kids in Welsh. Strangely, the only time she addressed Caratacus was randomly pointing at places of what she thought was of interest and barking out names.

'Cwm!'

'Dick the Fort's Fort!'

'John Trechannog was run over here in 1965!'

It carried on until Cwm Llechau.

Caratacus got out, got his case from the back seat, and then leaned through the open window of the car's front passenger side. 'How much?' he asked.

'What do you mean?' she replied.

'How much for the ride?' Here we go again, thought Caratacus. Maybe it was his accent, so he tried again. 'How much is this taxi ride?' he spoke like he was talking to a hard of hearing pensioner.

'I'm not a bloody taxi!' she exclaimed.

'For the sake of f...' said the internal voice of Caratacus Lewis.

'You stopped the car and asked me where I was going!' said the external voice of Caratacus Lewis.

'I know, I was just interested and then you got in and started nattering to me.'

It was face rubbing time again for Caratacus. 'Do you want some money then, tenner? Twenty?'

'No, let's say it's a favour, and anyway I always liked your mother.' And with that she pulled off with a 'tara', while Caratacus jogged alongside shouting, 'Wait, how do you know my—' but by that time he was already talking to the back end of the car shifting off in the distance, '—mother…'

He gave another sigh as he looked at the pub he was outside. He stared at its huge sign, a big nosed and weirdly large eared old man in a blood red tunic giving anyone who cared to look the 'V's'. Under him, in large Times New Roman script, were three capital Ts which he correctly took to mean Tafarn Tylwyth Teg, the pub of the fair folk in English, but never, ever, called that. The front door was already open, so he went through and pulled open the second, glass paned one and the noise and heat hit him like a train. It was packed, music blaring, standing room only which, by the looks of it, included on the pool table as well. There was no way he was going to get to the bar with his case.

'Evening, sir,' said a bearded man with arms like tree trunks. He looked like a wrestler and not since the sitcoms of his youth had Caratacus seen anyone wearing a string vest. Before he could reply the man carried on: 'If you are kipping 'ere with us tonight, sir, then it'll be easier for you to head around the back and get to reception there. I will take your bag through for you.'

'Cheers,' said Caratacus, who turned around and after a minute-long walk found the back entrance that indeed did say 'reception'. He was even more delighted to find the reception area actually looked like a real life on,e with real hotel stuff like keys and a phone.

As if by magic, a woman appeared. She was only just five foot, but her demeanour added another two feet in either direction. Her face was so stern that he felt like he was going to get a telling off.

'Be' ti'n moyn?' *'What do you want?'* She launched immediately into Welsh.

She said it in the same way you may hear the following in a particularly rum public house.

'Did you steal my pint?' Or 'Are you staring at my bird?'

'Errr, sorry,' he hesitated 'Speaking the English? Me siarad no Welsh.' Which was incorrect because he learned that 'siarad' was Welsh for speak from his mother.

She sighed. 'She' was Maggie Rosser, but she was always called Maggie Triple T. She had been born in the pub and by hell she'd die in the pub, and she would do so when she wanted, not when the reaper came. She'd make him wait.

'Name?'

'Caratacus Lewis,' he answered.

Only a poker player or a person with godlike observational skills would have noticed a relaxing of Maggie's pursed lips that may have passed for a very, very small smirk. For anybody else, a smile like this would have been the equivalent of one brought about after dropping a really good ecstasy tablet in 1996. It disappeared as she returned to her inquisition.

'Who's your father?' the way she asked made him feel as if answering, regardless of not wanting to, was mandatory. He was just about to reply when 'Who's your Grandfather?' followed straight after. Maggie asked everybody this. Knowing people, combined with a sense of place (even someone else's) is important to the Welsh; it means that they have a connection with you, well, the nice ones anyway.

'Erm,' said Caratacus taken aback. 'I don't know, I never knew him... them,' he corrected.

'Caratacus ap Neb eh? Where's your bag? Are you all the way down from London without a spare set of clothes?'

'No, I gave it to your porter when I came in,' he replied.

'Porter? We haven't got a porter.'

'Oh, then I've had my bags nicked.'

'Is that so? I'll have a little word and get you back what's left,' she said.

He wanted to scream 'WHAT'S LEFT!?!' but then he realised he just didn't care. It had been the worst day and he just needed a pint and food.

'Are you still open for food?' he asked.

Her: 'Jam.'

Him: 'Jam?' His mind told him she'd said 'jam,' but he thought it might be a Welsh word for something else.

Her: 'Jam.'

Him: 'Jam?'

Her: 'Jam.'

Him: 'Err, jam what?'

Her: 'Jam on toast or jam traditional.'

Him: 'What's jam traditional?'

Her: 'Between two slices of bread with marge.'

The white flag of his mind went up, the day had won, he surrendered.

'We also have Scampi fries or stout,' she added helpfully.

He picked up his key. 'Can I get a traditional jam sandwich. I just want to freshen up and I'll be down in five.'

'Gwd, your room is up the stairs at first left, breakfast between 5 and 9, it's all paid for.' And as if by magic, Maggie buggered off.

Caratacus leant down to pick up his case before realising that some arse in a vest had stolen it. Porter... he'd reached peak London. He found his room and thought, finally, that the magic had hit him and had transported him back to the seventies. The carpet was thick, and everything was coloured beige. The bed was a double with a bedspread that looked so flammable he thought it may ignite just by sitting on it.

Nothing to pack away meant he headed straight down. The bar was still absolutely heaving. In the seething mass of fun and noise Caratacus noticed some bloke at the bar with a pair of his pants on his head. He also recognised the giant porter wearing his Harlequins top. This wasn't paranoia. Sure, in the darkest parts of western Wales, it could be entirely plausible that a man, a huge man, could support the team Caratacus considered the aristocrats of rugby, a posh south west London club. It could also be possible that said huge man may have no appreciation that he was, indeed, a huge man and had bought his rugby jersey five sizes too small so it looked like a crop top that was going to burst at any given moment. But no, this wasn't paranoia. The shirt had Caratacus' name on the back, a present from his mother.

It was soon followed by the realisation that a lot of people had items of his clothing on their heads. They weren't even making a big deal about it, just getting on with their night.

He didn't know what to do. He obviously needed his clothes, but did he really need the aggravation of going around and asking drunk people for them back? And anyway, He didn't think that huge man could take that top off if he paid him.

'Jam!'

He knew the word was being addressed to him. He looked over and Maggie was behind the bar holding out a plate with his sandwich on. The bar was long and including the stern-faced owner, had five people working behind it, all dressed in the yellow polo shirts of triple T staff.

As she handed over the plate, a girl by the bar said; 'I didn't know you were doing food Mags, can I have a sandwich please?'

Maggie Triple T didn't even move her eyes, they were set on the plate.

'No, sod off, he's staying.'

The plate had a jam sandwich on it; cut in half, squares not triangles. It also held an apple and a Blue Riband chocolate bar. 'Drink?' she attacked.

'What have you got?' he replied.

'Beer, stout or whisky.'

'What sort of beer?'

'Beer.'

That sinking feeling was starting to become a part of him now. He stood there surrounded by people, some wearing his stolen clothes on their head, holding a plate containing a jam sandwich, an apple and a chocolate-based snack his mother used to put in his sandwich box on school trips in the eighties, and now he had to go through this again.

'Great, what sort of beer?' he said clearly and almost cheerfully.

'Beer? Well, beer. Wet brown beer.' she said, this time sounding a bit perplexed herself. It was then that Caratacus noticed there were no hand pumps on the bar and no optics on the walls. Just 3 barrels on their side and a load of jugs on the huge shelf behind. It made him think of a new craft brewery place that had opened near his house and that this is the sort of place they were going for. However, those bearded hipsters would have been horrified that there was only one beer, and it wasn't called something witty like 'Witch's tit' or 'Wizard's sleeve'. The bearded types also had tapas, featuring things artisanal, served on old CND placards reclaimed from a dead activist's attic in a clear out sale, not jam sandwiches on a chipped china plate.

He gave in 'Great! A pint,' and took a bite out of his sandwich.

She barked, 'Have you got your clothes back?'

He waved the sandwich indicating the whole pub. 'People are wearing them.'

'Who?' she asked puzzled.

'On their heads, including one of your barmaids,' he continued. She turned away and he thought that was the end of that and carried on chewing on the sandwich which he decided that he actually liked.

The music stopped and so did all other noise, Caratacus could see Maggie's head rise above the throng. He assumed that she was standing on a chair, but she was still only a few inches taller than the tallest person in there.

No one made a noise, breath was held. Maggie just stared out. Caratacus thought she was holding a rider's crop before realising it was an old orange fly swatter. She barked in Welsh first and then, 'Right. Any of you bastards who have acquired some items of clothing you have no reason to have, I want them back in reception ten minutes ago. Com-effing-prende?'

Everybody com-effing-prended.

Caratacus sat at the back of the pub, far away from the noise and the fun, brooding at the unfairness of life. He ate his sandwich and drank his pint before deciding it was time to give up on this awful day.

The stairs to his room were a struggle, the day had caught up with him. He crashed on the bed, managed to undress, and fell into a deep, dark, undreaming sleep.

CHAPTER FOURTEEN

YOU WILL MEET A TALL, DARK, HANDSOME, EVIL STRANGER...

It was the man off the telly. The politician, the handsome one. Here, in her flat. He was sitting back on her chair, with a smile on his face, relaxing as if he lived there.

She summoned Magick, hoping that some of it remained, anything, but there was nothing. She stiffened to defend or attack, even without Magick she could still snap his neck but did nothing, not wanting to scare Olivia.

'Hello Cassandra, or can I call you Cassie?' he asked calmly. His voice was lovely. She'd always thought that when she'd heard him on the telly, not that she ever paid any attention but yeah that voice. He indicated to the sofa and continued talking.

'Sit down please and who is this dear one?' He purred, his face was open and friendly, but it wasn't a request, it was an order.

Despite the smile, Olivia sensed the mood and became scared, hugging her mother's leg while in a baby voice told the stranger her name.

'Olivia? What a beautiful name for a beautiful little girl. Well, the apple doesn't fall far from the tree, does it? Come over here so I can take a proper look at you,' he beamed.

She squashed her face into her mother's leg and in turn the mother squashed her in as much of a hug as she could.

'What do you want?' Cassie said quietly and calmly.

He ignored her and continued to talk to the little girl but in reality, was addressing Cassie.

'Shy? Aww that's strange, your mother wasn't, otherwise you wouldn't be here. My name is Killian. You probably don't watch the news because you are a little girl, but I'm a very, very important person. Your mummy doesn't seem bright enough to watch the news, but she might have seen Uncle Killian on one of her dreadful day time shows that I go on so I can come over all real and nice. If not, Mummy may know me as one of the Dark Three.'

His eyes darted towards Cassie, his smile unchanging. Cassie's eyes opened wide for a split second, fear rippling through her as she put her daughter behind her.

Olivia, the coyness leaving her quickly as it did with so many children, peeked her head around her mother's legs.

'Oneofthedarkthree is a silly name.'

Killian laughed, a proper one. 'Yes, yes, it is. Oh yes, so much of your mother in you and a touch of your father I do believe.'

The last few words of the sentence demanded a reaction from Cassie, and she gave it. Time to move this conversation on to the end.

'I've done your job. You can go. Please,' she pleaded.

He tutted, still sitting, uncrossing and crossing his legs. 'No, it doesn't work like that, or have you forgotten so much since your move…' he looked around with contempt '…to live amongst the ants.'

Cassie's mind worked furiously. How could she end this? Attack now? Was he alone? She couldn't think straight, she was exhausted, the Magick having entirely left her body. She went back to basics and that was the basics of being a mother. 'Ok, what do you want? Leave her alone, I'll get a babysitter and come with you.' She was desperate, trying to think of any way they could leave her daughter out of it.

'That won't be allowed to happen. We'll look after your …spawn.' He said.

'No,' she replied. Was it the word spawn that did it? She knew it was this or the end, hers and Olivia's. It couldn't happen, she couldn't let it. She went for him.

He had a different view.

He'd been waiting for her.

'Yes.' He put out his hand, palm forward, his eyes glowing red. Olivia screamed at the sudden movement while Cassie's body convulsed in agony, frozen in time in the act of going for his throat, straining against the power that held her there.

The smile remained and he suddenly got up, moving like a panther. 'Hurts doesn't it? Imagine what I could do to her? I'm sure you can. That doesn't have to happen though.' He stood in front of Cassie, his face inches from hers. She was still but there was a little movement, the trembling of her body as she struggled to reach him and a single tear falling down her cheek.

His eyebrows raised a little. 'Oooh, all your Magick blocked but I can still feel you trying to break my spell. It's very interesting. The spirit of the underclass, eh? I suppose you must have picked up some of their values. Well, you obviously have because you live in a disgusting pigsty. A lifetime of training in the dark arts and this is all you have achieved.'

Still so very close he looked up and down her face, his eyes manic and then like a striking cobra he licked her, from below her chin, up the side of her cheek and over her eye. He stepped back a little, looked her up and down and then caressed one of her breasts, looking into her eyes as he did so. After an uncomfortable amount of time he stopped, stepped close and in a tender way leaned his head against hers.

'Mummy?' Olivia said, it was almost a squeak, but it tore through the silence. Penhalligon reached down, touched her head and said, 'sleep.'

She did and crumpled to the floor.

In that moment, Cassie's other rigid arm that had been stuck by her side moved, as if the hold for a split second had gone. The arm went up, her hand grabbing his throat before the invisible force re-took control. His eyes opened wide, there was no way she could break that spell. It shook him completely. He was a creature as old as time, he was born of Magick and this... this girl had broken his spell. He knew she was good, but this was different. He jerked his head back, the grip of her hand leaving a red welt on his neck. His face went serious, gone was the smile and he held her chin as he moved close again.

'Now listen to me, you little bitch. Playtime is over. She is fine, it's just a simple sleep spell. I am going to release you, but I want you to think carefully about attacking me.' He peered into her eyes then carried on. 'You will do a last job for us. We will keep your little girl and if you succeed then you will be reunited and maybe we can throw in something for you, as well. Consider it a little payment. Obviously, you messed up too much for us to reverse the banishment but maybe we could loosen the blocks on your Magick, make This World a little easier?' he paused. 'Alternatively, you could carry on with your little tantrum. I could release the hold and you could again attempt to attack me. I would stop you, again and then I'd get my men, the ones waiting outside this tip, to come in and I'd make you watch them take your daughter and then I'd make you watch me kill her slowly. I don't like doing stuff like that.' He smiled, 'Ok, I do actually. So, what's it going to be?'

He sat down, crossing his legs and clicked the fingers on his right hand releasing the spell.

She rushed to check on her daughter. Once she knew Olivia was unhurt, she picked her up and cradled her close, rocking her side to side. Her head whipped around and through clenched teeth she gritted, 'What do you want?'

Killian gave one of his smiles, the one that mesmerized most of the people he met, and clapped his hands in obvious joy.

'That's wonderful. It's nice to have you back in the fold a little more officially shall we say? Especially after your terrible mistake. You really did upset a lot of very important people once the tale of your disgusting behaviour got out. It was quite the news in both the Worlds, wasn't it? Made our side look a bit silly, a Dark Mistress getting up the duff – and even worse, you! The darkest of the Dark! The deadliest, the most accomplished, talked about in prophecy even.' The smile disappeared. 'Just another teenage whore.' He smiled again, about to go on before noticing she wasn't facing him but holding the comatose Olivia in her arms.

'She's only asleep girl. Best you focus on me,' he snarled.

She looked back then, the serenity of acceptance on her face making him check his anger. This girl was dangerous.

'Why me? You have six Nests of Mistresses to call upon.' she stated.

'That need not concern you, girl,' he replied.

He got up, straightening his jacket. 'You will leave tomorrow morning. Prepare and if you wish, spend some time with that,' he pointed at Olivia and continued. 'I'll send a car for you and we will look after her.'

'No,' she said.

'Sorry?'

'She stays with a friend not with you. You don't need her.' She looked through him.

He felt annoyingly disconcerted again, it was not a feeling he'd felt often, but he forced a laugh.

'Friend? You? Really? I didn't realise that Dark Mistresses could. How utterly disappointing.' He paused as if thinking to himself. 'Do you know what? I'm going to let you have your way as a token of my goodwill, especially after your service today which, incidentally, was amazing. I will allow your whelp to live with your so-called friend. Do not try and fool us, we'll know where they are, and will be watching very carefully. Don't deliver? We'll slaughter them, their family, their street and old sleepy head there. Understand?'

'What am I meant to be doing for you?' she asked.

He walked towards the door that opened automatically 'What you were born to do of course. Do our bidding and bring chaos. Small steps first though. I want you to kill one of Arthur's warriors and then I want you to kill the man himself. All you need to know will be given to you tomorrow. That block on your Magick will start dissipating in a few hours, our Magickers are working on it as we speak. Powerful spells! Can you imagine the blood that's needed?' He grinned and jokingly raised his eyebrows and then he left, leaving the door open.

Instantly, she carried Olivia gently to the sofa, moved her hair from her face and then got up and closed the door.

That night she phoned Katie and asked if she could look after Olivia for a week. She told her that a relative was very close to death and she had to go. She knew it was a huge ask and although she wasn't surprised when Katie said yes, it still made her feel strange. She felt overwhelmed again. That someone would do something like that for her was unthinkable. Saying thank you just didn't seem enough. New feelings assailed her again and she remembered how confused she used to get when she sometimes looked at Olivia and didn't feel anger and blame but felt something peculiar and so powerful it felt like bursts of Magick in her. It was love. Unconditional love and now it was in peril.

It wasn't too long before Olivia woke up and seemed unaffected by what had happened. She cried when Cassie explained her weeklong sleepover with her friend Bethany. The crying stopped when her mother promised that later that night, they were going to get fish and chips with real coke, and then she could watch 'Frozen' on DVD. Olivia did not cry after that, that was twenty Christmases come at once. That night Cassie sat with her daughter on the sofa, full tummies, both in their pyjamas with a snuggle blanket over them. Olivia had been quiet since the film started and Cassie smiled as her daughter sighed happily and without thinking held her hand. Twenty minutes later, with the film still going, she realised Olivia had fallen asleep and for the first time in her life, Cassie sobbed her heart out for this life, the one that she'd hated, the one she was about to lose.

CHAPTER FIFTEEN
GETTING TO THE ONCE AND FUTURE

A second is an amazing thing. It is a set amount of time, given a name to structure it, by you lot, people.

It's just a second but a lot of things can happen in a second. A life can end. A life can be transformed for better or for worse. It was during one of these seconds, the first one after coming awake, that Caratacus failed to remember. For that tiny second, that lifetime-lasting second, he was back in his own bed in leafy Twickers. He was snuggled in darkness, ready for a Saturday of quality Caratacus time. Then he remembered. He was at the farthest reaches of Wales, in a place ran by an abrupt, jam sandwich obsessed, midget Boudicca and on a quest given to him by a Northern Irish crime lord to find someone claiming to be King Arthur and take him to see a bird who lived in a lake. He wondered why Maggie had called him Caratacus ap Neb, he'd never heard of it before. He didn't know but you will now. It meant 'son of no one'; 'ap' means 'son of'. You've got your Macs in Scotland and your O's in Ireland and your 'Somethingsons' in England. Well, in Wales they all used to have 'ap', son of, but the English didn't like that, far too backwards. Aps and sometimes Abs meant that son of Harri became Parry, son of Owen became Bowen and others just used their first name or their Dad's name as a surname, which is why they have so many Evans, Jones, Davies and Williams in that tiny part of both worlds.

Caratacus ap Neb.

He reminded himself to text Mam later and ask if she knew something, although it may be too close to the discussing of his biological father which was usually met with her suddenly looking frail, staring into the distance and saying, 'that's all in the past', and even more fervent cleaning and organising. He checked his phone anyway, no messages, no texts, no missed calls, which usually happens when there is no signal.

The door opened – no knock – and in came Maggie Rosser, mug of tea in one hand and a slice of jam on toast in her other. Before he had chance to say 'bloody hell' she handed him the tea and the piece of toast.

'Tea and jam on toast, most important meal of the day.' She said. He took it, she opened the curtains, blinding Caratacus who completely 'tea and toasted' up, couldn't cover his eyes. Once his eyes became accustomed to the light of lights, he noticed his travel case on the floor by the sideboard. Even better was that on top of it were his 'stolen' clothes. They were folded neatly in a perfect square with his socks bunched on top.

He would have said something to Maggie, but she just barked 'Gwd thing!' before leaving the room. Despite his body screaming at him to do the contrary he bit a chunk out of the toast and was delighted to find it tasted normal. But while the toast and jam didn't kill him the tea was dreadful, Maggie must've strained it through an entire bag of sugar, and he could feel himself getting type two diabetes after his second sip. He placed it down on the side and, with his hands now empty, decided to get up.

Much later as he was leaving the pub, he saw Maggie, remembered he had questions and called to her as she was leaving the bar for the cellar.

'Hey, have you got Wi-Fi?'

Maggie didn't stop, turn her head or anything, just replied, 'No, no food until tonight now,' and disappeared into the cellar and out of range for question two. Question two was 'Where is the 'Once and future' pub? How he eventually got to it once he knew, was a different question altogether. In a moment of clarity, he realised a few things.

- He had plenty of time to find a local pub,
- Looking out the pub window he noticed the weather was lovely and he hadn't seen the village in daylight so how about a small explore?

And off he went.

After wandering around Cwm Llechau it didn't take long for him to realise that it was normal in this part of the world that people asked who you were and where you were from without any precursor whatsoever. It was a beautiful village and it made him think of his mother who had grown up here. The thought that she had walked these streets made him happy. He still missed civilisation though. Not for the first time in the past few days he was also confused.

Everybody had heard of the 'Once and Future' pub. Every single person he'd asked; and they all said that they'd had some of the best nights ever there. They could even tell you it was up in the Preseli mountains but whenever he asked them the exact location and how he could get there he was met with blank faces and frowns.

Despite the lack of progress and despite himself, he was starting to relax. Nothing strange had happened since leaving his room that morning and so he thought he'd make a final push to find out how to get to the pub. To his huge surprise he found a lovely cafe in the middle of the village. He tentatively asked for a cappuccino and was delighted to get one and they even had wi-fi! He was just about to check Twitter when a man came over to his table, turned the chair around and sat down. All the evaporated stress condensed back into his body but he managed a small smile.

'Can I help you?' he said.

'Actually, I've come to help you, Caratacus ap Neb,' he smiled.

Caratacus didn't return the smile he was too busy coping with a return to 'that sinking feeling' which was now probably closer to 'that plummeting feeling.'

Caratacus had a proper look at the man. He was well built, not huge but the way he carried himself was, how could he put it? Noble? The man wasn't too tall or too short, but everything about him even down to his pencil-like moustache looked, neat...precise.

'Why did you call me that?' asked Caratacus. This was a great chance to find out why people around here insisted on calling him this name.

The man smiled. 'Because that's your name.'

'No, Caratacus Lewis is my name, no middle name, no 'ap' no 'Neb', no 'ap Neb', Caratacus Lewis.'

The softly spoken rant helped Caratacus, he felt like the valve had relieved a bit of pressure, but it had no impact on the man opposite.

'I've come to help you Caratacus ap Neb,' he said.

'Go on then, help me,' sighed Caratacus.

'I've come to take you to the Once and Future.'

'How do you know that I need to go there? Who are you?'

The man straightened and power oozed from everywhere. He spoke, his voice powerful, like Richard Burton through a megaphone.

'My name is Geraint ap Erbin of the Dumnonii, I have been a King, a widower, a vanquisher, a murderer and many more but I will always be a warrior of Arthur.' And then he smiled, his voice returning to normal and casually added, 'Coming then?'

Caratacus looked down at his cappuccino with a swirl of chocolate powder dashed on the top and the little biscuit on the side of the saucer. It was Twickenham, it was his life and if he stayed right there and handed over the letter than he could keep that life. But he knew if he left with this man that much-wanted life was going to slip away.

'Sod it,' he said and stood up, leaving the cappuccino untouched on the table.

Geraint was about twenty steps ahead and walking towards the Triple T with a purpose.

Caratacus called to him. 'I don't need anything from my digs, I've got the message on me. Hey! Hey...you...I said I don't need anything from there. We can go straight.'

'I know,' replied Geraint.

'Can't we just head off and get this over with?' Caratacus had begun to whine.

'We are and we won't,' the reply came.

'Why does everybody talk as if they are the flipping dungeon master? Why can't I just get a straight answer…?'

Geraint ignored him as they walked through the second door of the Triple T. Geraint walked straight through the pub, naming some of the regulars as a way of greeting. He waved as he passed Maggie and smiled warmly, 'Maggie ferch Eira Rosser I see you,' and disappeared inside the toilets.

'I see you too, Geraint. Love to the boy,' she shouted after him.

Caratacus' eyebrow raised a touch as he heard Maggie use the word 'love'. It was like hearing someone say 'dildo' during Prime Minister's Question Time. He waited while Geraint was using the toilet.

The toilet door opened. 'Come on then,' said Geraint as his head popped through the space between door and frame.

'What?' said Caratacus.

'Let's get going!' Geraint urged.

'Through the toilet?' said Caratacus. He was already going through the door, despite everything screaming to the contrary. Caratacus thought there might be a way out the back of the toilet.

Of course, there bloody wasn't.

'In you go,' Geraint said, pointing into one of the cubicles.

'I'm fine,' Caratacus replied with a nervous laugh.

'Just go in. Trust me.' Geraint insisted. Caratacus surrendered and went in sighing and shaking his head. It's not as if Geraint was going to have sex with him.

Was Geraint going to have sex with him?

While he felt he should be questioning what was happening a little more he realised he just couldn't be bothered. He just wanted to get it done so he could sod off back to the bar, get a real drink and then look at finding that pub. He looked at Geraint who was now facing into the cubicle with his right hand on the top above the door. The man quietly chanted words Caratacus didn't understand before feeling a lurch as if the toilet had been struck lightly. As soon as the world returned to normal, he turned and yacked his guts up down the toilet.

'What happened there?' He said between spitting and flushing to stop it happening again.

For the first time Geraint laughed with proper humour, putting his hand on Caratacus' shoulder. 'I am sorry Caratacus. I forget how discombobulating the first few times are.'

Caratacus yacked again. 'I feel like I've got food poisoning, what happened?'

'We are here,' Geraint said simply, opening the door.

Caratacus groaned with feeling sick and groaned that he was being treated like an idiot again.

Geraint was gone, leaving Caratacus alone in the cubicle. He retched a few more times, flushing the toilet repeatedly and after a minute, knowing that no more retches were coming, he went back to the TTT bar.

He stopped.

It wasn't the TTT.

This was the Once and Future. I have been there many times and, on occasion, for myself, for a drink, to tell my stories. It is a place I like.

The pub's ceilings were low, but the room was large and at this time, full of people, enjoying a drink, a chat, a debate, and a laugh.

The walls were covered with pictures, portraits and old weapons: swords, shields and spears. The furniture was what you could call rustic and Caratacus was surprised to see rushes covering the floor. The bar was neither large nor small, but it was made the smaller by the huge man serving drinks behind it.

Geraint appeared through the throng. 'Drink, or head up and meet him now?' he said.

Caratacus needed to sit down first, he felt shattered and didn't understand that using Magick took it out of you.

'Any chance I can get some water, wash my mouth out a bit and then see him? I need to sit down,' Caratacus said to nobody whosoever because there was nobody there. He'd been talking to Geraint, blinked, then he was talking to himself. Geraint was lying on the floor. The remover of Geraint had been a punch victim. A fight had broken out between what looked like a load of large, Swedish, hipster bodybuilders. One of them had roared and punched one of the others who had been launched into Geraint.

Caratacus stepped back and chaos in blonde ensued. Everybody else in that pub just got on with their evening. Seen that, been there, done that.

The fight lasted seconds and ended with two conscious blondes and one unconscious blonde on the floor and one standing over them laughing loudly, head back like they did in old films, mouth open, looking like a Viking receiving an enema.

The conscious floor dwellers were also laughing even though they were covered in a lot of their own blood. Pub fights are usually little angry people bouncing two foot back and forth from each other, like they are playing on a bouncy castle. They jut out their chins and chests hoping that their friends have the sense to hold them back while they shout 'COME ON 'EN' while also hoping that the other person doesn't actually COME ON 'EN. If it ever actually breaks into physical violence, it's similar to a very aggressive hug with punches raining in from about one centimetre away as if they are stroking each other with their knuckles.

The fight victor suddenly stopped laughing as someone even bigger than him grabbed him by the top of his trousers and the scruff of his shirt and ran him about 5 metres through the pub before defenestrating him.

Despite the violence, Caratacus was surprised to see that everyone was still smiling or laughing. Even the man outside the window he'd been thrown through was manically roaring with laughter and bleeding profusely from the chunk of glass that was sticking out of the side of his forehead. Caratacus looked at the bloke who had done the throwing and recognised him as the big, bald, red bearded man from behind the bar. Geraint had stood up gingerly, but Caratacus could see he had a wry grin on his face as well.

The red bearded giant put his hands on his hips and said, 'You know I like a tussle, boys but next time, take it outside, ok?' before looking over at Caratacus. 'Caratacus ap Neb,' he stated, matter-of factly with a smile. 'Good to see you,' he said as if they'd been friends all their lives. Behind him, the inter big-laughing-blonde fight winner climbed back through the window and, completely of its own accord, the window repaired itself, pieces of glass flying from the ground into the four panes of glass and wooden frame it was before. The last thing that was heard was the 'Ouch' as the final piece of glass tore itself from the blond man's face back to where it had been moments before.

'Go and sit with Geraint over there and I'll join you in a minute. What do you want to drink?' the big man asked.

'Sparkling water or a diet Dr Pepper?

The man just stared as if he hadn't heard anything.

'Lager top?' Caratacus tried again.

'Ale it is,' he heard.

CHAPTER SIXTEEN
TIME TO MEET ARTHUR

Caratacus followed Geraint to one of the booths at the back of the pub and the two sat down opposite one another. Geraint smiled. 'Feeling better?' he asked.

'A little bit. My stomach feels a bit ropey though.'

'Drink?'

'I think that big barman is bringing something over now.'

On cue the man appeared and set down two tankards of ale and a shot glass containing an orange liquid on the table in front of Caratacus.

Geraint got up and the two men embraced. When they broke, they still held to each other, looking at each other smiling and quietly laughing.

The smiles cracked and it wasn't long before they both were crying back in a close embrace.

'Tommaltach told me about Bed, Peredur, Gwalch and Owain. My heart is broken. Is everybody else safe?' Geraint asked.

Galahad shook his head. 'Other than Cub, nothing. What news on the Three Kings?'

'The Druid King is around, I do believe he followed this one down,' Geraint nodded towards Caratacus. 'And Adda is found and is returning.'

'Some rare, good news there.'

'How have the deaths affected the old man?' Geraint asked, gravely.

'He'd already gone way before all this. You know he's been a shell since you all left—'

'We had to…' Geraint interrupted.

'Hisht, I am not judging. I'm just saying. I thought this news, the attacks on us would rouse him but it has sent him further into the depths. I fear he is lost for good,' Galahad said.

'I can't and won't believe that. Once we are together and we take some time to work this out, it'll get him back. Where is he?'

'Where he's been since you all left. Upstairs. He hardly leaves the place. In truth I've given up,' Galahad said, shaking his head.

Galahad looked at Caratacus. 'So, this is Tommaltach's message boy? What's this all about?' he beamed.

'Has Tommaltach not told you?' asked Geraint.

'Nothing.' A shake of the head from the big man.

'Tell him Caratacus.' said Geraint.

Caratacus replied, still a little embarrassed by it all. 'I'm here to get a bloke called Arthur and take him to a lady in a lake.'

Galahad stroked his beard. 'Why?'

Caratacus shrugged.

Geraint sat and shuffled over on the bench while Galahad sidled up next to him and smiled a wonderfully open smile. Caratacus trusted and liked him instantly, he oozed security. The big man offered his hand and Caratacus shook it, his hand tiny in comparison.

'Galahad ap Neb,' Galahad introduced himself.

'Sir Galahad?' Caratacus blurted out.

The smile was rueful, the groan was real. 'Not sir, never sir, none of that nonsense, ok?' He didn't shout it and it wasn't said in anger. It was stated, that's it.

Geraint laughed and Galahad's smile grew. He nudged his neighbour. 'Damned poets eh?'

'A pox on their stories and their bits,' Geraint replied and they both laughed. Galahad slid the small tumbler with the orange drink over.

Caratacus slid it back. 'No thanks. I don't think shots are going to help.'

'It's not alcohol boy. Ger here says you've never travelled before, and you are feeling the effects. This will help you.' Galahad slid it back.

Caratacus didn't like being called 'boy' one little bit. 'Fine,' he answered, in his best teenager voice and after a sniff of it, decked the drink in one gulp.

He waited for his stomach to lurch, his face rigid expecting the worst, but it didn't come. In fact, his eyebrows raised. Not only did he stop feeling sick he actually felt refreshed.

'Wow, what is that?' he asked.

The men opposite laughed again. Galahad answered, 'Like I said, just a tonic for people not used to the shudder after travelling.'

'Travelling by toilet,' Caratacus added.

'Pub toilet,' Geraint corrected.

'Of course…' mumbled Caratacus.

'Why didn't you email or text me to say you had arrived?' Galahad asked Geraint.

Caratacus' head shot up. 'You have signal HERE?' The importance of the occasion was broken as Caratacus suddenly came alive, struggling to pull his phone from his pocket. He unlocked it and noticed that there was 4G and it asked him if he wanted to sign up for Wi-Fi. A magical pub that didn't really exist in the real world had Wi-Fi! He laughed despite the utterly serious tone of the discussion so far. 'You have Wi-Fi! Have you got the code?'

'Once and future, one word, all lower case,' Galahad replied.

It was the most animated they'd seen him. 'Cheers!' he shouted as he bounced off to the bar.

'He's important?' asked Galahad.

'I actually don't know… Tommaltach sent him.' Geraint shrugged as if that was an answer.

Caratacus was delighted. Quick checks on social media showed nothing desperate to respond to. He had a few messages from friends and fifty-two from his mother. That combined with the thirty-five missed calls meant she was even more frantic with worry than usual. He looked up from the phone for the first time since heading over from the dark back of the pub. It was alive and loud. He recognised the Nordic four. They were in amongst people – well, sort of people – watching one of them arm wrestling a violet skinned person. There were some in jeans and other casual wear, but most people were dressed in clothing that had come from the costume department on the Lord of the Rings set. Some had cloaks, some had swords and there was even a bloke by the bar with a patch over his eye like a pirate. To Caratacus' delight, his phone vibrated, and he answered it in a flash.

'Hey, Hi Mam...I know, look there is just no signal around here and my phone is really playing up...Yep, all fine, still in Cardiff....No, no I'm not lying. The book fair was fine, and I'm here for a few more days. Yep, I've eaten. Yes, breakfast every day. Yep, love you too and see you next week. Mam? If you are doing any ironing (she was, he knew she was) could you do a quick run over my shirts? Yeah, I know there are a lot of them but just do the top two and I can do the rest... All of them? Oh, thanks Mam, you know you don't have to. I won't phone tomorrow because my signal is crap, but I'll call when I get back home. Yep, promise, and you, bye.'

He'd checked everything that needed checking and so went back to Geraint and Galahad at the back of the pub. They were deep in conversation but, when they noticed him, they stopped and got up.

'Come on then, young 'un,' said Galahad. 'Let's meet the old man.'

Caratacus followed Galahad and Geraint through the hatch of the bar and through a door to a room behind before they started to climb the stairs.

'NONE SHALL PASS!' This from a young man on the top of the stairs dressed as a medieval knight with a red cape, holding a giant broadsword in front of him.

'Shut it Neil, you know who it is.' Galahad called up the stairs at the young boy who now looked hurt at being told off.

'I don't know who they are!' the young man indicated with a nod towards Caratacus.

Galahad sighed 'I'll make introductions later.' By the time he finished the sentence he'd reached the top of the stairs.

Neil straightened and made his voice stronger 'You may pass Sir Galahad....'

Galahad growled quietly 'I've warned you to stop doing all of that nonsense, especially every time I come up the bloody stairs, I live up here for f—'

'B-but that's how...' Neil stammered, looking up at Galahad's face, but found a backbone from somewhere and straightened a little. 'That's how it's meant to be done. That's how we were told to do it.'

Galahad physically relaxed. 'Ok young 'un. You are right, of course. You are Fir C'Nu. I'll introduce the guests properly so you can do your thing.' He then grabbed the boy's chin in one hand. 'But you try this with me one more time and I will bend you, ok?'

Caratacus felt a little sorry for the kid because that's what he was, a kid. He looked about eighteen, if that. Just growing out of the gangly stage.

Neil gulped, nodded and then found composure. 'Strangers,' he called out like a Shakespearean actor, 'name yourselves before entering Camelot.'

'It's not Camelot,' Galahad said standing behind him. 'OK, look I will name them so you can do your bit for the old man. This is Caratacus ap Neb of Twickenham, Magicker, and he is on a quest, I thought you'd like that.'

'I'm not a Magicker,' Caratacus interrupted before being interrupted himself as Galahad continued, 'And this is Geraint ap Erbin.'

Geraint smiled. 'Come on Neil, while you've changed, I doubt I have in the last few years!'

Caratacus saw the shock on Neil's face when the name was announced and watched him go down on one knee, face down in supplication. 'Sir Geraint! Welcome home. I apologise, it has been many years.'

'It's OK, Neil, it's lovely to see you, but please why are we carrying on with the sir nonsense?' he said.

Galahad replied. 'I tell him all the time, but he doesn't listen or doesn't want to. It drives the old man to despair, but he still carries on.'

Geraint wearily started up the stairs again. Caratacus followed. Geraint put his hand on the young knight's shoulder. 'Up lad, let's see him,' he said even though he didn't look that much older himself.

As they tramped up the uncarpeted stairs, Caratacus started getting that knot in his stomach again, not the magic sick stuff but the anxiety knot which had been happening frequently since the death of Fanny Hill. He didn't do stress. In fact, he'd spent his life avoiding it, managing his life so well he barely came into contact with it. Since Tommy's visit it had been a constant companion.

He now understood that it was surprise at the constant mental crap arising that was driving that stress and maybe the best way to deal with it was to expect the unexpected. So, as he walked up the stairs of a magic pub, he remembered that – what was his name? Neil? – the Dungeons and Dragons kid had mentioned Camelot?

What then, could be through this door? *The* Camelot? The door at the top of the stairs probably opened into a different world. One, he imagined that would be bathed in the bright sunshine of midday rather than the time it was. It would be a glorious land of verdant pastures, rolling hills and castles with pointy turrets and knights having jousts and stuff while fair maidens watched, wearing pastel dresses and cone hats.

They finally reached the top of the stairs for Caratacus to enter Camelot. The door swung open and there, right in front of him was a living room.

'Of course, it bloody is,' he grumbled as they all went in.

It wasn't an entirely normal living room though. It looked like it belonged to a moneyed teenager who was having his first go at living on his own. On the far wall were three huge, fitted widescreen tellies, all of them were on but the two at the sides had their volumes off with subtitles furiously trying to keep up with what was being said. Caratacus recognised the news channel but not what was on the right screen. The middle screen, the biggest, had a game on it that he recognised as Call of Duty or COD as some of his mates called it. One huge sofa faced the screens while two smaller sofas flanked a huge low coffee table cluttered with half eaten or empty cartons of food, soft drink cans, magazines, books and bits of paper covered in scrawl. The noise of German soldiers being mowed down permeated the place while everything living stayed silent. You couldn't see the person doing the shooting just the top of his head on the main sofa.

'ANNOUNCEMENT!' Neil shouted, breaking the silence.

'JESUS!' Caratacus yelped. 'You scared the hell out of me!' he said, staring at Neil.

'Piss off,' said the top of the head.

Neil continued, 'My Lord may I introduce—'

'NO, PISS OFF!' this time angrier.

The second 'piss off' made Neil lose his train of thought so he started again, undaunted by being told to piss off.

'My Lord—'

'RIGHT! FOR GODS' SAKE, NEIL, WHY DOES EVERYTHING HAVE TO BE A BLOODY DRAMA?'

The figure stood up still holding the control console. A squat middle-aged man with a beard, wearing deck shorts, bare topped and footed and sporting a huge belly, stood before them.

The once and future King.

King Arthur.

'What?' demanded the King petulantly, daring a comment on his appearance. Neil dropped to his knee and without even looking down Arthur extended his arm and pointed to the young man. 'No,' he ordered. He noticed Geraint and a smile touched his face. 'Geraint,' he said with warmth.

Geraint strode over, a huge smile on his sharp angled, noble face but tears gathered in his eyes.

Arthur enveloped him in a huge bear hug and Caratacus could tell both men were crying. They touched foreheads, Geraint only a little taller. After a moment Arthur said quietly, 'I don't want to talk about it.'

Their heads still together Geraint responded, 'But what are we going to do?'

'I don't know, Ger, I don't have any answers anymore. Please, I can't deal with this right now. Come back tomorrow,' Arthur said.

'Arthur…' pleaded Galahad who had come over to stand next to them, one of his huge hands placed on Arthur's back.

'No. I told you I was not ready to see people,' Arthur replied, still in a quiet voice, sniffing a cry-induced snotty nose.

'Please, Geraint is here, the Kings are found and Tommaltach wants you to leave this place. There is something you have to do. Please.' The last word from Galahad was said no louder but the emphasis on it was as if it had poked Arthur with something sharp. Leaving the embrace of Geraint, he shrugged off Galahad's hand and exploded.

'No Galahad. I told you it's over! I told you to tell everybody to just go away and hide. I have nothing to offer. I told you I want to be left alone.'

'Lord…?' this from Geraint.

'No Geraint ap Erbin, I've had enough. I am fed up with being ignored and treated like this. You forget yourself…' He pointed at Geraint, then turned and pointed at Galahad '…as do you!'

Galahad's face twisted in anger. 'Forget MYSELF?' Caratacus could tell that this change had shocked Arthur, even more so when an equally terrified Geraint stood between them. Galahad kept coming, moving both backwards. 'Forget myself, Arthur ap Uther? Sat up here, hiding from the world. Hiding from yourself?'

'Fuck off,' from Arthur.

'You fuck off! Sulking up here playing games like a teenager when out there in both the Worlds things are changing, death and suffering is coming. Do you hear me?'

While Geraint grappled with the slow advance, Arthur started walking back to the couch. Caratacus and Neil just watched not knowing what to do.

Galahad laughed angrily. 'That's right waddle off...'

Arthur stopped and turned around. 'What do you want me to do, O Righteous One? Eh? Call bloody Excalibur and ride out and do battle? We tried that. We tried to find out what was happening, and nothing was. I'm still here! Everybody left me!'

'Why do you think that was? They saw the precursor to this! Constant sleeping, complaining, and eating. This waste of a life!'

'I didn't want all those lives! I don't want this one!'

'Well, isn't that fortunate, you spoilt fat arsehole! It's coming to an end. How you can stand there, like...like that,' Galahad gestured, 'when some of your brothers are dead and the ones that are left are next. Has everything we have struggled for been for nothing? I will not go to the next life like this.'

Galahad was crying with rage, shouting over Geraint at Arthur who was in a similar state. 'Stay up here. Hide and die. But I am not staying to watch you decay anymore.'

'Go on then, leave me like everybody else. You only stayed for yourself anyway. You only stayed because you were too scared to leave like the others. Go on, sod off,' Arthur bawled at the big man.

It was as if he'd been struck. Galahad's jaw tightened but his face went calm and that calmness made Geraint hold his friend's arms tighter, whispering 'Gal, please' three times.

Just like any married couple or close relationship they knew and pressed all the right buttons, but Galahad was hurt and exhausted. 'Let's go,' he said to Geraint and then, to Caratacus, 'We can try again tomorrow but I don't see much point.' Then he shouted, 'And why don't you put some bloody clothes on and tidy up you idle bastard...' and left just in time to hear, 'Piss off...' come from in front of a big screen as a graphic of a American Marine reloaded.

CHAPTER SEVENTEEN
THE CALM AFTER THE STORM

'He's a twat!' Galahad shouted back as he stomped down the stairs, quickly followed by a placating Geraint, a puzzled Caratacus and a terrified Neil.

'Twat,' Galahad said to nobody as Geraint's hand appeared on his shoulder.

'I know you are angry, Galahad but please with the swearing, you know I don't like it.'

Out of the dark of the flat stairway, they came through the door and into the hustle and bustle of a busy pub. Galahad headed behind the bar to help out the serving girl and immediately took an order. He nodded at the customer, looked over at Geraint who was looking at him. 'Sorry Geraint ap Erbin.' He poured a frothing ale from a large jug into a tankard and handed it over to the customer. 'He is a horse's backside,' and then he smiled.

Geraint's worried face broke into a smile, and he laughed quietly 'That's better,' he said.

Galahad poured three more ales and slid one each to Caratacus and Geraint, keeping one for himself. He looked at Neil. 'Have a break, young one. He's not going anywhere, and you need some time off that doesn't involve training or studying about training. Have a drink, I have one bottle of that lager piss you like.'

Neil was about to refuse but the last line made him pause. 'I haven't been for a run today, Lord.'

'Forget running tonight. How many times have you joined me for a beer?'

'I had a drink with you last Christmas,' said Neil thoughtfully.

Galahad chuckled 'Before that?' he asked.

Neil, still thinking hard 'I... think...it was...' he said.

'Christmas before?' Galahad asked in mock sincerity.

Neil knew it was in jest and, blushing, he smiled. Caratacus looked at him as if noticing him for the first time. He had the same honest face as Galahad with only continuous worry making him look different. The smile changed his whole demeanour, but it also showed how young he was. His smile was contagious, and it was joined with ones from Galahad, Geraint and even Caratacus.

'It probably was...' Neil agreed nodding.

Galahad brought a green bottle from the fridge underneath the counter, opened it and handed it over to Neil who thanked him, taking a sip like a young antelope at a very busy, predator-infested drinking hole.

'You have a fridge?' asked Caratacus.

'No, I have a magic hole to a lager brewery,' answered Galahad.

'Well, you might have!' Caratacus said.

Galahad and Geraint laughed and, two seconds later, Neil joined them, but he didn't know why.

'Fair enough,' Galahad said, 'I forget you are outside all of this.'

'Outside what?' asked Caratacus.

'You know, the Worlds, Magick, This World, That one.'

'I still don't know anything about what you are talking about to be honest. I've caught little bits but...'

'Don't worry about that now, boy,' Galahad said in a friendly way. 'You've had a hell of a few days by all accounts, well by his account,' he pointed at Geraint who nodded in response. 'Let's have a few drinks, forget today, and start again tomorrow. We've got a spare bed here, but you can travel to Maggie's straight if you fancy?'

Caratacus smiled, took a sip of the ale which, to his surprise, was drinkable. 'Yeah, I'd like a couple of beers. That sounds lovely. Can we sit and have them though and can we not be so close to those blonde, laughing mentalists?'

I don't think Geraint really knew what a mentalist was, but he smiled. 'Of course, let's go to the back, it's quieter there.'

'Who the hell wants quiet?' Caratacus, Geraint and Neil all jumped. Caratacus looked around at the face the voice belonged to; it was a stubbled, grinning face, almost close to insanity. The man was well built and tall like Galahad.

'Cai ap Cynyr!' exclaimed Geraint, throwing his arms around the taller man.

'Geraint ap Erbin,' answered Cai 'I see you, and shit, it pleases me.'

'Language,' stated Geraint smiling. Cai looked at Galahad behind the bar, still smiling but with a glint in his eye. 'Yeah Gal,' he said, 'no shitting swearing,' before breaking into a huge peal of laughter that Caratacus thought the blonde fighty people would be proud of.

Galahad handed over a freshly poured beer to Cai who lifted it to his mouth and cleared it in one.

'Another!' he said. He noticed Caratacus but kept his eyes on Galahad behind the bar and said, 'Who's dopey?'

'Cai…' Galahad warned. 'This is Caratacus, the messenger from Tommaltach I told you about.' He stared as if trying to pierce Cai's mind with his eyes.

This made Cai turn around and look Caratacus up and down, something Caratacus didn't appreciate at all.

Caratacus put on his best unimpressed, resting bitch face. 'Alright?' he said.

'Him?' Cai asked loudly, still as if Caratacus didn't exist.

Galahad and Geraint rolled their eyes in unison.

What he said in Welsh was 'lamb's penis' as he stared ahead, taking a huge draft of ale. Caratacus didn't know that, but he knew it wasn't anything nice.

Sod this, Caratacus thought. 'Listen mate…'

'I'm not your mate,' Cai replied, still facing forward.

Caratacus was about to give a traditional, south London 'Sod off mate...' when Galahad reached over and grabbed

Cai's face, squeezing his cheeks. 'Enough of your nonsense, ok? Just bloody behave!'

A dark cloud flew over Cai's face, a flash of violence in his eyes and just as quickly it disappeared, and a genuine smile appeared in its place. He held his hands out placatingly towards Galahad once he let go of his face. 'Hey...Old Cai was only joking,' he turned to Caratacus 'You can take a joke, eh boy?'

You may have thought that Caratacus had breezed through life. You were correct, of course but that didn't mean his pampered upbringing had kept him away from disruptive elements, what his mother called 'little bastards.' You didn't get away scot free when named after an old British chieftain from Roman times. He'd met many 'Cai' types in his life; dangerous, sometimes fun, bullying, befriending, life of the party or the end of it. You didn't go through life avoiding fights without learning a few tricks, and rolling over and showing your belly was one of them.

'Yeah, I know that,' Caratacus smiled and gestured to the tankard in front of Cai 'Another?'

Cai instantly calmed and turned towards Caratacus with a slight surprise on his face. 'I don't pay for ale here but very nice of you. Thanks.' He put out his hand, face serious but not angry.

'My name is Cai ap Cynyr. You may have heard of me – Prince of the plunder, the unrelenting warrior to his enemy. Heavy was he in his vengeance. Terrible was his fighting. When he would drink from a horn, he would drink as much as four. When into battle he came he slew as would a hundred. Unless God should accomplish it, his death would be unattainable.' He smiled.

Caratacus shook his hand '...Erm Caratacus Lewis,' he said lamely.

Cai noticed Neil behind Caratacus. 'Boy,' he nodded in greeting.

'Lord,' Neil answered looking uncomfortable.

As if nothing at all had happened, Cai turned to Geraint. 'How are you, Ger? What's the news? I am so sorry to see you in such awful times. I'm heartsick with everything, but Galahad tells me that the Kings live, and Cub? Who else?' Geraint was about to answer but Cai laughed again, 'Sorry Ger, I'm not giving you any chance to answer. Nothing changes eh? Let's sit, get drunk and forget life for a bit, yes?'

Geraint pointed at the booth at the back of the pub only just visible through the loud throng. 'That was already our intention.'

'I am going to serve for two minutes and then I'll join you,' Galahad called to them as he poured more ale into a tankard.

Caratacus followed Geraint and Cai before noticing that Neil was standing back. 'You coming?' he asked.

'No, Lord. I have to train...It was an honour to meet you...'

To his surprise, Caratacus found himself enjoying the night. These men obviously loved each other and even Cai stopped being an arse for a bit. The laughter and the stories flowed like the ale and Caratacus enjoyed the easy company. And, while listening to the tales of adventure – most of them featuring people he'd never heard of – he became drunker and drunker.

Drunkenness turned into 'being absolutely bladdered' and the rest of the night turned into flashed recalls before turning into the abyss of nothing.

CHAPTER EIGHTEEN

WAKING UP

Arthur gets up around half past six every morning. He'd love to sleep in, but his body and mind work together to stop it happening. In an instant his brain throws something out there to stop him returning to the glorious abyss of nothing. The scenes are mostly different, one of the many downsides from having lived so many lives. Once they happen, he doesn't want to think about them anymore. This morning his mind throws up the Battle of Mynydd Baddon which sounds grand. Even This World has heard of it. A moment in history that experts say someone called Arthur may have taken part in. Which is nice.

But what brought his mind from slumber and all the way here to bleakness was not the battle, the dreams never last that long. It was one scene and one moment of fear, it was the moment a Saxon spear rammed up into his mount's throat. It was the Saxon's scream of jubilation and Arthur's beautiful horse's strangled scream of pain and lastly Arthur's cry of loss as he was thrown.

Less than a second. Bang. Awake. This time it's a throw but yesterday it was a blow from a sword across the side of his face, and the day before a spear ripping through his flesh and deep into his body. It could be the face of someone three thousand years ago, contorted with rage, trying to crush his windpipe or holding his face under a small puddle of water until he drowns. Sometimes it's the faces of people he has loved but are long gone. Lovers, friends and family, all the way back to the beginning. Sometimes it is them in their death throes, the last struggling breaths of their lives, or sometimes it's just their faces, smiling or frowning at him and it wakes him, it still wakes him with pain. He is awake and he doesn't want to be and then the aches begin.

He is still tired.

He forces himself to get up. One of the Fir C'nu brings him up a cup of tea. He knows the boy's name is Neil. But sometimes he forgets. He is so bad with names nowadays. Galahad reckons it's all the tablets, but even when he's off them, he feels his memory is breaking down. The doctor tells him it's depression, the local druid agrees. His memory wasn't always like that. No matter how down or bleak he feels, he does try and say something to Neil. He feels sorry for the young man, this last warrior of the Fir C'nu but not so sorry that he does anything about it. He's glad he sent the rest of them away and he wants this one to be free as well, but Galahad will not have it. He understands they are of his blood and therefore he should make more of an effort with his great, great times a lot grandson but, honestly, he just can't be bothered.

Tea done, and with it tablets for blood pressure, depression and the numerous other ailments that afflict him. While he has bested dragons, giants, evil kings and warriors of dark renown, it seems that King Arthur will finally be destroyed by bad fats and a BMI in the far reaches of the thirties. What a song for the bards that will make.

He then watches a bit of breakfast television before listening to the news in Welsh on Radio Cymru.

He remains tired and he still aches.

Every single day either Galahad comes up and makes him shower or he sends the boy up to remind him. Whether it's the former or the latter, he wants to strangle whoever is in front of him. He knows he must shower! For the love of the gods, he knows that! But he just wants to be left alone. 'Can't a man shower when he wants?' he asks himself and even the question, the one about a simple task, a task so many of you do every day, helps him move down the spiral to even darker thoughts. Everything is a struggle, everything brings on the black dog, so he avoids doing anything but eating, shitting or pissing. Those are all things he can't avoid and having to do them and thinking about any of it pushes him closer to not wanting to wake up the next day.

Blessed release.

He has thought about it. Death. Real death. If this is his last life, then what's the bloody point? What has it all been for? What is the reason for him returning and fighting so many times? The Worlds are gods-awful places, this one is even worse than all the times before.

It's after the shower, or the absolute refusal to have one, and the subsequent argument with Galahad that he gets that inspiration, that infinitesimal spark that makes him think that the day ahead could be different, that he might do something worthwhile, and everything would be better. Maybe go horse riding, the Preseli mountains always made his heart soar, or possibly get out to the forge. Hitting the hell out of a molten bit of metal always helped. Or why not some sword practice? Lose some of this fat.

This flash tells him that everything is OK, he is back. But every time that happens his mind tells him, No. It tells him why he can't, and he listens, and he switches on the games console.

He gets up Call of Duty on one of the screens while the television stays on the other two and he lies on his couch stopping play when the news comes on. There is a small break for a sandwich and a can of pop (plus moaning by Galahad or moaning by Galahad through proxy with the boy) before more Call of Duty. By late afternoon it's game shows, the news on S4C until his favourite soap operas. He eats what he is given and watches television until about one in the morning and then plays COD until he falls asleep.

Most of the time he doesn't reach his bed but whether he does or not, it all ends in sleep and starts again at half past six the next day with horror.

Not this morning though. This morning he was woken up by the noise of laughter and the clanging of swordplay. He recognised the laughter of Geraint and Galahad as they practised with their swords. It gripped his heart and he smiled and then he chuckled for the first time in what felt like – and probably was – years and then he broke down and sobbed like a baby. The black dog does not go gently…

Same time, not that far away from Arthur.

It was movement that plucked Caratacus from the oblivion of drunken, unconscious deep-down sleep. He didn't know the movement, it could have been me, but immediately, consciousness brought pain, in head and in shoulders, then in stomach, and then in eyes. It brought dry swollen-tongued mouth, untouched by swallow and saliva. He moved his legs because they didn't hurt, they were barely attached to the living, slow death of everything alive above it. The first prodding of beer depression came then. What me? What where? Then he noticed that the movement that had woken him wasn't his legs or even any of the hungover parts of him, it was from the bottom of the bed. The pain that covered every part of his face and front part of his head would have made him cry had he any moisture left in his body.

He opened one eye. Someone tightened a vice around his head. He closed his eye and exhaled, his teeth shivering in pain.

He opened one eye again, it couldn't be two as the other one was squashed by his face against the mattress. His room's mattress? He hoped so.

There was a crow perched on the bottom of the bed frame.
It didn't sink in.
He groaned and closed his one eye against the agony.
It sank in.

''KIN HELL!' he cried as he jumped up into a sitting position on the bed. Pain, dull and deep, but also sharp, surface pain travelled through his face. That's pretty much all the pain.

His eyes, both of them now, looked at the crow but his screaming brain also registered the touch of skin on skin on his arm.

''KIN HELL!' he jumped away from whoever's skin it was and fell out of bed, narrowly missing the bedside table with his head. He leapt to his feet with the agility of a Russian gymnast and started to back away from the bed before releasing his third 'KIN HELL!' as he felt someone patting his backside which not only surprised him but informed him that he was completely naked.

He looked around to see that the patter, sitting in the room's only seat, was a short, very ancient woman dressed like his mother's friends did on bingo night. Feeling his nakedness, he tried to drag the bedcover over to cover his modesty, but it was currently being used by the girl in his bed and was tucked in tightly on the other side. His mouth dropped as he registered the girl. No, she wasn't a girl, she was a goddess, a beautiful, dreamy, innocent, dirty, perfect, sensual, proper goddess, and that wasn't the half of it. His brain was overwhelmed before righting itself enough to remind him that he was in the nip, so he gave up dragging the cover and, panicking, grabbed a free pillow, shoving it in front of him.

A crow, an old woman and a beautiful girl were in the room. His mind raced but the hangover reminded him it was there. 'Don't puke,' it said.

'Who are you?' he said weakly.

The young woman gently patted the side of the bed he had recently departed. 'Hey kitten come and sit back down so we can talk.' Her Irish accent purred. His legs weakened and he felt a knot in his chest, it wasn't his hangover this time, it was her. From nowhere his very being was telling him he wanted sex and he wanted to marry her, and he wanted to spend every single second of every single day with her, forever, and he wanted it now. He wanted to paint her or sculpt her, and he wanted to write poetry about her while holding her hand. He wanted to go shopping with her. That's how much he wanted her. He could feel his groin tightening and that brought him back to now and the room and his head telling his groin 'Please not now, groin.'

'I don't think you need anything that big to cover your phallus,' said the old woman, her voice the texture of late autumn leaves.

The word 'phallus' and his hangover combined to make him gag.

The crow cawed again. 'Mummy's boy, shitting his pants over a few girls and now he's gonna whitey.' It hopped around.

'What the hell do you want? Please leave,' he said.

'We have to talk, Caratacus ap Neb,' said the old woman, Ceridwen. 'You can stay standing, or you can get comfortable, it makes no odds to us.'

He ignored the 'ap Neb.' The choices he had were limited to staying where he was with a pillow over his willy or to tentatively crawl back onto his bed and under the covers, which he did. He perched himself as far away from the beauty as he possibly could without falling off and, with both the bed's pillows, he built a little wall between him and the hottest girl he'd ever seen in the world, ever.

He exhaled. At least things couldn't get any worse.

The door opened and in came Maggie Rosser holding a mug of dark brown tea in one hand and a piece of toast smeared with jam in the other.

'Morning,' she shot as she put the tea down and gave Caratacus the toast which he helplessly took.

Caratacus' mouth dropped, and he wondered if Maggie could see his guests. His hostess answered that question immediately by bowing to the three individually and snapping a 'Bore da' in her no-nonsense way. They all returned her 'Good morning' in the language in which it had been given, then she said 'Gwd thing!' and left. Caratacus' mouth stayed open.

This time it was the young maiden that sat up in bed, the covers covering her to the chest. Caratacus memorised every bit of skin that was shown by that movement. The air smelt of meadows, even though he wasn't entirely sure what meadows smelled of.

'We are being rude sisters,' she said. 'Let us introduce ourselves. I am Dannan of the flowers.' She held out her hand and he shook it as if in a trance. Once he touched her, he didn't want to let go but she pulled away gently with a giggle and, for that moment, that split second of a split second, he wanted to kill himself because of that loss.

'Shithead wee virgin,' said the crow which brought him back with a bang. He really didn't like that crow.

'That is my sister Badb. She is the shy one,' Danaan smiled.

The old woman remained in her seat. 'I am Ceridwen of Macha and I see you, Caratacus ap Neb.'

'Hello,' he said weakly.

'You need to take Arthur to the bridge,' Ceridwen said, suddenly.

'What bridge?' he asked.

'The bridge you idiot.,' this from the crow.

He looked at the bird. He did it in a slow, hungover seethe, and not just with his eyes but his whole head.

'I don't know where your stupid bridge is, you big, fat, ignorant chicken,' he said calmly.

The beauty by his side, the crone on the seat and the crow at the foot of the bed, chorused, 'Oooh hark at her,' in a high-pitched voice in unison, then laughed.

It felt like one of his being naked in school dreams.

'Sneaky Tommaltach has a plan for you and lucky for the Light our plans are aligned,' the crone said. 'We are in agreement. We want you to take Arthur King away, the Worlds are shrinking, and he must be kept alive, but unlike shining eyes we have a plan.'

'You must take the King to the bridge at Cantre'r Gwaelod,' Dannan said.

'Why? And why should I trust you?' he asked her.

It was Ceridwen who answered. 'Because, like you, oh lazy one we are part of this story and in this story something important will happen at the bridge, so you need to go there.'

'What will happen there?' he asked Ceridwen.

'Whatever will happen will happen.' answered Badb who hopped from the frame to the bed forcing Caratacus to pull in his feet in disgust.

'Can't you give a straight answer? I'm still going to the Lake lady or whatever. I'm not doing anything that will annoy Tommy McKracken. No way. Look' he said, 'I'll ask Tommy if it's OK and then get back to you. Have you got a mobile number I can get you on?' He knew he was being sarcastic, and it seemed that they did too as he felt the slap across the face from Ceridwen. His head rang, she certainly could move quickly for an old woman.

'Ow! What was that for?' he wailed.

'Do not tell anybody of this quest we have given you, child. Lives depend on it,' she warned suddenly, sitting back in the chair as if she hadn't moved at all.

'Whose?' he asked but he knew the answer.

'Yours if you keep asking stupid questions you pathetic waster,' Badb cried before cawing a stream of swearwords.

'Look, I don't want any of this! I want to go back to my life. I don't care about bridges or wizards or hobbits or any of that shit. I don't even think that this Arthur will go with me anyway. I'd love to be able to get this fat bloke to the middle of Wales, so Tommy McKracken doesn't throw me into the Thames with a concrete overcoat on.' He felt desperate now. 'Why not ask one of Arthur's friends like Galahad or Geraint? Why bloody me?'

Another slap made his head ring. This time it was from the beauty. 'Language, you naughty boy,' she said, pouting in mock anger. It was more Marilyn than even Marilyn but he didn't care, it stung and his head pounded and despite everything she still made his groin constrict. He felt like a chastised child wanting to point out that the stupid crow swore like a docker.

'Do the quest, my lazy kitten, take him to the bridge and make sure the task is done,' said Dannan.

'A task? What task? Why do I have to take him there?' Caratacus asked.

'You just do,' answered Badb.

'Then?' he asked, 'Will that be it?'

'Probably,' the young woman said.

'Possibly,' the older one added.

'It won't be it,' said the crow.

Then they were gone and Caratacus bit into the toast he was holding.

CHAPTER NINETEEN
A CHAPTER OF THREE KINGS

Caratacus got to his feet to drink his tea and polish off the toast. He stood up, put down his empty cup and started to rummage through his trouser pockets to find his phone. He'd ring Tommy and tell him he had a debilitating stomach bug and that he had to go home. He'd done the tough bit, hadn't he? He'd come all this way and delivered the message to Arthur, well not Arthur but his mates. There were plenty of them that could take him to the lake?

He checked his phone. No signal and battery low.

''Sake....' he said, sitting down on the bed. It wasn't just for the signal and the battery; he had remembered his new... ugh...quest from this morning. Even if he could disappear now, he still had to tell Arthur or one of the others the need to go to...oh God what was it called? 'Cantra gwaylot?' So, he would have to tell one of them anyway. How was he going to get out of this?

He had a grand plan, and the first part of that grand plan was to brush his teeth, have a shower and get dressed. He was yet to formulate the second part, but he could work on that during the first.

Five hours later no second part of the plan had been formulated. The first thing he did was walk around different parts of Cwm Llechau with his arm straight up in the air trying to get a signal until his battery went completely dead. His stomach grumbled reminding him that it existed and so he made his way to the café on the main crossroads. When he saw that the young girl behind the counter had a charger that was compatible with his, he wanted to offer her his shop as payment for half an hour of charge. She said yes, at the same time adding that the Wi-Fi wasn't working in the Café, so he'd have a fully charged phone that didn't work.

He stayed for a bit, having a sandwich for lunch but most importantly a cappuccino. Other than the girl, the cafe was empty. With no phone, Caratacus looked at the tourism brochures that were stacked untidily on one of the windowsills.

Amongst the usual local tourist attractions, that Caratacus didn't really care about he was surprised to see the leaflet for a museum in the village. What wasn't surprising was that it was a museum dedicated to doll's heads. He sighed, put it back on the pile and went back to drinking his coffee. The girl having finished behind the counter, she brought his fully charged phone back. He thanked her, adding, 'Got a museum then?' to break the silence.

'We got two.' She said straightening the chairs on other tables. 'We got the weird doll's head one at Mr Shellock's house and then we got the other one for you lot.' The 'you lot' wasn't said with a tone, it was matter of fact.

Caratacus couldn't think what lot he was. 'English?' he asked.

'No,' she answered, 'Magickers…That Worlders.'

'I'm not though,' he answered.

She stopped behind a chair, stood straight and looked right at him as if she hadn't seen him before. Then she shrugged. 'Oh, sorry, my mistake. Yeah, there's one museum in the village,' she said simply and carried on moving around the chairs.

He was about to ask how hard it was to be a youngster in a village that seemed to be encased in an impenetrable cocoon of signal blocking lead, when his phone started vibrating, making him jump.

That tiny spark of hope grew into a hot furnace of fear as he noticed the person who was calling was Tommy McKracken. He moved his hand towards the phone in slow motion, hoping that Tommy would ring off first. It was too late; his finger touched the answer button.

'Hello!' he squeaked. Far too cheerful he thought.

'Hello, Tommy.' he said sombrely.

'Good God I have just called him Tommy,' he thought.

'McKracken,' he added. 'Oh no', he thought but couldn't stop himself from adding…

'Tommy McKracken.' Shit, I've just called him by his full name and then he just kept on digging. 'Mr Tommy McKracken, Tommy, Tom, Mr McKracken, yes Mr McKracken, sir... that's you,' and then thankfully he went silent.

There was a long pause before a longer sigh and then, 'Have you been on the glue son?' Even when softly spoken, Tommy's Ulster accent ensured that everything he said was sharply delivered. He didn't wait for an answer. 'Never mind, I don't want to know. Where are you?'

'I'm in Cwm Llechau,' Caratacus answered.

'Why aren't you at Arthur's? You've been there though, haven't you?' Tommy McKracken sounded a little angrier than normal.

'I was there last night,' Caratacus said quickly.

'And?'

'He didn't want to see me.'

'What! Who did you speak to then?'

Caratacus felt like he was under exam conditions. 'I spoke to Geraint, Galahad, Cai and I think the young kid was called Neil.'

'Did you give them the message?'

'Yes.'

'And?'

'And what?'

'What did they say, you soft shite?'

Caratacus panicked again 'I don't know? Nothing?'

'Are they going with you?'

'I don't know!'

There was a pause before Tommy spoke. 'Get yourself back up there, talk to Arthur and tell him you both leave tomorrow. Ok?

'Err Mr McKracken?'

'Just call me Tommy, son. OK?'

'Err, OK but could you tell my mother I'm away for a bit longer and that she needs to sort out the shop? She'll know what to do.' Caratacus said.

'Don't you worry your pretty head about that. I had food with your mother and your wee shop girl last night.'

'You had food…?' His mother, a house cleaner, had dinner with Tommy McKracken which was bad before he groaned internally as he thought about how Marged had behaved.

Tommy cut in 'Shut up. Listen. As I said I had a lovely night with your Ma and the girl. It's all sorted. She knows you are away for a few more days doing some research for me. One of my wee men, Grak is going to keep an eye on the shop although between you and me I'm thinking of taking the wee girl on as muscle. She's terrifying…'

There was silence from Caratacus' end as he furiously tried to stop thinking about the meal...

'Get up to the Once and Future, get Arthur packed and out of there tomorrow morning. He knows where he's going. Once there he needs to get the gift back and then he has to go into hiding. Maybe get over to That World? Just stay safe until we know what's going on. Tell Galahad I'm meeting Adda off the plane and Cub will be with us in the afternoon. Got that?'

'Yes?'

'Right, I'll ring you tomorrow night. Don't mess this up…'

Caratacus blew out and leant back, happy to have survived. He quickly checked his phone to see if the signal was still there. It wasn't.

Someone sat down opposite him on his table. Instinctively Caratacus smiled at the person and he paused as he recognised the face. He just couldn't remember where from. His smile disappeared as soon as he remembered. It was that annoying tramp bloke from the train. Gone were the several layers of clothing as well as that ridiculous hat. He looked very different, but he was hardly dressed normally even now. His face was still one of happiness, his strawberry blonde hair sticking up in all directions. On his head, he had something that Caratacus thought of as a tiara or a silver band and he was dressed in a simple white tunic with gold lining.

Caratacus' head dropped. 'Oh God, what are you doing here? You're something to do with this aren't you? Go on then, what do you want with me? Annual paper, scissors, stone competition?'

The man laughed 'I am not exactly sure what you are talking about and no, the competition you are on about is at the beginning of the year.'

'Obviously.'

The man held his finger up to Caratacus for silence and spoke to the young girl in what Caratacus guessed had to be Welsh. They laughed out loud and for a flash he thought they were laughing at him.

'She asked if you wanted another. Cappuccino yeah?' the tiaraed man asked.

Caratacus desperately wanted another, but he wanted it on his own.

'Nah, I have to be somewhere.' Caratacus started to move.

'Yeah, I know,' the man laughed. 'I'm going as well.'

Caratacus sat back down. 'So you are here for me? I knew it!' Caratacus leaned on the table pointing an accusatory finger.

The man smiled. 'No, I'm not here for you, oh centre of the universe, but I know where you are going because I have to be there as well.' He offered his hand. 'We've been introduced before, but I doubt you remember. I'm Piogerix.'

He didn't. 'Caratacus Lewis,' he said, shaking Piogerix's hand. 'So how do you fit into all this?'

The girl put down a tray and put an omelette and a cup of cappuccino in front of Piogerix and a cappuccino in front of Caratacus. She smiled suggestively at the man who winked in reply.

'Good grief,' Caratacus grimaced 'You're old enough to be her Grandfather.'

'Actually, I am not. You stop thinking about age at about 1,500 years old.' He started eating the eggs with gusto. 'Go on then, big boy? Who am I meant to flirt with? Other 3000-year olds? Know any good dating apps for people in their fourth millennium? Immortal druids dot com?'

Caratacus didn't know how to respond so just shrugged and made a face while taking a sip of his coffee.

'So, you saw the King last night? How was he?' Piogerix asked.

'Dunno,' Caratacus shrugged again. 'Fat? Angry?'

Piogerix shook his head sadly 'That is not good news. We really need him back to his best as soon as possible.' It didn't take long before he finished the omelette and shoved the plate an inch away from where it had been. 'There! That's better.' He sat, still smiling and taking tiny sips of coffee. The smiling got to Caratacus.

'When are you going to the pub?' he asked.

'Later. I have a few things to collect around here first,' Piogerix answered.

Caratacus was relieved. He felt knackered from the nights drinking and had intended to go back to bed and snooze for a few hours. What Tommy didn't know didn't hurt him and more importantly didn't make him find someone to hurt Caratacus. 'Great, where shall we meet?'

'The Tafarn Tylwyth Teg and wait for me.'

'Time?'

'Is an illusion.'

Caratacus was still too hungover to get into anything he didn't want to, so he didn't. He finished his cup and yet again half stood to indicate he was leaving.

'You're going?' The blonde man asked.

Caratacus shrugged 'Well, yeah?'

Piogerix, laughed a short bark and shook his head 'Wow, Tommaltach was actually under selling you. So, after what has happened to you so far and everything to come, you are happy to leave here and head back to bed.'

'I'm not going back to bed,' Caratacus replied shiftily.

'Duh! Yes, you are.'

'So what? I don't fancy the doll's head museum so best I just get my head down.'

'So, you know everything about what's going on? Even though before yesterday you had never heard of Magick? Thought there was one world? Thought that humans were all there was? Thought King Arthur was from a film? And then you sit in a cafe opposite someone who does know all these things and a lot more I may add, and you want to go sleepy bo byes?'

Caratacus stood still, all parts of his body willing him to leave. 'Fine.' He sat back down. 'Go on then! Tell me.'

'What?'

'You know! What you said, those things.'

Piogerix laughed 'I haven't got time for all that! Weren't you listening? I have got things to do, I am off after this coffee is gone.'

Caratacus was surprised to find that he was starting to hate this man almost as much as that crow. 'OK, fine, just one of them.'

'Which one?'

Caratacus rolled his eyes, thinking furiously about what the man had said, especially when as usual he hadn't been paying attention. Finally, from the back crevices of his memory he remembered 'Magic! Yeah, tell me about magic.' he said.

'Magick,' the reply.

'Yeah magic.'

'It's Magick.'

Caratacus pinched his nose as his headache flared up. 'Whatever you say,' he said defeated. 'Have you got it?'

Piogerix's smile disappeared. 'I'm a bloody druid, of course I have!' Then his smile it returned, he snapped his finger, and vanished. A second later he was back, his smile even bigger. He clicked again and they, their chairs and the table were on a beach. 'Woah!' Caratacus said. He could smell the sea that was rolling in on the sand about ten feet away and he could feel a wind on his face before the man clicked his fingers and they were back in the cafe. Another click and the druid was a mirror image of Caratacus except Caratacus had never knowingly smiled like an idiot. Piogerix, as Caratacus, laughed and, in a mocking voice, said, 'My name is Caratacus and I'm a man child and I'm tired wah, my nappy needs changing.'

Caratacus rolled his eyes again. 'Hilarious,' he said sarcastically.

His doppelganger laughed with genuine humour, clapped his hands and all was back to normal.

'Fine,' Caratacus said. 'Can I do that? Have I got magic?'

'Magick,' the man opposite corrected. For once Caratacus was making an effort to get something right and for the life of him, he couldn't hear the difference between what he was saying and what the annoying man was.

'Yes,' he said, 'that.'

'We all have. Me, you, her,' he thumbed back to the girl behind the counter 'Everybody.'

'Then why can't I make us disappear back to the beach or... erm...fly?'

Piogerix shrugged. 'You possibly could. But I'll put forward two suggestions that may help you. Why are some people tall and others short? Have good or poor eyesight, have trouble losing weight or remembering things?' Before Caratacus had chance to answer he carried on. 'We are all born different, with different attributes and that's the same with Magick. Some people seem to have more Magick than others. But!'

The 'but' was louder and accentuated by Piogerix holding a finger in the air.

'It depends on what you do with it.' Answer me this? You have legs? Yes, a lot of people do. Why haven't you won the 100m at the Olympics? You've got a brain, like everybody else in the world? Why aren't you a physicist or biologist or a manager dealing with logistics?'

'I'm not very good at those things?' Caratacus answered weakly, unsure if an answer was needed.

'You may have been. What I am trying to say is there are numerous factors. Some may have small amounts of natural Magick, but they dedicate their lives to it and overcome their limitations. Others with a normal amount of Magick may have a natural talent with parts of it, like what I showed you a moment ago, one person could be very good at turning invisible but terrible at copying another. What sport are you good at?'

Caratacus thought furiously. They always said he could've gone quite far in football or rugby when he was eleven or twelve, not international but he was always considered to play for the county. That was all before he decided he didn't like training or playing in the rain or on a Saturday 'Pool,' he answered, 'I'm good at pool.'

Piogerix grimaced. 'I did say sports, but it doesn't matter. So, you are good at pool, does that mean you are great at all sports?' He didn't wait. 'Of course not, and it's the same with Magick. Some people have Magick coming out of the ears, they also have a natural talent for using it, but they don't use it, they don't care. I suppose to reach the top you have to have a mix of natural talent and dedication and maybe some love?'

'If we all have it then why do none of us use it? Caratacus asked.

'Oooh, a question? Wow, what an effort?'

'Fine, forget it.' Caratacus pushed his chair back for a third time.

'Sit, sit. My, you are sensitive. There is just less of it in This world. Ever since the two worlds separated, millennia ago, Magick seemed to start dying here.' He paused. 'Maybe that's not the right analogy. Magick here went into deep hibernation like plants when there is no sunshine. It's there but dormant.'

'What are the two worlds then?'

Piogerix slurped the last of his cappuccino, making as much noise as possible and got up. 'Too late, I'm off. See you later.'

He lifted his arm straight up and pointed his hand to the girl behind the counter. 'Bronwen! Diolch, money is in the till,' he said in Welsh and the till shot open. He put his arm down and opened the door to leave before turning around. 'Bron?' He clicked again and you could hear the noise of coins dropping into the tip jar. He winked and she laughed.

'See you later, Caratacus ap Neb,' he said and left.

CHAPTER TWENTY

FLASHPOINT

Once Piogerix had left him Caratacus headed back to his room and managed three hours of hangover sleep. He decided, as he showered, that there was to be no drinking tonight. His liver was demanding a night off and he was only too happy to oblige. Tonight, was planned. It was to start with meeting Piogerix, then travelling by toilet, being sick, telling a mythological man that they were headed off tomorrow, having some food and then spending the rest of the night watching telly.

So far, the plan was going well as he and Piogerix left the toilets of the 'Once and Future'. He'd spent five minutes heaving and swilling his mouth out with water while the druid king rubbed his back and said 'there, there' a lot. He was back to feeling human as they headed to talk to Galahad and Geraint at the bar. The pub was busy again and Caratacus tried not to stare at some of the non-humans he could see. At the far end of the room, he recognised the four plainsmen from the night before, still being loud, still drinking and still laughing.

Galahad smiled as they both approached. 'Ale?' he asked. Piogerix answered first 'No thanks Gal, I'm not staying. I travelled to make sure Caratacus arrived safely, but I am off. I have a mind to wander and a feeling I need to prepare for what's to come.'

Geraint looked concerned. 'You'll be back?'

Piogerix smiled. 'Of course, Geraint ap Erbin. I fear we'll be back together very soon and not for good reasons. I need to find out what is going on. There are too many factors that do not make sense.' His smile disappeared. 'Now is a time for caution. You are here and we know Tristan has been found. We have a list of lost friends, please don't let your names be added to it. Get Arthur away with Caratacus. Tommaltach knows what he is doing.'

Galahad leant over the bar and enveloped the slight druid in a huge hug while Geraint shook his hand, clapping his shoulder warmly. Piogerix turned to Caratacus and took his hand. 'Even with all my power, I haven't worked out why Tommaltach wants you here.'

Caratacus shrugged, unsure of what to say, while the druid continued 'I think this is going to be tough for you my friend but stay the course, there must be a reason why you are in the middle of all this.' And then, before Caratacus could answer (or in all likelihood, shrug again) Piogerix walked out of the pub and into the night.

'Ale?' This time, Geraint asked.

Caratacus was in no mood to chat. 'No thanks, I just want to sort out leaving.'

Galahad and Geraint looked at each other uncomfortably.

'Tommy McKracken messaged today, and it has to be tomorrow.' Caratacus whined.

Galahad looked ruefully at Caratacus and moved to serve a customer. 'Go up and give it a go. Cai is out doing whatever and I think Neil is in his room, so he's all yours.'

'I'll give you half an hour and then come up and see if I can help convince him,' Geraint added.

'Can't you just come up with me now?' Caratacus asked hopefully.

Geraint shook his head. 'Best not go in mob handed. He wouldn't like that. Go for it, you might get lucky.'

***

It wasn't anger but it was pretty close. It was as close to anger as Caratacus ever got but maybe it was more like frustration at having to do something he didn't want to do for maybe the fifth time in his life and the fourth time in two days.

It wasn't going very well.

'Tommy told me we had to go by tomorrow. Tomorrow!' Caratacus shouted the second tomorrow.

Arthur stood up. He was wearing a bright blue Hawaiian shirt with white swirls. It had fitted him a few years ago but was now riding up over his belly. He tugged it down self-consciously which made his temper worse. 'I don't know who the hell you are, and I don't know who the hell you think you are. Tommaltach is not the boss of me, and you definitely aren't. Nowhere near it. I'm not going anywhere. I'm in danger? Great! Bring it on!'

Then the wall behind him disappeared. It was the wall that had the three televisions on it. Well, it had been, but then it wasn't. It had been torn away like paper.

Arthur joined it soon after, as the floor he was on collapsed.

It had been ripped away by the club of a Giant. By 'Giant' I do not mean a really big bloke. It was an actual Giant. This one was called Cipgan Gawr. I know this seems like too much of an exciting time for an interruption but it's important you get some breathing space and some information. Giants are neither creatures of the Dark nor of the Light. What Giants have in common with each other is that they are big. Big, in size and in twattery. They are big twats. They are like those annoying people that think they are right about the next issue for discussion before they even know what it is. And just like those idiots, these single-minded creatures see the world in certainties. An example being if a Giant sees something that breathes, then that something is food. In this part of the world, they are called Gawr, that's the Welsh word for Giant but they were here thousands of years before that language was formed. The Gawr are just one tribe of giants that mostly lived on this island though there were others all the way down to the Pyrenees.

Interesting facts about Giants other than they are huge twats: they can move between worlds without the use of gateways of any type; and, if in proximity to Magick, they block it.

Magickers, spellcasters and people who do card tricks at weddings hate them. Evolution (it's a thing) has provided them with this tiny advantage in the 'hunted' stakes.

Now Cipgan Gawr – who, a few moments ago, had ripped the wall away and was now peering into the remains of a living room – was a one-eyed Giant. That doesn't mean he is one of the breed of actual one-eyed giants you may have heard about in Greek mythology, those are Cyclops, and they are doing fine thank you very much. No, Cipgan Gawr was an idiot, even in comparison with others of his own kind. He lost his eye while leaning down to grab some fast food in the form of a running goat and eye-butted the remains of an ancient oak tree. That was in 1832 when Victoria came to the British throne. Do you know that massive tree was stuck in Cipgan Gawr's eye for twenty-seven years? He didn't even think to take it out until the same Queen had become a Grandmother for the first time.

I best get back to the story. It's probably why you are here.

Caratacus hadn't been dragged down with Arthur. He stared in shock at how quickly chaos had descended, then common sense took over to remind him he was on very shaky ground which could, at any moment, collapse and take him with it. He tentatively climbed down the side of the wall just in time to see Arthur face the giant.

Cipgan sniffed.

'MEAN HORRIBLE ARTHUR HERE!' he shouted, his voice booming into the night. He had met Arthur before, and by 'met', I mean that Arthur had caught him raiding farms in the lands of the Dobunni, two and a half thousand years ago, and in what could be called an altercation, had cut Cipgan Gawr's little finger off. Another Giant fact I missed from earlier? They identify people and things as much through their noses as they do their eyes...or in this case, eye. They never forget a smell.

Arthur dusted himself down, and as soon as he saw the Giant his muscle memory shook him to action. He shouted a word of power, shooting his arm out to call Excalibur. When nothing happened, he remembered the Gawr.

'Motherf...,' he shouted in frustration.

Cipgan Gawr's face changed, now looking even angrier.

'CIPGAN GAWR NOT TOUCH HIS MOTHER!'

Cipgan Gawr thrusted his face towards Arthur and roared. Recoiling from the power and the fetid hum of the Giant's breath Arthur lost his balance and fell on his backside.

'CIPGAN EAT FAT ARTHUR.' Cipgan said with a laugh that vibrated through the night.

'Fat?' Arthur shouted, 'Who are you calling fat?'

'CIPGAN CALL YOU FAT. FAT ARTHUR. ARTHUR SMELL OF BEING SAD.'

With the grace and poise of a professional ballerina (if the professional ballerina had let herself go for a decade and didn't do any exercise, had bad ankles and ate Jaffa cakes every day. Yeah, with the grace and poise of that sort of ballerina) Arthur struggled off the ground on his hands and knees and stood up.

'I am not fat,' he said defiantly.

'TIME TO GO DEAD FAT ARTHUR.' Cipgan pulled his face away and held up his club which was the size of a medium sized horse.

You, my dear reader must have a very dim view of our hero Arthur, so far, and for that I am truly sorry. I have brought him into your life at a time when his is full of depression and sorrow and longing and anxiety. That isn't Arthur, it is just Arthur now. Depression doesn't really care about what you are or what you have done. Arthur had never met an opponent like depression, and he didn't have the weapons to fight it. Depression told Arthur to lie down and take the club full on. Wouldn't it be great, he thought, not to have to wake up tomorrow? He had wanted it to end but he didn't want to do it himself. He wanted it to just happen and then he wouldn't have to feel like he did anymore.

Back in the pub, it was quickly clear that this wasn't a random Giant attack, something that can and does happen. The wall downstairs had also been taken down and there was fighting everywhere, Galahad knew an orc squad when he saw one.

He could see the Gawr outside and knew there was no point trying to call his sword. He reached underneath the bar, pulled out an 'encouraging good behaviour amongst customers' club and yanked a decorative shield from the wall. Then he went out to meet the pub's attackers.

Most of the patrons of the pub were hiding behind overturned tables. Orcs in a situation like this are like foxes let loose in hen houses. They are there for a reason – to eat a chicken – but that doesn't stop them killing every single thing in the place. The orcs had rushed in, fast, clinical and brutal and by the time anyone could react many were dead.

Geraint, who had been talking to a local, was up and at them in an instant. He wore his sword whenever he could, and now he pushed it through the throat of one of the orcs that had been amongst the slaughter at the first table. He was joined by unexpected allies. Well, unexpected to the orcs. The laughing plainsmen were bloody delighted at what was happening. They loved damage and they loved punching orcs.

Despite help, the numbers fighting the orcs dwindled until an exhausted few survived, their backs to one of the pub walls that was still standing.

'We need to do something,' shouted Galahad.

'I am open to suggestions,' Geraint replied.

***

Caratacus lowered himself from the second floor of the wrecked building in time to see the Giant's club rise and Arthur fold his arms in defiance. Caratacus felt helpless as if his feet were stuck to the floor. Arthur was going to die. He then saw a blurred shape speed out from the periphery of his vision, somersault into a ball shape and hit Cipgan square in the eye. The shocked Gawr, roaring in agony, dropped his club and covered the point of his pain. He stumbled back once, then twice, and then fell, the back of his head cracking on a boulder. The big stone had been minding its own business since it had been deposited there and covered with ice about 21,000 years ago. Then a mere 11,500 years ago as the ice retreated north it was released from the glacier and re-introduced to the world. It was here millennia before the pub was Magickally placed here and the locals called it Carn Arthur, Arthur's rock and it was. It had saved his life.

Cipgan Gawr died then.

Don't feel bad, he was nasty.

The ball shape stood up and Caratacus recognised Neil. The young knight recovered into a fighting stance from the tumble of the attack, sword recalled now the Gawr was dead, and ready to go. 'LORD?' he shouted and then looked at Caratacus. 'Take him and run.'

'Where?' asked Caratacus in a desperate shout as he could see the fight that was taking place in the bar of the pub. He wasn't looking at a gawky teenager anymore, he was looking at a young warrior. Two orcs ran out. Neil didn't charge; he danced towards them and their deaths were quick. He went back into a fighting stance and looked over to Caratacus who was now by Arthur. 'Go or we all die!'

The intensity of Neil's order – even his voice had changed – shocked Caratacus and he grabbed Arthur's arm. For a second, Arthur didn't move. He looked at the body of Cipgan and then at Neil as the young warrior shouted at them, once more, to go.

'Come on,' shouted Caratacus, which woke Arthur from his stupor. He turned, looking lost. 'What do we do now?'

Caratacus was already moving. 'Run,' he shouted. And so they did, into the darkness.

***

Same darkness, different place. Galahad was face down in the grass outside the pub. He lifted his head.

He saw that 'The Once and Future's wall had been removed revealing a look into a life sized doll's house; his empty room upstairs, and downstairs in the pub, his friends and others fighting for their lives. Yet again he struggled onto his knees and then to his feet. While the last of the orcs had been defeated, he'd come out to help Neil. He'd taken a blade through his body but had finished them before he fell. He whispered the words and with the Gawr dead, his sword appeared in his right hand.

He stepped over what remained of the wall of the pub that he, himself had built. Their home was in pieces and the bodies of customers, people who had become friends, and orcs, lay strewn on the floor.

The plainsmen were not laughing, one of the two on the floor was dead, the other unconscious. The two remaining cradled one each and they wept as they laughed, unabashed and with feeling. The wailing seemed to accentuate the carnage before them.

Another noise made him turn. It was the noise of gathering battle and it was coming from the pub car park. Out of the dark, another squad of orcs appeared from the wilds of the Preseli mountains and into the light of fire from a few remaining gaslights. They stood, not moving, just waiting and watching. The only noise, other than the groans of the dying and the wails of the Plainsmen, was the heavy breathing of the living. Galahad didn't know where Arthur was, but deep in his heart, he had to hope he was alive, and he had to stop these orcs so his friend could get to safety. Without him there would be nothing.

His hands were on his knees, and he was sucking in deep breathes in preparation for a last stand but then he saw Geraint lying near him, a knife stuck in his chest, his dead eyes staring at the night sky.

Neil ran over to help up Galahad who waved him away as he struggled to stand.

'Neil?' he said.
'Yes, Galahad?'
'The end?'
'Yes, Galahad.'

The Once and Future could not fall into the wrong hands and so 'The end' had been placed in the cellar. The end was just that, an orb of such power that, when ignited through Magick, would destroy the pub. He knew that he needed to destroy every orc here or they'd chase after Arthur.

The orcs ran at them. Neil knew that death was coming from below, but instinct made him run to meet this attack. Galahad started the final chant, the little Magick he had stirring in his stomach, just as he said the final syllable of the last words, he heard from the darkness, the voice of Piogerix shout 'NO!' and then the orb blew, vacuum black sucked air out of the world before firing a funnel of light hundreds of feet into the sky and everything below was reduced to atoms. Arthur had been given time but at what cost?

CHAPTER TWENTY-ONE

CULHWCH AC OLWEN

He was Culhwch ap Cilydd ap Celyddon. He still is. The titles they used when challenging him were: Culhwch, wound giver to the Gawr Ysbaddaden. Cousin to Arthur. Champion of the forty impossible tasks that included the catching of the legendary wild boar Twrch Trwyth. Culhwch, England's bane in the wars of Glyndwr. 'Heaven's sender' he was called by the French when he sailed for Nelson. And still, after millennia, he called himself only one name: Culhwch, husband of Olwen.

Like the others, he'd lived so many lives and right now it was looking to be the end of his last one. The most headstrong of Arthur's warriors, it was very rare that Culhwch walked back to the cave of the long deep sleep. For he was sent; blade, arrow or bullet, he was sent there cheering or screaming. None of the calmness of Geraint, the vision of Arthur, the guile of Tristan. Not for him going gently.

'Don't include us Cul, we don't die all the time…' the voice of Bedwyr, trying to get a rise, which he always would.

Husband of Olwen.

There was never another. No one would or could ever match up to Olwen. He never gave them the chance. Even Tristan had moved on eventually, but not him.

He smiled.

Blood bubbled from his mouth.

It was the smile, not the blood, that stopped the blade removing his head.

'Why are you smiling, you old fool?' asked Cassie Newton, breathing heavily.

'Pass me my sword... I am too weak to call him. This is death and I want to see the Hall of Heroes.'

She looked around and saw the sword where she had disarmed him a minute before. She picked it up and placed it in his hand.

'Why are you smiling?' She asked despite not knowing why she did.

He coughed, more blood dribbling from his mouth. 'I am thinking of better things, of true love, of holding hands, of laughing, of love making so intense you would think you were one body, of a smile that made you think that you were the centre of the world. Memories I have put from my mind since I was the age I look now not the age I am.'

'All bollocks,' she said. 'Live, win or die. Time to say goodbye.'

He tried to prop himself up on his elbows and failed, slumping down onto his back. He stared at the sky and laughed again. 'Sod off, young one. I know who you are. You're the one who is talking bollocks.' He coughed again 'I know who you are…'

Cassie's face changed from impassive to momentarily confused. She changed from fighting stance to standing over Culhwch still holding her sword to his throat. 'You know nothing,' she said with a confidence she was beginning not to feel.

'Your name. You named yourself at the beginning of the fight. Cassie? You're...the Outcast.' Culhwch was starting to fade.

After trying to end his life with every part of her being, she now needed him to live a little longer. It had not taken her long to find him. The information given to her was that he was working as a farmhand in the middle of Pembrokeshire. Culhwch of Arthur working on a bloody farm. Her time as a Mistress had not disappeared completely and the thought of a warrior of renown, even of the Light, tending livestock filled her with contempt. Once in the vicinity, spell casting had put her one or two farms away and then it was just a matter of waiting.

'I know who and what I am. What's it to you?'

Culhwch laughed and when the pain of doing so hit, he laughed even more. 'Shhh,' he mumbled as if drunk. 'Don't be angry with me, it's not my fault you know what I'm talking about.'

Cough, blood, pain, groan.

He continued ,'I never realised you still lived. I thought they'd killed you.'

With no fighting, no wars, no glory, no one would have foreseen how happy Culhwch was working on a farm. He was born into the ruling caste so long ago. Farmers had been invisible to him. He knew they were important; it was Arthur who always reminded him that they fought so other people could grow things like food and family. If you fought just for yourself, you were on the wrong side. When they left Arthur, told they were to live their last lives, everybody thought Culhwch would find a fight, maybe get some work from Tommaltach, accompany Adda on an adventure or go and fight other people's wars with Gwalchmai and Owain.

When everyone said goodbye that morning, when some went to live their last life, Culhwch picked up his pack that contained all he had and walked. He decided to put his journey into the hands of the gods and goddesses of the countryside, the rulers of streams, of hedges and junctions of roads. He'd always been respectful of the small gods, the *Bachod* as they were called, and as he walked, they talked with him and sent him the way they saw fit.

By the evening he'd found a small pub in a small village and the *Bachod* advised him to drink this night which he was happy to do. He found easy companionship that evening, easy talk and easy laughter and all speaking in the Welsh that he thought in. A phone call from one of his new friends led Idris and Enid Harries from Hendre Dyffryn, to pop in the pub and offer Culhwch a job and a caravan to live in to boot. The *Bachod* don't mess about when they gift-give. From that point on, the Harries family was his family and his life never went outside the borders of Hendre Dyffryn and the pub in the village up the road. They had two daughters, Poppy and Ellie, both teenagers, both beautiful, one wilful, one caring, both wonderful, who mothered him as much as their mother did them. He was surprised to feel how much Magick flowed through them all, untapped and hidden. Every day he was amazed that he enjoyed farming. Getting up early and having to do things all the time, he loved it.

This morning he was up even earlier than usual as he wanted to get to Cae Isaf and check the fences. He'd walked rather than taking the 4x4 and when he arrived, he saw a slip of a girl waiting for him with a sword and knew that it could be the end.

It was.

Blood bubbled again and he lifted his hand and pointed weakly at her while still smiling. 'You know exactly what I'm talking about,' he repeated. 'Smiles, touches, passion, happiness. That's why they cast you out. You'd felt it and you'd been tainted by it.'

'Shut up...' she said but he just talked over her. 'I knew him... Bit awkward. Keen... he reminded me of a foal, weak legs, trying to find his feet but full of energy. I really liked him, Cassie.'

The blade dug in as she pushed down 'SHUT YOUR FILTHY MOUTH!' She screamed; her face contorted in anger.

'SHUT YOUR MOUTH,' she screamed again, this time closer to and into Cwlhwch's face before the anger leached out of her. She was no longer talking to Culhwch anymore, just the body that once held him.

Cassie Newton was on her knees over the lifeless body of her foe.

'He broke my heart,' she whimpered. Then she leant her head on the chest of the dead warrior and for the second time in her life, cried until she had no more tears to do so. Her voice hoarse, her eyes half closed, and her heart sick with pain, she looked up in time to see a bright light at the edge of the field. The spirit of Culhwch was walking away, surrounded by other points of light. What she saw was the moving on of Culhwch ap Cilydd accompanied by his friends, the Bachod of the nearby streams, hedges and road junctions, the ones he'd prayed to and left things for, the ones that loved him. They took him as far as they were allowed and then waved him on to happiness.

   To Olwen.

CHAPTER TWENTY-TWO
THE JOURNEY TO THE TROLL BRIDGE

They ran through the night – if you could call it running – not knowing if they were heading from danger or towards more of it. For Caratacus it was stumbling terror in the dark, worrying that he was about to be attacked and killed at any moment. It was also continual fear that his sneakers were being ruined. For the first ten minutes, Arthur ran alongside him. That was until they heard and felt the blast from the Once and Future. It stopped them both and they stared mutely as the bright orange light died slowly and was replaced by darkness. It robbed Arthur of energy, of life, as if what little hope he had, had been purged from his body. They started running again but it was Caratacus who was doing the leading, sometimes having to drag Arthur along. Arthur did not respond to a single question and Caratacus felt desperately alone. His sneakers were sopping wet and covered in mud as they traversed the moors and fields of the Preselis, as were his hands, elbows and knees, the first points of contact during the many falls. They'd moved for hours, taking small breaks where they slumped. The last one had lasted a little longer because, both exhausted they had fallen asleep; Arthur hunched, chin on chest, Caratacus's head on the King's shoulder.

One of them must have moved as they slept, causing them both to jump awake in shock, looking at each other like strangers for a moment.

'I can't believe we fell asleep,' Caratacus said as he stood up and began stretching the hard night out of his body. Arthur just sat there, staring into nothing. Caratacus' morning thought process, glacial in speed at best, started to slowly awaken. He wondered if he should phone Tommy for help. He pulled his phone out of his pocket for no reason other than the need to do something normal. No signal – shock. He put it back in his pocket and looked around, the sun was up but there was still a morning chill in the air.

Arthur still wasn't moving.

Despite everything, Caratacus looked at the view. It was awe inspiring. He could see the towns of Cwm Llechau and Newport with a beautiful light blue sea behind them. He turned to look at where they'd slept. What they'd had their back to was impressive. Caratacus would have described it as a load of huge stones with a massive flat boulder laid on top of it. I'm telling you it's a Neolithic burial chamber. He nodded in a weird acknowledgement of being impressed.

He wondered what was he was going to do. Tommy wanted Arthur safe and with the Lady in the Lake, while the women and the crow wanted Arthur at the bridge to Cantre'r Gwaelod. How to get there? He knew he couldn't travel by magic, not for himself, he still didn't know how to do it. But maybe Arthur could? Caratacus didn't really know what Arthur could do other than drink, eat and play games. Was he magic? He must be something or he'd been seriously overrepresented in some of the stories and must have had some hell of a PR team.

Arthur grunted as he struggled to his feet. He looked how Caratacus felt, his face wan and his eyes puffy through exhaustion. 'You ok?' Caratacus asked.

Arthur didn't answer, he just looked around the giant stone edifice. Then he looked at the younger man. 'Come on then,' he said simply before walking in between two stones.

Caratacus paused, sighed, and followed.

Two hours later they were walking along the grassy verge of a main road. This early in the morning it wasn't busy, only a lorry and two cars had sped past them so far. Arthur was walking purposefully ahead of a complaining Caratacus who was struggling to keep his feet.

'It didn't send us very far,' he whined, 'Why just here if the stone gateway thing was magic?'

'Magick,' Arthur corrected, still walking.

'That's what I said. Magic.' Caratacus replied seeing Arthur shaking his head.

'It's Magick,' said Arthur.

'I said that.'

'No, you said magic and it's Magick.'

Caratacus stopped exasperated 'Magic!' he shouted 'Magic, magic, magic. There! Ok?'

Arthur carried on walking, and it wasn't too long before Caratacus realised that the conversation was over, he wasn't going to win and so, shuffled down the road to catch Arthur up.

A few more cars had passed them, and all had tooted, wanting to acknowledge a portly, bearded, middle-aged man, dressed in a bright blue Hawaiian shirt and basketball shorts who was walking up the side of the A487 in deck shoes at around seven in the morning.

Caratacus was as close as he was going to get to Arthur. 'So, is there another magical portal cave near here?' he asked.

'Getting a bus,' Arthur replied matter of factly.

'A magical bus?'

'Yes, it's taking us to a magical school for mythological warriors,' Arthur replied and even though he was exhausted Caratacus recognised dripping sarcasm.

He sullenly mumbled to himself, 'Yeah because that would be the weirdest thing that's happened to me,' showing that he was no stranger to the world of sarcasm himself.

Arthur stopped suddenly, Caratacus just managing not to walk into him. They were by a post which Caratacus took to be a bus stop here in the wilds of Wales. They stood in silence for a five-minute period that felt like a day longer than eternity. Lorries and cars continued to toot as they passed, Arthur raising his hand in response whenever they did.

Caratacus couldn't decide what he hated more, talking to the miserable old sod or the uncomfortable silence. His mouth made the decision for him. 'Is this bus is going to take us to this Cantre place?' he asked.

'Cantre'r Gwaelod,' Arthur said lifelessly as he stared down the road in the direction the bus would eventually come from.

'Whatever it's called,' said Caratacus.

Arthur gave a grunt which might have been a yes and that was enough for Caratacus. He snapped. 'Jesus! I don't want to be here either, so give me a break yeah? I asked for none of this. I'm knackered, I'm cold, I stink, my new sneakers are ruined, and I left my charger in the pub.'

Arthur turned. There was no shout or snap, just him with his hands on his hips as he emanated sarcasm from every pore of his body.

'Oh, I am so sorry mate. Battery a little low on your posh phone? Up a bit earlier than usual, love? I don't know if you noticed on planet what-ever-your-name-is but last night my home was torn down and people I love were killed! And now I am stuck with you, correct me if I am wrong, a bookshop owner? Who doesn't know the difference between Magick and bloody magic and who is going to guide me to safety at a place he's never heard of? All of this while being chased by orc death squads. Yeah princess, I feel your pain. I'll stop messing about and get planning. How about King Arthur and the quest for the little twat's phone charger?'

Caratacus turned towards the hedgerow away from Arthur, folding his arms. 'Fine I'll shut up.'

'Fine with me.'

'Fine.'

The bus pulled up ten minutes later. Bickering began again in earnest firstly about who was to pay, and then between the bus driver and Caratacus about the bus not taking cards, the latter railing at the former about how on earth a bus in the 21st century only took cash. The driver, Mike, didn't respond once. What Caratacus didn't know was that Mike had two teenage daughters at home and therefore this wasn't a rant in his mind, it was a Tuesday, or a Wednesday or a Sunday or one of the days in between.

Caratacus waited for a response but as the doors of the bus hissed closed and it began to move, he understood it wasn't to come so he placed his money down and sloped off to the back where Arthur was.

Arthur was sitting with his legs akimbo in the middle of the back-seat row forcing Caratacus to squeeze into the window seat. After about five minutes, and despite fatigue and the chafing of his damp clothes, he couldn't help but stare at the beautiful countryside the bus journey was showing them at forty-five miles an hour. He'd never seen so many greens and that wasn't just in the patchwork of the fields but the sea that stretched as far as the sky. What this scene didn't need was the pig snort snoring of Arthur who had fallen asleep as soon as Caratacus had sat down. Caratacus was jealous because try as he might, he couldn't fall asleep himself; he just leaned his head on the window, yawned continuously and worried about what was to come.

'Wahey!' Arthur shouted himself awake, making Caratacus jump and the three other people on the bus turn around. The big man ignored them, yawned and turned to Caratacus.

'Where are we?' he asked.

Caratacus shrugged. 'It's just fields and hills.'

Arthur looked out the window and nodded. 'Ah we've got a bit of time yet.' The tone of his voice signified that the argument earlier was forgotten.

'Tell me what Tommaltach said again?' he asked. Caratacus had not forgotten the argument and was still in a deep sulk, but the question had momentarily caught him off guard. It was also the first time that Arthur had spoken to him like a human being. He paused as he remembered the lies he'd decided to tell, but he started with the truth.

'He sent me down to take you to the Lady of the lake.' Caratacus winced internally as he said the bonkers sentence out loud. 'Then he texted me the night before last to say that we needed to stop off in Cantre'r Gwaelod first. He didn't give a reason,' before quickly adding 'I am so annoyed I deleted it,' in a way that would make the hammiest of actors cringe. Arthur went quiet and, out of the corner of his eye, Caratacus could see the old king deep in thought. He wanted to move Arthur quickly away from asking any more questions so asked one of his own. 'What is Cantre'r Gwaelod?'

Arthur folded his arms and they rested on his belly. 'So you know by now there are two different worlds, This one and That.' Caratacus wanted to put up his hand and ask questions on that one small sentence but while Arthur was explaining he wasn't asking difficult questions. Arthur continued. 'There are plenty of little places where you can sometimes cross over, standing stones, caves, forests and in certain built-up places where Magick and stories build up,' he looked up at Caratacus. 'None of these are official places where travel between the worlds can happen but one that is, is the bridge to Cantre'r Gwaelod.'

'Why don't you live over there?' asked Caratacus.

Arthur went quiet again, really thinking of the answer. 'I've spent time over there but it's a nice place to visit, if you know what I mean? I haven't been there for over a century. The last two times we returned were the wars and those were here and for a short amount of time.'

'You fought in both wars?' Caratacus looked at this bearded fat grumpy man sitting not a foot from him and couldn't imagine him in a soldier's uniform. He shook his head, trying to shed the doubt that was there. The first world war was black and white and grainy like the few films of the conflict that survived while the second was the colour of movies like 'Battle of the Bulge' or 'A Bridge too Far'. Neither seemed real and even less likely was this man being part of it.

'Where did you fight in the Second World War?' he knew little of the first one so there would have been no point of reference to nod at. Because of the films, he knew more about the other one.

'We were back for about six months and most of that was training. Never had seen a plane properly so jumping out of the bloody things took a bit of getting used to. Once we were ready, we took ship to North Africa, were dropped off in Italy and then we were dead about a week later.' He laughed.

Caratacus looked out the window, somehow uncomfortable with the blasé way the man was talking of his own death.

'We're here,' Arthur said, getting up and making his way off the bus.

CHAPTER TWENTY-THREE
SHOPPING FOR SOUVENIRS...

Caratacus was surprised to have to push through a throng of blue skins, elves and dwarfs who were waiting to get on the bus he was getting off. Arthur seemed to know where he was going and so he followed him on a well-worn path through a copse of large trees. He hadn't known what to expect on the other side, but it wasn't this.

Before them was a large stone building which had the look of a three level warehouse. From the centre of what looked like the middle floor, a stone bridge rose about a hundred feet in an arch, the other side seemingly disappearing into the sea.

'Cantre'r Gwaelod?' asked Caratacus.

'Nope, Cantre'r Gwaelod Bridge visitor centre and troll toll office,' replied Arthur walking towards it.

To Caratacus' surprise the doors slid open; surprised because the entire building had that oldy world Harry Potter feel about it... except for the doors and tourist shop which was in a modern annexe to the right of the entrance. The left-hand side was a visitor centre with glossy brochures on shelves while the main part of the building was what an airport departure lounge would have looked like in the 13th century. At the back of the building were queues of beings waiting to see green trolls behind large wooden desks. Let's go over there in a minute.

There are two main types of trolls in the Worlds. Wild trolls are like little green giants, they live in any wilderness they can get to and then spend a lot of time going around like demented toddlers putting everything they come across in their mouths.

The others are the ones we see before us. Same size, about eight or nine feet tall, fat, boulder-shaped hands, same green skin, same jaundiced tusks protruding up from the side of their lower jaws. These Trolls love a bridge. I don't know why, and I suppose neither does any troll because there aren't many troll philosophers thinking great thoughts on the big questions about being a troll. While the wild trolls love space and freedom, these trolls are bridge-lovers. They are called Oomoom-Ufs. I don't suppose you are an expert in the languages of the trolls, but it's pretty simple.

'Ooo' means gold, as in 'Oooh, some gold', 'Mmm' means loving something as in 'Mmmmm, I want that', Oom means anything smaller than them who are not Trolls as in 'look Oomans - let's eat them,' and Uf-Uf means sex as in...well you get it. The wild trolls derogatorily used to call them 'Gold loving people shaggers' and in a very subtle act of empowerment these gold loving people shaggers started to use the name for themselves and eventually became Oom Oom-Ufs. They were just wild trolls that became as civilised as a troll possibly could. They loved their bridges and instead of eating anything that came over their bridge they occasionally robbed them then ate them.

Progress is inevitable unless you lived during the second decade of the twenty first century and the Oomoom-ufs decided that they would charge things to cross their bridge and take payment in meat and/or gold. Which leads us to a lot of people waiting to get tickets to cross the bridge.

'So, where to next?' asked Arthur. Caratacus looked embarrassed 'I'm sorry, I really don't know. I was told to get to the bridge but nothing after that.'

The chat on the bus had changed things a little between them, they weren't friends but there was some sort of truce between what were, basically, two children in middle-aged men's bodies.

Arthur scratched his beard in thought. 'I'm going to have a look around and see if Tommaltach's contact is about. They must be expecting us,' Caratacus felt uncomfortable knowing they were here because of the two women and the crow and not Tommaltach as Arthur continued, 'There's a part of this place that also sells supplies we could do with for next part of the journey, but I've got no money. You got any left?'

Caratacus shrugged, 'Can't you just pay by magic? Spell them or something?' he asked.

It was Arthur's turn to shake his head, 'One, it doesn't work like that and two, Trolls will absolutely not have Magick anywhere near them. It's banned here... except for up there…' Arthur pointed up to the open second floor where they saw three people pedalling furiously on exercise bikes. They weren't 'people' though, they were wizards and Caratacus could tell they were wizards because they were dressed as if an 8-year-old had been asked to draw a wizard. They were men with long grey beards and had on flowing, silver robes with large cones like hats on their heads. Cones and robes decorated with gold stars and crescent moons.

'Shift wizards,' Arthur continued. 'It's a strong spell that's needed to block Magick from a building. What happens occasionally is that places with money could keep a Gawr like the one you met at the pub but either the smell is awful, or they get bored and then get destructive. There is no way one Magicker could keep a blocking spell going for too long and even with three it's tough. So, three do it for however many hour shifts.'

Caratacus saw that two of the three were wearing fake beards. 'Why are they dressed like that? Isn't one of them a woman? Is that really what wizards dress like?'

'Nobody dresses like that,' Arthur answered. 'It's for the tourists that come through, they love it.'

'Why are they doing this then? Wizards can just do a spell and make money or rob banks invisibly. They must be minted,' said Caratacus.

Arthur shook his head. 'It's not as easy as that. Those poor sods are, as likely as not, in debt, gambling probably, usually is. A lot of Magickers get bored and need a release. That usually ends up with Magick exhaustion and breakdown ,or drugs and breakdown, alcohol and breakdown, or gambling, then destitution and breakdown. There are a lot of them in situations like this, 'working for the troll' as they say.' Arthur walked off towards a wooden booth near the back with a small queue in front, and a sign 'Bureau to Change' above a troll who looked more likely to put salt on you and eat you than facilitate a transaction.

'Bye then…' Caratacus said sarcastically to himself.

He headed over to the gift shop, fascinated at what could be there. The layout and the bright decor could've been lifted from gift shops at the Empire State Building, the Roman Baths in Caerleon or Tower Bridge in London and any tourist attraction in your world. It had the same stuff as well, key rings, guides, fridge magnets, stationary, T shirts and all the wonderful knick-knacks you panic buy near the end of a visit because you haven't got anything for the kids, your partner or your parents. What says 'I couldn't be arsed' more than a keyring? A step up would be a keyring with what your name means on.

Matthew meaning Gift of God. You are adventurous but don't suffer fools, you are inquisitive blah blah blah.

Of course, some of these keyrings were for Trolls with troll names.

JHAT BCOS YOR CALD JHAT.

DRET BCOS YOR CALD DRET.

Caratacus sauntered around the shop flicking through the travel guides. Amongst the Aberystwyths and Londons he smiled at the others; Cantre'r Gwaelod, the firepits of Jaylahezi, the resort islands of the Mer and the Orclands of the north. He flicked through the latter, surprised to see the front page telling the reader not to ever go there. He put it down and another shelf caught his eye. A little sign told him it was King Arthur memorabilia. He walked over and smiled as he looked at the heroic pictures of his travel partner. All a little younger, all a lot thinner and taller. He picked up a figure that must have been Arthur. It was a knight, all armour except for the bearded face of an Arthur that was not his. He looked more like the white Jesuses of home and then he realised he was only in bloody Wales. Twickenham seemed as far away as a comfy bed or sanity at that moment, but instead of feeling his usual anger or despondency, he felt a little energised, maybe even a bit excited...

Tommy McKracken had asked him to do something and he was doing it, and pretty well if he was being honest. He still didn't want all this; he wanted to go home and get back to his life, but he did want to see Arthur safe. Maybe after the lake he could take him back home. His mother could hide him and look after him, take over from Caratacus. Mam would love that, a Welsh speaker to take care of. He didn't know if he could tell her all about the King Arthur bit. She didn't have that much of an imagination. Yeah, he could put Arthur in his mother's spare room.

'Psst...' and with that psst his tiny bit of positivity flapped its wings and flew away. He could almost see it leaving through the sliding doors. He looked down to see a crow.

'Limp dick,' she cawed.

Sorry. THE Crow.

'Black chicken,' answered Caratacus matter of factly.

'Where is Arthur?' asked Badb.

'Bureau de change. What do you want?' Caratacus asked while looking around the shop to make sure no one was watching. Somebody was. The crow's sisters were behind the counter. They both blew him a kiss which he ignored as the repulsion of the older woman countered the beguiling hotness of the other.

As he walked over, the crow flew over and perched on the shoulder of Dannan. Ceridwen, the crone smiled, 'Ah, Caratacus ap Neb, how goes the quest?'

Caratacus rolled his eyes, 'It's not a quest. You asked me to do something, and I have. So I'm sure it's time for me to go home now.' All three laughed at him, the crow jumping up and down as if insane. Caratacus exhaled. 'Fine, what next? Fight a dragon, rescue a princess on the top floor of a castle or find true love's kiss?'

'You have brought him here because he needs to find someone who believes in him but also something else needs to be done.' The beauty said matter of factly adding a wink right at the end. His groin tightened.

'Why can't you tell him all this?' asked Caratacus.

'Because we've told you, you arse biscuit,' said Badb.

Caratacus wanted to strangle the bird more than he wanted to have sex with the beauty and he had never felt a power as strong as wanting to have sex with the beauty in his life. He didn't reply, his jaw went rigid and he looked at the other two.

Then he sighed. 'Ok! What?'

Ceridwen spoke. 'This is important, Caratacus ap Neb. You are reaching a junction. The Dark has risen further. Armies assemble in This world and That. Ensure you complete Tommaltach's demand, but you must ensure the safety of the chosen one. As long as they live then Cromh Du will continue to weaken. They are the only one who can send him back to exile. Keep Arthur safe.'

'Can't I just tell him everything?' Caratacus interrupted.

Ceridwen shushed him aggressively before carrying on. 'You have a tough path ahead. You have done well, unambitious one,'

Caratacus rolled his eyes.

'But you need to stay the course. These are things I task you with, once you survive here...'

'IF!' the crow bounced laughing again, 'IF!'

The crone ignored her, 'Get the once and future king to the Lake and a gift returned will be given. Stay with Arthur. You need to be at the end for the end.'

'Can't you just tell me like an adult? Like a list with instructions? Why is everything so cryptic with you three all the time? Also, why me? Why are you picking on me?'

'Because we like you, kitten,' said Dannan. Caratacus deliberately did not make eye contact but still felt his stomach flip when she spoke.

'Well, it doesn't feel like it.' Caratacus started to feel sorry for himself. 'I haven't got a sword... not that I want a bloody sword. Everybody has magic in them except me and whenever I'm near it, I end up being sick on the floor!'

All three sisters said 'Poor Caratacus,' at the same time. One angrily, one sarcastically and one sympathetically. I will leave it up to you to decide which one was which.

The crone was first to speak then. 'Why should anything be easy for a no one like you? Have you bothered to ask anybody about your particular set of skills? No! Just moaning, whining or running from one disaster to another! Why ask for a sword and in the same breath say you don't want one? Why on earth do you want to use the gift of Magick? What reason when all you want to do is to go home and suckle on your Mam's teat!'

The maiden leaned over and touched his face 'You can do this honey bunny, maybe you can learn something about yourself while you are here.' It was a suggestion more than a question.

'Learn what!? I don't know what any of you are talking about! Please give me a straight answer! I just want my old life back! Tell me how to get home!'

Ceridwen shuffled forward, Badb now on her shoulder until her face was an inch from his. She smelt of soil and decay. She paused as if she was about to say something vital and he leaned in because of that importance. She spoke, 'My advice to you now is… go and get a cup of tea…'

Caratacus was about to swear again, then reared back in shock as the crow flapped its wings, aggressively cawing in his face. He tried to stay upright, stumbling over one of the displays before falling into the shelves that held the Arthur toys. He jumped up embarrassed as people watched him, then looked back to where the Morrigu had been. But they were gone, replaced by two shop assistants who stared at him in annoyance knowing it would be them and not this idiot who would be clearing up that mess.

'Are you taking the piss?' Arthur asked, making Caratacus cry out in surprise as he didn't know the man was there.

'What?' he replied.

'What do you think?' this from Arthur.

'What?' asked Caratacus, really confused.

Arthur pointed at Caratacus' hand and to the latter's embarrassment realised that he still had the Arthur figure in his hands.

'I didn't realise I had it,' he said embarrassed, 'honestly...I'm sorry.'

Caratacus had been holding it up and Arthur gently took it from him and looked at it. He smiled to himself. 'I don't look like this now eh?'

It was a question but Caratacus knew it wasn't to anybody but for Arthur himself. 'I actually fought with all this rubbish on, you know?'

He knew this question was for him. 'This is the Middle Ages yeah? You've never mentioned this time before.'

'We weren't alive for long,' Arthur started talking, slowly walking out of the visitor's centre, Caratacus following. 'It went a lot like the second world war story I told you about. It was during the Hundred years war. Some bastards of the Dark were going around villages in Normandy slaughtering people and sacrificing the children left alive to Cromh Du. We woke up, Merlin told us what he thought we needed to do so we joined the retinue of Matthew Gough and within a short while we were involved in the war. It took us a few months, but we found them, we lost no one that time, the portal opened almost straight afterwards.'

'Wouldn't you prefer something quick like that?' Caratacus asked.

Arthur stopped, as if weighing up what he wanted to say. 'Sometimes, but going back to the cave isn't something to look forward to. It's not like sleep, it feels like death. Get stabbed in the throat, then it's blackness, it's nothing, and then you open your eyes on a block of stone in the cave. I don't know how it works but sometimes the quest ends but the portal doesn't come, so you live the rest of your life and while that can be lovely, it's hard too. But having to go into the cave off your own back, lie yourself down on that same block... it's horrible. So, when you come back sometimes you just want to live – not be alive, anybody can do that – actually *live*. You are returned to fight for something, and I have been happy to do that but sometimes I wanted to get drunk with friends, meet new ones, see places, fall in love but all you had was that quest and then darkness.'

'Couldn't you have done that this time? Especially if you think this is it.' Caratacus asked.

Another pause and then Arthur answered 'You'd think so but before you can actually get on with living you have to know why you are back in the first place. It's really hard to explain,' he paused to think. 'I told you about the Second World War, that was easy, we woke up, the world was at war, the Dark was everywhere, they were showing themselves in everything they did. We were needed. Sometimes we came back for a number of quests or the fight against the Dark was more than a mission. We fought against the Saxons back in the day, but we never won, and we never lost, nearly all of us died of old age, there was no portal. I grew old and saw my grandchildren grow and then suddenly, I was awake on the stone. What I am trying to say is that sometimes it's one mission and then it's back to the cave, or maybe it's a war or a period of time and then a portal appears and you are back in the cave, or it's old age and then back to the cave. Sorry. Do you understand what I'm on about?'

They'd left the centre and were walking away from the crowds by the bridge.

'I think so. As long as you knew what you were back for, you could stop thinking about it and get on with the mission and the living that came with it,' said Caratacus.

'Yes! Something like that. This time we didn't know why the hell we were back and neither did Merlin. The more I didn't know the worse I got. The boys just got on with things, but I couldn't, and being stuck in the pub made things harder. I know now that it's depression, but whatever its name it's always been near me, all the way back to my first life, but this time it was allowed to grow.'

They found themselves outside a row of buildings. It was a small town that had grown out of the bridge area. There were two shops bordered either side by two larger stone buildings. Caratacus had been listening, desperate to ask questions but not wanting to stop Arthur talking like this. They both looked up when they realised they'd been meandering, and that meandering had gotten them somewhere.

The buildings were old, brick and lopsided. There were two shops. One was an upmarket Elven clothes store which was all the fashion now. It was closed. Elves could be a stuck-up bunch, long lived, not given to shows of emotion but given to shows of loving themselves. Elves loved themselves so much that at the point of orgasm they often said their own names. The shop sign – in Welsh, English, Troll (by law near a bridge) and Elven – told whoever saw it that it only opened for an hour every day and that hour had passed.

The other shop front looked like it had sicked up random items. Outside the front door were things like a tin bath, elaborate but broken mirrors, a candelabra and hideous statues of people and creatures. Surrounded by his stuff was the owner, a large human-looking bloke but with two ram horns adorning his head. He sat on a large, wicker chair, you know, like the one Jane Seymour sat in, in 'Live and Let die.' I like Jane Seymour. I met her once in Tesco's. I liked her a lot.

Next to the shops were two bigger buildings. One was a pub called 'The Flying Chair' which boded well. The remaining building was the largest but with a smaller entrance through which you could see people...peopleish people drinking hot drinks and chatting, but whatever actually happened there was further inside. While the pub looked dangerous it was this building that had a neon-lit skull and crossbones over a gridded sign above it. It looked menacing but the flash on and off every three seconds made it doubly so. Caratacus was about to ask what it was but was interrupted by Arthur asking if he fancied a drink indicating the pub. Before Caratacus could answer, a man came flying out of the swing doors, stumbling before going over on his backside with a thump, making both Arthur and Caratacus inhale with that ooooing noise that accompanies seeing a fall that you know really hurts.

The swing doors, the ones they used to have in the wild west to easily facilitate people being thrown out were still swinging which helped the two men see inside. Every opening swing allowed them to see different scenes from the almighty fight that was taking place in there.

'Sod that,' said Arthur, 'Tea?'

Caratacus made a face. 'In the skull and crossbones place?'

Arthur smiled 'In That World that means a bingo hall.'

'Why the skull and cross bones then?' asked Caratacus.

'Have you seen people playing bingo? I've seen some fighting in my time, but bingo is brutal. Come on, let's have a sit down and think about what to do next.'

The cafe part was up front, (wo)manned by two well-groomed, bored looking women who generated energy by chewing gum at a rate of knots. To the side was a modern amusement arcade with a good selection of arcade games and gambling machines. Behind it was a large open corridor leading to a giant hall with about 200 people sat at tables playing bingo.

The men sat down.

'Happy staff,' Caratacus said and Arthur raised his eyebrows and smiled.

After minutes of being ignored, Arthur lifted his fingers to his mouth and whistled loudly. One girl was out the back but the one who remained lifted her head, looked over as if nothing had happened and Caratacus swore she hissed at them like a cat, but what she definitely did was tut loudly and threw down her book. She wasn't a young girl either, she was a beautiful woman in her thirties, her skin kept flawless by a strict regime of having no expressions.

'Yessss?' she said chewing stroppily.

Arthur was about to answer when a woman sidled over from another table. 'It's you!' she said excitedly.

'Probably not,' Arthur said, instantly.

'My Lord it's me, Betsan Gwenifans, we fought together a few years ago?'

Arthur looked embarrassed but inwardly he panicked and became angry with himself. He'd never considered he'd be recognised here. It had been a long time and he'd changed…a bit. He smiled, 'I am so sorry I get this all the time…I'm not him.'

It was obvious she didn't believe him and stood there grinning. She looked over at Caratacus.

'This is Arthur King, isn't it?' it wasn't loud, but it was clear.

'No, of course not,' Caratacus laughed sheepishly with a lie that wouldn't even convince his mother who believed everything he said.

The serving woman sighed loudly 'Teas?' She said as if she was doing them a favour.

Arthur just nodded and waved her away, worrying about the situation.

He leant forward as soon as she'd gone and the girl, still grinning, leant to meet him. 'Betsan Gwenifans, it fills this old man's heart with joy that I see you.' He tenderly grabbed both sides of her head and planted a tender kiss on her forehead. She looked up and he matched her grin for grin, but he had put his finger to his lips, so she knew to keep their conversation quiet.

The grin disappeared when she realised, she may have put him in trouble. 'Lord, I am so, sorry…' He was still smiling when he replied, 'Don't be silly, I have to be careful but how could I forget someone like you? Are you well?'

She was about to answer when an almighty crash of crockery breaking came from the kitchen followed by 'ARTHUR AP UTHER?'

Caratacus jumped from the sudden noise and then saw the blood drain from Arthur's face.

Arthur sighed and turned to Betsan. 'I can't speak now but I think I'm going to need you very soon. I don't know how but please wait for my call.' She nodded and they embraced. They came apart and she smiled at Caratacus, as if apologising for not acknowledging him and left.

'Shit,' Arthur said quietly as he banged the table with both hands like a nervous drum roll. He looked towards the kitchen door in expectation. A woman appeared in a washing up pinny, sleeves rolled up and her dragon-red hair tied messily into a bun.

She moved forward out from the doorway a step, put her arms on her hips and announced to the café: 'Everybody out please. We are closed,' followed by, 'Not you, you bastard,' when she saw Arthur was getting up to go.

Arthur stopped, sat back down, and wiped his hands on his sides nervously. 'Gweni?' he said, apologetically.

'It's Gwenyvere Queen to you, you arse.'

CHAPTER TWENTY-FOUR
THE TWO TRIALS OF CARATACUS

Nobody seemed to react badly to being told to go, some without touching the drinks they had wanted and paid for. Gwenyvere stood over Arthur and Caratacus, with the two girls who worked there standing not too far away. They had stopped looking uninterested but remained sullen.

Gwenyvere glanced at Caratacus for less than a second. She nodded. 'Go away,' she said.

While it seemed to be happening a lot recently Caratacus still hadn't gotten used to being talked to and treated like a piece of rubbish.

'Erm, no I won't, thanks,' he said sarcastically. 'Sod tha,t' he thought. 'Sod you,' he thought.

Gwenyvere did nothing but the two girls instantly fell into fighting stances and hissed likes cats, confirming what Caratacus had thought earlier. Arthur leaned over and whispered. 'It's ok. I need to sort this out. I'll find you when I'm done.'

'If you are still breathing,' Gwenyvere said to herself. Then she took what looked like a credit card from the large pocket at the front of her apron and handed it to Caratacus. 'This won't take long. Why don't you go to the arcade? This card will give you games for free and some free spins on the slot machines.'

He felt like a kid being sent away from an adult's conversation. He didn't need or want the card, but he had to go somewhere. He felt embarrassed when he took it and walked off, followed closely by the two women.

***

She reversed the chair and sat opposite him. Gwenyvere staring at Arthur, Arthur staring anywhere but at Gwenyvere.

He broke first. 'Gweni…'

'Nope,' she cut through him, 'I meant what I said. Friends have earned the right to call me that, you are no friend.'

He glanced up at her. As striking as ever, even when sweaty and dishevelled after a morning in the kitchen. He noticed a tiny strand of silver in the copper hair. He'd missed her, and for a moment he thought he was going to cry. He stopped himself. These emotions! Since his first life they were never far from the surface, but he kept them mostly in check. He was King Arthur; people shouldn't see too much of what he felt. That wasn't what people wanted from a leader. But, since the depression, it felt like he had lost control of his emotions, they ran riot, making him feel embarrassed and then, in turn, more depressed. He wanted his friend to hug him and then he remembered that she wouldn't know about the others, her sword brothers who loved her and who she loved with every bit of her being. How was he going to tell her? He looked up and she sat there staring at him, judging him again. He felt a different emotion then, another one always so close to the surface.

'You left me!' he said angrily.

Gwenyvere raised an eyebrow. 'Wind what's left of your neck in big boy.' She responded calmly, but when he looked at her, the muscles around her mouth and those green eyes had tightened. 'I hope you remember why I left. How I tried to talk to you for a year before.'

'I didn't know where you'd gone,' he said.

'You never asked though, did you?' she said accusing.

'No one knew!'

'Galahad knew.'

'He never said.'

'I bet you never asked.'

He looked down again, knowing when he was defeated. He didn't want to talk big stuff. 'So, you work in a kitchen?' He didn't care, he just wanted to avoid what should be said.

She knew what he was doing. 'I own the kitchen Arthur ap Uther, I own the whole building, the cafe, the bingo hall, the arcade, everything but the arena.'

'I didn't have you down as a businesswoman,' he said with a smile.

'Well, times they are a changin…' She answered with a smile of her own, and that break in hostilities broke his defences and he started sobbing. Gwenyvere got up and hugged him. The words broke out of him, unordered and in bursts, but she understood, and when she heard about the deaths of her family, especially as she believed that this was to be their last life, she sobbed too. She asked questions and he answered them as best he could and then he told her everything that had led up to her standing, comforting him.

'Who's he then?' She asked when Arthur told her about Caratacus.

He shrugged. 'No one.'

***

'Pert bottom,' said one of the girls. He turned around. They were good looking women, although he had to admit that being looked at like he was something they should avoid stepping in wasn't as sexy as you'd imagine.

'I agree,' said the dark haired one, meaning that the blonde haired one must have made the remark.

'Thank you,' Caratacus said.

'What job do you do?' the blonde asked suddenly.

'I own a bookshop,' he answered, puzzled at the change of conversation.

'Where?' The blonde this time.

'Twickenham.'

'Where is that? New York? London?' asked the blonde again, but while her voice was as toneless as before, her eyes had gone from completely dead to mostly dead with a quantum of pleading.

'I suppose you could say London,' Caratacus answered. In an instant, the brunette had grabbed his hand, pulling him away from the blonde who, less than a second, later grabbed his other arm.

'MINE!' The brunette shouted.

'NO MINE!' The blonde replied.

'Hey!' Caratacus said. They each started pulling him towards them while hissing at the other. As he tried to pull his arms away, their grip tightened until it hurt.

'ENOUGH!' He shouted. He never shouted, it took too much effort, but their grips were so strong and painful he'd started to panic.

'I SAW HIM FIRST, YOU STUPID BITCH,' said the brunette.

'PISS OFF, ALEXANDRA. HE WANTS ME!' This was from the blonde, followed by more hissing and more pain.

He was starting to feel overwhelmed, and claustrophobic, and when they started using both their hands, the pain was excruciating. A feeling gathered in his chest, started to spread, and then exploded out of him. The two women flew as if shocked by electricity, one into the arcade the other into the bingo hall.

Picture this. You are playing bingo. A dishevelled, screaming woman is thrown past your table and crashes into a wall. What do you do? That is correct. Absolutely nothing, you carry on playing bingo. The players didn't even look up. If you want to learn mindfulness, fall in love with bingo, you won't think about anything else again.

Caratacus looked at his hands in utter shock, before bending over and emptying his guts on the floor. By the time he'd stood up and his stomach had settled they were standing before him, quietly hissing at each other.

'Please! Will you pack it in? What's the matter with you both?' He asked weakly.

'He wants me, Kimberley you moose!' Alexandra the brunette said spitefully.

'Get lost he can't stand the sight of you,' Kimberley spat back, and then to Caratacus, 'can you?'

Caratacus wished he knew how he'd made them fly away because he wanted to do it again. He saw the door of the amusement arcade which, three minutes and forty-nine seconds ago he had had no intention of going into. It looked like escape.

They continued to hiss at each other until they realised he was no longer there and followed him into the arcade.

He walked through the gambling machines just inside the entrance and into the main arcade. Games were dotted everywhere; riding, racing, jumping and shooting were available as well as space hockey and, weirdly, ping pong. In the middle was a grandiose booth with a girl around the same age as the two who were escorting him. She looked at him with as little interest as humanly possible and then, as she saw the two girls behind him, stood up and started hissing at them as if deranged.

'GET OUT YOU SMELLY BITCHES! YOU'RE NOT ALLOWED IN HERE!'

'I CAN DO WHAT I WANT YOU LITTLE COW AND I'M FOLLOWING MY FUTURE HUSBAND, SO COME OUT AND STOP ME!'

Caratacus could feel his eyes roll back into his head as he stood there with these women shouting at each other, followed by an inordinate amount of hissing. Again, he walked off and the hissing weirdos were soon forgotten when he noticed the old arcade game Time Crisis 2. He remembered it from his younger days. He'd loved it. A smile crossed his face and for a moment the dark cloud lifted. He looked at the card Gwenyvere had given him. It was blank on both sides but with a shrug he waved it over the money slot and the screen with the light blue gun showed his credit. He picked it up and fired at the screen to watch the opening story.

Funny thing nostalgia: the grip, the game, everything; like a time-machine for emotions. His first game went by in a flash, and he'd just started a new game when he felt a presence next to him. Caratacus knew it wasn't one of the girls as he could hear them fighting at the entrance of the arcade.

The man didn't say anything and Caratacus didn't see any reason to speak either. If you start with that sort of nonsense, you must accept the consequences. A thought flashed through his head. 'I have actually learned something…' It soon left when the bloke next to him spoke.

'One's coming up top left.' It was said in such a monotonous voice that Caratacus thought it had come from the machine. An 'enemy' did appear where he said it would and Caratacus soon dispatched him with two shots.

'There will be another one in a second,' the man said and then, 'I would reload if I was you.'

More points and hints followed. 'Do you really want to choose that? I would have chosen something different. Are you going to keep shooting in that stance,' were a select few. I am a storyteller and yes, I want to tell you as much as I can, but I am not putting you through all of that. I am fond of you. The ones you've just read and the ones I left out were delivered so boringly that Caratacus felt an urge to turn the plastic gun on himself.

'Pilkas Ritter.' The man didn't say it as if he was introducing himself, he just said it.

Because there was no inflection, Caratacus thought he had carte blanche to ignore him.

'Pilkas Ritter,' he repeated four times, and every time was the same as the first.

Caratacus relented. 'Caratacus Lewis,' he said, shooting a load of barrels coming down a hill at him on the screen.

'Fancy challenging me?' Pilkas said. 'You aren't awful.'

Caratacus didn't want to play him, but he did want him to shut up. He was about to move onto another game anyway or try and sneak further away from those women, but he relented. 'Go on then, one game.' He looked over at the man for the first time. He was in his late fifties, about five foot two inches, overweight, and bald except for a few stray brown hairs growing from the sides of his head.

'You challenge?' asked Pilkas.

'Yes! Whatever,' Caratacus said and moved the card over both the money slots. It was then that he noticed the top scorer board. It had nothing but the name 'Pilkas Ritter' on it.

'Pretty good then?' Caratacus asked.

'I play a little,' Pilkas said simply, followed by, 'Let's do this shit,' in the most un 'Let's do this shit' voice in the world ever.

It seems teenage muscle memory is a thing, because moments later Caratacus was playing the game of his life. They had both managed to survive well into the game, but both their character's energy levels were dipping dangerously low.

Duck, rise, bang, hit, duck, rise, bang take hit, bang, hit, bang take hit. One more injury and it was all over.

Pilkas tipped up to fire a shot and... bang. He was hit. Game over player two. Caratacus felt the pressure leave him, his avatar was on empty, but he managed to take out a few more bad guys before a final hit ended his game.

Deadpan, Pilkas stood at his sie, face on. Caratacus smiled. 'Good game eh?'

'You improved immeasurably during that game did you not?' It was a statement, delivered like white noise, but Caratacus couldn't help but think there was an accusation there.

'Beginner's luck after so many years, I reckon,' he replied, amiably.

'That wasn't luck. Next.' Pilkas said. Again, no question mark.

'Nah, I'm fine thanks. I might just have a look around.' Caratacus said.

'No,' Pilkas replied.

'Damn.' Caratacus thought and replied, 'Yes,' a little more emphatically.

It went back and forth for a bit.

One of the No's or yes's, I can't really tell, was interrupted when Caratacus saw that the two women had stopped arguing and had come to stand next to him. They were silent, but blonde Kimberley had taken one of his hands while Alexandra was behind him caressing his hair. They were both performing what they thought a smile looked like because they had done it so rarely before.

'I will let you feel me up in the toilets,' Alexandra whispered into his ear.

Caratacus winced. Pilkas was still saying yes without Caratacus saying no.

'Why are you wasting time with boring Pilkas and his stupid challenges? No one bothers! Let's leave. Take me to Twikingem with you. I will kiss you on the mouth,' Kimberley whispered, her lips just touching his ears. He would have shivered but his head was being snapped from side to side by the girl behind. He looked over at the racing game and saw temporary escape. It was the old car game that you could sit inside and race like an actual car. It would give him a break from the girls before seeing if Arthur had finished. He said to Pilkas while pointing, 'OK one go on this?' He walked fast and got in.

Pilkas joined him, then he turned his head like a robot and spoke like one. 'Are you ready for a right royal arse kicking?' He even said arse not ass...

Caratacus sighed and waved Gwenyvere's card over both slots and the game came to life but not before he noticed that, again, Pilkas' name occupied every slot on the leader board.

This was another game that Caratacus had wasted a lot of hours on in his younger days and nostalgia struck again as he felt the seat, the small, fat steering wheel, and saw the graphics that flashed up counting down for the race to start. Caratacus looked over at Pilkas' intensely calm face and realised he wanted to win. Yes, he hadn't done this for a while but surely, it's like riding a bike or driving a pretend rally car? He felt that there was something on this race but decided it must be how competitive Pilkas was being. Caratacus wasn't bothered enough to be competitive, but the man was making him. He could feel his hands starting to sweat.

3-2-1. The game started.

A lifetime of wasted man hours again came in handy and after the first big jump they were neck-and- neck and Caratacus heard a grunt from Pilkas. He moved a little bit ahead and positioned himself better, preparing for the last bend before the finish line. He angled across to Pilkas just edging him out too far on a tight corner. Another grunt made him look across at the other screen to watch Pilkas's car roll over before coming to a stop. Caratacus crossed the line with a quiet, but audible, 'Yesssssss.' He didn't care, he felt great winning that. Pilkas looked over at him, still with no expression. 'You didn't tell me you had raced on this game before.'

'You never asked,' shrugged Caratacus. He was about to get out, but he had been so engrossed in the game he hadn't realised that the girls had been by the side of the pretend door, watching him and jostling for position. Now he'd finished, Alexandra started stroking his hair with just as much physicality as before. He looked over at Pilkas who was still staring at him. Caratacus was desperate to leave, but he couldn't take another hammering to his ego by running away from some girls that wanted to...wanted to do something to him.

He looked at them and they did that rictus smiling again which was absolutely terrifying. He moved Alexandra's hand. 'What is it you actually want?' he asked them both.

'Marry me and take me away from here.' They said it together and couldn't have got it more in time if they'd been having rehearsals. The moment they said it, all hell broke loose and this time they went straight into fighting, while Caratacus looked on with shock and a tiny bit of fascination.

He looked over again at Pilkas who seemed to telepathically understand what Caratacus wanted. 'I will hide you if you play another game against me.' It sounded like one note being continually played on a recorder.

'What? This?' He pointed at the steering wheel.

Pilkas shook his head. 'No, not this. You must choose another.'

It was instant. 'Get me away from these and you're on.'

'On what?' Asked Pilkas.

'Never mind,' Caratacus replied, getting out and gingerly stepping over and around the hissing women.

They'd reached the other side of the arcade and could still hear the girls fighting. Caratacus knew he was stuck here until Arthur had finished so he may as well do something. He saw Pac-man and Asteroids, but he didn't fancy them. He saw some blue skinned teenage girls playing Mortal Combat while young guys stood behind trying but failing desperately to look cool.

'Pool!' Caratacus smiled with inspiration.

'What?' Asked Pilkas his head jerking up and showing the teeniest, tiniest flicker of shock.

'Yeah, I fancy a game of pool,' Caratacus smiled. He'd wasted many hours on the arcade machines, but nothing compared to the time he'd spent around a pool table. He looked over at Pilkas. He had stubby legs, his arms were equally so, and he had a big protruding belly. He could have him.

'Killer?' Asked Pilkas.

'Yeah, if you fancy.' Caratacus answered with a shrug.

'Obviously, the pool table is in a separate place,' Pilkas said, walking off and leaving Caratacus to look like a lemon on his own before he followed.

'Obviously,' Caratacus answered wondering how obvious it was.

***

'I honestly don't have a clue, Tommy sent him down to the Once and Future. He hasn't been specifically mentioned in prophecy,' Arthur told Gwenyvere.

'You know our chosen one has been killed?' she asked. 'I was told this morning.'

He shook his head.

'Lexie was a lovely girl and had grown to be a wonderful woman. I can't believe she's gone. Did we do something wrong? Did we miss something? Things have changed, the Dark must have been planning this for years and now they are moving. I am doubtful it's about us either, it's something bigger. There are already refugees moving into Cantre'r Gwaelod so maybe the stories of armies moving aren't so far-fetched,' she stood up, taking her pinny off. 'They have killed our brothers and tried to kill you. Our messenger of prophecy has been killed and armies move in That world,' she paused and started pacing, 'I felt something big was coming but they need us out of the way first. This is why we're back! Maybe this *is* our last time, but we aren't meant to just wither and die!'

'You don't know that Gweni,' he said quietly. Deep down in his soul he knew she was right, but he didn't want to be a saviour any more.

She ignored the 'Gweni'. 'Yes, I do. I'm sorry but it's time. You have to fight.'

Arthur slowly got up from his chair. 'Say you are right? What can we do? Half of us are gone already. I know nobody in This or That World any more. I have not spoken to any leader over there in years. We have no army! Look at me, am I really what you think the saviour of the Worlds looks like?' His head dropped, and he felt the knot of anxiety in his gut.

She walked over to him and for a moment he thought she was going to slap his face but instead she lifted his chin. 'It doesn't matter what I think, it's what you think that's important. Now shift yourself. I have to think about what we do next, which means rounding up squabbling girls.'

As if they'd been called, Kimberley, Alexandra, and Mali from the arcade all appeared, looking sullen. Gwenyvere looked to Kimberley and Alexandra. 'I thought you were keeping an eye on the boy?'

Mali smiled. 'The stupid cows lost him.' Which gained her a lot of hisses from the said stupid cows. Kimberley looked panicked. 'The Grey Knight had him before we even got to him! It wasn't our fault!'

'Pilkas was in the arcade and not in the arena?' Gwenyvere asked worried. 'Where is he?'

They had stopped hissing and were all looking at the ceiling or the floor or anywhere that wasn't Gwenyvere's face.

'GIRLS!'

'Killer pool…' Whispered Alexandra.

'Oh gods…' Gwenyvere grabbed Arthur's elbow and led him out of the café.

'What's the matter?' He asked.

'I don't think your Caratacus can be that important to our story,' she said.

'Why?' he replied.

'Because he is about to die.'

CHAPTER TWENTY-FIVE

KILLER POOL

Pilkas led him past the beeping, whirring cacophony of the arcade machines before entering a long, wide corridor where a throng of people were queueing for something. The queue was full of beings from both worlds; dwarves talking loudly, plainsmen like the ones from the Once and Future, armed to the teeth, and Elves cloistered in small groups, desperate not to have the slightest brush from another creature in the place. It was a queue of excitement, like a concert except the only squealing came from a group of half-orcs as he walked by.

'What's going on there?' asked Caratacus.

'That's not our queue,' said Pilkas as he carried on walking.

As they made their way down the corridor, people started shouting at Pilkas who walked past them as if they weren't there.

'It seems like they're excited,' Caratacus said, conversationally.

'Oh, they are,' came the reply. Caratacus was just about to ask about it again when they reached the start of the queue. There were two serving hatches and, either side of them, two doors. The left-hand side was the entrance the queue was waiting to get into. The right-hand side was empty, with just a twenty-one fingered Curill sat at the hatch. Pilkas walked straight up and before Caratacus could join him, he felt a tap on the shoulder. It was a girl with whiskers, and stubby horns protruding from the top of her head. She folded her arms, 'You aren't thinking about pushing in old man. We've been here for an hour.'

Ignoring the 'old man' part Caratacus answered. 'Ok chill. We aren't here for your thing, we are just going to the pool room.'

'Oooh, hark at him,' she said sarcastically to her friends, 'the pool room.' They laughed.

Pilkas cut in, standing about six inches away from him and making him jump. 'I've put you down as Caratacus ap Neb. I hope that's ok?'

Caratacus was about to correct Pilkas, but when he turned around the man was already walking towards the door.

The horned girl shouted. 'You aren't playing, are you? What are you? Towel holder? You have to be a colour.'

'Sign here,' from the hatch, the white skinned Curill pushed a bit of parchment towards Caratacus with his ten fingered right hand and then offered a quill with his eleven fingered left one. It was then that Caratacus felt that now-familiar sinking feeling. He turned to Pilkas who stood by the door holding it open.

'We are just playing pool, yeah?' he asked.

'Yes.'

'It's in Welsh,' Caratacus said and the Curill just looked at him and shrugged. Caratacus dipped the quill into the dish of ink at the right-hand side of the hatch and scratched his name.

'Just pool?' He asked again but this time it was to the back of Pilkas' head as he walked through the slowly closing door.

'Sod it,' he pushed back the parchment and went into the darkness.

'Who was that with The Grey Knight?' He heard from the queue before the door closed.

***

The place stank of Deep Heat and sweat. It was like he'd come through a door to a different world, and the only reason he knew he hadn't was because he wasn't on his hands and knees throwing up.

He was in a changing room, a sports changing room. He remembered the atmosphere and smell from his school days. This giant concrete cave with lockers and benches stank of liniment, sweat and competition. The sinking feeling went up a level. He moved back to the door he'd just come through and pushed. It didn't move and after a few, small, embarrassing pushes he gave up, leaning his head against the door.

'Please, give me a break,' he said to the door. He felt a presence behind him but kept his head on the door, his eyes closed.

'Yes?' he asked, impatient to get the next crazy thing out of the way. He felt the small nudge on his shoulder, but he still didn't move.

'Who the hell are you?' came a voice like gravel.

Caratacus sighed. 'No one,' he replied.

'I know your name. I mean who *are* you?'

Caratacus groaned, realising that he'd signed the parchment 'ap Neb'. He looked up and carried on looking up into the bearded, helmeted face of a very large man.

Gravel Voice growled. 'Where you from? I've never heard of you.' He turned back to the changing room, 'Hey Varkuuz? You heard of this one?'

The Elf he was talking to was a dark Elf, one from the numerous tribes of the Zed Mountains, dark in attitude and often in deed. Paler than the other elves but just as stuck up. He was sat on one of the benches, topless and hunched forward as another of his kind massaged his shoulder. He looked up and spoke, his voice quiet and sibilant, 'Just a colour. Another debtor, Galfinas, ignore him. Let him enjoy the last few minutes of his life.'

Galfinas was wearing a war helmet, but everything else he wore screamed Tuesday night darts league chic. His shirt was almost shining black, and his short sleeves had tiny orange lightning bolts embroidered on. On his shirt's small, chest pocket his name was embroidered in yellow. He sniffed, harrumphed and stalked off.

Caratacus looked for Pilkas who was at the far end of the changing room looking as if he was stretching. He rushed over, avoiding any possible contact. He brought his face about an inch from Pilkas's,. 'What the hell is going on?'

Pilkas who was in the middle of a lunge replied, 'You challenged me to killer pool.' He stood from the lunge. 'This is killer pool.'

Caratacus looked around. The changing room was like an ant hill of commotion. Galfinas was banging his head against a locker, the dents getting bigger and deeper after each contact. A short, bald-headed woman with a stubby nose was staring in the mirror telling herself that she *'had this'* over and over again. Someone he couldn't see was screaming. There was exercise, stretching, contemplation, amiable chats, psyching out and praying, a load of praying. In the corner, there were four gods cooing and ahhing, gradually becoming larger, younger and more colourful as more prayers were dedicated to them.

'I am not fighting anybody!' Caratacus said quickly. Not said, actually. He squeaked.

Pilkas stared, then blinked. 'You don't have to fight. You have to play pool. You have to play killer pool like you said you wanted to.'

Caratacus' voice rose a few octaves. 'Why is there a changing room? Who are all these people? Where is the pool table? I think our ideas of killer pool are completely different. Can we forget about this? I'm going to get back to my friend and let you carry on. Sorry for messing you around. How do I get out of here?'

Pilkas ignored Caratacus. He tied his shoelaces tight with a middle-aged man grunt, stood and sprang up and down gently on his knees before holding out his arm and whispering a word. A pool cue appeared Magickly in his hand. Caratacus was relieved to see an actual pool cue. 'Ok, explain to me what the rules are and how do I get a pool cue?'

'You haven't got one?' This from Pilkas.

'Of course, I haven't bloody got one!' Caratacus said through clenched teeth.

'You can get one from the spares rack over there.' Pilkas pointed and Caratacus went over, tried a few and once happy... or as happy as you can get in this situation, came back. 'Rules,' he demanded.

'Ten of us play, five champions, five newbies. We all have three lives each, the purpose of the game is to pot a ball. That's it. If you fail to pot one you lose a life, if you lose all three you are out.' Pilkas spoke as if he was reading from a manual.

Caratacus's head jerked back in realisation. 'Oh, that's the same as where I am from. Hold on, are you a champion?'

'Yes,' Pilkas said simply.

The torches on the wall suddenly spued forth green fire. A big wooden door opened and a smartly dressed woman – as in smartly dressed woman from Caratacus's world – walked in. She had a clip board which meant she was in charge.

'FINAL PREPARATIONS PLEASE,' she bawled.

Pilkas walked off. 'Are we meant to follow her?' Caratacus called over to the back of his opponent's head. Pilkas stopped, turned 180 degrees and said simply, 'Yes.' Then, as if an idea had been teleported into his head, he continued, 'Good luck, and I hope you are not in the bottom five.'

'POSITIONS PLEASE,' came the clear voice of the woman in charge.

Galfinas was suddenly at Caratacus's side, trying to manoeuvre himself in front, earning him a swift 'sod off' as the latter shrugged him off. Caratacus was about to ask about bottom five when he saw a slight, pale man screaming and fighting against two officious creatures.

'NO! PLEASE! I'LL PAY BACK WHAT I OWE, PLEASE!' he shrieked.

As Caratacus followed the struggling trio through the door, he found himself in a cauldron of noise. A pool table at the centre was lit by giant floodlights. He looked up and covered his eyes as the floodlights temporarily blinded him. His stomach lurched. Surrounding the pool table, rows of seating going up to the ceiling were full of hundreds of people watching, cheering, standing, shouting and jeering.

He spewed. Not Magick. Nerves.

'You've been sick,' Pilkas was by his side.

'Thanks,' Caratacus replied sarcastically but said nothing more as the crowd had stopped their cheering and had started humming. For a brief moment, the whole place was shrouded in darkness as the spotlights went off before flashing on a moment later, centring on the green-topped pool table. The humming became louder.

Pwff! A body appeared. So bright was the man-shaped creature that it reflected the spotlights back. The humming turned into cheers as the spectators broke into whoops and screams. The guest MC for the big, weekly event, 'Monday's Killer pool', was almost as big a deal as the game itself, and Anastasiana Anastasiana-Anastasiana III was one hell of an MC to have. Translucent and white skinned as were all from the tribes of the frozen south in That World, Anastasiana was one of the few that had headed north. Evolution – again, it's a thing – meant their people were white skinned to make it easier to hide from big snow animal things that eat them. Camouflage was usually deep in their psyche, but not for our Anastasiana. He wanted to be seen and he wanted to be seen by as much of the world as possible. All parts of his flesh on show – which was quite a lot – were covered in bright, light- reflecting sequins, but they also covered his cloak, the beautiful leg-split dress he wore for the night and that night only, and his top hat. His heels were not sequined, they were silver and sharp like his all-canine teeth which he showed now with a coy smile.

He rose in the air, floating up to the middle point of the full stands, the lights following him, the crowd suddenly falling silent in expectation. Silent until a 'We love you Anastasiana,' broke out of the quiet, followed by a peal of laughter and a few more affectionate shouts until Anastasiana held his manicured hand out. Another 'pwfff' and a microphone and stand appeared before him, which he cradled in both hands and tenderly brought towards his full, sensual lips.

'Denizens of both Worlds—' He stopped, his smile getting bigger, he could feel the excitement, he fed off it... literally...then carried on. 'Big of beard and bosom, sharp of claw, sniffers of smells, wound givers, wound healers, rampagers, soft-speakers, carers, axe wielders still, dancers and storytellers,' he paused looking at the audience, every one of whom thought he was looking directly at them, 'what on earth are you all here for, darlings?' he asked conversationally.

'KILLER POOL,' the crowd shouted back.

His face feigned sadness, he bowed his head in mock hurt and sighed. 'Oh,' he said in a small voice, 'a quiet crowd. How upsetting.'

Anastasiana had been entertaining the people of That world for more years than he would ever consider mentioning, and they had expected this response. In fact, they had been waiting for it. Laughter and applause rippled through the audience followed immediately by a louder and longer 'KILLER POOL.'

Still floating, Anastasiana started laughing maniacally, the pitch getting higher while he pirouetted. Fireworks went off on the outskirts of the amphitheatre and trumpets sounded; there was a madness to it all and the crowd reacted accordingly.

It affected the competitors around the pool table. The stubby-nosed girl from earlier – who, before this point, Caratacus had thought was rather attractive – started walking around and screaming into her opponents faces. The ones who looked like they had volunteered to be there either screamed back or pushed her away. The four that hadn't were all crying now. When she came to Caratacus she screamed, 'You're dead, pale man!'

'Thank you,' Caratacus replied nervously, not wanting to provoke her even more.

He was literally sweating and figuratively shitting his pants. The light, noise and heat by the pool table pressed down on him. He stepped over to Pilkas who was warming up his right arm by rotating it like a propeller. He put his hand on the tubby man's shoulder to get his attention and shouted even though he could barely be heard over the crowd noise, 'get me out of here! This is ridiculous! I wanted a game of pool!'

Pilkas didn't answer and even if he had, Caratacus doubted he would have heard him anyway. He was about to shout again before hearing his name being called behind him. He turned in the direction of the shout to see Arthur at the bottom of one of the stairwells close to the pool pit. As Caratacus reached him, Arthur was remonstrating with one of the burly security team who was telling him to return to his bench. Arthur looked at Caratacus, his face furious, 'What the hell are you doing?'

'I don't know! I just said I wanted a game of pool! Now I'm here! Get me out of here!' Panic had overtaken Caratacus now. A security— Caratacus looked at who had placed a hand on his shoulder. A security ogre started to guide him to the pool table. Caratacus looked pleadingly back at Arthur and mouthed, 'Help!' The King leant over and was about to speak but was interrupted by Anastasiana as the crowd again quieted.

'Now my lovelies, you know the rules but, as always, they are worth repeating. How many competitors?' he asked.

'Ten!' came the shout back.

'That's right darlings, ten competitors, five professionals, five...' he paused as if talking about cat sick. 'Five willing volunteers.' The audience laughed at that and Caratacus's sphincter contracted.

'It's always pro, not, pro, not, in the turns. Everybody has three lives, miss a ball, lose a life, the first five eliminated are...well, eliminated, while the remaining five compete for the prize money. We don't allow people to leave the pit or excessive physical contact, bombing, diving or heavy petting...' The crowd knew it was coming and laughed nonetheless, 'and what else can we not have?'

There wasn't even a pause. 'MAGICK!' was the answer.

'And how do we do that?' Anastasiana asked.

'BRING IN THE GAWR!'

'I can't hear you Dahhlins!'

'BRING IN THE GAWR!'

'Yes, my adoring fans, let's bring in the Gawr!' The lights left Anastasiana and lit up an entrance to the side of the pool table. Naked slaves from various races entered first, pulling on taut ropes which eventually led to a bed the size of a basketball court with a fat, pallid looking Gawr on. The spectators went mad, but the Gawr didn't seem to care, it just lay there like some sated Roman emperor burping, yawning and eating.

'STON-KAR, STON-KAR, STON-KAR,' the crowd chanted until, with an effort of sod all on the effort scale, he raised his hand in acknowledgment. The lights turned away from Ston-kar and back on Anastasiana who changed his pose to a wonderful archer-like flourish.

'That is right. No Magick. No cheating here, my little swamp ducks.'

Caratacus realised he was the only competitor standing and walked, embarrassed, to the remaining empty seat between the skinhead from earlier and a mulleted man with a thin moustache, in a Roman toga. The next five minutes was Anastasiana announcing the competitors. It became pretty obvious to Caratacus that the five favourites always progressed and the remaining five were always out. The favourites were introduced by their name, the number of competitions they'd won and the numbers of seconds and thirds they'd placed. It took a couple of minutes and while they were being announced they walked around the pool table taking in the cheers like wrestlers.

He had already unfortunately met the helmeted massive half-Goblin, Galfinas, as well as the slight, dark, pale skinned elf Vaarkuz. The shouty woman was Princess Treanna, the toga'd man next to him was called Wayne Evans. Caratacus knew that Pilkas must have been a name but was still shocked to find out that his name was Pilkas the Grey Knight, and wondered if he'd been played. Galfinas and the princess stomped around during their introductions as if they were about to have a fight rather than play pool. Pilkas just stood up when announced and immediately sat down, Wayne waved, clicked his fingers and pointed a lot, while Vaarkuz was obviously the pantomime villain who was booed and jeered with good humour. When the others were announced there was derision.

Caratacus didn't even stand for his, the others, when called, just hunched in their chairs crying. He hadn't noticed that he was the only other competitor given a name, the others being called by a colour assigned to them.

The lights went off again and you could feel the buzz in the darkness. The place went silent before, out of the vacuum, boomed Anastasiana's voice.

'My darlings, it's time for the main event. You've met your entertainers, so all there is left for me to do is count you down.' The crowd joined in. 'Five, four, three, two, one!'

The drums stopped, the lights burst on and there, floating just above the pool table, was our Anastasiana, a smile as wide as can be on his radiant face.

'BREAK SOME BALLS!' he shouted, then disappeared as everyone in the place went wild.

CHAPTER TWENTY-SIX
THE TWO DEATHS OF CARATACUS AP NEB

The man who'd been given the name Red was now covered in red and didn't have a head and wasn't alive anymore. Red's head had been cut off after losing his three pretend lives, leading to losing his actual one. It had been stuck in a sack and carried out of the main arena at the same time as his body was dragged the same way. Caratacus had been appalled at the casual butchery and the memory of the crying man on his knees as Galfinas, the fat bully, danced around before chopping down with an especially presented sharp sword, would stay with him forever.

Red, who had directly followed Galfinas was the first to go. Green, who was following the dark elf and could barely hold his cue never mind pot a ball, surprisingly stayed in one round longer before losing his last life. His wretched end, witnessed by a baying crowd, was literally at the hands of Vaarkuz who strangled the life out of the poor man. I think that was it for Caratacus. Rather than loosening his bowels with fear, that was the point when he stopped being scared and got angry. How dare they take these poor people's lives for entertainment! Where were the laws in this place?

Still, he could barely stand for his first shot, a relatively easy one made a lot harder by the circumstances. But he made the shot and, in a very un-Caratacus like way, he shouted in anger and relief.

'Have that!' he spat at the table, but it could've been for anybody and everybody in that place. He looked into the throng of people and found Arthur and Gwenyvere. Arthur smiled and put a thumbs up and Caratacus, despite the fear, smiled back. He sat down and immediately stood up, too nervous to settle.

Five minutes later, he lost his first life. There were a few balls left on the table and the princess made an easy shot and left him with nothing easy to pot. When his ball ricocheted off the top pocket, she jumped up from her seat, screamed and pushed him. Wayne joined in with the pushing as Caratacus backed off and officials got between him, the princess, and a taunting, laughing Wayne. Only Vaarkus had lost a life from the professionals. Caratacus had now lost one and the man named White, who followed Pilkas, had one life left. The other non-favourite, given the name Blue, also had one life but that only lasted for two minutes after Caratacus had lost his first.

Caratacus looked on in horror as Blue, a man who looked to be in his sixties was dragged back after trying to make a break for it. He was brought before Wayne who waved to huge applause from the crowd. Unlike the others there were no tears from Blue, no grovelling, there was just defiance in his face, and it made Caratacus want to cry. The sadness lasted until he saw Wayne put the noose around Blue's neck and tighten it.

That was it. Caratacus didn't think, he sprang from his seat, took five steps forward and smashed his cue across Wayne's back. It didn't break but it made that wonderful thwack noise to show that it had made contact properly. The spectators went bananas as Wayne hit the deck. Galfinas roared and ran at Caratacus as did the princess. A loud siren rang out and security guards managed to place themselves between Caratacus and the players who were baying for his blood. Caratacus, who had never known such rage, tried to move his arms but they were being pinned in the melee. He looked over and watched as Wayne got to his feet, tidying up his dishevelled toga before getting hold of the end of the loose end of rope. He looked over at Caratacus and smiled his sibilant smile.

'No!' Caratacus shouted.

'Yes!' laughed Galfinas who joined Wayne and started to pull on the rope that had been thrown over a beam made for the act of hanging, very close to a now sleeping Ston-kar Gawr.

The crowd noise got louder as the death kicks of Blue grew weaker. Caratacus had already shaken off anybody around him, turning his head away from the pathetic spectacle. The lights went off and, again from nowhere, Anastasiana appeared.

'Wonderful fanatics of Killer pool – a challenge of foul play has been given against Caratacus ap Neb.'

A spotlight shone on Caratacus, blinding him, he covered his eyes trying to look at Anastasiana.

'Excessive physical horseplay is the charge and what is the penalty for such a charge?' Anastasiana opened his arms as if to accept the answer.

'LOSE A LIFE!' shouted the crowds in unison.

Anastasiana looked down at Caratacus and smiled. 'And that's what's going to happen.' Then he disappeared in another 'pwff', accompanied by some jeers.

Some shuffling creature wiped off another chalk stick man from Caratacus' name on the giant score blackboard.

It wasn't long before the last newbie lost his life. The man they'd called White now fitted the name as the blood left his face. He had fallen to his knees as he'd missed the shot. Caratacus' stomach turned over, wondering how Pilkas was going to end this poor young man's life. He couldn't understand why Pilkas was here playing this and how many people he must have killed to get to this level of fame. The announcer had said that he'd won numerous competitions. It wasn't as if he'd fallen in love with the pan faced man, but he hadn't disliked him. The noise of the crowd built up again while Pilkas walked up to the tearful man. Pilkas spoke to the officials who were awaiting his decision. Caratacus' heart was going like a train. Pilkas shook his head, a slight one, his face still as dispassionate as ever. Security came over and picked the man up who instead of crying for his life was now crying his thanks to

Pilkas, leaning out to touch him in some form of gratitude as he was carried away.

It was then that the realisation hit Caratacus like a train. Not a rubbish British one but one of those snazzy fast ones they have in Japan. The killing was optional! It was up to the person who knocked them out whether they lived or died and every one of those bastards except Pilkas had made the decision to end someone's life.

Inside something shifted, moved, expanded and he knew that the anger he felt had made something magical inside of him stir and the only reason nothing was happening was the massive, dribbling Giant, twenty feet away.

How the hell was he going to get out of this? He sat up and looked at Arthur. Why wasn't he intervening to help? Would he just let him die? He obviously didn't think that his mother would in any way be able to sort this situation out, but he still wanted her here. He missed her and, again, he felt that stab of guilt that he'd taken her for granted. Blood left his face as he thought about himself dying here, punched to death by one of these bastards and her never knowing about it. A sharp slap at the top of his head brought him back to real life. It was the Princess Treanna, who looked at him with disdain. 'Get on with it you loser,' she snapped poisonously, then laughed, joined by Galfinas and Wayne.

He ignored her. He felt calm, his brain seemed uncluttered, he looked at the pool table, and for the first time since beginning the game it just looked like a pool table. This was simply a game of killer pool like he used to play against the boys in the Turk's head. The boys, a pint, a jukebox, a pound on the table and him playing like a pool playing machine. All he had to do was survive longer than just one of these bastards. He didn't walk around the table, he strutted, looking at angles, he even smiled, and he didn't have a bloody clue why. He saw the shot he wanted, he lined it up, took it and potted, leaving Wayne in trouble. The look he gave Caratacus could have turned milk sour, the one he gave when he missed would have curdled it.

It was clear that all the players except Pilkas and Caratacus were working together to get rid of them. It didn't matter though, Caratacus was on fire and had brought an increasingly unhinged Wayne down to one life.

The princess played one of her shots that was meant to leave Caratacus in trouble, but hubris saw the shot rattle the pocket leaving him with an easy pot. She swore and threw her cue in the corner. He forced a smile at her as she passed. He didn't take the easy shot; he took a harder one which left Wayne little chance of making his. He looked up at the Toga'd little twat and Wayne knew it was over for him. The spectators went silent at this rare humbling of a champion. Wayne bent for a shot and then stood up again quickly. He walked around the table and tried again. I was going to say that Caratacus thought he saw fear in Wayne's eye, but I'd be wrong. He didn't think. He definitely saw fear in Wayne's eye.

He missed.

Ha. Bloody Ha.

It had been pleasing to see how sick the man looked and when he missed the shot he remained in situ and started to cry softly. There was no shout of joy from Caratacus, he remained calm as he leant his cue against his seat and went to talk to the officials.

Wayne was lying face down on the table, he still hadn't moved but the shaking shoulders showed that there would be a wet patch on that part of the table afterwards. The officials came over with Caratacus and when Wayne saw the noose, they brought with them he screamed and was quickly grabbed by security as he tried to run. His 'friends' looked away, embarrassed at the scene. Snot bubbles blew and burst as they put the noose around his head. He screamed again; it was so high-pitched, dogs who scavenged for food by the Troll bridge outside howled in answer. Then the official that Caratacus had talked with whispered in Wayne's ear. The falsetto scream stopped and through sobs he nodded.

After being told what was going to happen, Galfinas roared. He took off his helmet in disgust and shouted at Caratacus who stood, doing an impressive impression of an expressionless Pilkas.

There was no cheering in the crowd just a buzz of puzzlement as Wayne still lay on the table while two security guards came either side and held him down. One reached back and lifted the toga, the other pulled down his underwear. People gasped as Caratacus lifted his pool cue and swung it like a baseball bat making contact with Wayne's bare arse.

The thwack was audible, replaced by Wayne's pitiful scream and followed by one or two confused cheers by the crowd. Caratacus wasn't only punishing a murderer, he was venting everything that had happened since leaving Twickenham.

Thwack - my weekend.

Thwack - tasks.

Thwack - magic.

Thwack - running.

Thwack - my lovely sneakers

Thwack - sweating.

Thwack - mental women.

Thwack - mental men.

Thwack - stupid sweary crows.

Thwack - hijacking my bloody life.

Caratacus was panting when he finished. They carried a weeping, limping and cringing Wayne back to the changing room and the game continued. Unburdened with not having to be literally killed, Caratacus ended up knocking out Pilkas and a furious Galfinas before losing his last life. Princess Treanna was the winner and she stood on the pool table taking in the cheers of the crowd.

Caratacus stayed on his chair as Pilkas sauntered over and handed over a small purse of money.

'What's that?' Caratacus said not taking it.

'Prize money. A very impressive third. You can play again now. I am so glad you got through.' He didn't look glad, but then he didn't look anything.

Caratacus felt exhausted, he wanted to shout at this man, but he just couldn't summon up the energy. 'You should've told me,' he said instead.

Pilkas blinked. 'You challenged me, and you stated pool did you not? You won. You won it all. Not many challengers succeed. Not bad and especially not for one with such muddy shoes.'

Caratacus didn't know how to answer until he realised this was Pilkas's attempt at humour and suddenly he started laughing. Pilkas didn't join in, but his eyes shone as if he was smiling. It was then that Arthur appeared with Gwenyvere.

Caratacus thought that Arthur looked genuinely pleased to see him. The king clapped him on the arm in a friendly manner, but Gwenyvere looked concerned. 'We need to get out of here, now.'

'What's the matter?' Caratacus asked.

'Too many people, too many of the Dark, and there is something wrong. Some people are leaving fast. There is something happening. I can feel it.'

Caratacus turned to see Pilkas walking towards him. 'I'm going,' Caratacus said. 'Thanks for the company and no hard feelings.'

'Hard feelings about what?' replied Pilkas.

'The whole me nearly dying thing which was entirely your fault,' Caratacus said. Then, 'Doesn't matter. Take care and maybe I'll see you again.'

'I have your prize for you,' said Pilkas.

'I've got the money,' replied Caratacus holding up a bag of coins. Pilkas grabbed his hand as if to shake it and whispered words in his ear.

They stepped apart, their hands were still together, and they shook. Caratacus stepped back, a nervous smile on his face, and mumbled some words. In his hand appeared a pool cue.

'Now, with that,' said Pilkas 'and your skill, you could beat anyone.' Caratacus smiled, a little confused. 'Thank you, Pilkas the Grey Knight,' he said.

'Congratulations, Caratacus ap Neb.' And with that, Pilkas turned and walked off.

'So, you know Pilkas the Grey?' asked Gwenyvere sarcastically.

'Some bloke I met this afternoon while you two were catching up.'

'Maybe you aren't a no one?'

'Oh I am,' he answered. 'Can we go somewhere so I can fall down please?'

CHAPTER TWENTY-SEVEN

BEGINNERS LUCK

Caratacus hadn't slept well. It wasn't the bed, that was wonderful. It wasn't a lack of tiredness, because he was absolutely shattered. It was the intermittent knocks on the door throughout the night from Alexandra and Kimberley wanting to come in.

A broken night obviously had no effect on them, because when he shambled downstairs that morning, they were sat at the breakfast table with Gwenyvere and Mali as if they'd had the sleep that Caratacus had wanted.

'Good morning, Caratacus,' they said in unison, like school kids greeting their teacher.

'Sit, have some breakfast,' Gwenyvere pointed to the empty chair with the knife she was buttering her toast with. 'Tea? Coffee?' She asked.

The normality of it all relaxed him and he pulled the chair out and plonked himself down. 'Tea would be lovely, cheers,' he said.

'Mali. Another pot of tea please,' Gwenyvere said.

'It's Kimberley's turn!' Mali cried.

'I made the toast you silly cow!' Kimberley shouted and hissed like a cat.

'You're the silly cow, you silly cow,' spat Mali and then hissed in return.

The hissing lasted about ten seconds. Gwenyvere folded her arms, closed her eyes and winced, tapping her fingers, waiting for them to finish. Caratacus felt a foot rubbing against his groin and jumped. Alexandra looked over and smiled seductively mouthing, 'I love you.' He saw the seductive eyes but not the smile or the mouthing of 'I love you' because Alexandra was on the far end of the table and to reach his groin, she was virtually under it.

Gwenyvere swore and clapped her hands. 'For the gods' sake, girls, you're in your thirties! Can't we have a day without arguing? Alexandra, stop messing about with our guest and finish your breakfast. Kimberley, go and prepare for morning training and Mali grow up and make a pot of tea.' She paused then barked, 'Now.'

The 'now' was enough. They knew that particular now wasn't a normal now but a now now, a proper now, a right bloody now.

Gwenyvere relaxed when the girls left but nowhere near as much as Caratacus did. He smiled apologetically. They had met properly the previous night after they'd returned from Killer Pool and both had been surprised to find they liked each other. The girls not being there had helped. He, Arthur and Gwenyvere had eaten together, had a few drinks and talked until bed. He'd relaxed enough to talk about his life and when they talked with him about what was happening, he didn't feel like an outsider anymore. He didn't understand all of it and he couldn't tell them much about why Tommy had chosen him. He wanted desperately to tell them about the crone, crow and maiden but remembered their warning.

Gwenyvere opened up about leaving Arthur and the others. 'I had to get away, you know that. I never agreed with you that our last life was meant to be one of self-indulgence. I thought the Dark were not organised, but I knew they were out there. I couldn't go away with the boys to fight. You know what some armies are like with women in. I haven't the energy to willy wave. I travelled to That World for a while, cracked a few heads before learning this place was for sale and so bought it.'

Arthur asked how buying a bingo hall was fighting the Dark. They'd had a few drinks by then, not a lot but enough to be more open with each other. She got up and beckoned the men to follow her. She pushed through a door at the back of the kitchen to reveal a large training gym.

'All this is for you?' Arthur asked walking around, his feet echoing with every step.

'No! Not just for me. It's for my girls.'

'Who are they?' Arthur asked.

She smiled, 'They are of my line, like your Fir C'nu. They are all from the same town in That World. My descendants were not ones to roam it seems. After all my searching, of my only direct line, first female to first female and of an age to be trained, there were only those three. I was always impressed by the Dark Mistresses, and I thought I'd train my own and set them up to do some good.'

Caratacus winced. 'They're deadly?'

'Very.'

'Great.'

Arthur was at the far side of the gym, touching equipment as he walked past it. 'I'm not very observant, but they don't seem to like each other very much,' he said.

An old gymnastics horse stood nearby, and Gwenyvere jumped on it, backside first, and sat. Caratacus looked away a little embarrassed. He found her beguiling, beautiful, and dangerous. He still had trouble believing in everything that had happened to him, but without doubt he believed this woman was royalty, it was the way she carried herself.

She sighed, then answered. 'I think they are a bit touched in the head and yes, they don't get along. It's more than frustrating. I've been training them for five years, and they behave like teenagers when – as I feel like I shout at them every day – they are all in their thirties. Not only do they dislike each other but they hate it here.' She shook her head. 'They are among the best warriors I've ever seen, utterly deadly, but honestly, I would've let them go back to their lives if nothing had happened soon. They are driving me insane.'

When they had moved back to the front room, Gwenyvere looked at Caratacus and smiled. 'So how is the Magick feeling? What has he taught you?'

Caratacus felt embarrassed, as did Arthur ,and it was he who spoke first. 'He's not here for training. Tommaltach needed him away from London and it won't be long until he's back there.'

She side-eyed Arthur, still smiling, 'He has some Magick in him. Surely even you can feel it.'

Arthur looked at her, uncomfortable with the subject. 'Of course I can feel it Gwenni, but plenty of ordinary people have it.'

'Hi guys, I am right here,' Caratacus said sarcastically, sad, to be demoted to outsider again.

Gwenyvere laughed. 'I am sorry Caratacus. I can be rude sometimes.' She leaned over and grabbed his right hand. 'Have you tested your powers? Your Magick?' The last two words she asked sarcastically.

He was embarrassed. 'I'm sick whenever I'm near it.'

She held out his hand, palm up as if she was about to read it. She gently traced her index finger down his lifeline. He felt dizzy but wasn't sure if that was the Magick again.

'I want you to concentrate on the feeling of my finger but also acknowledge that sensation in your stomach. You've got that sensation, yes?'

His mouth was dry, he was staring into those green eyes as if bewitched by the calm way she was talking to him. He nodded. 'I've had an annoying pressure in my stomach since this all began. I thought it was acid reflux.'

'Concentrate on it. Feel it, but feel around it. Can you do that?' She asked.

It wasn't pain anymore, it was a feeling and he understood that it could be lots of feelings at once. It was a pressure. Was it like nerves? Excited expectation? It was all of them, all at the same time.

'I feel it,' he said in a whisper.

'And my finger?'

'Only just...but more,' he closed his eyes as the feeling transfused his body.

'Gently now, Caratacus. Look at your hand, look at my finger and then concentrate on the place where it was touching. When I take it away, move that pressure from you, allow it to slip away like a little fart…'

He hadn't expected the word 'fart', so he laughed but he'd already been allowing the pressure to move. A small, solid-looking bubble of yellow light rose from the palm of his hand. He felt his body tingle, the pressure that had built in his stomach disappearing for a moment. Pleasure and relief took its place.

'Concentrate on the shape now,' her voice broke his concentration, 'Go into its centre. Feel its centre. Now, feel it into a hundred different balls. Go!'

It was so easy, his mind did it like it was asking his body to breathe. He stared in delightful awe as the orb broke into tiny versions of itself. He laughed, and so did she. He looked over at Arthur like a child who'd won best actor in the school play. Arthur smiled back.

'That is just the start,' she said. 'You just need to train your mind first before any of the big stuff but sorting out the Magick in your body is always the best way to start.'

He didn't know why he asked then. Maybe he had fallen a little in love with her, 'So… you two? You know? The stories? How come you are still good friends?'

They both smiled, she laughed. 'What? When Arthur committed incest while we were married or after I ran off with that glorious manifestation of chivalrous manhood, Lancelot?'

Caratacus smiled in embarrassment, 'Well...either…'

Arthur walked past, he was a tipsy. 'You must know that's all bullshit by now? We are back with bloody bards again, aren't we? Peredur, Cub and Gwalch thought it would be great to have a bard with us and tell some of our stories, a bit of PR but you can never control a story or their ego. Hardly any of it happened like they said.'

'You were never in love?' asked Caratacus.

'Not in love. Oh yes, I love him. I love him very much but like that? Ugh,' she smiled.

'You should be so lucky….' Arthur replied and then he giggled, then she did, and then it turned to laughter so contagious Caratacus caught it.

It hadn't been long before Caratacus felt beyond tired. He didn't know if it was the wine or a few days that would've tested the endurance of a primary school teacher. Half an hour later he was in bed and had the best twenty minutes sleep he'd ever had before Kimberley, the first of his callers, gently knocked on his door. Real Caratacus, the old Caratacus wanted to open the door. This Caratacus, this new one who had done lots of new things, even producing a ball of light from his hand, took over and reminded all the other Caratacuses that while beautiful, the girl outside was a trained killer and absolutely mental. New Caratacus was victorious and after five minutes of knocking, silence fell, and he fell asleep for thirty-five winks before the next desperate tapping on his door by Alexandra.

Back at breakfast, Caratacus asked where Arthur was. 'Chopping logs,' was the quick answer from Gwenyvere. 'He knows he's carrying a few pounds.'

'Do you need logs?' Caratacus asked.

'Hell no, we use gas.'

He paused. 'Gweni?' he asked.

'Woah there tiger! You're a nice guy, but we aren't at that point in our relationship yet. I think Arthur had known me two hundred years before we got to Gweni.' She said it smiling which took a lot out of the sting Caratacus felt.

'Sorry,' he mumbled.

'Forget it. Anyway, what was the question?'

'Can you teach me a bit more magic please?'

'It's Magick but I'm not sure we'll have time. I think you have places to be and so do I.'

'We're leaving?'

'Like we talked about last night. Something big is happening and it's clear that Arthur is not safe. He needs to get to the Lake, but he also needs to be defended. I am sorry handsome, but I'm not sure you are enough to help the Once and Future King on your own,' she smiled.

He returned her humour. 'What? Even though I can shoot a non-aggressive ball out of the palm of my hands?'

Mali came in with the large pot of tea, Arthur close behind, his body drenched with sweat.

'Great! Tea!' he exclaimed.

Caratacus saw that the change in Arthur was continuing, he was obviously stiff from physical work, but he was moving differently. Gwenyvere smiled, 'Good workout?' she asked.

He smiled back, 'It wasn't a workout. I just fancied chopping logs. I'm keeping myself busy.'

'Of course,' she said to herself. A second later, the smile had gone as a breathless Kimberley rushed into the room. The blonde woman stood straight to compose herself and when she looked at Mali and Alexandra she smiled, 'I've just heard a herald from over the bridge. It's war! An army of the Dark has entered Cantre'r Gwaelod!'

'WHAT?' Both Gwenyvere and Arthur shouted.

'What else did he say? Was it surrender or has Gwyddno King been defeated? How haven't we heard of any armies massing?' Gwenyvere and Arthur were in utter shock. Caratacus didn't know what to think except that this was the happiest he had seen these three girls since his arrival.

Kimberley's smile grew further, she spoke like she was telling a very exciting bedtime story. 'It's mental out there! People are fleeing across the bridge, even the trolls from the centre are leaving. I just punched some man in the face,' she clapped.

'So, looting has started?' asked Arthur.

Kimberley's smile changed to a look of puzzlement, 'No, he knocked into me.'

Gwenyvere ignored her, 'I've heard nothing of war in the kingdoms. Yes, there are skirmishes further north, they've always happened and always will do, but what the hell is an army doing this far south?'

Arthur stopped pacing, 'What if this is all part of the same plan? What if it's about me? What if it's about those bastards going after all of us? This world is on the edge of chaos, and it seems That one is as well! What if it's all connected?'

'There are too many coincidences for me to argue against but what do we do? The need to keep you hidden still stands,' said Gwenyvere who held up her hand as if knowing that Arthur was going to disagree. 'Listen, we have no warriors except me and the girls. We also have no idea what's going on, what the threat is, and while we have a bloody good idea, we don't know who the enemy is.'

She stopped speaking, going into deep thought. Not for the first time, Caratacus felt out of his depth, not being able to add anything.

She turned around the chair and sat opposite Arthur, 'I'm out of ideas. You need to get to the Lake like Tommaltach wanted. You need Caledfwlch but they might have something else for you.'

'I haven't needed her for thousands of years. I have Excalibur,' Arthur replied.

'Do you honestly think that?' Said Gwenyvere, 'Do you know what I think? This is it. This is the end of the worlds. The Dark have made their move. What would King Arthur the Once and Future King need at the end?' She pointed directly at Arthur's face and when he didn't answer she repeated her question, jabbing her finger into his forehead gently on each word.

He lazily swatted her finger away and mumbled. She lightly slapped his swat away and repeated, 'What would King Arthur, the Once and Future King need at the end?'

'Caledfwlch,' he said, a little louder and a little clearer.

'We know where she is, so that's where we are going,' she stood up. 'I need to close everything, you lot need to pack, and we can meet here after lunch.'

She looked to the smiling girls, 'Go and close everything and prepare for a journey.' Then, she said to herself, 'I'm more afraid of the reaction to closing the bingo hall than I am of the end of the world,' before following her descendants out.

Caratacus looked over at Arthur, 'She doesn't mess about.'

Arthur smiled, 'Never did. The strongest, the most decisive, the most just, she is more the King Arthur of stories than I ever was.'

Caratacus returned the smile, 'I think you're doing great,' and went to get ready to leave.

An hour later Caratacus heard his name being called. It was one of the girls, Alexandra he thought, and for once it didn't sound like she wanted to kidnap him.

'Yes?' he shouted. He was right, it was her, dark haired like Mali but with wider doe eyes.

'Go to the kitchen, you are needed. We aren't coming with you. Something big is happening.' And then she stepped away.

He thought it must have been something important as she hadn't tried anything on. He felt Magick ignite in his tummy as fear and excitement mixed.

He made it down the large stairs and suddenly she was there again in front of him. Before he could do anything, she kissed him sensuously on the mouth. He was about to push her away when she stopped. She smiled and winked. 'Goodbye Caratacus ap Neb.'

He didn't have chance to reply as she was gone. He walked into a kitchen of bustle and asked what was happening.

'We have just been told that an army is crossing the bridge, maybe two. You have to leave. We have to hold them,' Gwenyvere said as she walked through the room.

'No,' said Arthur, 'We all go together. What the hell will you four do against an army?' There was no answer just the girls joyously packing things away in cupboards. Arthur looked stressed; he leaned on the table. 'No army from over there has set foot on This World for...what? I can't even remember. Three thousand years? What the hell are they doing?'

Gwenyvere breezed through again, 'Arthur, you and Caratacus are important in whatever is happening. You need to head to the Lake. We've kept you here too long. Me and the girls are not going to charge an army so don't panic but we have to do something to slow them down.'

'This is just panic! They aren't going to send an army over the bridge. It breaks ancient laws that even the Dark abide by,' Arthur complained.

'Know that do you?'

'No but…'

'Then that's decided,' she stopped moving and exhaled. 'I am going to slow them down, give you a chance to get away. If my plan works, we'll join you at the Lake or we'll head to one of Tommaltach's safe houses in London and lay low. You think I haven't made plans in case of an emergency?'

Mali moaned as she walked quickly past. 'We are trained for one hundred and forty-three scenarios and yes, armies on the bridge is one of them.'

Arthur paused, thinking, and then nodded. 'OK. let's go,' he told Caratacus who nodded back.

Gwenyvere stopped in front of Caratacus and smiled, her green eyes shining, 'Cati, good luck and I'll see you soon. Remember what I've taught you, remember the feeling in your stomach and my finger on your hand.' Caratacus nodded finding it hard to say anything but she continued, 'I think you are actually a big part of this story, so stay alive. Look after the old man and yourself, OK?' She kissed him, softly on the cheeks.

'Thank you, Gwenyvere,' he said blushing.

She tapped his face in a friendly way. 'Call me Gweni.'

Her goodbye with Arthur was longer and with tears. Caratacus didn't notice as he was surrounded by Kimberley and Alexandra.

He sighed. 'Can't we just say goodbye properly?' he asked, slowly stepping backwards.

'That's what we are doing. We don't want to marry you now, Caratacus. War is here, we are happy, so you are no use to us now,' blonde Kimberley said.

'Goodbye, Caratacus ap Neb. Don't die,' said Alexandra.

'Err that's nice,' Caratacus replied and without another word they moved away and continued to prepare.

CHAPTER TWENTY-EIGHT

IS GALAHAD DEAD?

Of course he bloody isn't.

He wondered for one second if he was waking up back in the cave. How many years had passed this time he thought? Five? Five hundred? It didn't feel like the cave and usually there was silence and now he could hear bird song. The up and down of blackbirds, the high pitched ratatatat of the chaffinch and above all the carrion, clarion call of the crow. He was face down again but this time there was no getting up. He couldn't even open his eyes. He started to remember sharp shots of recall, the orc squads and how he thought it was the end. He recalled Geraint and the crying of the living because of the dead and finally he remembered the explosion.

He willed his eyes to open, but his will was ignored, the same with moving his head, his arms and his legs. He would've panicked if he hadn't fallen back into the sleep of the exhausted.

He groaned as he was lifted. In his delirium, he saw the orcs lining up ready to charge, then he didn't. He saw Arthur smiling. He smiled himself. He felt a soft bed underneath him. He felt the explosion again. He saw his deaths, all of them. Catrin kissing him tenderly. He cried because he knew she was gone. Did he cry? He wanted to.

He saw Carys, his daughter, and in an instant, he was throwing flowers in the river where her ashes had been scattered. He missed her. Why did she die? Anger. Loss.

He saw his friends sat around, battle weary. Did they have swords or guns? They left and he felt a longing for lost laughter and love. He saw a tunnel of light. Was this death?

A shape came towards him, a huge man who dwarfed even himself. He could see the antlers that came from his head, a skull-like grin. He felt dread and revulsion and it, he, her stepped faster. 'It's over', it said, eyes flashing gold. 'It's my time. I have come for you.'

Galahad put his hands up to protect himself. He couldn't. He tried to run. He couldn't.

The thing came closer…

'I am coming to end you and everyone you love,' it said.

And closer…

He couldn't move.

It stopped and reached its hand to touch Galahad's face. He screamed and this time his eyes opened and light flooded in. He grabbed in fear as he shut his eyes against it. He clawed his face trying to remove the dark stain that covered it. He felt strong arms holding him back against the bed which made him struggle further.

'Gal,' he heard.

'Get Piogerix,' he heard.

'Thank the gods,' said Tristan.

Tristan.

He stopped struggling.

'Who is there?' he cried. Or tried to. What he heard was a croaked noise.

'Shhh, Galahad. Rest.'

'No please, no more rest. Talk to me,' Galahad said. He was panicking again.

'Take a drink.'

'Tristan?'

'Who else, Galahad?'

'Cub! When we heard you lived, I was so…so,' he croaked. Tristan placed a hand on the big man's shoulder.

'Hey, come now, all is well. I think the gods watch over me. Fortunately, the messenger found me before I returned to my room and now, I am here, to save you, to save all the other old men and save the worlds. Good to see you awake. We've been worried.'

'I haven't been worried,' another voice.

'Cai?' Galahad asked.

'I'm sorry I wasn't there, my friend. I'd gone for a walk and ran back when I saw the explosion,' Cai answered, and Galahad felt a hand take his and he squeezed. He slowly opened his eyes. They were getting accustomed to the light, shapes appeared above him as he lay on that comfy bed he had dreamed of.

Hours later and after periods of snooze he was sat up in bed, ready for company. He still felt drained, there was still pain in his joints when he moved but he did feel better and for the moment, safe. Around his bed were people he had known, trusted and loved for so many lifetimes. They were in one of the large rooms at the back of the Triple T. Cai sat next to the bed while Tristan stood the other side. At the foot of the bed were the Three Kings.

Piogerix sat on the end of the bed. Behind him stood Tommy McKracken, hands in the pockets of a suit so sharp you could cut paper with. Next to him and taking up two people's spaces was Adda Mynyddmawr. The big man was dressed straight out of a Tolkienesque taproom, red trousers and a fur jerkin which at that very moment was being covered in cheese and onion crisp crumbs as he emptied the remains of the packet into his mouth. If you thought the jerkin was getting messy you should've seen the beard.

Galahad was told of what had happened immediately following his black out. He was right at the time, it was going to be the end, the grand sacrifice that would have destroyed all within that Magick infused blast.

Piogerix had, for reasons only known to himself, returned to the pub in the middle of the attack and immediately felt the build-up of Magick. He had no time to stop the blast but, in that microsecond, had managed to suspend time around Galahad and the men, so the blast did not impact them...so much. It still sucked life out of them and cast them around like rag dolls. Galahad cried again for Geraint but knew there was little time for proper mourning. When he asked about Arthur or Caratacus, he was met with silence. There was no news, and he didn't know whether to be relieved or worried. But they couldn't wait for everybody to heal properly; they had to plan. The news the Kings had brought meant that everything had changed. They had their last task.

'Where's Neil?'

Piogerix smiled, 'He's just back from his run.'

'Weirdo,' snapped Cai.

'Leave him alone, Cai,' said Galahad and then he smiled as he remembered Neil on the night of the attack, 'He really can fight, can't he? I thought the old man had felt sorry for him keeping him while releasing the rest of the Fir C'nu, but bloody hell, he was like a man possessed, and it seems he can recover faster than us old codgers.'

'Talk of the devil,' said Adda as Neil pushed the door. He bowed, 'Highnesses, my Lords…'

He was cut off as Maggie Rosser bustled in behind him with plates of sandwiches. Two boys followed her, one carrying two plates of small biscuit-like snacks, the other with two jugs of orange squash.

'Ale,' demanded Adda.

Maggie Rosser set down the plates on the side table next to Galahad's bed.

'Jam. Peanut butter,' she said as she wiped her hands on her pinny. Another boy came in and set down plastic glasses for the squash.

'Ale,' repeated Adda.

Maggie walked through the door, 'Breakfast. No ale. Ale isn't for breakfast. Squash is good for now unless someone would like a cup of tea.'

'I'll have a cup of tea?' said Tristan.

'Well, you know where the kitchen is don't you, g'boy,' and with that Maggie left.

Adda mimicked her as soon as he made sure the door was properly closed, 'Well you know where the kitchen is! Ale isn't for breakfast. It bloody is! Anyway, I could've had a mimosa or a bloody Mary. Pass me a jam, Cub.'

Tommy had been silent so far, his face grave, and when he spoke everybody listened. 'Enough of the chit chat. We are in so much trouble I don't know where to begin. When your boys started dying, we thought it was about us. It's bigger. Our messenger of prophecy has been killed by the Dark.' Grumbles started from different sides of the room before Tommy held up his hands. 'That's not all. We have reports of armies of the Dark – orcs, elves, the lot – coming together in That World. We also have word that there are armies of the Dark here as well.'

'Bigger than the orc squads sent against us?' asked Galahad.

'I am talking Armies, not squads,' answered Tommaltach.

'They can't just bring armies from That World here! I don't have to tell you all this. There are laws! The nations won't stand for it!' Galahad exclaimed.

'I don't get it either,' Tristan said in agreement, 'I can see why they want to kill us, but we have barely seen them properly since our return. Yes, they were in Syria, Libya and the day-to-day stuff but there was no plan. What are the world governments saying?'

Tommaltach folded his arms. 'We've been stupid and lazy. The Dark didn't go to ground when you all appeared. You must have appeared because of what they were doing in the shadows. They wanted us to think they were doing nothing. They've been empire building. I know why governments aren't angry with the breaking of truces, they've been infiltrated by Dark.'

'What about That World?' asked Galahad.

'Banners are being called. Peace for a generation means they've also been unprepared. Standing armies in the lands of the south are at their lowest in history.'

'So that's it then?' Cai stood up. 'We're all going to die?'

'I don't think so,' Piogerix replied and then he glanced at Tommy. 'We don't think so. They aren't as confident as they should be. Something is missing.'

'Arthur?' from Galahad.

'Maybe,' Tommy shrugged.

'Caratacus ap Neb?' asked Galahad, 'Where does he fit into all this?'

Cai stormed, 'Yeah who the hell is he? I'd never heard of him and then he's here as if he's one of us and then the little bastard is the only person with Arthur. I don't like it.'

'You don't like anything, Cai, so why don't you keep that flapping piece of skin beneath your nose shut while we think about what we have to do, eh?' Tommaltach didn't snap but Cai was told.

'We should know,' Cai mumbled, unhappy at being chastened but unwilling to push a man who regularly sent people on a one-way trip to the bottom of the Thames.

Tommaltach sighed, 'To be honest, I don't know what to make of Caratacus's part in all this. He was mentioned in a very small prophecy from a crackhead at the same time as I was going to get in touch with him regardless. The boy has been told to get Arthur to the Lake. If they've survived, that's where they're headed.'

'Right then,' said Adda, 'we let Gal rest for another day and then we head off after Arthur.'

'Actually, no,' Tommaltach said. 'The boys' – he always called Arthur's warriors that – 'will have to set off as soon as possible. But we and Piggy need to play a bigger game and see the bigger picture.'

Adda folded his arms, 'I don't do strategy, Tommaltach! You know that! Let me go with the boys. Cub will cach his pants if he has to have another fight without me.'

Tristan smiled but said nothing.

'No, Adda. We need you.' Then, before the big man could reply, Tommaltach added, 'Also these boys will be doing a lot of walking.' He was serious, but he said it as a joke, and it lightened the mood.

Joke or not, that decided it for Adda. He smiled. 'Fine. I'm with you then.'

CHAPTER TWENTY-NINE
CASSIE COMES AS GWENYVERE GOES

As Gwenyvere had told Caratacus, there had been no pitched battles for her during the Second World War, there had been no point trying to go through the rigmarole of being part of male only units. The constant personality battles would have been more draining than the real ones. They had been brought back for a small role that time; the war had been something that the people of This World had to do themselves.

It was very easy to blame the Dark for the rise of the Nazis, but it let people off the hook. Because it hadn't been Dark overlords in cloaks that had led to the murder of millions, it had been ordinary people.

Hitler was a man. The people who brought him to power were mothers and fathers who loved their children. The guards at the camps were also people. Just people.

A month after 'the boys' had dropped into Italy it had been Gwenyvere's turn to go into France. It was there, amongst the Resistance that she had learned how to kill with guns and blow things up and now she needed the latter skill. Her plan had formed as soon as a worried herald had crossed the bridge to inform people what was happening. An army was crossing and there was word that there were another two following. There was panic everywhere. Horns were being blown which added to the chaos. Fights broke out as people who could use them clamoured to the pub toilets to escape.

The toilets had been her first plan for Arthur – Magick away and hide – but she knew that portals could be watched and would be even more so at a time when the Dark moved.

She'd also thought about sending the girls away with Arthur and the thought remained. But why would she do that? She had found, recruited, and trained them for exactly this situation. They were ready. They'd been ready for years. They were here to lay down their lives for others.

But, in the end, Gwenyvere hadn't been able to send them after Arthur or into battle. For hours they'd hidden in the tunnels below the bingo hall, Gwenyvere furious that events had overtaken her planning.

Her revised plan was to take out the officers. Leave them leaderless and let them flounder.

But she soon realised that it was time that was needed, not winning. So she changed her plan again.

They weren't just tunnels; this was an armoury. She'd built it along with the training gym when she'd recruited the girls. When Gwenyvere decided to train warriors of the Light she was going to do it properly.

She looked at them stretching, helping each other prepare and she felt an ache in her stomach. She loved these annoying girls. She needed them safe and wanted them to have happy lives. She hadn't told them the original plan so there was no reason for them to know she was changing it. They had wanted to leave this place since the day they had been brought here so she was going to make that happen.

'We are staying with you Mother,' Mali said, folding her arms.

Gwenyvere's stomach lurched with pride at being addressed as 'Mother'. It happened so rarely. Her jaw went rigid to stop herself from showing her emotions.

'You are not sending us away when you need us most,' Kimberley added, face angry at hearing Gwenyvere suggest they should take the portals out.

'But you've never wanted to be here anyway. Go and get yourself free now, while you can!' Gwenyvere pleaded.

'We've never wanted to be here because it's been so bloody *boring* here. We didn't want to be training, serving tea or calling the bingo. You trained us to fight but never let us! You told us we were meant to be like the Dark Mistresses, you told us all about them, but you never let us go out and do what we were trained for,' Alexandra said, insistently.

Gwenyvere was embarrassed because Alexandra was right. She'd wanted warriors of the Light, but she'd kept them penned up and hemmed in. She put her arms around them, pulling them into an embrace. Gwenyvere was angry, that here, when the end was close, she had this. Their heads were leaning on each other and for a moment the young girls' faces cracked a little bit. 'You aren't going to die?' asked Alexandra.

'No,' she said convincingly to all but herself.

***

There were no more desperate creatures trying to use the portal in the toilets of the Flying Chair. The ones that hadn't got through were now being stacked up with other dead bodies just outside the visitor centre. An orc squad from the Black Jackal tribe had been tasked with guarding the toilet. They weren't expecting any attacks, but they had been told to expect two important visitors: Dark Mistresses.

At-Jakazad had enjoyed the slaughter as part of the first squads to arrive and while he was nervous about any visit from the strange and – even by his standards – cruel Mistresses, he was pleased that his squad had been honoured to guard the portal for their arrival. Beating the squad from the weakling Fat Jackal tribe was an even sweeter prize.

He had been horrified when he'd seen the mixture of orc tribes that had been chosen to be part of the first army. It showed a lack of knowledge about their people's history. It was hard enough to see other Jackal tribes but the coming together of Wolf, Hawk and Axe tribes almost resulted in a battle before they crossed the bridge.

The door of the toilet flashed briefly, and two Dark Mistresses walked out.

'Report,' was all Cassie said. He bowed his head and did. Every pub that this one could travel to had warriors on the door. They were looking for two men approaching middle age, one bearded fat man and a thinner one with stubble and nice but dirty shoes.

'They have not come through any of the portals, Dark Mistress,' he said.

She looked at her partner. 'Then they're either here or on the roads,' she said before addressing the nervous orc again. 'Anything else?'

Cassie had a feeling inside and it made her uncomfortable. She was enjoying this power, she enjoyed being in charge. She could, without any comeback, kill this orc in front of her. She shook her head suddenly and the orc flinched.

'Anything else?' She barked to hide her embarrassment.

If he had bowed any lower, he'd have cut his stubby, green nose on the floor, 'I only know my own orders, Dark Mistress.'

'Who is in charge?'

'Human called Barrat Skee. He has set up Headquarters in the bingo hall.'

'Where?'

'Out here and then to the left. You will see it when you leave.'

***

Barrat Skee shook the match he'd used to light his cigar then threw it on the floor. The march over the bridge had been easy. Now, all he had to do was wait until all his forces crossed and then move towards London. An army from That World in This World! He'd never thought he'd see the day.

He sucked on the cigar, blew the blue smoke out, and laughed. He'd been in the army of the Dark all his adult life and now things were finally happening. He'd waited long enough although he'd never thought about coming over here. What he'd always wanted was destruction of the southern states in That World, those stuck-up Kings, Queens or whatever they wanted to call themselves.

He'd been the senior commander when they accepted Gwyddno King's surrender. He sneered when he thought about the old man and his wife – all high and mighty, all regal looking. He'd wanted to execute them there and then, but he had orders. His only consolation was the look on their faces as he personally ran through their personal retinue in front of them. Shit on the parasites. Of all the generals of the Dark, only he had come from nothing. He'd grown up on the streets of Dinas, an orphan thief before he'd been caught by the authorities. He'd been sentenced to death, but he'd escaped, joined the armies of the Dark and never looked back.

Knock knock.

'Yes Major,' Skee said, as a straight-backed man in uniform came in.

'Dark Mistresses to see you, sir.'

Shit.

'Of course, show them in,' he said and stood up, straightening out his uniform.

Two women walked in, both, to his eyes, incredibly young. He couldn't help it; he knew most of the Dark Mistresses were dangerous, but he hated their confidence.

Cassie was impressed with the man in front of her. He hid his fear well but did little to hide his contempt. What she wasn't impressed with was having to work with another Dark Mistress who had met up with her in the pub portal before traveling. Gretchen L'nteel was the name but Cassie was sure she would soon forget it. She was as all Mistresses were: cold, calculating, and efficient. L'nteel had updated her before arriving in the General's office. Cassie's mission, however, stayed the same. Find Arthur and kill him.

The walk to the office made her angry. It was obvious she'd changed and while her companion strolled through the bodies of innocents caught by the army of the Dark unworried, Cassie felt ashamed. It made her even more certain about getting out of this alive and taking Olivia far away.

'Barrat Skee,' he said formally. They introduced themselves as stiffly as he did. It was Cassie who spoke next, 'We are not here to join your army, General.'

Skee nodded, trying not to show his relief, while Cassie continued, 'We need all intelligence about sightings of Arthur.'

Gretchen L'nteel interrupted. She had been the one who had told The Exile about what had been going on, and she was not going to lose authority to a whore. 'He has been seen here in the days before the invasion. Separate reports state his company was a human male and 4 human females.'

The name Arthur caused a ripple of excitement in the General and the thought of bringing back the bane of the Dark in chains or in bits appealed to him, 'What do you need? You have whatever of my advanced party that are here, or you may wait for the rest of the invasion armies to arrive over the bridge.'

Unsure, the two killers looked at each other, before a warning horn was heard.

Genuine shock appeared on Skee's face. 'That can't be right!' He started to move to the door to find out what was going on. 'That means we are under attack!'

***

The flare flew into the sky, straight from the visitor centre where the bridge entered. If everything hadn't had been completely awful because of the brutal, invading army who were there to kill and enslave everybody, it would have looked really pretty.

The horns that had blown in terror at the army's arrival were now blown by that very army as they realised that they were under attack.

Minutes before, Alexandra had walked into the visitor centre like she was on a morning stroll. Two guards stopped her inside the door. They said one and half suggestive things to her before being deaded. The hundreds of soldiers who were coming off the bridge stared in horror as a small girl calmly pulled out grenades from her shoulder bag, plucked out the pins and threw them in all directions, watching explosion after explosion tear walls, ceilings, and flesh.

When the smoke cleared, Alexandra stood in what she thought was a pretty cool fighting stance, legs apart, spear in both hands facing towards the debris she had created. She stayed like that for a minute before accepting that anybody who was keen on killing her was digging themselves out of a collapsed building. She shrugged, fired the flare to tell her sisters she'd done her bit, then unwrapped a bit of chewing gum, lobbed it into her mouth and sat on the end of an undamaged table checking her socials.

The flare had gone up as the second army passed the top of the bridge. Underneath it, Gwenyvere had finished planting the explosives she'd recovered from the armoury. She saw the flare and smiled knowing that at least one of her daughters still lived and was following her plan.

By the time they had fully formulated the plan the army had been in full control. All the buildings were being used as command posts while soldiers continued to cross the bridge, move through the visitor centre and out to make camp until they received their next orders. There were thousands already here and thousands were on the bridge.

Returning from a final scout around, Gwenyvere had faced the girls who sat on a table swinging their legs like they were in primary school. They'd looked expectantly at her, and she'd shaken her head slightly bemused that they weren't on their phones or arguing.

'Just so we are clear. Alexandra, make your way to the visitor centre. As soon as you see the banners of the second army reach the very top of the bridge, fire the flare gun for me to set the timer,' Alexandra nodded.

'Mali? Kimberley? As soon as the flare goes get in amongst them. Cause carnage, make noise and make them think they are under attack by a bigger force. Don't get caught!' They also nodded, their faces full of concentration.

'I will be on the gantry just below the top of the bridge,' she continued.

'How?' asked Kimberley.

'You do know I'm a Magicker?' She answered, sarcastically.

'Yeah, but you never told us you were that good,' came the response from the blonde killer.

Gwenyvere smiled. 'I have love. You just haven't been listening.'

Kimberley had the grace to bow her head and smile.

'Listen, this is important,' she said, as they leaned forward, beginning to look worried. 'As soon the flare goes, I'll set the timer and we'll have minutes. You two have to create chaos immediately.'

'I want the pub!' said Mali and Gwen's heart sank as she waited for the arguments to start.

But Kimberley stuck her hand out. 'Agreed.' As Mali shook it, Gwen fished out three necklaces and handed one to each of the girls. Their faces were sceptical, and she rolled her eyes.

'Stop it before you start,' she warned, 'I just want to say how proud I am of you. I know it's been tough, and you haven't wanted to be here since you arrived.'

'That's not true!' exclaimed Alexandra.

'You could've fooled me.' Gwen's laugh changed immediately to a sad smile. 'I'm proud of you and you need to know I love you and if you have any affection for me…'

'We love you, too!' Mali snapped, and the others agreed loudly.

'Please,' Gwen pleaded, 'this is hard enough. If you do love me, you will promise to stay as safe as you can, regardless of whatever else is going on. I need to know you'll be ok. I've had these necklaces made; they are sapphire because that is my birthstone. Wear it for me. It contains a small part of my Magick that should boost yours. I initially made them to aid you in combat. They can transport anywhere, once, using line of sight. BUT,' she emphasised holding up her finger, 'please don't use it for that today ok? If you are in trouble at any point during the fighting you must use them to take you directly into the cubicles of the Flying chair and then you can portal to Welshpool. When our tasks are done, we'll meet at the cockpit in the town. Are we all clear?'

Mali grabbed Gwenyvere's hand, putting it on her cheek. 'We understand, mother.'

'So, again! Once everything is set and you have caused chaos, we'll meet at the cockpit then we disappear. So, what are we doing?' She tested, 'Alexandra?'

'I blow the visitor centre and if I there are too many guarding the portal then I use this,' she held up the necklace.

'Mali?'

'We make chaos, then pub.'

'Where to?' Gwen asked.

'Welshpool,' they said it together.

'And where then?'

'You'll tell us?' Kimberley said nervously.

'What if I can't?'

'You will,' Kimberley said again.

'No! Stop this! Anything could happen! What if I don't make it for a week? What do you do then? You have to be grown-ups.'

Silence.

'GIRLS!'

'We stay alive and then we get to the address for the sly King.'

Gwen nodded, 'Good.'

'Everything is going to be ok though,' Alexandra said

'I know that.' It was said with no doubt and the girls smiled at the certainty.

***

Gwenyvere tied off the last bit of dynamite and smiled. It reminded her of Amiens, of the Resistance and of being utterly alive. She stopped to watch her descendants fighting, hundreds of feet below. Not one looked or behaved like Gwenyvere but these past few hours, after all the years of being together, they reminded her of Anwen, her first daughter. She blew hard as if it could expel the painfully joyous memories. She attached the detonator to make it ready.

The soldiers fighting Mali and Kimberley were experienced, they had raided the enemy and had stood in battle. But they didn't know how to deal with repressed, well trained and unhinged thirty-something women in open combat. The bodies stacked up as they ran out of ideas on what to do next. They had rushed these hissing girls and it hadn't worked; they had ventured forth in groups, and it had ended just as badly.

'This is awesome!' Kimberley shouted while sucking in air and struggling to pull one of her daggers from the stomach of her last rival. Her face streaked with blood, her eyes shining maniacally, she looked around at her sword sister who smiled in return and answered, 'This is easy! Can't we just kill them all one by one until all the armies are dead?'

Kimberley chuckled, it was almost time to go but she quickly glanced at the bridge, worried about Gwenyvere. Her mouth dropped 'Mali? Look!' She pointed, 'She's been seen! Soldiers are starting to get to the platform. They'll kill her.'

Mali paused for a moment thinking about everything that Gwenyvere had drilled into them then she looked at Kimberley and smiled viciously, holding her sapphire necklace, 'Let's get up there.'

***

Cassie had also seen the interloper under the bridge. When she saw warriors start to stream over the side to deal with them, she thought it would be dealt with. It was the appearance of two fighting women out of nowhere on top of the bridge that changed her mind. She pointed up and said simply to the other Mistress, 'We are needed.'

***

Gwenyvere had fired five arrows and five bodies lay on the ground before she called her sword. It didn't matter that she'd been found. All that was needed was for her to set the timer and transport out. Fewer warriors were lowering to the platform to stop her, and she knew why when she recognised the battle screams of the girls above.

She swore in anger, helplessness touching her.

She couldn't let them die up there, but it meant she couldn't set the timer.

When she reached the top, it was clear that it was the entire second army that were the ones in trouble. The warriors on the bridge had felt a sudden surge of excitement when the two women first appeared. That was soon replaced by panic then fear then panic and fear. Now they hung back, a huge circle of men formed, unwilling to join the pile of dead bodies surrounding the howling women.

Gwenyvere was furious with them; the power of their necklaces was wasted now. 'What have you done?' She screamed.

They both flinched still facing the enemy, but Mali shouted, 'You couldn't see that they were coming to kill you!'

'I'd have managed,' Gwen shouted thinking furiously of an escape plan when to her dismay two female warriors, landed with the grace of cats on the bridge and immediately fell into crouching fighting stances.

'I see them,' shouted Gwenyvere, her heart sinking at the sight of the Dark Mistresses, 'Kimberley! Hold that army back while I help Mali.'

She swore in anger, she had to rethink everything, and had to do it fast.

***

Mali had never been hit like that before. She looked up at Cassie from the floor, initially in shock but then in anger. She spat blood and hissed.

Gwenyvere's decision to deal with the Dark Mistresses quickly was made through logic rather than over confidence. The explosions below, the horns, the flare had all helped to spread panic amongst the squashed soldiers on the bridge. Keep one of the girls on them and keep them quiet for as long as possible. She would defeat a Mistress quickly while Mali held her ground against the other. It wasn't working. These two were deadly. Mali was being overwhelmed and even Gwenyvere was struggling.

Dodging yet another blow from the Mistress opposite, calm entered her head. She knew what she needed to do. She parried another attack from Gretchen, the sweep that followed was timed to perfection and it was only the quick reflexes of the Dark Mistress that stopped a follow up killing blow. Instead, Gwen's sword cut deeply into her opponent's back. Gretchen rolled away to give herself breathing space to fight again but Gwenyvere took that time to find a way to save Mali who was moments away from death.

***

Mali was sure she was going to die. She felt like a child opposite this girl. On her knees, exhausted, she struggled to lift her head but managed a last lift of her sword to block another killing blow. It drove her onto her back.

***

Cassie felt a moment's doubt when she stood above the girl. She'd fought better opponents, but she hesitated as she went to finish it. It was half arsed and the girl, with one last effort blocked it, pushing herself sprawling onto the floor. Now it was time for this girl to die.

***

A Magick word and a blast came from Gwen's free hand, it was a weak blast but that was the intention. Knock the Mistress back, gain time. It worked and Gwen reached Mali's side.

***

As the shockwave hit, Cassie hesitated, waiting for the next move.

***

Gwenyvere leant over Mali who was about to apologise for letting her down. Gwenyvere shushed her, put her hand onto her chest over the necklace, her eyes glowing. Mali then realised what she was doing and cried out. Gwenyvere smiled, 'Love you,' and whispered words of Magick.

Mali was in the toilet of the Flying chair; Alexandra was already there.

***

On the bridge, the soldiers hadn't moved, not one, not even the most gruntified grunt wanted to risk being maimed or worse at the hands of this blonde woman. Kimberley hissed at them before turning her head briefly to see Mali being tended by Gwenyvere before disappearing. She got it. They weren't getting off the bridge. Their necklaces had one journey in them, and they'd used theirs to get up here. Mother could not have that much Magick left in her so the bridge would have to go but with them on it.

She shrugged and with a terrifying scream, ran at the Mistress in front of Gwenyvere, swinging her sword for a killing blow.

Cassie heard the scream and back flipped away landing delicately on the wall of the bridge.

Kimberley fell as the expectant impact disappeared. She rolled into a defensive stance, sword facing Cassie.

'Wait!' said Gwen and years of training permeated through Kimberley's anger, she hissed automatically.

The Mistresses were back on their feet now and slowly approaching.

'I'm not going,' Kimberley spat.

'Fine,' Gwen shouted back, 'Listen to me. Go down to the platform below, get the detonator and bring it here. Don't argue, just go.'

'But them?' Kimberley asked incredulously. She knew her mother could fight but after using Magick and against these two? A final 'Go,' made her move.

'Mine,' said Gretchen.

Cassie shook her head, 'There is no point risking anything here, let…'

'Mine,' said Gretchen cutting off Cassie who shrugged. Their opponent moved well but she was clearly weakened by Magick use. Even an injured Dark Mistress should finish this fight quickly and then she'd find and kill the other.

Cassie blinked, astonished as she saw the point of a spear out the back of Gretchen's head. The speed of the red headed woman was something to witness, and she wondered who the hell she was. It had been so fast. The woman had clumsily thrown her sword at the Mistress, an old tactic but usually used by Magick users against less talented opponents. Throw weapon away and call another weapon to use when closer. There is no way any Dark Mistress would have been fooled but it was the speed with which this woman had approached that was astounding. Two massive sidesteps, a duck inside a blow as the spear appeared in her hands in time to be driven up through the neck.

Gwenyvere pulled out the spear, looked at Cassie, smiled and winked. She felt the deja-vu of death and like every time before, hated it. She wasn't ready. She wanted to spend more time with the girls. Why, right at the end, had they become everything she'd wanted? Years of watching the sullen little sods sulk their way through life, begrudgingly doing the tiniest things. She realised that the voice in her head sounded exactly like her daughters when they were being sullen little sods. I wonder where they got it from, she wondered.

Cassie had thought that the blonde woman had escaped, and that the older woman was giving her time. It confused her when the former appeared and moved to the other's side. Cassie looked at the hundreds of warriors who were stood back watching. You didn't get to see Dark Mistresses fight often in a lifetime, so why not?

Cassie pointed her sword at the two women and shouted over at the warriors, 'Don't just stand there. Kill them!' Before looking in horror at the detonator in the red head's hands.

Kimberley saw that Gwenyvere's nose was bleeding from over-use of Magick. Tears came to her eyes with shame as she knew, she'd done this. At any time, Gwenyvere could have Magicked away. It was only by them coming up to defend her that she'd been forced to use up her energy which meant they were stuck, 'I'm sorry,' she cried and Gwenyvere shook her head. 'It's ok,' she groaned as a spasm of agony ran through her body.

'Are you ready?' Gwen asked Kimberley who, sobbing, nodded while she was brought into an embrace. Gwenyvere was crying now, 'I didn't tell you I loved you enough, but I do.'

'I love you too,' shuddered Kimberley.

'Ready?'

'Yes?'

'Bye.'

'No!'

Kimberley slumped to the floor of the Flying Chair toilets with a sob.

Back on the bridge, Cassie watched helpless; panic almost overcoming her as she tried to recall the right words.

They happened the same time; the press of the detonator, the right words, the sending away of Kimberley and the last heartbeat of Gwenyvere, Queen of a land long forgotten.

The bridge exploded.

CHAPTER THIRTY

THE LADY OF THE LAKE

The car door slammed closed which made Caratacus jump. The car pulled off, leaving him standing, half asleep, by the side of the road, staring down at the floor, exhausted after only fifteen minutes of sleep.

Arthur tapped lightly on his arm.

'What?' Caratacus groaned.

'Nice, innit?' Arthur said conversationally.

Caratacus looked up. A large, becalmed lake of lay ahead, framed by hills of greens and the sun climbing over them. It was beautiful.

Caratacus regroaned, face crumbling. 'Why did you make him stop? There's nothing here! There is a parking spot by the lake over there. We have to walk again now!'

Arthur ignored the moaning; he had a smile on his face. This view, this place made him feel better. Fresh air and a view that reminded him of his first life, here in his last. He inhaled a huge gulp of air and exhaled as if he was receiving, then giving, a gift.

Caratacus' permafrown was replaced by a look of realisation. 'Ahh it's an actual lake, as in Lady of the Lake? Where are we exactly?'

Arthur scratched his ginger beard, 'Hmmmm, I haven't been here for lives, but it was Llyn Vyrnwy when I was here last.'

'When you threw Excalibur into the lake?'

Arthur looked at Caratacus as if he was an idiot. 'You've seen Excalibur.'

'I don't know. Maybe?'

Arthur went quiet, picked up a stone and threw it into the water. It plopped with no importance. 'It was never about Excalibur.'

He held his hand out and mumbled a word, a bright silver sword appearing into his hand. The moment it arrived he swung and spun in it in one simple action, 'I was given him in the wars against the English for Glyndwr, but my sword, THE sword, was always Caledfwlch. Excalibur is a nice-looking sword that does a job. Caledfwlch was mine and it was everything. At the beginning there was me and him, given to me by her,' he indicated in the general direction of the lake before continuing. 'The promise? That I handed it back when she wanted.'

He paused confused, looking around, 'I think it was over there...it was the first time, after maybe ten times of coming back, that I actually died. I mean not of old age or going back to the cave. I'd fought Mordred and as I killed him, he stabbed me in the gut. She...,' he pointed again, 'She told me that before I died, the sword would have to be returned. It was a time when our enemies were strong. Most of us were dead except for me and Bedwyr. I knew I was dying. We had fought on the shores of the south, in the lands of the Silures and we'd travelled by horse all the way here. Even now, thousands of years later, I remember the exhaustion of that ride and the pain of dying. It was a slow death. When we arrived here, Bedwyr took me off my horse and asked me what to do.'

Caratacus stayed still and barely breathed, worried that any noise he made might break the spell and end the tale.

'He argued with me. He didn't think we needed to give the sword back because he thought I'd pull through. I knew differently and I'd made a promise. I begged him and in the end he agreed. He took it and I watched him walk to the lake's edge. He swung and threw it with such force... Caledfwlch flew much further than the throw, straight into the middle of the lake. The last thing I remember before waking up in the cave one hundred and twenty-three years later was an arm rising from the waters and catching it. She brandished it three times and then slipped below the waters. For thousands of years, I've heard and seen stories about me, about Gwenyvere, round tables, and holy grails but the tale of the Lady of the Lake and the way she reclaimed the sword was even more beautiful in reality. Except for the last bit of course.'

'What last bit?' asked Caratacus, expectant and enthralled.

'When one hand went down, another came up flicking the V's before disappearing under the waters of the lake,' Arthur said.

'Sod off!' Caratacus laughed.

Arthur joined him, 'Seriously. She could be bloody nasty sometimes. What's the time?' He asked suddenly.

Caratacus had a quick check, 'About nine.'

Arthur looked around, 'I don't think she's here yet, but she should be appearing soon.'

'The Lady of the Lake?' Caratacus asked.

'That's her,' replied Arthur still looking out.

Caratacus realised Arthur wasn't snwering his question but making a statement. He was pointing.

Initially, when Caratacus saw the lake shining with bright light, he thought it was the reflection of the sun rising over the hill behind him, but it wasn't. The lake's shine increased in brightness until the two travellers couldn't face it and turned away.

In an instant, the light disappeared.

Caratacus blinked for a moment, trying to get his vision back. He squinted at the lake, expecting to see some sort of goddess in light at its centre. But there was nothing out of the ordinary that he could see.

'What happened? What was that for?' he asked.

'There she is,' Arthur pointed and started off towards a white burger van that had not been there five minutes earlier. He was a bit out of breath as he walked, still feeling the after effects of inactivity over the last few years. He stopped. 'This place is in This world and That World,' he said, 'right on the border of Magick. They come together at different times.'

They both carried on walking, 'Just this place?' asked Caratacus.

'Nah, lots of places. Usually places of big Magick...erm... battlefields maybe? Places that were Magickal originally and places where lots of things have happened. History keeps moving on and on, with all those lives and hopes and laughter and tears and tragedy and life and death—' Arthur had stopped again and was putting the flat of his hand on top of his other pudgy hand and repeating the action with every word as if he was building a mime tower, 'Until it's like...like an opening, a gateway...a different place that is This and That,' he shook his head, 'Merlin would be able to explain this better.'

'Merlin?' Caratacus asked, more excitedly than he meant. The wizard's name had, again been dropped casually into the conversation and unusually Caratacus became inquisitive.

Arthur carried on walking, 'Not now. Let's just deal with this bit first,' he said with finality.

By the time they came to the clearing where the white burger van stood, it had become busy. Carts were parked up by the side; horses and what looked like a woolly mammoth were tied at the far side of the cartpark. An ogre dressed in a loin cloth and a peaked cap was collecting the parking fares. From the van to the side of the lake were tables full of people...I say people but y'know... Anyway, they were all sitting, tucking into breakfasts and drinking hot drinks.

The burger van wasn't just white, it was bright, shining, white, totally incongruous against the natural colours of the land. In the space between the top of the serving hatch and the roof was the legend, 'The Lady of the Lake,' in red painted pretend handwriting.

'The Lady of the Lake is a burger van?' Caratacus asked.

'Mobile food emporium,' Arthur replied.

'Burger van,' said Caratacus.

'Burger van,' agreed Arthur as they both joined the queue.

'Tommy McKracken wanted me to take you to a burger van? What do we do now?' Asked Caratacus.

'Gods, boy, what are you worried about? We are here and we are hungry. Well I am. So, let's eat. Let's order some food and then we'll ask why we are here,' said Arthur, not angrily but like a parent after 5 minutes in a car with an infant asking whether they were there yet.

'Ask who?' asked Caratacus, joining the queue.

'The Ladies of the Lady of the Lake!' He said, moving closer conspiratorially with his back to the van, hiding his pointing gesture and mouthing, 'Them!'

Two women could be seen in the serving hatch, one cooking on the hot plate behind the other who was taking orders and money from the gathered throng. Caratacus thought they were twins or sisters who closely resembled each other. Other than a pinny, both was dressed for a very posh ball rather than flipping burgers.

The queue shortened until Arthur and Caratacus were up next.

'Yes love?' said the woman taking the orders. She didn't look up.

'Two bacon sandwiches please, Nim,' Arthur asked in a cheerful voice. Her eyes flashed up from the serviettes she was removing from plastic packaging. A smile came over her face, before a look of fear as she turned around. The woman at the hotplate turned around fast. 'YOU!' she said,

'NO!' said the other.

The cook's arm came out and a flash of lightning flew from her fingertips, hitting Arthur in the chest with a sharp cracking noise. Arthur shot back, landing on his back on the soft wet banks of the lake. The customers enjoying breakfast stopped eating to witness the commotion.

A smoking Arthur got up and wiped his muddy hands on the arse of his trousers. Caratacus ran over to him shaking his head in shock. 'Have you upset every woman you've ever met?'

'Vivien, leave him alone and let him speak...please.' Back in the burgervan the woman Arthur had called Nim pleaded with the other.

'Of course! Defend him! Every bloody time, Nimue...' They continued bickering as Arthur stood next to Caratacus. He looked up at the bookseller, 'Cheers mate, you were a great help, then,' he said sarcastically.

Caratacus rolled his eyes, 'What could I do? Attack the two burger van women with my magic sword? Oh no, of course not! I can't magic one up. Maybe I could do shooty lightning bolts from my eyes.'

'No one can shoot lightning bolts from their eyes,' Arthur said as if it was the most important thing to make clear at this point.

'Try me,' Vivien said, looking at him.

Arthur looked from her to Caratacus and shook his head. 'No one can.'

'What do you want, Arthur ap Uther?' Vivien said sharply.

Arthur went down on one knee, head bowed. 'Vivien, Nimue, Goddesses of Lake, I see you and dedicate myself.'

Vivien folded her arms, a cynical look of anger still on her face. Nimue, smiling, winked with the eye her sister couldn't see. At that moment it started raining. Caratacus noticed it was only raining over him and Arthur who was still on one knee in front of him.

The two grandly dressed goddesses in the burger van didn't say anything for what seemed an eternity. Arthur was still on his knee and the queue they were in was getting larger. Two tall, thin creatures with very sharp teeth were making short barks and they didn't sound like they were discussing the weather.

Vivien made a decision and spoke to one of the sharp toothed ones, 'No Terry, I am sorry, but we are closed,' she told him. 'As of when? As of when I bloody well say so,' and then to the rest, 'Sorry folks no more food for a while. Maybe longer. It all depends on this massive waste of space.'

Arthur rolled his eyes but still blushed.

She shouted sorry a few more times as the queue members grumbled off to the rest of their day.

'Who's he?' Vivien nodded at Caratacus. 'I feel like I should know him.'

'He's no one,' said Arthur dismissively.

'Cheers,' added Caratacus glibly.

'Tommaltach sent him to me,' Arthur continued.

It stopped raining and Vivien's eyes softened, 'How is the sly King? He comes here?'

Caratacus could hear the hope in her question.

'No Vivien. We are in desperate times…' Arthur began.

'Think we do not know this, Arthur King? This and That World are in chaos, war has begun here, the Dark gathers its forces, the Kingdoms gather theirs, poverty begins, despair follows and soon after, death. We feel the pressure building like a storm. Why are you here and how do you think you can come back to see us and not expect a punishment that befits your crime?'

'Leave him alone sister, I have told you there was nothing to spurn,' Nimue said softly, 'let him speak.'

Dark clouds gathered again, Vivien opened her mouth, then closed it again. She rolled her eyes, 'Go on then,' she said as the clouds disappeared.

Arthur looked up questioningly. 'Can I get up? Can we talk properly?'

She nodded, 'And him…?' She asked.

'Like I said, just a very unimportant human mortal from Tommaltach,' Arthur replied as he struggled up from his one knee.

'Charming,' said Caratacus.

Vivien pursed her lips. 'He has Magick in him, Fat King, I can feel it. You'd better not be lying to me.'

'Let's talk and find out what he wants first,' Nimue said, smiling at Arthur who smiled back like a coy teenager.

'I know what he wants,' scowled Vivian, taking her apron off, bundling it up and throwing it in the corner. 'Come around the back,' she snapped and slammed the serving hatch closed.

'So, you and the sister, eh?' Caratacus smiled, conspiratorially.

'Yeah, but not now,' Arthur replied.

Just as they reached the back and saw the Goddesses, Caratacus felt the shudder of going through a portal.

'Please no,' he said, then was sick on the floor.

'What's the matter with him?' Asked Nimue.

'He's not used to traveling between the Worlds,' Arthur replied.

It was only after the last retch and final spit that Caratacus realised that they weren't at the back of the burgervan. They were in an opulent dining room, high walls painted white, lit with large electric chandeliers. The centrepiece of the room was a table that could fit about fifteen diners, maybe more. An array of servants were positioned by the walls awaiting a call. Drinks had been served to the three who were sat on the far side of the table.

Recovered, Caratacus could see as he approached that Arthur was bent forward, Nimue by his side comforting him. Even the stern-faced Vivien, her arms folded defensively looked a little concerned. Caratacus stopped, he didn't want to intrude. They talked for about five minutes.

Nimue looked up and smiled. Caratacus had liked her straight away anyway, her face was kind, and it was matched by her gentle mannerisms.

'It's ok,' she said, 'Come. Sit,' Arthur sat up straight and looked up at Caratacus with an apologetic smile. Carataus returned it as he pulled out a grand looking chair and sat down.

Vivien fixed Caratacus with a look like Mrs Bradley his old French teacher. The terrifying Mrs Bradley hadn't been the greatest teacher, but she did had got great results from her pupils. This was done by scaring the language into them.

'Arthur is an idiot. You may look like a plain no one...'

'Thank you,' said Caratacus.

'...but you are here for a reason. The Sly King does nothing by accident.'

'I don't know why he sent me. I wish he hadn't. All he said was that I had to find him,' he pointed at Arthur, 'and take him here and then somewhere safe for a few weeks.'

'Why you?' Vivien asked.

'You don't ask Tommy McKracken why,' replied Caratacus.

Vivien smiled and looked over at her sister, 'McKracken still. Such a vain man,' she said warmly. 'But what are you to him?' She pressed.

'Well, he said he's my Godfather and wanted a favour, and like I said, you don't ask questions of Tommy and you don't say no either.'

Arthur interrupted, 'You didn't tell me he was your Godfather.'

Caratacus shrugged.

'Mammoth shit King,' Vivien said, formally ending the former line of questioning, 'it's clear to me that we are at a special point in history. We mourn your warriors, and while I do not give even one shit for you, your warriors have always been at the nexus for things decent in the Worlds. For you to be here, guided here by this unremarkable…'

'Cheers,' said Caratacus

'…man sent by the remarkable Tommaltach means that we are also part of the story. You have asked for our gift, once returned, and we are happy for to give it.'

Nimue stood with Vivien and held hands, their bodies glowing bright white like the lake had outside the grand room. They held their free hands in front of them and an equally glowing sword appeared. To Caratacus it had none of the grandeur of Excalibur, it looked like an ordinary sword. He shook his head at the thought that now he could make comparisons about swords.

'Time to go, Arthur. The bridge at Cantre'r Gwaelod has fallen and an army approaches,' Vivien said.

Arthur looked at Caledfwlch. He smiled and closed his eyes as he felt his old friend in his hands once again. He whispered his words and the sword disappeared. 'So, it's me and the boy against an army of the Dark. What am I going to do against an army?'

'You aren't, fat King. Your job is to stay alive and that means running. If you can.'

'Beli's balls, do you want Caledfwlch back so I can use your tongue as its sharpener?' Arthur was exasperated by the relentless attacks of the Goddess.

'I wouldn't let you near my tongue, you rutting hog.' Vivien smiled an icy smile and slapped the King gently across the face before walking away. 'Good luck, fatso. And good luck to you especially, lazy turd.'

'Me then,' Caratacus said to Arthur and they both smiled at each other.

Nimue moved to Arthur. 'I have a gift for you.'

Vivien turned, 'He has had the gift!'

'That was from us sister, this is from me,' she said, sounding stern for the first time. She moved close to Arthur and Caratacus walked away a few feet to give them privacy.

Nimue placed her hand on his cheek. 'Some of your warriors are only a few miles away from us. I doubt it's a coincidence. As my gift, I will send you to them.'

Arthur's eyes opened. It was the first time he'd heard any mention of his warriors since the attack on the pub. 'My warriors? Who?' he asked, desperately.

Nimue shook her head. 'I do not know; you know it isn't like that. All I know is that they belong to you Arthur, my wonderful Arthur.'

Arthur smiled and nuzzled her hand like a cat. 'Thank you Nimue. Why haven't you told your sister the truth about us?'

'What's the point? It's our story not hers, and anyway she wouldn't want to understand.' She took away her hand. 'Even we do not know what is to come. If you win and this is your last life, why not come and spend it with me? I am due some holidays.'

They laughed together. 'Are you serious?' he asked.

'Very,' she answered.

'Just me and you though not…?' He left the question unanswered.

'Just me and you,' she laughed again, 'but she gets to visit.'

'Fine,' said Arthur, mockingly, and before he could say another word, she kissed him tenderly on the mouth. He grabbed her as tenderly as the kiss and they embraced, kissing, until Arthur and Caratacus disappeared.

'Disgusting,' Vivien said coming back into the room.

'Oh, do give it a rest.' Nimue said it gently but it was enough to chide Vivien. Then she continued, 'While I expect you to be harsh to Arthur, you should not have been so hard on the boy. He is important and has power and lineage.'

'I know but he needs to step up,' Vivien replied.

'He'll get there.'

Vivien harrumphed. 'Not quickly enough and I am sure he is being encouraged by someone other than Tommaltach, but I cannot sense who.'

'You are correct sister. I sense it too. I also sense that our part of this story is over.'

They looked over at me. Both nodded but only one smiled. I nodded and smiled in return.

They were correct.

Then I was somewhere else.

CHAPTER THIRTY-ONE
FROM A LAKE TO THE HILLS

They found a clearing to spend the night, somewhere to build a fire and get some shelter. It wasn't just Arthur and Caratacus anymore. Nimue had been true to her word and her gift was to transport them to people who were linked to the King. Arthur gave thanks when he saw Galahad, Tristan, Cai and Neil before him.

Caratacus was happy that there was less responsibility on him now and happier still that he had other people to do stupid stuff like be brave. He was also surprised that he was happy to see the others regardless. Galahad brought him into an embrace, and he didn't know what to do, but he wanted to acknowledge it, so he uncomfortably patted the large warrior's back.

'Not dead then?' Cai spoiled things as always.

Initially, Arthur had insisted there was no time to talk and that they must push on west away from the forces of the Dark that the Ladies had warned them of. Galahad had beckoned Arthur to the front of the procession, away from the others and told him of the death of Geraint. Arthur didn't stop but asked to be left alone. Galahad watched his friend walking ahead with concern, hoping another piece of bad news wouldn't mean a return to his personal darkness.

After a few minutes Arthur slowed to let the others catch up, Galahad could see that Arthur had been crying but, now, his face showed no pain, 'I think we should do something for those we've lost, he said, quickly adding, 'When all this is over.'

'Of course,' Galahad replied and then, as if nothing had happened, Arthur told the group about the dash from the pub and the meeting with Gwenyvere. Caratacus could sense the delight and relief felt by these men at the news. Even Cai seemed happy. There was laughter at the story of the Lake Ladies, especially of Vivien's welcome.

'How long did you stay with Nimue?' Cai asked, with genuine humour for once, and when Arthur blushed the men laughed and Caratacus found himself joining in.

Arthur learned that it was Piogerix who had saved so many at the pub. The explosion had wiped out the Once and Future, but his spell of protection meant they had lived.

The evening wasn't warm, but it wasn't uncomfortable. Cai and Neil were with the group they'd gathered as they travelled, while Arthur, Galahad, Tristan and Caratacus relaxed around the fire. Caratacus lay on the ground and within a minute was asleep, shattered from the day.

Arthur sat on a fallen tree trunk and stared into the fire, poking it occasionally with Caledfwlch which seemed to make it spit and crack in anger at the attack.

Here, under the stars in the old kingdom of Powys, surrounded by danger, he felt right. Scared, in pain after hearing about the death of Geraint, yes, but there was also excitement.

He wondered why he felt like this. Was it freedom? Was it that Galahad, Cai and Cub were here? Was it because there was an impossible fight ahead? Maybe it was all those things. Add to that seeing Gweni and Nimue again and even Vivien. Add to that a purpose, a real enemy at last. He still wasn't sure what he was doing or where they were going, but now, he didn't feel alone. Now, they had people to look after. The army that had landed over the Troll bridge from Cantre'r Gwaelod would be moving slowly, but they had sent out scavenger squads. Communities in Powys from That World knew what these squads could do and so they moved east. They were joined by confused and frightened families who had also been the victim of the monsters. Each new person helped build a picture and it was worse than Arthur and his men had realised.

I left them for one moment. I wanted to see for myself what they were being told. They didn't know the half. Riots had broken out in major cities, fear was rife as news percolated through about terrorist attacks, border closures, food shortages and even war. The Government had fallen, and the Monarch had asked Killian Penhalligan to form a new one in their name. His first acts were to shut the borders, put soldiers on the streets and to ask for volunteers for his new Patriot-militia, a new civil defence force that he had pushed hard for during the last election.

The last thing the free media had reported before all but one outlet was shut down due to 'security concerns', was the surprising news that over a hundred thousand people had already signed up. True, many people had volunteered, but in reality, the new militia were all ready to go and had been for some time. It was made up of an army of the Dark that had been waiting in This World for precisely this moment. People were unable to get online between 10pm and 6am, which coincided with power cuts and curfew. There was no international condemnation because every country was doing the same thing.

My heart broke as I witnessed the distrust and the hatred built, not just by the big machines of Government but by individuals. The world is fed by acts of trust, kindness and love, and from what I saw in the brief time it took to get an overview, it was beginning to starve.

Then I was back in my story. Arthur and his men knew so little, but still, they knew enough.

'We've seen this before,' Galahad spoke as if he knew what Arthur was thinking about. He was sat opposite Arthur, sprawled out, leaning back on his elbows, the fire making his big red beard look even more vibrant.

'The Nazis,' Arthur said looking up.

Galahad sat up, cleaning whatever was on his hands. 'Yes and No. We've seen this plenty of times. This is the same crap, different time. I bet you my next horse that this Penhalligan is of the Dark.'

'Have you got a horse?' asked Tristan.

'The next one I said,' Galahad replied, laughing.

Cai walked into the clearing and spat into the fire. 'There are thirty people out there now. I've told them to bunch up or we won't be able to defend the camp if anybody comes at us.'

Galahad looked up, 'We couldn't defend this place anyway. I'll sort a rota. Have any of the incomers got weapons and the knowledge of how to use them, Cai?'

'There are a few. The young one is giving them advice as we speak.'

Tristan sprang to his feet, 'Stay here, Cai. I'll go and help Neil, then bring him back. The boy needs to remember to eat and sleep. He doesn't stop.'

'I like him a lot,' Galahad said to himself.

'And I do,' Arthur said, adding, 'It's been a long time since one of Fir C'nu have reminded me of myself. He's a nice boy. I'm proud of him.'

'He's boring.'

'Oh, do grow up, Cai. Haven't you ever got anything nice to say?' Galahad countered.

'Enough,' Arthur spoke quietly but sharply knowing how these little spats built up into something more annoying.

Cai spat in the fire again, 'Well, here he is,' he said as Neil entered the clearing, accompanied by Tristan. He carried himself more confidently, but it didn't stop him walking in as if he was asking permission. It'll come, thought Arthur. 'You ok?' he asked.

'...err yes my Lord…' Neil said but Arthur could tell he wanted to say more.

'Out with it then, lad.'

'I hope you don't mind, Lord, but I've taken an inventory of weapons, food and some other things that we may need. We are running low on everything and there aren't enough blankets for people to sleep under tonight. It'll get colder.'

Arthur stood, walked over and put his arm around the shoulders of his many-times- great Grandson, 'Well done, son. Why don't we go and talk to them, reassure them, and then set up a rota for guard?' Neil smiled. This was the Arthur he'd heard about before he started with the Fir C'nu. One he had wanted to serve. He thrust his chest out and smiled a broad smile, 'Yes Lord.'

Galahad got up. 'I'm going to make a pot of tea.' And on the word tea Caratacus opened his eyes.

'I'll have a cup of tea,' he said and then groaned as sleeping on the damp ground caught up with him.

'Ooh, look we have found his power at last,' Galahad said, 'He springs into action on hearing the word tea!' The others laughed and Caratacus grunted into a sitting position with the grace of a dancing hippo with a sore leg.

He yawned and rubbed his face, 'Has anything been decided then?'

'We're getting more stragglers and it won't be long until we are caught by the army that crossed the bridge and if they don't find us, maybe one of the army units that are hunting for people who break the curfew will,' Galahad said.

'We are in the middle of nowhere. Why would the army bother out here?' Caratacus asked. They'd heard that, after dark, only military vehicles and people on official government business could travel. The amount of traffic they'd seen so far meant that there was a large military presence in the area.

'Because they are looking for us,' Galahad said gravely.

'Come on, why would the Government be after some people claiming to be King Arthur and his men, haven't they got their own disasters to deal with?' Caratacus tried to sound confident but didn't feel it.

'We talked about it earlier. I think the Dark have taken over Government,' this was from Tristan. 'We have to have a plan. We can't wait for them to find and slaughter us. The Kings are out finding allies, but how are they going to find us? We don't even know where we are!'

'We just need to head north-east, away from the horde that crossed the bridge,' said Cai.

'What is there though, Cai?' Tristan was angry now. He was one of their best strategists. They always thought him young because he looked the youngest, but he was a thinker and the thought of just running away without a plan was driving him mad.

'Woah,' shouted Cai, as a crow landed in front of him making him jump. 'Bastard!' he said, embarrassed about how he'd reacted. The others laughed which made him angrier. Caratacus stopped laughing as soon as he thought he recognised the crow. If you could indeed recognise a crow. Didn't they all have beady eyes? Weren't they all just black crow-like birds? But this one? He stared. This one had a face he wanted to punch, and he could tell you from deep down in his heart that he'd never had any inclination to punch a crow, or any other bird for that matter, in the face. His eyes narrowed. The crow walked as if it owned the place. He knew it was her.

It was the bird's turn to jump when Cai shouted 'AARRGGHHH!' and leapt at the crow who hopped just out of reach as if taunting him and then opened its wings and cawed twice into its supposed assaulter's face before bouncing into the undergrowth.

Caratacus knew the crow was there for him, so he stood up with another grunt. He looked down at his ruined sneakers, the ones that he'd loved that had been through the puddles of the Preseli hills, the bogs around Lake Vyrnwy and, for the last 3 hours, the valleys of Powys. He sighed, 'I need a pee' and followed the crow.

His stomach moved, a slight lurch. He went from nighttime on the side of a valley into the alcohol section of a brightly lit and relatively busy supermarket aisle.

People were passing him, going about their business and by the rosé wine section was the beautiful Dannan, Badb on her shoulder with Ceridwen squinting at a bottle label.

'This one!' she said to the beauty.

'Caratacus ap Neb is here, sister,' Dannan said. She was looking at Caratacus, then winked. He closed his eyes and groaned as he felt his legs start to weaken.

'Shit shoes, virgin,' Badb squawked at him.

Caratacus was about to say something but some bloke pushed his trolley between him and the women.

'Can people see us?' He asked as a woman leant past him to pick up a one glass rosé bottle.

'I can see you,' she said rather grumpily, 'because you're in my way.'

He shifted with a quick apology, then to the Morrigu, a quiet, insistent but totally miffed, 'What the hell is going on? We're on the run! I'm shattered. Are we going to die?'

Ceridwen laughed her heaving, wheezing chuckle and her gnarled hand tapped him on the head. 'Caratacus ap Neb, I do believe I am proud of you!'

The compliment was as shocking as the knock on the head. He didn't know what to say. He shrugged uselessly.

'Kitten, you are doing so well,' Dannan of the flowers said, stroking his face as he closed his eyes. For a second he didn't feel aroused. He felt overwhelmed. He shouldn't be here, he should be back with Arthur but there was a small part of him that wanted to stay, to stop being chased and hurt or worse.

'Can't you stop these armies?' he asked desperately, 'Or tell us how to escape?'

The crow had thankfully been silent but now started cawing like she was laughing again.

'I've done everything you've asked, and we're in even more trouble! Can't you do something for me?' Caratacus continued.

Ceridwen prodded Caratacus in the chest, 'You think we haven't been helping you already? If you had taken Arthur King when we said, he would not have been there for the attack.'

'You would not have met Gwenyvere and learned of the army if we hadn't have sent you to the bridge…' Dannan added.

'And now we have pulled you out to tell you how to get to safety,' Ceridwen finished.

It hadn't crossed his mind that these three had been helping and not moving him around like their personal plaything.

'Who are you?' he asked.

They laughed again and he knew why. This was not their first meeting, but this was the first time he had been bothered to ask who they were.

'Show him!' Badb cawed.

Crone and maiden moved one to each side of him, holding his arms and looking into his eyes. The crow hopped on to his shoulder. He flinched but didn't move as he could feel the weight of them holding him down.

Their eyes changed to black, and he felt fear. They spoke as one.

'We are the Goddess, we are the Morrigna, the Morrigan and the Morrigu.'

Flash!

He was in the middle of a battle, men with painted faces were going at each other with sword, spear and shield but the fighting was also done with fist, thumb and teeth. He could hear the roar of battle coupled with the screams of terror and the stink of piss and shit.

Two fighting men fell at the feet of Caratacus. Both weaponless, they grappled, punches flying. The blue painted man had succeeded in getting into a superior position and now started to choke the red painted man.

Caratacus stared at them as Dannan casually walked past him. She leaned over and spoke. Their voices still combined, 'I have many names. For now We are Dannan,' she pointed down at the fighting pair. 'I am the Goddess of war; I wander the field of battle and push men to bravery and renown. Before this fight many of these warriors prayed to me for their protection.'

A horseman rode past, and a swing from his sword saw the blade knock a chunk out of the blue faced warrior's skull, killing him instantly and allowing his opponent to breathe again.

Dannan pointed at red face, 'He was one of them.'

The world shuddered. They remained in the same place, but the noise of battle was gone; replaced by an even more terrifying one, the sound of the aftermath. Bodies dead or close to it were strewn in all directions. Carrion was everywhere, birds enjoying the feast while women moved amongst the bodies looking for plunder or for people they loved. The smell made Caratacus baulk as they walked amongst death. He noticed the red-faced man who had been saved before, lying below them, lifeless eyes staring at the sky, mouth opening in a final silent scream.

Dannan had become Ceridwen who stood over the corpse. 'We are the Goddess of Fate. He prayed for protection and we delivered. He met someone who also prayed to us. Prayed a little harder.' Ceridwen became Badb who immediately landed on the dead warrior's forehead and started pecking away at his eye.

Caratacus looked away in disgust.

The crow looked up at Caratacus. 'It isn't all valour and glory, it's hardly ever that, although it is joy. I do love that joy.' She paused as if enjoying the moment. 'But it is fear, it is pain, it is loss, it is blood and the end of things. I am the Goddess of that too. I accept the glory and the lust, but I also want their dead eyes and my hunger is insatiable.'

Shudder. They were back in the supermarket, this time in the biscuits section.

'THEM!' called the crow and immediately Dannan put the digestives in the trolley, 'We are all one person, Cati.'

'But different,' said Ceridwen.

Caratacus had stopped listening for a moment as he realised that if they were all the same, he was becoming aroused not only by a vixen but also a very, very old woman and a crow. After all the reasons he had felt sick since the start of the journey he was surprised to find a new one.

They walked along the aisles like a really weird family out for a Friday big shop. The two women were picking things from the shelves and putting them in the trolley.

'It's near the end you know, Caratacus ap Neb?' said Dannan, looking at the price of a tin of corned beef before making a face and putting it back.

'Sacrifice time!' Badb looked at him. 'The end, Faceache.'

'You want our help, Caratacus?' asked Ceridwen.

'Yes! But you brought me here,' Caratacus responded and there was a flicker of surprise on the faces of the two women and the crow flapped her wings.

The Crone spoke. 'You are growing, lazy man. Not even we foresaw how much. Such a shame.'

'Why is it a shame? I'm getting the hints, you know? It's cruel! I'm going to die, aren't I? Why not just come out and say it? Help me? Tell me what I need to do to live!'

'If that is what you want? We can send you back to Mam and Twickenham right now,' Ceridwen asked innocently.

Caratacus blinked, 'Right now?' *'I want to go home,'* he thought.

'This very minute,' Dannan said, 'back into your house, back to comfort, back to routine.'

He paused, 'Can you save Arthur and everybody?' he asked.

'Why do you care? You will be home; safe and sound,' the crone replied spitefully.

Dannan moved alongside and stroked his face, 'You've done your bit, kitten, and you have been amazing. Time to go home.'

He wanted that so badly his stomach started hurting. He'd asked for none of this, he'd done everything he'd been asked by these three. He just wanted things to be normal again but at the back of his mind…

'What happens to Arthur and his men?' He asked a little more strongly than he intended.

Dannan smiled, 'Well, it's not looking hopeful, is it? You already know that you are being chased by an army, but you don't know about the other army approaching from the north. The Dark God, Cromh Du, has risen again and he makes his way with his chosen ones to watch your friends crushed.'

'It's the end?' asked Caratacus.

'It's an end.'

'What if I go back? Do they live?'

'If you go back, they have a chance,' Dannan replied with a shrug.

Every thought rose to the surface, demanding attention and solution. He could feel the worry and the Magick rising up within him and it reminded him that things had changed so much in so little time. He became angry as soon as he understood he couldn't leave them and that meant he would die. Fear flashed as he remembered the sword cleave through the blue faced man a moment before. His head showed him the different ways he'd witnessed death since leaving home and his legs shook, but he could feel the Magick grow stronger inside him.

'If I go back, can you promise me we'll get through this alive?' he asked, knowing the answer.

'No,' replied Ceridwen.

'A chance?' he asked desperately.

This time Ceridwen smiled. 'There is always a chance.'

'Can't you just help us win?' asked Caratacus.

'It doesn't work like that, Cati,' said Dannan, sadly.

He started shaking, 'Tell me what to do, and send me back to my friends,' he said. Immediately, he felt a strong grip on his arm. It was Ceridwen. They looked at each other. She nodded and he knew it was a grip of reassurance. Dannan hugged him; not a hug of sexuality but one of friendship.

She broke away and kissed him tenderly on the lips, 'You are one of my favourites. Now have you got your phone on you?'

Aware that his little man was at attention he fished around for his phone before getting it out. The phone I mean.

'Battery?' she asked.

'12%,' he answered.

'Then write this in your notes...'

Once they were done, both crone and maiden smiled at him, the crow hopped from the trolley bar to Ceridwen's shoulder. 'If you die, I am going to be sorry to eat your eyes Caratacus,' she said.

Dannan laughed and looked at Badb. 'So soppy! Get a room…'

And Caratacus was outside the clearing but this time without the bird.

'Bit quick for a piss? Forget something?' Asked Cai as Caratacus walked back into the sleeping area. Caratacus laughed but he felt scared again as he lay down, putting his hands behind his head.

He stared up to the sky, 'A chance,' he said tiredly.

'What?' Asked Galahad but the exhausted Caratacus was already asleep.

CHAPTER THIRTY-TWO

ALL THE KING'S DAUGHTERS AND ALL THE KING'S SONS

It was Tristan who broke the morning silence, running into the camp in such a rush that it brought everybody but Caratacus to their feet.

'Lord, you need to see this,' he said breathlessly.

Twenty minutes later Tristan, Arthur, Galahad, Cai and Neil were in a field, crouched into a hedge outside the small village of Bwlch-y-Cibau. Armed men were dragging terrified people from their houses.

Arthur turned to Tristan and whispered, 'Cub, I want us to protect everybody, but we can't take on anybody on our own. We need to get the people we have with us to safety first.'

Tristan shook his head. 'This isn't what I wanted you to see. Move down here and I'll show you.' They didn't have to walk too far down the line of the hedge before they could see what had brought Tristan running into camp.

The next field held two large, gated sheep pens and in them were about forty children, some as young as three or four years old. Many were silent, showing signs of shock, others were quietly sobbing while being consoled by some of the older children.

'Those guards are wearing Nazi uniforms!' said Galahad in a sharp whisper.

They were. There were only four of them and at that moment they were arguing furiously but the warriors couldn't hear what was being said.

I could.

'If you want to take the Captain's torque from me, then challenge me,' the man – and he was a man –said. His name was Robert Cavaney. Though he had a captain's torque around his neck, he had neither the attitude nor the ability necessary to wear it. If brutality was a calling, then that was his. He was second in command of the infamous Hitler battalion, a mercenary group from That World that consisted of like-minded Nazi fetishists from both Worlds.

Cavaney's job had been simple: bring these little rats into This World with the army from Cantre'r Gwaelod, take them to the only drinking hole and, within two pubs, be in London to hand them over. But he hand't been prepared for an attack on his small force by three hissing bitches.

'I didn't say that, Captain,' his subordinate said, 'I just said we can't stay here.'

Not only had the women managed to kill some of his best men, but they also followed them through one of the portals. The confusion of those horrible wasps attacking them in the confined space of a pub toilet in Welshpool, while he'd been trying to herd children in small groups, meant that he'd panicked and spoken the wrong spell, destroying the pub toilets. So, instead of London and safety he was stuck, gods knew where, in the middle of nowhere.

'I don't need you to tell me things I already know!' Cavaney snapped. 'My orders stand. We stay the night, three on guard here, and the rest of us will guard the villagers in the church. Tomorrow morning, early, when they have a bit less fight in them, we gut them and move back towards the bridge to Cantre'r Gwaelod and the safety of the army.'

'This is a stupid job. Why aren't we with the main army gaining plunder?' asked another of the guards.

Cavaney looked over. 'We all volunteered for this, so shut it.' They would have had a reward once the little bastards were safely in London, though now Cavaney wasn't so sure, which is why he had to rescue the situation.

'Can I be a part of the group to get rid of the villagers tomorrow?' said one.

'And me,' said another.

Cavaney smiled, 'OK, take a long first watch here and that'll be fine.' He pointed to the one who hadn't spoken. Sezzast the Dark Elf didn't say much. 'I'm leaving you in charge, but no interfering with the prisoners, you can have as much sex as you want when we finish this task. Agreed?'

They nodded and as one, arms raised, saluted.

Cai saw the salute. 'Nazi bastards! They've stopped arguing and the man with the torque is sodding off,' he said, feeding the information to the group who were sat behind him.

'We can't leave them,' Neil said.

'We won't,' Arthur answered, 'but we have to think about this. Cub, you say there are about fifty warriors guarding villagers in a church?' Tristan nodded.

'That officer was probably setting guards so we either wait until the next change or we do this now,' Arthur continued.

'I say we do this now. We get the children up to our position and go,' Galahad argued.

'How will we survive with all these kids plus the stragglers we've already picked up?' Cai shot back.

'We aren't leaving them,' Galahad stared.

'But you are happy to leave the villagers?' Cai was starting to enjoy himself and getting angry as well.

'Piss off, Cai…'

'Shut up,' Arthur stopped them. 'I agree with you, Galahad, but Cai is right to worry. However, these children must be important, or they'd be dead already. If we manage to rescue them and move fast, then we will drag the guards after us and maybe they'll leave the villagers alone.'

'So, what's the plan?' asked Galahad before a loud rustle made them turn to see Neil sprinting across the field towards the pens and their guards.

'Shit…' was everybody left remaining thought. They knew they couldn't get there in time to support him. Tristan whispered a word of Magick…

Sezzast's head rolled to the floor and another of the guards had Neil's sword through his throat. The third reacted quickly after the shock of watching the head of his comrade roll past his line of sight. He at least managed to pull around his machine gun and cock it before thinking that he'd been punched in the chest. He stopped thinking about it, closed his eyes and went to an afterlife he deserved.

Tristan pulled out the arrow from the dead Nazi's chest, nocked it to his bow, whispered words of Magick and the bow and arrow disappeared.

Arthur, having run from cover with the other warriors, was bent over trying to gulp in air so he could show the anger he felt, 'You...don't...You don't…. disappear without....'

Galahad took over and grabbed the young man by the arm, 'What the hell were you thinking? What if they'd seen you? Those children could be dead!'

Neil looked hurt but he lifted his chin, 'My Magick, Lord. I used invisibility and silence in the lead up to my attack.'

Galahad was impressed, the quick use of two spells before attacking and killing two men was impressive and reminded him that Neil was no longer a kid, there to make tea, but a trained warrior. All the Fir C'nu had their own Magick, and he was embarrassed that he didn't know Neil's skills sets were invisibility and silence. It was a tough Magick to have. He was still angry with him though. 'That third guard would have killed you if not for Tristan.' He paused. 'You did ok though.'

Arthur, his breath back, stood in the middle of the men, 'Galahad, Cub, go and talk to a pen each. Find out who they are. Tell them they are safe, that we are here to take them to safety and that we have to move quietly and quickly.'

Galahad smiled as he walked over to the pen. It wasn't just to reassure the children who were staring in fear at the latest danger to come into their lives, it was because in the last half a day he had seen Arthur return from wherever his head had sent him. His instincts were returning. Look who he didn't send to do this job, quick-to-anger Cai and a worried looking Neil.

Tristan and himself looked less of a threat and Arthur knew that and had sent them without thinking.

Galahad explained to the children that they were safe, they had to leave, they had to be quiet, and they had to listen to what he said. A little girl of no more than four came over and lifted her hands up, demanding action. He picked her up, she cwtched in tight, head nestled into his neck, and off they went.

Three hours later, when Arthur, his men, the stragglers and the children were miles away, Cavaney and two of his jackbooted men found the empty pens and the bodies of their comrades.

The blood drained from the Captain's face 'We are dead,' he said to himself before barking at the man next to him, 'Go find Constance the tracker. Now!'

***

They had barely made a mile after leaving the clearing. Breaking camp and getting people and the children organised had taken longer than they thought. It was during a short break, while they passed their strictly rationed water around that Caratacus decided to go for broke and explained to everybody what the Three Goddesses had told him.

'Please believe me but we have to get to these hills,' he showed them the notes he'd taken from Dannan.

'Breiddin?' Asked Arthur squinting as he read, 'What's there?'

Caratacus checked his notes. 'It's a fortress of safety. I promise. We'll be safe there. It's called the Forty-eight-hour fort.'

'How do you know all this?' asked Galahad putting a reassuring hand on his shoulder.

'I'm sorry, I can't tell you, but please trust me on this,' Caratacus pleaded, looking into the faces of the famous warriors.

Arthur stared at him for an uncomfortable while. 'Do you trust the person who gave you this information?'

'I think I do but do we have much of a choice? Do we die here or try something then possibly die later or maybe not at all?' replied Caratacus. He lifted his phone and saw that his battery was down to 7%. 'The Breidden Hills are about 8 miles directly west of here according to my maps app.'

'We've been in worse situations. The last time was horrendous,' Tristan said matter of factly.

'How did you get out of that?' asked Caratacus hopefully.

'We didn't get out of it, we won and then we were all slaughtered by Nazis,' Tristan replied.

'Oh,' Caratacus let it go.

Arthur paused then looked at Galahad. His second-in-command and best friend shrugged in a 'let's give it a go' rather than an 'I don't know' way.

Arthur smiled. 'So, here we will probably die, but up on that hill we will possibly die?' A small pause followed before, 'Ok let's do it. Has everybody had a bit of food and water?'

Tristan stepped up, 'The inventory is low. If it is as far as Cati says, then it's quarter rations once for us and twice for the young ones. We have no choice but to go really, even if there is no fort coming to save us. If we run out of options and need to make a last stand, let's make it on high ground.'

Caratacus would usually have worried about that news but was too busy glowing inside hearing Tristan calling him Cati. He felt like a kid who had just learned how to ride a bike in front of a proud father.

Hours later he wished to God he was a kid. He was exhausted. At all times, two of the warriors were at point, watching for attacks, while another two were rear end guards. Every other adult was carrying a child. Galahad and Caratacus were the only two that stayed with the youngsters the whole time, Galahad because the children loved him and wailed whenever he wasn't in sight and Caratacus because he didn't have any weapons.

'Has anybody got anything I can have?' he asked when the journey began.

'We are bonded to our weapons and know the Magick that calls them. Unless you are carrying something then you haven't got anything,' Arthur told him, 'Just stick to carrying children.'

He would have given anything to fight. Just in the hope he may get knocked out, anything rather than this. He was covered in cuts and bruises from exhausted stumbles; he was close to breaking but struggled on. He wasn't glad but he was relieved that everybody else seemed as drained as him. He found himself wishing his mother was there. Mrs Lewis was proud if Caratacus made his own tea or hung up a jacket, so he wanted her to see this. He wanted her to feel pride because it was something he was feeling. That was when tears came and looking up while a little boy hugged his neck hard, he prayed to whatever god was around that he would be kinder to his mother if he ever saw her again. *'Maybe I'll buy her flowers?'* he thought before deciding that maybe he wouldn't go that far. She'd think it was the end of the world.

Neil, who was on point, ran back to the main group, 'We've hit a block. We don't know where we are going. We can go west but we don't have a detailed enough map. Also have you seen Cai? He was on point with me, and he's disappeared.'

Arthur shook his head, 'We can't worry about Cai now. He's a big boy and should catch up. I'm more worried about us,' he said.

'We are going to have to move quickly because those Nazis are catching and it's getting late,' this from Galahad who arrived at the same time from the rear. Arthur looked worried then clicked his finger in a 'Eureka' moment.

'I never do this. Well, I haven't for a few thousand years. You just forget, don't you?'

'What? Get on with it,' said Galahad, curtly but with no malice.

'We ask the gods. Well not so much them as the Bachod. They know the holy places nearby and how to get to them.'

'They're annoying. They'll ask too much,' said Galahad and Tristan nodded in agreement.

'Needs must,' Arthur walked over to a clump of trees and fell on his knees. Bachod were all around but to call one with a tiny bit of power, sometimes you needed a little sacrifice. He called forth Carnwennan his knife and made a nick in his hand. A single drop of blood flowed down one of his lifelines that had ended so many centuries before and dripped to the ground.

As soon as Arthur started mumbling words Caratacus felt Magick in his stomach, surprised at how it felt strangely good rather than making him throw up. Arthur opened one eye and nodded at Tristan. 'You have a bit of Magick, Cub, place your hand on my shoulder.' Tristan did so and the air became electric. Arthur looked at Caratacus. 'You know that Magick you were feeling? That control? Feel it and put your hand on my other shoulder.'

A second drop hit the ground.

Caratacus homed his senses in on the Magickal pressure. He concentrated on the feeling of a finger tracing on his hand and then he smiled and put his hand on Arthur.

Arthur's eyes pulsed a bright blue, his back arched as he spasmed.

'Good gods!' he shouted.

A third drop of blood hit the ground and, 'SMASH' a wave of energy exploded from Arthur, knocking all of them to the ground.

You see, a couple of drops of blood from any of you coupled with a bit of Magick would have brought forth one of the Bachod, possibly a river sprite or even a god of a hedge or a break in a hedge, if there was one there. Arthur hadn't thought. Three drops of his blood were powerful anyway. Three drops of King Arthur's blood coupled with a bit of Magick was unbelievably powerful. Having Caratacus lend his newfound Magick to it was like draining a nuclear power station to make a cup of tea.

Everyone was on the floor, laying there unhurt but unable to move after experiencing such power. As one they leant on their elbows to look at what Arthur had called.

'Bloody big water sprite!' Said Galahad.

That's because it wasn't a water-sprite. It was a goddess. To be exact it was a Celtic goddess called Latis and she was not happy. She stood in the middle of the clearing in her pyjamas, wearing a face pack, her hair tied up in a towel.

She was not amused.

'WHAT THE HELL ARE YOU IDIOTS DOING?' She sounded more exasperated than shouty, but she was a goddess for goddess' sake, you are going to feel that voice never mind hear it.

All of them immediately moved a kneeling position, except Caratacus who followed a nanosecond later.

She stood glaring at them; arms folded. 'Well?'

All their foreheads were touching the ground, but they started to look up slowly, first at the goddess and then at each other. Their eyes widening at the realisation that they didn't know the name of the goddess they'd called.

'You do it!' mouthed Arthur at Galahad who shook his head vigorously. Arthur tried to look at the others.

Tristan immediately sensed what was coming and moved back to prostrate himself, his forehead touching the damp grass so he wouldn't be called.

'Go on!' Arthur whispered even more insistently. Tristan shook his head and knowing he'd been defeated Arthur groaned, dropped his head and spoke.

'I am Arthur, King, ap Uther ap Beli Mawr, many lived for the Light and I beg your forgiveness for your calling.'

She made THAT face – she knew he didn't know her name.

'You called me. So, who am I?'

Every warrior except Arthur and Caratacus tensed up. Arthur did the reverse and let out a massive sigh and answered. 'We beg your forgiveness, goddess, for we are ignorant fools and do not know whom we have called.'

Arms still folded, her eyes closed, her chin dropped to her chest, she exhaled for what seemed an age. She mumbled to herself, 'First time I have been called for about 2000 years and they don't know who the hell I am and it's bloody pamper night.' Her eyes opened and her chin shot up.

'Fine! Let's just get this done shall we, Arthur ap Uther? I am the goddess Latis, once part of the pantheon of these islands, of water and of beer and now of watching films with a glass of wine and wasting my time dating idiots who continue to let you down and don't deliver on simple promises they made when you first met, and don't get me started on what they claim to be gods of on their dating profiles. Gaulish god of thunder, my arse.' She stopped, realising she'd said more than she needed. She straightened her posture to look more goddess-like which is tough when you are dressed to watch a boxset and eat chocolates.

'So puny mortals, why have you dared use such Magick and call Latis to…'

She stopped talking and looked around like a hawk, head darting, looking for the sound.

'I can hear snoring! Is someone sleeping? You imbeciles have called a goddess and one of you falls asleep! Get up! Come on! Up!' she demanded.

They all looked up reluctantly and then slowly got to their knees. All except Caratacus who was still softly snoring in the praying position.

Tristan glanced to make sure Latis wasn't looking, nudged Galahad and sniggered. He hid his smile as Arthur looked over in his best scowl. The king had a great 'stop messing about' face when he wanted.

'Divine one, may I address you?' Arthur had stepped forward gingerly, 'This is a mortal of Magick who has never really used it before, has no control over it and it was his power with my blood that called you.'

She stood there, arms still folded, lips pursed, staring at them.

'Fine,' she said in a tone that a teenager would have been happy with...or fine with. 'You have called me, and you have done so with blood and with Magick. You call...you dare call and I have answered. So what can Latis, Goddess of the pool, possibly do…'

Caratacus' snoring was getting louder.

'Can someone wake him?' she sighed.

Tristan shook Caratacus by the shoulder and he jerked awake with a 'Not my beautiful face!' and then coughed with embarrassment, mumbling a quick apology.

For the next half an hour, Arthur told the Goddess their story and their predicament. They were joined by all the travellers, children included, who sat in awe looking at the Goddess who was now a lot more relaxed, sitting on a high stool and sipping the glass of red she had summoned to listen to the story. She asked questions of some of the children and even asked about some of the tales she'd heard of Arthur.

'So, you have called forth a goddess of great power to the mortal realm for the first time in centuries to move you and a bunch of children eight miles?' She said in a mock disapproving tone. The group laughed and she smiled.

Arthur looked at the floor like a scolded child and smiled, embarrassed. 'Yes, Divine One.'

She laughed. 'I like you, Arthur ap Uther. I had heard of you and your men and what I see, I like.' She looked over at Galahad whose eyes opened wide in surprise when she winked. 'Like a lot.'

She stood and they all rushed to their feet. 'I will get you to the Breidden Hills and ….' She stopped as she noticed Arthur with his hand up, 'Speak, Arthur ap Uther.'

Calling a goddess mattered, and it bothered Arthur that he had called one by mistake. He thought the Arthur he remembered would have done something to apologise properly and he did so now. He dropped to his knee, followed by everybody in the group, and, a second later, by Caratacus who rolled his eyes. His knees were soaking and every time he was down there, he noticed the state of the sneakers.

Instead of the usual whisper, Arthur spoke aloud the word that called a weapon. In his hand was Excalibur, beautiful and bright sword of myth. He laid the blade on his forearm.

'Divine Latis, Goddess of the pool and probably goddess of quite a few more people gathered here after today, this is the sword Excalibur. It is a sword of much power. I feel it is the right thing to offer to you. I give it gladly as a sacrifice.'

Even if they had wanted to, the people in that place would not have been able to look up, the light from Latis had become too strong for mortal eyes. Arthur felt Excalibur being taken. She spoke and the words were loud.

'Arthur ap Uther, I am humbled by this powerful gift given freely and I accept. I am genuinely surprised that you are giving this away. I grant the gift you ask. To you all I wish the best for the hard times to come.'

The light dimmed but the last thing they heard in the normal voice of Latis was a faded, 'Call me!'

All who were there felt a shudder as they found themselves in a different place.

What Latis had done was indiscriminately transport the group to the foot of the Breidden hills. And by 'indiscriminately', I mean she moved Arthur, his warriors, the people they were protecting and twenty of the closest Nazis who'd been about to catch up with the group.

'There's the fort,' shouted Neil, pointing before hearing the shouts from the soldiers of the Dark.

'How did they get here?' asked Caratacus.

'Go! You need to run, I'm staying to defend. Go!' Shouted Tristan.

Arthur swung him around. 'No! We can all make it. We've lost Cai. I can't lose you as well.'

Tristan wanted to argue but he knew his King was right. 'Run,' Arthur shouted. Many of the children started to scream but the warriors didn't care, let them, let them run in terror because if they didn't make it up this hill, they were dead anyway.

I could say that they did run but they didn't, they couldn't, the gradient was so steep that it was just crawling at times. The cries of the kids turned to exhausted whimpers and then it turned to fear-induced keening as they heard the Nazi dressed warriors shouting as they reached the bottom of the hill. Some started shooting, others started climbing.

'They're shooting!' cried Caratacus, 'They're shooting at kids!'

Galahad shouted over, 'You know that feeling you had in the glade and the anger you are feeling now?'

He nodded as he felt it build inside him, he felt the finger on his palm, but for the first time he felt red, he felt anger and he felt release.

'Throw the anger at those bastards!' Screamed Galahad, 'NOW!'

Without the right words, it's uncontrolled but Galahad knew that. It didn't matter, something had to happen. It smashed out of Caratacus down the slope. The lead Nazi was stooped, trying to stand on the steep hill to fire his luger pistol when he was incinerated by the blast, and everybody behind him was felled to the ground.

Caratacus wasn't surprised. It was as if he knew that blast was coming and was glad it did.

'HAVE THAT!' he shouted.

The first of the children had reached the top and were running across to the large door of the fort.

'Wait!' shouted Arthur who reached it just after them. He ran forward. 'We don't know anything about this place. Cub? Cover me.'

A simple word and an exhausted Tristan had a bow with an arrow notched at the ready.

Galahad was swamped with crying children, he made encouraging noises, but it wasn't making any difference.

Arthur banged on the hard-oak door. 'Open the door,' he shouted. 'We need help!'

A hatch opened and a man's voice said, 'Who requires entry?'

'Arthur ap Uther.'

They were interrupted by Caratacus, delirious after loosening his Magick, running like a drunk man, past Arthur and full pelt into the door.

'Who's that idiot?' the voice asked as Caratacus slumped to the ground.

'Does it matter?' said Arthur.

'To me it does,' the voice was affronted now.

Arthur looked down, 'Caratacus ap Neb.'

'Lewis,' wheezed Caratacus as he slipped into unconsciousness.

The last thing he heard was a woman's voice, one he recognised, shouting, 'From Twickingham?' followed by the creaking hinges of a large door opening before he fell into darkness...

CHAPTER THIRTY-THREE

THE FORTY-EIGHT-HOUR FORT

Cassie had watched the chase to the fortress from a copse of trees at the base of the hill and wondered what to do next.

She had only just survived the collapse of the bridge. Casting protective Magick a moment before the explosion had ensured her survival but it had taken time for her to climb out of the rubble. After producing a spell that powerful she had needed to rest before carrying on with her task but there were things that needed to be done first.

The Dark armies' headquarters had been set up in what seemed to be in an old bingo hall. There was the usual bustle of activity as Cassie strode through to where she had been told she'd find General Skee.

'My congratulations on your survival, Dark Mistress,' he said with a bow.

'My thanks, General, but I believe we have larger concerns than small talk?' She was amazed by how easy it was to fall back into the old patterns of speech. She thought back to the school gates. 'Greetings, Chantelle, how goes young Corey? I notice a love bite on your neck, was fun had last night?'

'Firstly, I feel it important to report the death of my Dark sister. While I cannot recall her name, I am sure you will need to note it in your report'.

'My deepest condolences, Mistress,' he bowed again. 'We didn't really bother with digging out bodies, seeing as they were mainly fodder class, but would you wish for me to send out a party to find her remains?'

'That will not be necessary. A situation report, if you will. It seems you have lost some of your army, General. Plans? Where is Arthur?'

Dark Mistresses had a knack of terrifying people and while the General was no exception, he had been around, he had survived, and he had some pride.

'I am well aware of the situation…Mistress,' he added quickly, he wasn't that proud. He inhaled deeply, finding some sort of equilibrium before reporting, using the ancient names for Wales and England when he did. 'Things have obviously not gone to plan. Instead of three armies heading east we are just over one and a half. Our orders have changed. We are no longer heading towards major habitations in the south east of Cymru and midlands of Lloegr but moving east as we have something major to deal with.'

'Arthur,' she said. Not a question, a fact.

She was met with silence as a worried Skee stroked his chin, a throwback from when he had sported a small, trident beard in his younger years.

'There's more.' Again, not a question.

'The reason for the surrender of so many kingdoms and peoples in That World was not solely down to military might. We have strengthened our hand in the last few months and have taken certain hostages.'

'Hostages?'

'Brats from the royal families. All races, north, south, east and west. All of them,' he answered.

'Every family?' This time it was Cassie who broke character. She knew how the Dark moved. She, herself had been part of it, but to have that much power in That World? It made her feel uncomfortable.

Olivia.

She wished it would stop happening. The name leapt, unbidden. That's what they wanted to do with Olivia. She'd phoned Katie and spoken to her daughter straight after getting out of the rubble, taking a phone from one of the senior officers outside the bingo hall.

There had been no hello, just, 'When you coming home Mummy?' But for once she didn't mind the question. She was glad she was missed, and that Olivia was safe. She'd spoken to Katie and, afterwards, felt a weight had been lifted. She needed to finish this, do the job, go home, get her girl, disappear, get cable TV, have a life and eat takeaways.

'What has Arthur got to do with the hostages?' she asked.

Still rubbing his chin, Skee said, 'The squad that was escorting them to London have been attacked and now the hostages are with him.'

She knew immediately what she had to do, but first she needed to prepare properly for what was to happen next.

'You are billeted?' she asked.

'I am in the main house…'

She was already walking out the door. 'That will do, send someone to show me where it is. I need to rest. Send food immediately and rations for two days travelling. Set two guards on me and then I will leave.'

The General was tired and had hoped to catch some sleep himself but knew now that it wasn't going to happen. Well, not in the bed he had chosen. He watched as the striking, young, brown-eyed, brunette walked out of sight, and he sighed.

'By your command,' he bowed low to nobody.

By the time Cassie woke it was dusk. She'd needed more sleep than she'd thought and was annoyed. Her annoyance was increased when she found a piece of paper on the bed stand. She became angry with herself as she had not heard anybody enter. A lapse in her defences like that could and should mean death but she cast those worries aside as she unfolded the note. It simply read: 'Breidden Hills now.'

She sat, lit her first cigarette for days, and planned.

She questioned the guards, and they were adamant that no one had left or entered her rooms and from the fear that sweated from them as she interrogated them, she believed they were telling the truth.

She travelled through the night. Determination and a return to fitness drove her to make those miles in a time that few humans could have done. By early afternoon she had arrived and for a moment panicked that the note had been put there to help her enemies rather than her. She didn't have many options but to trust it, however, so she waited, preparing food and catching up on a bit of sleep. For hours, all that could be seen on the summit was a large pillar and she sighed as she checked it for maybe the tenth time that hour. This time, the pillar was gone, and in its place a large fortress.

She didn't feel tired as she watched the panicked retreat up the hill. She felt anger and confusion at her anger. The hostages were nothing to do with her, but her anger came when she heard the terrified cries from the children. There was no thought when Cassie called her bow, arrow notched. One of the soldiers had reached the slope first and was firing. She breathed, nocked and fired, watching the arrow hit deep through his neck below his ear.

Cassie cursed, angry that she could've given herself away.

She lay on her back immediately hiding herself from the fort. As was usual with Cassie in situations like, this a plan formed, and she acted. She needed to get in there. There was no point getting into a pitched battle between two armies. She had to get in and kill Arthur. Her bow disappeared and as she heard the bells ring out from the fort, she set off to find a way in.

***

The large door was opened, and Tristan helped to heave the unconscious body of Caratacus onto Arthur's shoulder. They were still under fire, bullets whistling past their heads and thudding into the wooden walls of the fort. Galahad herded the children in.

Arthur, evidently struggling with Caratacus's weight, called to Galahad, 'Gal, stop the enemy gaining a foothold up here.'

'Only Cub and Neil have bows,' Galahad shouted back.

Three shapes ran past like a blur. A brunette stopped, returned to where Galahad was standing and looked up into his face, her expression resolute. 'We have bows,' she said simply and then Mali ran off to join her sword sisters.

***

Arthur called over to anybody who could hear, 'Keep an eye on him,' he nodded to the body over his shoulder, '...and look after the children while I see who's in charge. Neil you are with me.' He lowered Caratacus to the ground and was rewarded with a groan.

'That will be us, then,' a voice came from the darkness. Four tall soldiers appeared then halted with precision, making way for a figure who stepped forward.

'Welcome, Arthur King. I am Bellerophon,' said the man.

***

Tristan had already shot two of the hill's climbers before the girls arrived. It stopped any more attempting the climb, but it meant that more fire was being laid on the defenders.

Four more dead in less than thirty seconds saw the Nazi uniformed attackers pull back to safety.

Tristan whispered the words and his bow left him. Exhausted, he slumped heavily on his backside before lying back. He felt someone sit next to him. Looking over, he saw one of the girls that had come to help him earlier. He smiled his smile, 'Hiya,' he said cheerfully.

Alexandra smiled back, 'Where are you from?' she asked.

***

King Bellerophon, bronze of skin, large of shoulder, big of belly with a voluminous beautifully curled beard, smiled bright.

'I have heard of you, Lord King,' Arthur said, bowing his head in respect.

'As I of you, Arthur King,' Bellerophon smiled and mirrored the bow. He continued, 'Two sets of guests in one visit? We barely get them at all. I knew something was happening. Let us go to my main hall and talk.'

'Thank you, Lord King, but can I ask what this place is? Are you here to help?'

'This, Arthur,' Bellerophon said, a large smile on his face, 'is the Forty-eight-hour Fort. We spend our days moving throughout this world and throughout history, appearing then disappearing, sometimes providing help, sometimes shelter and sometimes nothing. Sometimes we are just simply there.'

'And you stay for forty-eight hours?' asked Arthur.

Bellerophon's grin changed from joyful to sheepish. 'Err no, it's about forty-three but it doesn't sound as impressive.'

While Arthur chuckled, the fort's master continued, 'Is there anything else we can do for you other than provide security? We are already feeding your people and I have set aside rooms. You are in the royal guest room, there are two rooms either side for your retinue. Are we expecting trouble?'

Arthur had seen many halls in his lifetimes, but this may have been the largest. He kept looking around in awe as he told Bellerophon everything that had happened up until he and the others turned up at the fort.

Bellerophon leaned back on one of the oak tables, his sandals on the bench 'We only let you in because the three women asked us to.'

'Four,' Arthur corrected.

Bellerophon looked confused. 'No, just the three.'

'Gwenyvere?' Arthur asked.

Bellerophon answered, a little puzzled, 'I'm sorry my friend, none of them are called Gwenyvere.'

Arthur frowned, 'Then she won't be far away. I'll send out a party for her.' Bellerophon got up quickly, his face almost in pain. 'Arthur King, I think you should wait for the women to tell you themselves. While they have not mentioned any Gwenyvere, they did talk about their mother?'

'I never heard them call her that but maybe?' Arthur offered.

'She did not survive,' Bellerophon replied, adding quickly, 'I am sorry Lord King.'

The world left Arthur, life left his heart and pain took its place. He blinked, then he opened his mouth to speak but closed it when he didn't know what to say.

The logic of clutching desperation took over, a survival instinct to stop pain we all have.

'They don't call her mother!' He exclaimed and turned on his heel. That logic also moved him out of the great hall of Bellerophon as quickly as it could before reality could destroy the remnants of pathetic hope.

'Neil!' he shouted as quickly as he was walking, 'Let's find everybody and see what's going on.'

As moved through the sprawling corridors of the fort, asking directions, Neil could see Arthur's face change. He recognised the look; it was the haunting, hurting one he'd worn for so long, trapped upstairs in that living room.

Finally, after trying countless rooms they found the soldiers' mess hall. They were pleased to see that Caratacus had regained consciousness and was tentatively slurping some soup at a large table. Galahad and Tristan sat at the table while Mali, Kimberly and Alexandra stood talking to them.

Arthur looked at Galahad and, seeing the hurt on his friend's face, knew immediately that his worst fears were confirmed.

'Gone?' he asked, his voice weak.

Galahad nodded; a tear rolled down his cheek into the red hair of his beard. He brought in Arthur into an embrace, heads tucked into each other's necks as they sobbed.

'Gone,' Arthur managed to say again.

CHAPTER THIRTY

REINFORCEMENTS!

It was that sweet moment of waking and Caratacus had forgotten where he was. A zeptosecond of joy before his aching body reminded him. He wasn't waking up in the fresh smelling comfort of his huge bed as the whirr of the electric blinds introduced him to the delights of an easy day of not doing very much. But it wasn't just his body that brought back harsh reality, it was the mattress made of sacking and stuffed with straw and hay, and the sleeping noises coming from Tristan. They had one of the rooms next to Arthur's, having taken guard duty alongside Bellerophon's men between 12 and 2.

Caratacus was exhausted. He didn't know why he was awake, especially considering how quickly he'd fallen asleep. He shifted into a more comfortable position on his back, eyes trying unsuccessfully to pierce the darkness.

He'd been rocked by the news of Gwenyvere's death. He hadn't known her long, but he'd liked her and enjoyed their time together. To think of someone so vibrant not being here felt bewildering. He was glad that he'd been given that first guard stint after midnight as, no matter how tired he'd been, he would not have slept. He rolled over, trying to get comfy and swore quietly to himself, to which the sleeping Tristan replied by grunting and rolling over himself.

A minute later, warning bells pealed throughout the fort. Caratacus scrambled for the lamp that was next to his bed but was beaten to it by Tristan shouting a word at which the wall lamps burst into light. Caratacus sat up, unsure of what to do, while Tristan had already put on his boots and opened the door.

He turned to Caratacus. 'Let's go! It's an attack!' he shouted urgently.

By the time Caratacus and Tristan arrived on the ramparts, the bells had stopped and there were nervous murmurings amongst the defenders of the fort. Bellerophon, Arthur and Neil arrived and placed themselves on the balustrade above the main gate. It was Galahad's watch that had sounded the alarm and he was there, waiting.

'What's happening?' Arthur barked, squinting to see something. The sun was rising slowly behind them, so the slope they were watching was covered in shadow. Before an answer came, Arthur could see for himself. A first force of about twenty men were attacking up the slope with a secondary force consisting of the Nazis coming up in support behind them.

'Galahad? Neil? Remember the orders from last night? Do you have your twenty men?' Arthur asked. Galahad nodded.

'Ok, go and defend the east wall against any surprises,' he ordered. Galahad and Neil shouted to their men as Arthur turned to Bellerophon.

'Lord King, are you sure you are happy with me commanding your men?'

Bellerophon smiled grimly, 'Arthur King, While I look forward to the battle ahead, I have a feeling this fort...my fort, has been sent here to help you in your quest. Therefore, I am happy to put it under your command. As for my men, I have been banished here, but these men have been selected.'

'For what sire, and by whom?' Asked Tristan.

'The guards belong to the fort. In life, they were the best, the bravest and the fiercest, and at the point of their deaths they were brought here to serve. It is a final honour for a life bravely fought,' explained Bellerophon.

'They're dead?' Tristan asked again.

'They are neither dead nor alive,' Bellerophon shrugged nonchalantly. 'For the fight ahead, you couldn't ask for better warriors to assist you.'

'I don't think we are going to need them right now,' said Arthur, suddenly excited as he pointed towards the men that had reached the summit, 'That first group isn't attacking! They're running!' And then, recognising them, he shouted, 'It's the Three Kings!

'Archers to me,' he hollered. In seconds, he had ten in front of him. 'You five stay on the battlements. As soon as the front group are clear start peppering those bastards.' He turned to the others. 'You five. Follow me.'

Caratacus could just make out Tommy and Piogerix who were both struggling up the slope. It was strange to see Tommy McKracken doing anything other than sitting down and looking menacing.

By the time Arthur had come through the gate, the pursuers had decided to give up taking casualties from the archers on the fort's walls and had retreated once again.

Tommaltach shouted to his men as he, Adda and Piogerix stood before Arthur sucking in air. 'Go straight in. Get your breath back and we'll come and sort you out.'

Arthur grinned, 'Boys!' He opened his arms and they all stepped in together, hugging each other before breaking apart. 'I don't know what god, prophecy or itch brought you here, but you are a sight for sore eyes. We have an army approaching and we need help to keep them at bay for just under two days. Up for it?'

'Two,' said Piogerix through heavy inhales and exhales.

'Yes, two days, sort of, and then we are safe,' replied Arthur.

'No, two armies...two armies are headed here.'

'And Cromh Du,' put in Adda.

Arthur smiled grimly. 'Is that all? Let's get you in then. It seems we have some talking to do.'

Adda held back. Dragging his massive frame up to the summit had hit him particularly hard. He sat down, still breathing heavily, before hearing a shout behind from the fort's walls: 'Shift your arse, fatty!'

He didn't move, just growled to himself and then chuckled.

'Fatty?' Another shout.

Adda, still facing down the slope shouted, 'Tristan, when I get in there, I'm going to snap your neck.'

Tristan laughed as he watched his old friend and sparring partner struggle up from the floor and wipe the bits of grass from his behind. Adda looked up and smiled to see Tristan, a woman standing very close to him. 'Meet me at the bar and get me a drink,' he snarled.

Tristan leaned on the wall, still grinning. 'It's a fort, you human dreadnaught. There isn't a bar.'

'You don't think I haven't been here before, idiot? Of course, there's a bar.'

Tristan was about to shout back when Bellerophon interrupted, 'There is a bar if you want one. The fort seems to know what people want and then tries its best to provide it.'

Tristan frowned while thinking then asked, 'How come the fort didn't show me the bar?'

Bellerophon smiled and nodded towards Alexandra. 'Maybe the fort has already given you something you want.'

Tristan blushed before Alexandra playfully slapped him on the backside and walked in to find her sisters.

An hour later and back in the main hall there was much hugging, introductions and shows of anger and tears at the news of loss. Bellerophon and his guests sat on benches to catch up on what had happened and what was to come.

'Get me an ale,' Adda shouted at a server, 'and a milkshake for my girlfriend,' he indicated to Tristan opposite.

Tristan folded his arms and smiled, holding in a laugh.

Arthur stood and all individual chats stopped. He was at the end of the large table. At the head of the table, Bellerophon lounged on his throne. On Arthur's right sat Galahad, Caratacus, Neil, Tristan and Kimberley. On his left, Tommy, Piogerix, Adda, Alexandra, Mali and the chief of the Royal Guard, Jawhar Al-Saqli, easily recognisable in turban and flowing royal blue robes.

Arthur addressed them. 'Warriors, we find ourselves, yet again, at the end of the world. It seems clear that the Dark have been manipulating all of us to get to a point where they'll finally succeed and drag This World into chaos. I'm sorry to say that I unwittingly allowed them free rein, for which I am sorry.'

Murmurs grew louder, and Arthur held his hands up. 'We were all fooled, but while they have manoeuvred us to their will, I do not think they are the only power in play.'

He paused.

'Look around us. What have they done?' He laughed suddenly, 'They've brought together the last remaining warriors of Arthur. And more – they've reunited them with the Three Kings!' He pointed at them individually, and chuckled to himself. 'Or isn't it the three bastards? That's what they call you?'

'And proud,' answered Adda with a laugh.

Everyone on the table laughed and Arthur stood up, warming to the subject, 'Fate has brought together the Dark's greatest enemies and thrown in three warrior women trained by our magnificent sword sister Gwenyvere, and a weird, moaning man who seems to have a bit of Magick in him.'

More laughter followed and Caratacus smiled, blushed and waved, not embarrassed by the insult but by being mentioned in that company. He looked around and couldn't believe he was here, couldn't believe how much his life had changed.

Arthur continued, 'So, not only have we all found each other, we have found each other in a Magick fort, protecting the sons and daughters of kings and queens. A fort, I may add, that is defended by some of the greatest warriors in This World's history. Come on!' He was pacing now, making eye contact with whoever had their heads raised, 'COME ON!' He shouted again. 'We can hold here. We can keep out the Dark because we all know what will happen once there is no one to stand against Cromh Du – the scales tip to darkness.'

He sat down and everyone remained silent. Arthur looked at Bellerophon. 'How many hours do we have to last out before the fort moves?'

Bellerophon looked to his second in command. Jawhar stood up and bowed his head. 'Twenty-nine and a half, sire,' he said before sitting down again.

Arthur paused. 'That's all we have to hold out for. We need to stay alive, move and then start planning properly to fight back. Mali? The situation from the west please?'

Mali looked uncomfortable with the attention, but it was plain to see that she'd taken on the leadership of her sisters since the death of Gwenyvere. 'When we blew the bridge, I would guess that maybe 10,000 soldiers made it over. They are beginning to arrive here.'

'We know there are thirty thousand troops in This world heading to this hill from the north,' said Piogerix soberly.

'How?' Asked Galahad, 'How have they so many warriors over here without being noticed? How are they so near to us when we didn't know we would be here, and the fort certainly didn't?'

Tommaltach smiled grimly. 'Fluke. Those soldiers weren't intended for us, they were intended to bolster the real army when Cromh Du brought in martial law.'

Galahad shook his head. 'This is crazy! He can't do that. How has he managed to gain so much power?'

'They've planned properly, and they've been patient,' Tommaltach answered. They have people everywhere and, until now, they haven't made any huge, stupid moves.'

'Stupid moves?' Bellerophon interrupted. 'They seem to hold all the cards.'

'That's my point, Lord King,' continued Tommaltach. 'There's rioting in major cities, rumours of war, law and order is breaking down. They have a man now, Killian Penhalligon, who has been asked to run the country. Do you hear me? He *has been asked*!'

'That politician? How has he ridden so high in the Dark as a mortal?' asked Tristan.

'He isn't. He's one of the hated ones, the Dywylldri. The Dark Three.'

While the girls and Neil were none the wiser, Caratacus could see how the news affected the others.

Arthur stood up again. 'Gods, they are so much more advanced in their planning than I thought. It's not just about surviving here, we have war in That World, and I have no idea what'll happen here when orc or goblin armies are revealed.'

He stopped, noticing that Caratacus had his hand up, like he was in school. Arthur sighed and grunted permission for him to ask the question.

'If they control the armies in This World and That, as well as the government, then why are they spending so much effort to destroy us?'

'That is something we don't know, but I believe we are to find out,' said Piogerix, standing as the warning bells started to chime.

They all looked to Arthur. 'I don't think this is the final battle any more. I think it's the start of the final war,' he said, and went to the walls.

CHAPTER THIRTY-FIVE
HARK THE HERALD TEPETI SHOUTS...

Since midday, soldiers of the Dark had streamed in from the north and the west into the valleys below the fort. Arthur could see how it was worrying people, so he ordered only lookouts on the walls and made sure the others stayed busy and away from the views of impending doom.

Adda had been correct when he told Tristan that the fort provided what you needed. While exploring for a place to hold the children safely, Galahad had come across a hall the size of Bellerophon's which had a giant screen and a projector, and instead of wooden benches and tables, a floor covered in bean bags. Arthur stepped into the hall to check all was well and laughed when the children dragged him to a beanbag that they had kept for any warriors who blundered in.

Back on the wall he smiled at the memory. He'd stayed to watch cartoons with them for a while and joined in their laughter. He would remember it forever, because those young people were bonding. The families of many of those children despised each other, often for actions that had taken place hundreds of years before they were born. If they could get through this, if they could live, then the next generation of rulers may decide not to wage war on friends.

A horn sounded, lazily, from below, waking Arthur from his daydream. He folded his arms and looked at what was to come next.

'Oooh,' said Piogerix, 'How traditional. They've sent a herald.'

The herald was neither human nor orc but a feathered Tepeti. The Tepeti had skin the colour of a clear summer sky. A slender race, on average a foot taller than the tallest of you humans. They were of That World, living as clans in their tribal lands deep in the tropical forests of Tepet and they rarely left. When they did, they weren't only conspicuous by their blue skin and bright plume but how loud they were. How loud? As loud as certain American or British tourists when they are abroad.

Unlike the much-needed selective deafness of a lot of the people who deal with the tourists I mentioned above, the Tepetis' hearing was extremely poor, hence their need to shout, and because of that, their villages were not hard to find. Every Tepeti's feathers were different, and that came down to personal choice and status. Some were traditional and were covered from head to foot, while others plucked themselves, showing their arms, their legs, their heads or a selection of limbs.

The Tepeti below was of high status. He had kept his legs, arms and back feathered, but his chest and head had been plucked. His plume was vibrant, a mixture of bright, primary colours which contrasted with the black of the giant shire unicorn he was languidly riding towards the foot of the slope.

'Arsehole has slaves,' Tristan stated as he saw that the Tepeti was accompanied by two human slaves on a leash he held. They were topless and head-shaven with colourful trousers and chests adorned with a feather tattoo. The top of the feather was yellow, the bottom, blue, to indicate the clan that owned them.

The warriors on the wall fell silent for a moment before Caratacus asked lightly, 'Slavery is allowed in That World then?'

'In a lot of places and amongst a lot of races it sadly is,' answered Galahad bitterly.

Arthur turned to his warriors, 'Right, they are doing this properly, so I'm going down. Who's with me?'

'Three kings?' suggested Galahad.

'Sod that,' growled Adda, 'I'm not walking down that hill.'

'Me and Piogerix are with you,' said Tommaltach, already moving. 'I'll do the talking. You two are far too honest.'

The three made their way carefully down the slope. Below, the Tepeti looked around at the view as if on a morning stroll. The kings reached the bottom, all panting heavily, especially Arthur who was struggling to suck in air. The Tepeti looked at them. His blue face, with its wide, flat nose and eagle like eyes, broke into a broad, gracious smile showing tens of small, sharp teeth. From the back of his saddle, he brought out a large golden ear trumpet.

'KING ARTHUR AP....' he began.

'Wait!' Arthur shouted and gulped in another few breaths, his hands on his knees. 'I'm not ready,' he groaned and then he retched, a vain, pulsating, dry heave which was followed by another.

Piogerix put a supportive hand on Arthur's back, but both he and Tommaltach looked away, embarrassed, while the Tepeti just stared with an appalled look on his face. Arthur stood, staggering slightly and spitting on the floor. Finally, he looked at the herald.

'KING ARTHUR AP UTHER...' The herald began and then stopped as Arthur started heaving again. He stumbled into Piogerix and looked up at the druid for help. The whiff of Arthur's breath made Piogerix wince and turn away.

Eyes wetter than a puddle, Arthur looked at Piogerix pleadingly, 'Have you got any water?' he asked.

'You need some mints, my old friend,' Piogerix replied.

Arthur rolled his red eyes. 'Funny. Have you got any water?' He asked again.

Piogerix was already handing over an old army water bottle from his belt and as Arthur went to grab it, Piogerix pulled it away. 'Don't let your lips touch the rim though!' he said.

'Alright, don't panic!' Arthur said with exasperation and grabbed the bottle. After much tipping, swilling, drinking and spitting he handed it back, 'Have you got any mints on you, then?' he asked quietly.

The Tepeti stared at the inanity of the conversation before the battle to end wars.

'Nope,' Piogerix replied shaking his head. Arthur looked over at Tommaltach who also shook his head.

He looked up at the herald, 'You?'

The Tepeti's eyes widened in shock and his look in response was as if he'd stepped in something brown that had been shot from an animal's anus. He was so taken by surprise that he was about to respond before a lifetime of experience kicked in. He looked with disdain and waited to see if any further retching was to be forthcoming. He decided to chance it.

'KING ARTHUR AP UTHER. I SEE YOU. I PRESENT MYSELF, TEE-TEH-TEH AMLYANNTHAN, TOP OF THE TREES OF THE YELLOW CLAN, A BRIGHT LORD OF THE TEPETI AND YOU SEE ME TODAY AS A HERALD OF HIS HOLINESS CROMH DU.'

He bowed low, eyes down, his head even below his unicorn's. Then he put his trumpet to his ear and waited for the response.

And waited.

Looking confused, Tee-Teh-Teh sat upright, repeated his greeting and again fulfilled his bow and waited.

And waited.

He looked up again, confused. The kings before him were clearly waiting for something. Tommaltach broke the silence.

'A king does not talk up to a common herald,' he growled.

After a series of humiliations in a space of ten minutes, the veneer cracked.

'I LIVE AMONGST THE TOP OF THE TREES,' he snapped quietly – albeit quietly for a Tepeti – indicating that by 'top of the trees' he meant that he was at the highest point of his clan and Tepeti society, the equivalent of royalty.

'Get off the horse, you lanky blue arse!' Adda's voice echoed down the slope.

Standing behind Adda, Caratacus recognised the feelings of confusion and pride- destroying frustration on the feathered blue man's face and, for a moment, felt some sort of cross-species solidarity.

The Tepeti admitted defeat with a loud sigh, followed by loud clicking noises. Immediately the two slaves shifted into action, one went down on his hands and knees to become a step while the other moved to the side as something to lean on while the Tepeti dismounted.

Once more he repeated his greeting. This time, to make certain he was not rebuffed, he added Piogerix and Tommaltach's titles and lineage.

Arthur responded in formal fashion ending with, 'I see you,' and followed by a bow in which he was joined by the other two.

Tee-Teh-Teh gestured towards the gaggle on the slope.

'YOU ARE A MERE HUNDRED…'

'One hundred and ninety-nine…' Tommaltach interrupted.

Another large SIGH.

'STILL, WE ARE MANY TIMES THAT. YOU MUST SEE THERE IS NO WAY OUT OF THIS ALIVE IF YOU DO NOT GIVE US WHAT WE DESIRE.'

'Go ahead then, speak now. Tell us what you want.' said Arthur.

'THE CHILDREN, AND YOUR SURRENDER, ARTHUR AP UTHER.'

'What else?' asked Tommaltach.

'THAT'S IT. NOTHING MORE.'

Arthur shrugged, told the Tepeti he'd have an answer in two hours' time, and the three walked back up the hill.

CHAPTER 36

FIRST BLOOD

For a moment, the ten stared up at the fort. Two commanders of the armies, the rest were senior officers.

'I say we attack immediately,' shouted one of the commanders. General Vynar Borthos was dressed in the field uniform of a British Army General. He removed his peaked cap – revealing thinning, strawberry-blond fuzz that matched the colour of his bristling moustache – and tucked it under his arm. He pointed his swagger stick up the hill. 'Skee, they have given their answer to the herald. Let's just get on with this. Send our troops up there and finish this before the Three arrive... or worse.'

He flickered then as if the broadband was rubbish and the signal had cut out.

General Skee looked over, 'Borthos old chap, why don't you revert back? I don't think subterfuge is needed now do you?'

Borthos shrugged his shoulders and, with ease, the ageing general grew and expanded, shedding his disguise to reveal a much more solid figure. Skee raised his head to stare at the now seven-foot Borthos. Green skinned, rough like sandpaper, and bald except for what you might call a hipster bun. His four, muscled arms brushed himself down as if the Magick he had used was something he could touch.

He grunted at Skee in some sort of thanks, 'I keep forgetting I am that little pale man. I quite enjoy commanding This World's British soldiers, they're good when they stop moaning. There'd be trouble if they realised they're fighting for us and taking orders from a Garkanarian.'

'Are there any original senior officers left?' asked Skee.

'Some who have always belonged us, a few that have come over and some very senior officers who don't know what's going on but who are coordinating down in London,' answered Borthas.

'The others?'

'Tribute for the Dark Lord.'

Skee looked back up the hill. 'Powerful Magick I'm sure,' he said to himself, and then to Borthos, 'With all due respect, General, not all our armies have arrived. We aren't at full muster. We should wait.'

The growl from Borthos was not for his colleague, just an expression of disgust for the situation. 'They are few and no match for us. I say we attack. Use my elite guard.'

'It would be a waste of good warriors,' Skee turned to him. Both were old soldiers and good at what they did. Unlike many of the Dark, these two respected each other. This wasn't an argument; this was a disagreement on tactics and strategy.

'Skee, we have the bulk here already. Send them up. My guard will finish it. They are a few hundred, weighed down by a group of children.'

'Arthur and his men are there. One of my sections has also reported that, this morning, the Three Kings broke through and are with them.' Skee started stroking his chin.

Borthas smiled. 'That makes it more interesting. All of them?' Seeing Skee's short nod, he said, 'I like Mynyddmawr…' before shaking his head, 'Let us get this done, let us attack quickly and end them.'

Skee looked up again. He wanted to wait, he was a controlled officer, he didn't do rash, but he also knew that his army had had too many reverses since hitting This World and an army ran on morale as much as anything else. They needed a quick win. Still stroking his chin, he realised that Borthas was waiting for an answer and nodded. 'Send in the auxiliaries and then your guard.'

Borthas clapped his two sets of hands and turned to the officers, issuing the orders for an immediate attack.

***

Boom. Boom.

The drums began, the deep thumping pushing the armies of the Dark to move. The part that was made up of slaves didn't need such encouragement, the whips and threats of violence did that.

Boom. Boom.

At the foot of the hills, it was those slaves that formed ranks first. Death awaited them, but if they lived and were noticed there was a chance they could be freed. By 'freed' I actually mean they would stop being slaves and, instead, be recruited on a fifty-year contract into the army, but when you have nothing, a day off a month and money that is yours is incentive enough to face certain death on a hill.

Boom. Boom.

In front of them, five giant horses pulled five thin wheeled carts into view before stopping. Each horse was ridden by a black cloaked figure. Their faces were hidden but all who witnessed the slow procession knew these were Dark Magickers. They dismounted as one, as if choreographed. The noise of spitting came from the ranks. The slaves did it to ward off evil and, in this army of the Dark, they knew it when they saw it.

Boom. Boom.

Whatever had been hauled on the carts was hidden, covered by tarpaulin, a different colour for each cart. The Magickers moved like dancers, slow and deliberate, to stand behind their respective covers and, as one, pulled them away, letting them slip to the floor at their feet.

Boom. Boom.

On each cart, three cages were revealed, the type you saw on cartoons, the type you saw Tweety Pie the bird living in, safely away from Sylvester the cat and his Machiavellian plotting. Size-wise they could fit a human head... because each had a human head in it, eyes closed, facing towards the slope.

The drums stopped.

The noise of a silent army is not actually silent, but it is hushed, broken by shuffling feet, bodies agitated by nerves or excitement, armour knocking armour. Through it came the noises of the animals – horses, cattle and sheep for food, mammoths and horned Dreestenders from That World for battle – but, over it all, came the deep mesmeric chanting of the Magickers.

As soon as that chanting began, the eyes of the heads opened as if sharply awakened from a deep sleep, then shock turned to horror at the realisation of their reality. They had been kept alive for one reason and that was to call the army of the Dark to attack.

They screamed.

As soon as they did, slaves ran to each head and in front of each screaming mouth placed a megaphone, magnifying the noise and sending it to speakers throughout the camp to be heard by their forces and, most importantly, by the enemies on the hill.

It was five long minutes. The heads shrieked until they couldn't any more and, when the last head stopped, Generals Skee and Borthos looked at each other, nodded, raised their hands and dropped them as one. The slave army roared and charged Arthur's hill.

***

Listening to the screams was excruciating. Even after thirty seconds it was affecting the defenders of the fort. The screams of the children deep inside joined that coming from down the hill and not even Galahad could calm them.

On the wall Adda spat and shouted over to Arthur ten men down from him.

'They are cocky, they're only attacking this side of the fort.'

Arthur grunted in acknowledgement then raised his arm. 'ARCHERS!' he bellowed. For a flash he thought about the poor slaves that were being forced up that hill but his next thought was about the people in the fort. His hand went down. 'FIRE!'

With a commander's eye, he nodded in satisfaction that so many had gone down. These first volleys had to count because they didn't have enough arrows to keep it up. He let three more volleys go before the enemy were checked by the dead and by fear. The volleys would not work as efficiently now the first ranks of the Dark were thinned.

***

Wave after wave came at the fort. Only one of the enemy had reached the top of the wall so far, and he and his ladder had quickly been pushed away. With few arrows, Arthur ensured that no further enemy soldiers scaled the walls, his warriors pushing ladders away when they were thick with attackers. Others threw rocks or anything else they could to dislodge down on to the soldiers of the Dark.

Caratacus was terrified, a feeling he was now used to. He'd thanked whatever god was listening when Galahad had come over to him as the first ladders hit.

'Cati, please don't take this the wrong way, but you are no use up here.'

'I agree,' Caratacus nodded with conviction.

'Get some of the older children and help give out water during the fighting. Keep your head down and look after the others.'

Caratacus nodded. 'What if they get in? What do I do then?'

Galahad was already moving away but he looked back and grinned. 'Fight or die,' he said.

Caratacus rolled his eyes. 'Marvellous,' he said and ran to get water.

Despite Arthur's best efforts, another attacker made it on to the ramparts, then another, and while they were being killed as fast as they found their footing, it was only a matter of time before the dam broke.

A matter of right now.

Arthur's sword was knocked from his hand and, with no time to Magickly call it back, looked helplessly as his opponent lifted his sword high for a killing blow. The man's scream of triumph stopped in an instant as Arthur punched him square in the face. Arthur picked up the now befuddled man by the seat of his trousers and his collar and threw him off the wall with a roar. Thousands upon thousands of the Dark continued to attack, the noise like storm waves against cliffs.

'Good gods,' Arthur groaned and leaned heavily against the fort's wall. He'd always thought his last death would be different. I mean, fighting to the death trying to defend children was good, but he'd always liked the time he'd died after falling asleep softly. He bowed his head again and closed his eyes. 'Gods, can't you just give me a break? Can't you just help me?'

He felt a hand on his shoulder, and he stood up straight, ready to fight again. A female voice said calmly in his ear, 'What's the magic word?'

He turned to see the goddess Latis smiling back at him. Gone were the pyjamas, face pack and towel and before him was a warrior dressed for battle, her dark ringleted hair bound on top of her head. I would say she looked like a goddess but... well...y'know.

Arthur dropped to one knee. 'Holy one,' he said.

'I see you have forgotten about me already.'

'No! Of course not! I... we...' he blustered.

'I told you to call me. You did and I am here.' She held up her hands before Arthur spoke again. 'I am feeling quite invigorated. Things that we deities love—' she started counting on her fingers, '—worshippers, being worshipped, receiving offerings, are looking up. Since you called me, I have noticed that I have some new worshippers amongst the children of your group,' she smiled, 'I have been hearing their prayers. It's wonderful! And as for offerings,' she stretched out her hand and Excalibur appeared. She swung it and held it aloft, looking at it almost with love. 'This...' She blew out her cheeks. 'The moment you dedicated it to me, I felt like one of the bigger gods, you know like Thor, or Nodens or Fukk.' She carried on looking at it, then shook her head as if coming out of a trance. 'But anyway, I am here, and I want to return it.'

'I gave it gladly,' Arthur replied reverently.

She looked from the sword to Arthur, 'I know, that's why it was important and that's why I return it. Give it to the snoring boy or something. It worked and now I've come to help you and my new followers.'

She put her arms on her hips, looked at the attacking army and took in everything as if she was measuring up a kitchen.

'Quite the situation then?' she said to nobody, continuing as if to an invisible ally, 'so it's Arthur, his warriors, the Dark... oooh and Cromh Du is on his way? The chosen one is here as well? Wow!'

She looked around and stared directly at me. 'Quite the story, Garan?' she said, smiling. I returned the smile and nodded.

'Who is that?' Arthur asked, noticing me for the first time.

Latis ignored him and helped him get up. 'It doesn't matter. I have accepted your call. You have my help. I accepted your gift in that glade and now I give one in return,' she tapped his cheek gently and disappeared.

***

His name was Clatack-Ror, and he was a pretty handy warrior of the Blood Axe Tribe. On this occasion, he'd pulled ahead of the other attackers from his tribe. Death, plunder and rape were at the front of his mind, not to mention the back and all the bits in the middle. He looked up at the walls and recognised one of the human females who had killed so many orcs at the top of the bridge before its destruction.

'Bitch,' he shouted and increased in speed, 'I'm going to make it slow and painful,' he thought, 'and then before you die, I'm going to fu…'

His train of thought stopped moving at the same time his legs did. His head hadn't stopped moving though, because it was no longer attached to Clatack-Ror's body but was sailing through the air, about 50 foot above it.

A moment after Latis disappeared Arthur heard a change in the noise of the attackers. It went from the roars that promised violence to the cries of people who were on the wrong end of it. He also heard a lot of swearing from the warriors on the walls.

The orc behind the headless Clatack-Ror stopped. A human-looking woman had appeared ahead of them. This one was about forty-foot-tall and was smiling nastily, like she wanted to hurt lots of people. She calmly thrust out her arm towards part of the attacking army, palm facing them, and immediately they burst into flames. The orc stopped in horror but was shoved forward by the oblivious warriors behind. The shove forward became a panicked push back as realisation hit hard. What hit even harder was a nonchalant smack from Latis that wiped out fifteen of them. That orc behind headless Clatack-Ror stared, unsure what to do. That was immediately rectified by Latis' small-van-sized right boot connecting with him, and him ending up as a piece of meat about five foot away from Skee. The General looked up, sniffed, and nodded at Borthos who nodded back.

Skee looked over to one of the waiting officers. 'Sound the retreat,' he said calmly and, a minute later, the screams of the headless began.

CHAPTER THIRTY-SEVEN
THE DEATHS OF WARRIORS, THE END OF KINGS

'They're forcing us back again!' Shane shouted incredulously as he, his siblings, and the senior officers watched their forces scatter down the hill from their command tent below.

The Dark Three had arrived just after the appearance of the goddess, and their helicopter had touched down into chaos. They'd expected to arrive in time for the capture of Arthur, his men and the royal brats, and, more importantly, a few hours before the arrival of Cromh Du. Instead, they witnessed the desperate retreat of their armies while their enemies remained safe behind the walls of a mystical fort that had only arrived the day before.

'Bastards!' Cate spat as their warriors piled down the hill. She had spent the past few days appearing on official television channels stirring up hatred towards anybody who entered her sights, even accusing Killian's Government of ignoring the people. They'd both laughed at the plan, but they weren't laughing now.

Killian didn't show his anger, but his siblings knew it was there. He turned towards Skee and Borthos, 'Generals, it seems your tactics are failing. Tell me why you should remain alive?' It was said calmly but no one was in any doubt as to the reality of the threat.

Skee answered quickly, knowing his fellow general would not respond in any way that could help them remain breathing. He went onto one knee. 'Dark One, we can only apologise. Our orders did not include a retreat. I will order the deaths of a tenth of our officers involved. It may inspire better leadership for our final assault.'

'No more chances. Darkness is only a few hours away and with it comes the Master. I want this finished and I want their dead bodies, bar the child hostages, arranged outside the fort.'

Shane sat on one of the chairs in the open command tent. 'All of our forces are here now. Why don't we send them all up?'

Borthos had calmed since the rebuke and bowed before Oriole. 'Dark One, we have been attacking by regiment because there are just too many of us. More warriors would be a hinderance.'

Shane was about to answer when his brother intervened, 'My brother is correct. Send all our forces up there. No one stops until we are inside. I don't care if the bodies of our dead pile up to the top of those walls. Let them be the bridge that brings us victory. Sound the attack now!'

Skee and Borthos bowed stiffly and, moments later, the heads started screaming.

***

Caratacus sat with his back to the wall on top of the battlements. He was hunched over as if the pressure of life was bearing down on him. His eyes were open, but unfocussed. On his knees lay Excalibur and even its shine didn't draw his eyes.

After the intervention of Latis, Arthur had called him over. 'You ok?' the King asked. Caratacus nodded, relieved that the fighting had stopped. Arthur smiled. 'Not long to go now. We're going to be ok. Hold out a day or so and we are gone. Here,' he held out his hand, mumbled, and a shining sword appeared.

'Excalibur?' Caratacus asked shocked.

Arthur nodded. 'Latis didn't need it any more, so she gave it back and now I think you should have it.'

Caratacus shook his head. 'I won't need it.'

'Maybe not, but take it anyway. For me,' Arthur said as Caratacus took it reverentially.

Arthur leant over and whispered some words in his ear. 'The first word calls it,' he said, 'the other sends it away.'

Caratacus looked up at him, 'I…I don't know what to say. Thank you.'

Now, one small fight later he wished he'd never seen the sword. He was numb with exhaustion and heaviness lay on his soul. He knew why. He'd killed someone. Now, when he closed his eyes, the orc's face loomed – the hatred, the shock and then the terror. It had been laughing moments before, having reached the battlements, causing death and chaos. Caratacus wanted to run but screamed in fear, pushing Excalibur into the attacker's throat. Now, he wanted to cry but couldn't as the attack screams began from the valley below and Caratacus finally closed his eyes, hoping it would shut out the noise and the terror it brought.

It didn't.

'They're coming!' Someone shouted from the opposite wall, 'From all sides!'

The screams were now being drowned out as the roar of thousands of warriors came to destroy them.

High on the largest wall above the main gate, Adda could feel the fear emanating from the defenders. Despair was contagious and he had to do something to stop it. Heads turned towards him as he struggled to stand on the wall. He steadied himself, his legs wide apart, before unbuttoning his breeches and pissing off the wall towards oncoming death.

The warriors around him started laughing and the laughter spread quickly as others turned to see what was happening. It was a moment that paused fear.

After shaking himself comically, Adda slowly buttoned back up, called his giant sword and bellowed, 'Come, you sons of whores! Come and die!'

It wasn't the screams, or the attackers' roar, but the laughter that brought Caratacus from his torpor. Arthur went down on one knee in front of him a look of concern on his face.

'Cati, please, go and protect the children.'

Caratacus looked up and shook his head, too choked with emotion to answer. His face said no with much more force and Arthur understood. 'OK, stand away from the walls and plug the gaps,' before running to defend the walls.

It wasn't long before all four of the fort's walls were covered with ladders full of attackers, time and luck disappearing fast. Piogerix used no Magick defending his section of the wall. People forgot that he'd been a warrior king decades before taking the druid's staff. His white robe was wet with sweat and streaked with the blood of others but still his sword arm kept moving, cleaving and hacking, ensuring no one managed to gain a foothold.

As a druid, his life of millennia was one of searching for balance and that is what he sought as death was close. He'd held back his Magick, trying to find the best time to use it. Too soon and he would be too tired to continue fighting, too late and he may not have enough energy for any useful Magick, and too late would be just that. He'd been waiting for something else to save them, but now he understood that it had to be him.

Two of the fort's defenders had managed to push away a ladder from the wall. It gave them a welcome lull of a few seconds before another ladder was placed and the bloody murder would begin again. Piogerix blew hard, using his sleeve to wipe the sweat from his eyes. When they were clear, he looked out at the blanket of marauding soldiers that seemed to cover every part of the land. It was time. He looked over to Tommaltach. He was commanding the wall to Piogerix's left and had stepped back to assess where the next threat was coming from. He turned when Piogerix shouted his name.

'Call the reserves! Call them all!' Piogerix shouted.

Tommaltach was about to ask if he was sure, but he didn't. He could read the situation and he could read his friend. If this continued, they'd be dead within the hour so he nodded and shouted to his messenger to blow the horn that would call the reserves.

Piogerix took a swig from the ladle in one of the water buckets and beckoned Tommaltach to walk to the wall with him. Instinctively, they put their arms around each other. 'Come,' the druid king said conversationally, 'defend me while I give them hell.'

'Try and stay alive,' Tommaltach said.

'I'll try. But please, if I can't, make sure Adda is ok. You know how emotional he gets.'

Caratacus was on the wall on the other side of the fort with Arthur when the horn sounded. He glanced over and did a double take when he saw Piogerix climb to the top of the wall. It looked so out of place amongst the chaos of battle.

Piogerix spread his arms and rose ten feet in the air, his eyes blazing a bright yellow.

Above the druid, pitch-black clouds formed and multiplied until they covered the sky, making the day into dusk. The fighting on the walls continued, but the warriors attacking up the hill stopped, sensing that something was about to happen and it probably wasn't going to be anything nice. The wind whipped up and a huge peal of thunder was the starting pistol for rain. It was light at first but, like the wind, it quicky got stronger.

The fort's defenders seemed to be protected from the worst of the weather, but they were still being drenched by rain. Caratacus didn't care, as long as it stopped the fighting. He leaned on the wall and watched as a ladder of four attackers was lifted by a gust and thrown back. Lightning followed, sheets of it at first to light the chaos, and then forked strikes came from the gathered clouds randomly hitting groups of soldiers.

Any warriors of the Dark that weren't lying on their stomachs in fear were running for their lives down the hill as more and more bolts of lightning struck amongst them.

Piogerix screamed, his head lolling in exhaustion.

'Enough, druid!' Adda shouted up, over the din of the storm. And he and the men on the wall watched Piogerix slowly land and slump to his knees. It was when he fell over on to his back that they saw the arrow protruding from his chest.

'No!' shouted Adda.

Far below, despite the rain, the wind and an army retreating in disarray, Cate watched, smiling. Her eyes red with immortal power, she whispered the words of Magick, and her bow disappeared.

Adda, Galahad, Tristan, Arthur and Caratacus stood in a semi-circle as Tommaltach kneeled down next to Piogerix, pulling him close, gently telling his friend that all would be well. Blood seeped from the side of the Druid's mouth. 'Stop fussing Tommaltach,' he chided with a laugh and then grimaced as a spasm of pain hit.

'Heal yourself,' pleaded Adda.

Piogerix shook his head. 'Too late my old friend, I've nothing left.'

Galahad went down on one knee and gently ripped the fabric around the arrow to look at the wound. Piogerix placed his hand on Galahad's arm before it slipped off weakly.

'No. Stop. Please. I'm done, and I need to say something before it's over.'

'It's not over!' Adda growled but Piogerix ignored him. 'This storm won't last much longer now that I'm not powering it and that means you still have seventeen hours to hold out. You must get away and regroup. Unite the kingdoms in That World and begin the fight back in This. I am afraid that the Dark rules here now.'

Tommaltach hugged him closer. Caratacus, unsurprised, was still deeply uncomfortable at seeing the gangster with tears running down his cheeks.

Piogerix coughed again before continuing. 'Arthur, I am afraid it's all on you yet again, my dear old friend.'

Arthur dropped to a knee and smiled sadly. 'Isn't it always?'

Piogerix grimaced again. 'Arthur. Don't ever isolate yourself again. The depression feeds on it and it's as bad an enemy as Cromh Du himself. The worlds will need you more than ever in the days to come. Keep your warriors close.'

Tristan, as ever, looked to lighten even the darkest of times. 'Warriors? There's only me and Gal left.'

'And Caratacus,' Piogerix pointed at the quiet man standing just a little further back from the rest. Caratacus was so upset to see the druid in pain. He'd grown to care about Piogerix, but he felt awkward being part of a group that had known him for thousands of years. He blushed and shrugged when he realised that they were all looking at him, 'I'm not a warrior,' he said weakly.

'Make him one Arthur. Make him one now, for me,' Piogerix asked.

Arthur looked confused. 'What do you mean?'

'You're Arthur. You can do whatever you want,' the druid reached over and gripped Arthur's podgy hand. 'Do it for me, knight him, swear on Caledfwlch or whatever and when I am gone, burn my body so my spirit goes to Otherworld. I'd say I'd wait for you, but I hope that will be a long time yet.'

Arthur nodded. He called Caledfwlch and held it blade down. He looked at Galahad and Tristan, 'Put your hands on the pommel boys,' and then to Caratacus, he smiled, 'Come on then, place your hands on top.'

He paused for a moment and looked at Piogerix for inspiration which didn't come. 'Caratacus ap Neb, from this moment on you are part of us...' he paused, 'We aren't called anything though?'

Without thinking, Caratacus whispered, 'Aren't you the knights of the round table?'

Piogerix laughed weakly, blood ran from the side of his mouth. Galahad and Tristan groaned, and Arthur let out a little laugh. 'That'll do. Caratacus ap Neb from this moment on you are one of the knights of the round table.' He nodded at Caratacus and then looked at Piogerix. 'You happy now?' he asked.

But Piogerix had already gone.

CHAPTER THIRTY-EIGHT
THE BLOODY REUNION

Cassie had been in the fort for twenty-four hours. With the situation so fraught, the constant attacks and so many strangers within the walls seeking its protection, it was no wonder she wandered the corridors unchallenged. That changed as soon as she recognised the girls she'd fought on the bridge to Cantre'r Gwaelod and she moved with more care. That concern meant that it had taken her longer to find the room Arthur had been assigned. When she arrived, she could hear him inside so hid herself in the joists above the corridor and waited until it became quieter.

An hour later, he was either asleep or tired, but regardless, he would not be ready for an attack. It would be a risk using Magick to enter but any warning could be enough. She remembered from training that the place to Magickly transport to surprise someone was always just behind a closed door, it was a space that was usually free of anything and therefore any danger. She prepared herself and then leaped.

***

He'd fallen asleep as soon as his head hit the pillow, but a few hours later he'd stirred for no reason and then couldn't get back to that safe warm place. He decided that sleep wasn't going to return and, rather than look at nothing, he'd stretch his aching muscles. That's when he heard the noise, the gentle popping of someone arriving through Magick. His response was instant, a word of power and he became invisible. The new arrival approached the bed and seeing it empty, fell into a crouch as if expecting an attack. He moved quickly to block the door before dropping the Magick and calling forth his sword.

'Looking for someone?' he asked.

Fear and anger touched her. The noise of his quiet question almost deafened as she changed stance. She knew it wasn't Arthur as soon as she saw the figure before her. Too slight for the chubby king.

She prepared to attack, and her opponent's face came into the light of one of the torches. It looked like...but it couldn't be...her chest tightened. The shock was so much she felt her legs go. How could he be here? Now? She dropped both her short swords. All she could do was say his name.

***

He moved to the right quickly, putting the large bed behind the warrior he was facing, giving them the chance of moving to the left or an attack that he was ready for.

'Neil?'

Ready for everything except that.

***

The shock of seeing Neil incapacitated her for only a moment. Her body felt empty before it filled with hatred and blind fury. Every single swear word she knew she threw at him in a scream. In a second, she'd rolled forward, expertly picking up her discarded swords in a single movement. This was the man who she'd fallen in love with, given herself to and then been discarded by.

He had destroyed her life.

This was Olivia's father.

***

This was a trick surely? That wasn't her? How could it be? The bastards were playing games. The shock was stopping him move! This was twisted! This was sick!

She shouted at him and it forced a reaction. 'Who are you?' he replied and two mouthed words later a spear appeared in his hands, anger filling his body.

This girl, the only girl he'd ever loved was here. In front of him. But how? The girl he had decided to throw away duty for, to change his destiny for. The girl who had been brutally murdered because of him was about to attack him.

***

'Who am I?' The thought exploded in her head, 'WHO AM I? The training pens of her youth had taught her to harness hatred in everything she did. They had prepared her to use it but not to let it take over. It did now. Her first blows flew in with such power and speed.

Neil blocked them with ease as he didn't look to counter. He needed time to think. He'd asked the question because the person before him was dead and if she was dead, who was attacking him?

He stepped back from the blows this time. 'Cassie?' He asked quietly.

It was the way he said it that stopped her, the swords lowered slightly, for a moment. Hatred started to rise again in her before he spoke again.

'You're alive,' not a question, a simple statement. Despite everything he smiled a small unsure smile.

'Of course, I am!' She spat, 'Not that you care!' Inside she winced, that was weak, she sounded like Olivia.

'Care?' he answered, 'I was told you were dead!' It was his turn to raise his voice, anger touching his words.

They circled each other but their weapons were down. Cassie felt overwhelmed, her anger was pushing her to attack but she was confused.

She remembered the words at her trial. 'The father has been offered a chance to see her but does not accept the unborn child is his. He has returned to his order.'

He was hurt. 'If you knew I was alive why didn't you look for me?' he shouted.

The anger made her react again, it was pure reflex and she used Magick to push him back. He hit the wall and instantly rolled to the left; her sword hit the wall a moment later.

It was all hatred for Cassie now, tears fell down her face as he blocked blow after blow.

He ducked another, just managing to get close and grab her arm as she tried to stab down into his shoulder. Their faces were inches away from each other. 'Cassie please,' he pleaded while forcing the sword to drop from her hand.

'You left me and Olivia! You left your daughter to rot!' she shouted.

'Daughter?' He asked, his arms dropped to his side, just before she headbutted him in the face. He hit the floor, unconscious.

The door crashed open, Galahad came through first followed by Tristan and Arthur.

She flew at them, Galahad moved quickly towards Neil. A flying kick from Cassie hit Tristan square in the chest knocking him and Arthur back through the door. She kicked the door closed and with a scream and a word of Magick, snapped the key and turned on Galahad with a snarl.

'You're dead.'

'Try it girl,' Galahad pointed his sword at her. He didn't know who she was, and he didn't care. All he knew was that she was trying to kill Neil.

A whisper and one of her swords disappeared, and a spear replaced it. She threw it. Galahad avoided it by a hair's breadth and moved to attack as the spear clattered against the wall behind him.

It was her turn to defend. Her initial fury faltered as she struggled to defend herself. She tried her Magick push to give her time, but he used his own and the blow passed through him, his ginger hair blowing as it did so.

She went at him again but this time her anger was mixed with fear and desperation. She hadn't fought anybody this talented, this deadly, in her life. He moved so fast for someone so big.

He parried another blow and before she could strike again, his fist hit her cheek sending her to the floor.

She went to jump up, but he was on her too fast, he grabbed her by the front of her tunic, lifted her and slammed her hard against the wall knocking the breath from her. She tried to spit in his face, but she didn't have the energy and it struck below his chin, a strand of it remained in her mouth. It was about to end, but all she felt was embarrassment because of the spit. Her feet were a foot off the air and as she tried to kick him weakly, he slammed her against the wall again. While he'd been calm throughout the fight, he now looked angry. She heard the banging against the door as he moved his hands around her neck.

The last thing Cassie saw as she was about to lose unconsciousness was Neil standing up behind the bearded man and then nothing.

Pain woke her. Jaw, neck, legs and head and then concern hit at the same time at the realisation that she was tied tight to a bed.

Calm.

She took a breath, the air making her throat sore, reminding her of what happened during the moments before losing consciousness. She remembered Neil and her heart began to beat faster. He'd been genuinely confused when she'd mentioned Olivia. She didn't understand. And then from the darkness, she heard...

'Olivia?'

She felt her heart expand so much it hurt and then it jumped as Neil stood out from the shadows at the back of the room. He came to the bed, his face impassive but she knew that face, had loved that face and knew that he was in pain. Her heart ached as she saw him without her anger and the pain grew as she remembered how she'd once felt about him.

'Her name is Olivia?' He asked.

Her wrists were tied together, as were her ankles while a leather strap covered her chest and arms. She tried to say yes but could only muster a croak after Galahad's attack, so nodded.

His face was still expressionless but then a single tear rolled down his cheek. When he spoke it was dull, without feeling. 'They told me you had killed yourself because of your shame.'

She shook her head and wanted to wipe the tear from his face, take that pain away. She was on the verge of tears herself. She tried to speak and then cleared her throat grimacing with pain. 'They told me that you abandoned me when you found out I was pregnant, that you were ashamed of me, that you thought I had tricked you.' She became angrier as she understand the lies they'd both been told.

'I didn't know,' Neil said quietly and calmly. Silence ensued and both understood that this natural break might be a chance to talk properly, without the anger and confusion that they still felt. Easier said than done when hate and loss had been at the centre of their young lives for years.

'Is that why you've come to kill me?' Neil asked, a big sentence in a small voice.

She laughed. 'You?'

'What?' he asked playfully, not with anger and she felt her heart lurch with love. The expression, THAT expression was the one that had broken through the barriers of her heart when they had been thrown together those years before. The first person that had made her – a Dark Mistress of such power and prospect – smile at something that wasn't cruel.

His expression changed; it was still soft but there was steel there. 'Who then?' A pause, then, 'Come on, Cass.'

He clenched his teeth to help him remain rigid because if he did not, he'd fall to the floor as broken as his heart. He felt yet another tear roll down his cheek, but he didn't cuff it. Any movement would break his concentration. He wanted to release her, for her to take him in her arms. She was the only person who made him feel like everything was going to be ok. He'd forgone his duty once and looking at his love...his former love, made him doubt if he wouldn't do it again but she was here for a reason and if it wasn't to kill him what was she here for? It was obvious but he wanted to hear it from her.

'Cass?'

She knew there were powerful Magick wards placed on this room. Because of her, because of what she could do. She could feel them, but it was nothing to what she was feeling in her soul. The love, anger, helplessness and confusion were so great that despite the wards, she could still feel her natural Magick, repressed for so long, growing inside her, pushing out. She wanted to scream, hit something but more than that Cassie Newton wanted Neil to hold her and do what he did best, give her hope. She didn't want to lie to him anymore, so she answered.

'Arthur,' she said.

He felt himself relax a little at the truth he already knew, 'I can't let you do that,' he said gently.

'It doesn't matter any more. I never wanted to do this anyway,' she said. Then, 'She is more like you than me.' It just came out; she didn't mean to say it.

'Not now, Cass,' he said, shaking his head.

'I'm sorry, but I'm here because of her.'

Neil's face hardened but he remained calm. 'You are a Dark Mistress, you don't need reasons.'

Cassie shook her head. 'I haven't been one since you left, since Olivia. I'm doing this for her. Please Neil, I feel stupid, untie me so we can speak properly. The Magick wards will still work, and my arms are still tied in case you feel scared?'

They laughed.

After Neil released her from her bondage, they sat on the bed and told each other everything that had happened until that moment. It hurt. Life had been stolen from them, time had been cruelly wrenched away but hours later, sitting closer and holding each other's hands, they understood that, now, they had been given more time and an opportunity to live the life that they had dared to dream of when they had first fallen so hard in love.

They kissed.

CHAPTER THIRTY-NINE
END'S BEGINNING

Dawn was breaking but the sun's summer rays seemed to struggle to make it over the hills and show themselves to the land. There was a chill in the air to remind all who were awake that, while summer was here, this was Wales and the land always pushed back. Down in the valleys below, mist snaked, sticking close to the ground, as if snuffling for food. It obscured the army that Arthur knew was there and, every so often, the mist would thin, and cooking fires could be seen, tiny dots that showed there was life, that there was bustle. The army of the Dark had started to stir.

He'd walked out from the fort just to feel the earth under his feet. After a minute, he sat down, slumped, leaning on his knees on the dew-damp ground of the slope below the fort. His eyes were puffy from little sleep. Worry was etched on his face as he stared into nothing, facing towards the throng in the valley. He sighed. This was it; this was the day it ended. They had done way beyond all their expectations. He was still alive and if he was still alive then there was hope, it was just that he didn't feel it.

So, after – what, countless lives? – this was the last. Had they been good lives? Wasn't part of this depression he'd been feeling these past few years a direct consequence of them all? Constant bloodshed, continual struggle against the Dark, and then death. It hadn't been death though had it? Because he and his warriors had always known they were coming back.

He shook his head angrily, trying to rid himself of these morbid thoughts, but he couldn't. Those times they'd died but hadn't really? It had still felt like death. He'd never got used to it but how many deaths would it have taken for him to do so? Another twenty? A hundred? How many more battles?

Battle? A word to summon the gods, conjuring up valour and glory and the nobility of the warrior. Battle. The stink of sweat and shit, the mewling, agonised cries of men begging for their mothers. And what if you actually lived? You still had to enter that cave eventually, losing people along the way. Rarely a chance to say goodbye to loved ones who you knew would be dead when you next returned.

'Stop,' Arthur said knowing that the depression was starting to strengthen its grip, and not wanting to venture further down the road of despair. The faces of the people he'd loved and who had left his life carouselled through his mind: lovers, friends and family.

'Stop what?' Arthur turned around to see the two remaining kings walking towards him. It was Adda who had spoken. He sat down heavily next to Arthur, rocking back with the effort, legs kicking up in the air before returning to the ground.

Arthur grunted, annoyed that his silence had been broken but glad his depression was silenced. Tommaltach sat next to him, lowering himself with a little more panache. No one said a word, they just looked out, taking in the army below but also the view as the sun gradually pushed itself further up into the sky.

After a short, comfortable silence, they all stretched their legs out, leaning back on their elbows.

'Beautiful, isn't it?' Arthur remarked.

No one answered but the other two nodded.

'Hell of a backdrop for the last scene,' Tommaltach commented.

'We haven't lost yet,' warned Adda.

They barely acknowledged Galahad as he joined them, sitting next to Tommaltach.

Tommaltach picked up a blade of grass and put it close to his face as if he hadn't seen one before. 'I know that but still... If this is it?'

'We've been in worse spots?' Adda asked, unsure.

Galahad sat up, rubbing his hands together. 'It feels different though. You all feel that?'

Tommaltach nodded slightly, 'Yup, everything has felt different for a while now. It does feel like an end,' he said.

'I have to admit that I have felt that too. A buzzing, like nothing will be the same again,' said Adda. He turned to Arthur, 'What about you?'

Arthur looked into the face of the big man next to him. He paused, then smiled sadly. 'I haven't felt anything for years Adda, nothing at all, nothing until the attack on the pub.'

He went silent again and faced down the slope, 'And since then I've felt alive.'

Adda hated all this serious talk. 'So you think we are going to win this? Another victory against the Dark for King Arthur?' he pushed.

Arthur's shoulders moved with a little chuckle, and then, still staring down the hill, he shook his head. 'No, I think this is it. I think I'm here to die for the last time.'

Adda didn't know what to say and was relieved when Tristan sat down next to him. They looked at each other and smiled. There was no need for quips, or insults. This moment was too big and too perfect for their usual back and forth.

Alexandra then sat next to Tristan, he took her hand and kissed it tenderly.

'Hiya,' this from Kimberley who was walking towards them with Mali and Caratacus who sat down just behind the main group.

Arthur nodded with warmth at Caratacus who smiled and threw an easy-going salute in return.

'How's Neil and the girl?' Arthur asked.

'Reacquainting,' Caratacus replied.

'They should have left last night. Gone to get their daughter and live their lives,' said Adda.

'We all have lives to live,' exclaimed Kimberley quietly. Mali turned to her and silently shook her head in warning.

Knowing that the Dark Mistress they'd fought on the bridge was here had opened up the recent wound of losing Gwenyvere. It had taken stern words from Arthur to stop them attacking her in the room she and Neil were in.

'I suggested it to him,' said Galahad, 'but he wouldn't hear of it. He said his place was here.'

'Better a living coward than a dead fool,' Tristan said bitterly.

Galahad smiled. 'You don't mean that.'

'I wish I did,' Tristan answered and squeezed Alexandra's hand once more.

Caratacus looked up, noticing for the first time, the swallows darting back and forth, chirping in ignorance – or maybe delight – at the death and desperation below.

Tristan noticed him watching them and looked up himself. 'Oh to be one of them,' he said.

Caratacus nodded, smiling and making a noise that seemed like a laugh, but that Tristan could tell wasn't. 'Are you OK my friend?' He asked and, from nowhere, Caratacus felt trapped and small and found himself too choked up to answer. He coughed to clear his tightened throat, to clear the blockage of grief, and bowed his chin to his chest in embarrassment. Tristan shuffled his backside over and put his arm around him, lowering his head to Caratacus's. 'You've done great, lad.'

Galahad, sitting on the slope in front of them, leaned further back, reached his hand out and squeezed Caratacus' foot. He was still staring, admiring the view but understood in that moment how this confused man may be feeling.

'Cub is right, Cati, you have done so well.'

Caratacus' head was still on his chest, but the movement of his shoulders showed he was sobbing, tears running down his face in a rictus of release. He cried for everything that had happened and everything he had done. He wept through fear and through exhaustion and the dread that if there was to be one more fight, he may be called on to kill again and he didn't know if he could do that.

How could he explain how he felt to these people, who had fought and killed for so long? Tristan hugged closer, Galahad squeezed tighter, and everybody had stopped talking. The wind had changed direction and for a small moment the noise of the army below was silenced so all that could be heard were the swallows above.

Tommy McKracken looked over and saw his Godson breaking and felt remorse at involving him.

'Long way from your wee shop,' he said with his full-on Norn Irish accent, matter of fact, but full of humour.

Caratacus could tell how it was meant and he nodded vigorously, hoping the movement would stop him breaking again.

Arthur broke in, 'Cati, I'm still not sure why you were sent to me but, regardless, I think we still have one fight left before the fort can take us to safety. You've done more than enough, and I thank you for it, I really do.'

Caratacus peeked up again and saw Arthur was looking directly at him. The King looked adamant. 'This isn't your fight, and you shouldn't have to die here. I want you to keep Excalibur and I want you to defend the young ones in the main hall. Even if we fail here, it'll be the last room they will come to, by the time they get to it the fort will be gone. Right Bellerophon?' The last sentence was directed at the ringlet haired King who had come to join them and was standing behind the group.

'Of course, Lord King, I have ten of my men stationed there now. Maybe I will join them,' he said, smiling.

'That's decided. Cati, you've done more than enough,' he repeated.

Embarrassed, Caratacus cuffed tears from his face and lifted his head, his eyes squinting at the light. He looked over at Arthur and gave his crooked smile. 'Nah,' he said with mock bravado, 'I'm a Magick bookseller, wielder of Excalibur, champion of Killer Pool, who called forth a goddess and saved King Arthur. Where else would the great Caratacus ap Neb be but battling a Dark god, his psychopathic children and forty or so thousand soldiers?'

There was a pause before everybody started laughing. Adda barked with an almost biblical guffaw which seemed to make the situation even funnier and within a few seconds they were all roaring with laughter.

Down the slope to the fields below, the Dark god that Caratacus had named, his three psychopathic, long-lived children and those thousands of killers stopped what they were doing as the soft summer breeze carried the noise of friendship, freedom and carefree laughter down the slopes to them and, in that moment, every single one of them felt doubt.

***

Cromh Du, devourer of souls, heard that laughter. Cromh Du, supreme being of the Dark, listened to the music of friendship rolling down the hill. Cromh Du, living god of chaos, heard their love and, worst of all for him, he felt it.

His hate and his cruelty were elemental so wouldn't it follow that something as pure as what came from those on the slope hurt him?

His head pounded. He wasn't used to feeling weak but that's what he'd felt from the moment he'd commanded the death of Arthur, weeks before. Gods did not have headaches or sore joints and more than all either of these, gods never felt doubt. What had happened? Was this his doing? Had he, by his own actions, turned Arthur into the very chosen one who could destroy him?

He'd arrived a short time before, already vexed because his children had forbidden him to travel through his Magick, stating that they could not afford any more lives to sacrifice for something a helicopter could do. The death of Arthur was all that mattered now but doubt assailed him again. Arthur should have died in the first attack, his men should all be dead. Well, all but one, and that wouldn't have to be for long. Two of the Three Kings still remained.

He knew little of the kings and cared less, but they brought about a sense of such blinding anger amongst his children.

He rarely spoke to any outside a small circle but when he did, the Three Kings were often brought up. They seemed to have been more of an obstacle to the plans of the Dark through the millennia than Arthur.

Now, in his command tent, Cromh Du sat on an elaborate throne. Before him stood the Morrigu: hunched Ceridwen, loathsome Badb on her shoulder, and next to her the scheming Dannan. They stood as they had done weeks before when they had told him of the danger to his plans, to his very existence.

He had known the Morrigu as the weavers. They worked at the loom of life, using their skills to create the tapestry. They could be lying bitches, but he knew they had told him the truth about the prophecy and what he needed to do. Sbut still he felt doubt and it made him angry.

'Kill Arthur and no one will defeat you! Deepen your breathing, Crippled God,' warned Ceridwen pointing her arthritic finger at him.

'Steel your cold, speeding heart, Lifebleeder,' said Dannan stepping from behind him.

'Don't shit your breeches, Empty One,' Badb's wings flapped as she teased. They were as old as him, they knew the names that mocked, the ones he hated, the ones that hit. The thought flashed through his mind. Crush her head, rip the other's throat out and violate the last.

It was replaced by another, but this thought wasn't his, it was them, all three united as one, and the pain made him drop from the throne to his knees. For a second, he was sure their voices were going to split his skull, it couldn't contain their voices, their power.

'MAKE YOUR MOVE. TAKE THE STEP. REACH OUT. DON'T THINK. YOU'RE A GOD, AREN'T YOU? MAKE THOUGHTS FLESH, DESTROY US, KILL US, TAKE US!'

He screamed again. God he may be, but the body he inhabited was mortal flesh and his scream tore his throat. The pain subsided and he looked up. The Morrigu were gone, replaced by the worried faces of his dark children as they rushed into the tent.

'It's time!' he shouted angrily.

***

'What are they building?' Asked Kimberley.

'Gallows,' replied Galahad.

'For hanging?'

'For hanging.'

'Who though? It's not big enough to hang us all.'

'I think we'll find out pretty soon.'

'I can hit that handsome man from here. One arrow and,' she made a dying noise, tongue protruding out.

'Go on then,' he smiled.

'No arrows left, only the Dark Girl has one left,' she said simply, shrugging, the Dark Girl being the name they had given Cassie.

'I thought the fort provided everything?'

Kimberley smiled. 'We used them all.'

It was mid-morning and every single person alive in the fort was now on the walls watching the action below. Instead of an attack, a few hundred warriors had made their way up the hill and gotten to work.

Just 300 metres from the fort, a large tent had been pitched in front of the entrance. As Kimberley had learnt, gallows were being constructed before their eyes. It was like an ant farm, busy, with people running back and forth. Caratacus pointed out the TV cameras to Arthur and Galahad.

'This is something new,' Galahad mused.

'I don't think it's good,' answered Arthur. 'Why don't they attack and finish us?'

'I honestly think they are scared,' said Galahad.

'Why? We've nothing left,' said Arthur, leaning heavily on the battlements.

'They don't know that. They didn't know we had a Magick fort, the help of a goddess and the dying power of a powerful druid,' answered Galahad.

Down in the valley, large TV screens were being pulled upright. The shouts of the troop's commanders could be heard as they marched thousands of soldiers and halted them in front of the screens.

***

One moment there was a large tent, the next it had faded into nothing. In its place was Cromh Du sitting on an elaborate throne, Cate, Shane and Killian looking resolute behind it. The throne was flanked by 3 red-garbed warriors, elite killing machines to guard a god. Behind them, two Dark mistresses.

In a semi-circle behind, encompassing them all, were the Generals and the leaders of the Dark. All arranged as if sitting for a portrait. To the left and right, television cameras faced the throne. The only movement were the various green, blue and pink skinned creatures involved in the filming. They bustled about with final preparations before disappearing to their prearranged positions. All but the floor manager, who looked to Caratacus like a 4-foot Hamster. She stood at the centre, bowed to Cromh Du, put her three fingered hand in the air counting down with each finger and the moment it reached one, she clicked her fingers and vanished.

Say what you want about evil incarnate, but they really can put on an impressive show.

From the fort you could see the giant screens flickering into life all over the valley. The first vision to fill them was a close-up of Cromh Du. A gasp of forty thousand could be heard as the forces of the Dark saw the face of a god. For many peoples of That World such as the dark elves, goblin and orc tribes, this wasn't a military leader or even a god, it was *their* god, it was their parents' god, their people's god. They had prayed to, left tribute to, and sacrificed to him, many in a shrine dedicated only to him in their dwellings. His worshippers dropped to the ground, followed by every single creature watching.

One or two started to shout his name. Others joined in, repeating it, over and over in unison, rising in volume.

'CROMH DU! CROMH DU!'

The god smiled as he heard his forces chant his name. The war leaders and generals behind the throne joined in. It went on for five minutes and it would have been longer had it not been for Cromh Du raising his arm. The chanting stopped and silence settled in the valley.

The chanting unsettled them all in the fort, all they could do was stand and listen.

Then Adda shouted, 'Who are you?' and the people on the wall broke into laughter again, the one shout breaking the spell of the chant in a flash.

Cromh Du lowered his hand and settled back on the throne, still smiling.

'Arthur ap Uther,' he announced grandly, his voice echoing from the large speakers positioned with the screens.

The army of the Dark heard the name of the man they despised and howled. Cromh Du chuckled to himself before raising his hand again to silence the multitude.

'Arthur ap Uther. Dark-Bane. I see you,' he said formally.

Arthur was no stranger to showing off. He picked up the cloak that he'd draped on the wall and swung it over his shoulders to fasten it. He was smiling and as the cloak settled, he caught Caratacus' eye and winked. He put one foot up on the battlement, looked at the view as if he was noticing the Dark forces for the first time, and then, in a voice that needed no microphone, shouted.

'Cromh Du, Dark God of chaos, Deathbringer, Soul Devourer,' he deliberately left a gap as he saw Cromh Du nod. He watched the Dark God inhale to speak, then spoke again.

'Maggot King, Foot Dragger, Imprisoned One.'

Cromh Du stood up fast, furious. On either side, swords appeared in the hands of his red uniformed bodyguards. The Dark mistresses placed their hands a foot apart, blue bolts of miniature lightning springing from palm to palm.

Cate, like her brothers, stood still. 'He wants anger,' she said, not directly to Cromh Du but loud enough so he could hear.

He did and just like she intended, it stopped him flying into a rage. 'Dear Arthur,' he said mockingly. He walked forward as if his standing up had been deliberate and not in reaction to the Once and Future king's taunt. 'Firstly, would you care to give the cameras a wave? Not only is your timely and pathetic end being broadcast to my loyal warriors whom you see aligned before you, but also tuning in are the forces of the Dark in both Worlds. It seems your death is compulsory viewing.'

He smiled, shook his head and addressed the Fort's defenders. 'You have all fought bravely, and against all odds, you live. And while you have been brave, you have also been fortunate. So far, you have faced but a fraction of my army but now they are all here. You are what? A hundred? Your druid king is dead. You have no more goddesses to help you. One word from me and we will sweep you away,' he used every part of the space in front of his throne, the cameras changing shot for the literal army of viewers.

His expression changed to a taunting surprise, 'Oh, do you think your little castle will disappear before then?' He shook his head dramatically. 'No, I can tear your toy fort down inch by inch in 45 minutes.'

Arthur still posing on the wall kept his face impassive as they all realised that their enemy knew what they were holding out for.

Cromh Du continued, 'Did you think that I did not know about your one and only way out of this alive? However, there is another way,' he paused, 'Arthur, surrender yourself to me and I spare the fort, your friends and the children.'

He stopped pacing and shouted, 'You have one minute.' The screens went dead and the chants of 'Cromh Du' began again as he stalked back to his throne and sat down. No one knew that his proximity to Arthur was weakening him. The king was the threat that he'd been warned about, and he had to stop him before he weakened further. That strange feeling of doubt hit him again and he growled softly in anger.

'Father?' Killian had heard it.

He forced a smile, 'Nothing my son, I am just excited about what is to come.'

***

The screens came back on and the chants stopped.

'Your answer Arthur ap Uther?' Cromh Du asked.

Thousands of eyes stared at the close-up of their enemy.

'I think I'll pass,' Arthur answered conversationally.

Unable to hear, Cromh Du's forehead furrowed. He turned to his minions. 'What did he say?'

Cate stepped forward, snapped her fingers at the producer. 'Send up a microphone to that fat fool. Now!'

Time wasting was almost a superpower to Caratacus, and it had been his idea to stall for time by getting Arthur to speak softly. A ladder was brought forward and one of the production team climbed the ladder and handed the microphone to Arthur who smiled and thanked him.

Arthur tapped the microphone. 'Hello? Hello? Is this on?'

Cromh Du responded, 'Speak, Arthur. We can hear you. Have you made yo…'

'Helloooo? Can you hear me?' Arthur asked his voice bellowing from the speakers.

'We can hear you…'

'Hello…'

'SPEAK!' Cromh Du shouted, losing his composure, his anger growing as he heard laughter from the walls again.

'Calm down, Dark One, you don't want to give your stolen body a heart attack,' Arthur responded glibly, reminding everyone that Cromh Du's body was as mortal as theirs. Arthur continued, 'I hear you and I decline your offer. Even one step backwards against darkness is one too far. Instead, I give you an ultimatum. Take your armies back to That World, they do not belong here. Stop your destruction and then, in due course, let us meet in battle, just me and you. I do not trust you. If I surrender, you'll slaughter all here. You are a worm.'

He expected such talk from the weavers, but Cromh Du had not been spoken to like that by a mortal for millennia. Pent up rage at feeling weak and having to deal with this situation with guile and not mass murder was too much.

'YOU DARE!' He might have a mortal body but he still had the power of a god. His rage blasted from him, knocking some of the defenders of the fort from their feet, his evil shaking them. Their newly found confidence disintegrated in a flash.

Caratacus shook his head as a wave of nausea hit him. He could feel the Magick reacting in his stomach, as if wanting to do something, pushing him to act but all he could do was stare down from the walls.

Cromh Du didn't know how his rage had affected the people on the wall, nor did he care. He stormed forward, way past the chalk marks that had been drawn on the floor for the cameras. He pointed up, 'YOU DARE TALK TO ME LIKE THAT? YOU WILL REGRET THAT, KING OF ANTS!'

He spun around and barked at the Dark Mistresses. 'Bring them out.'

Within moments, two people were being led out. One was tall, one seemed like a child, both had hessian sacks on their heads with their hands tied in front of them. They were taken on to the wooden stage of the gallows.

Angry murmurs came from the fort, heads dropped in expectation of what was to come.

Cromh Du looked up. 'Where are your funny comments now, Fat King? Speak!' He leapt onto the stage, placed the noose around the neck of the tallest, tightened it a bit and then pulled off the hood, 'Haven't you anything to say to Cai ap Cynyr?'

Most of the defenders didn't know who the man was but they knew immediately that he was important by the reaction of the leaders of the fort. Of those who knew him, the heads of Arthur, Galahad and Tommaltach dropped as if resigned to the worse. Caratacus, Neil and Adda shook their heads, but it hit Tristan. Other than Bedwyr it was only Tristan who could really be called close to Cai. They were family, and just like family, there were members they could spend days with and there were members they wanted to punch in the face, twice.

Tristan leaned on the wall shouting in shock in the language of their youth, 'Cai! Don't panic! We'll get you out of this.' He looked across at Galahad, 'Save him Gal,' he pleaded. 'I can't… Not one more of us.'

Galahad cut the distance between them in a step and grabbed him. 'Hey Cub, not now,' he shushed Tristan who was about to speak. 'We have to keep our heads.'

'Silence, Arthur?' Cromh Du laughed and was joined in genuine laughter by all behind.

Arthur lifted the microphone to his mouth. 'Speak your terms, Crippled God,' he said bitterly.

Cromh Du ignored the insult. 'Drag your fat carcass from the fort and prostrate yourself before me. In return, I will return Cai ap Cynyr.'

'What of the other person?' Shouted Arthur, his heart sinking.

Cromh Du laughed again. 'Of course, How could I forget?' He walked to the end of the stage where Killian had placed himself and handed over the microphone. Up until that point Cassie had stood unmoved and unperturbed at what was happening.

Even seeing the Dark Mistresses only stirred anger but that one action of the microphone being passed to Killian made her stomach flip, dread creeping into her soul and she gripped Neil's hand tight.

'Are you ok?' he asked.

She didn't answer. She just stared at the wooden gallows.

Killian looked directly at her and all blood left her face.

'Good morning, Cassie. I see you decided to forgo the little task I set you,' he indicated to Arthur further down the battlements. 'You always were a stubborn little whore. But I did warn you there'd be consequences.'

He turned and smiled at the camera and laughter came from the armies watching on the big screen. Killian continued,

'I warned you. You've seen my election posters! It's there in black and white! I am a man of my word!' And, without even thinking, he looked directly into the camera and winked. 'Remove the hood.'

You may have guessed that it was Olivia under that sack. It was lifted off and there stood the young girl, her face already red from crying.

Cassie crumbled, the pain in her heart so large she thought it would explode and the only thing stopping it, was releasing it slowly to the universe through the mad keening noise coming from deep within her. I have witnessed, I have told stories. I have been there for the beginnings of greatness and the end of empires. But then, right then, I wanted to drop down from the fort's walls where I was watching, get onto the gallows, take Olivia Newton in my arms and make everything ok.

'No!' Screamed Neil as he realised who the young girl was. A whispered word, and his sword appeared in his hand. He vaulted the wall without a thought.

He was caught by Galahad and Tristan and hauled back over to safety. He struggled while they held him tight. 'Neil!' Galahad said, his face right up to the young knight's. 'Let Arthur do what he has to, I promise she'll be safe. See to Cassie,' he said, noticing that the girl was on her hands and knees, her breathing shallow, spit dangling from her mouth in a silent scream.

Arthur shouted down forgetting to use the microphone but not needing it, 'Release them now and I will come to you.'

'You do not dictate to me, worm. The terms have changed. I don't want just you, I want what remains of your pathetic warriors. Who is there? I see Galahad but who else? I can see the flames of your auras. I see yours Tristan of Cernow! But there is another I do not know. Have you been recruiting, Fat King? Come out, new warrior. Name yourself and die with Arthur.'

Neil, still cradling and rocking Cassie heard what was said. He gently kissed her forehead and stood up.

'No please don't. Don't go,' she pleaded, gripping onto his sleeve.

'I have to, Cass. I have to get our daughter back.' Saying the word daughter made him pause. He went on one knee, looking into her eyes, willing her to understand, 'When you get her, get away from here, go and see my mother, she can help you. She has my money. Don't tell her I'm dead, tell her I love her and show her her granddaughter.' They were crying, forehead to forehead. She didn't speak but answered with a nod and a strangled sob. He wiped his eyes and stood, his face impassive.

'I am here,' he shouted, 'now release my daughter.'

Cromh Du shrugged, 'I have no need for an ant. I want the last warrior. Step forward, scum of Arthur! I see your aura. Do not waste my time or Cai and the brat will be doing the rope dance.'

Arthur shouted, 'Only three of us remain. You see us here. Enough! We are on our way.'

Cromh Du sneered, 'I am not a fool, Arthur ap Uther. Your auras betray members of your order. I can SEE your souls, they are like fire. I want you three before me on your knees and I want him.'

Arthur followed the Dark Lord's finger, they all did.

It rested on Caratacus Lewis.

He looked over at Arthur. 'Me?' he said pointing at himself.

Arthur understood and his shoulders slumped. He nodded and mouthed, 'I'm sorry,' understanding that by agreeing to the dying request of Piogerix, Caratacus was now one of them.

'I can go instead,' Tommaltach said but he knew it was an empty offer. He clapped Caratacus on the arm, pathetically asking, 'you ok?'

Caratacus looked his godfather in the eye. 'Yep,' he nodded. It was a strange thing because he actually was. No fear, no dread. He felt utterly fine.

Arthur smiled at Caratacus and brought him into a hug. 'Stay behind us,' he said before embracing Galahad and Tristan. Adda and Tommaltach soon joined them.

'Hurry up, Arthur King, or I may change my mind and despatch one of my gifts,' came the gleeful voice of Cromh Du.

'I am sorry, Lord King,' cried Neil who came to stand in front of the man he'd promised to protect.

Cassie pushed passed her lover and spoke to the man she had promised to kill. 'Please get my daughter back safe. I'll never forget you for this, never. I'm sorry for everything,' she broke down.

He hugged her briefly and then to them both. 'When she's safe and this fort takes you away, go and forget the life of duty and find happiness.' He walked off, then stopped and turned. 'Don't forget me?' he asked simply.

Neil couldn't answer, he just shook his head while Cassie lifted her chin. 'Never,' she said and Arthur, Galahad, and Tristan from the depths of time and myth, and a book seller from Twickenham went to face a god, rescue their friend, save a little girl, and then die.

CHAPTER FORTY

AN END

The moment the gate opened, and the four men stepped out, the army of the Dark roared. Revenge was coming. Smiles grew on the faces of Cate, Killian and Shane. This was it. The plans they had put in place after the second World War were coming to fruition. Killian and Cate held hands without realising they were doing so; the anticipation was almost sexual. Shane was making a noise; this was definitely sexual for him but, at the back of his mind was the determination that once Arthur was gone and Cromh Du master was happy, he was going to make every single one of the army behind him break the fort and drag Adda and Tommaltach out in chains.

The warriors stopped ten metres before Cromh Du who bowed low in mockery, the noise from the crowd getting louder.

'On your knees,' he ordered.

'Release Cai and the child,' Arthur replied.

Cromh Du nodded at the Dark Mistresses who touched the thick ropes around the prisoner's wrists. They disappeared and both rubbed away the pain. Olivia started crying again.

Cromh Du gently grabbed her chin. 'Shh, little one, you will see Mummy and Daddy very soon.' He looked over at the four, 'but first you get down on your knees.'

Cai took Olivia's hands and walked slowly towards Arthur and the men.

Cromh du pointed and, in his hand, a flaming spear appeared. 'I said get on your knees.' His eyes narrowed.

Resigned, they lowered themselves to the floor while two of the red garbed warriors carrying large axes moved to stand behind them.

Cai walked over to Arthur, slumping to his knees in front of him, letting go of Olivia's hand.

'Take her to the Fort, Cai,' Arthur said with a reassuring smile, 'Everything is going to be ok.'

Cai looked away; his friends took it to be embarrassment. He was proud, his capture must have hurt. He looked at Arthur.

'I'm sorry,' he said.

'Don't be…' Arthur's smile turned to surprise as Cai plunged a dagger into his chest, screaming, 'I can't die! I didn't want to die!'

Arthur fell to the ground, shock replaced by sadness before exhaling his last breath. Galahad and Tristan screamed in despair while Caratacus stared in shock at what was happening.

Olivia screamed and ran to Caratacus who was the closest. She hung on to his neck for dear life.

Cai, his face in pain got up and, still facing his friends, stumbled back a step as Cromh Du walked towards his prisoners. 'Oh dear,' the god put his lip out, 'is King Arthur dead? Like I told you, not one of my men would hurt you. But then, Cai is one of yours. Cai?'

The warrior looked over, pain and hate in his eyes.

'Heel.'

'You bastard,' shouted Galahad 'Why?'

Cromh du smiled sibilantly, 'It's quite the sad story. Your old friend became very scared when he believed that this was to be his last life. He's petrified of the dark of nothing. So he came to me. And, for the simple gift of revealing the whereabouts of you all, I offered him immortality.'

Cai looked at his sword brothers, a pleading madness shining in his eyes. 'I didn't want to die! I can't face a forever of darkness!'

Cromh Du looked at a camera. 'It is over!' he bellowed, to renewed cheers.

In that moment, both Tristan and Galahad moved with purpose. However, before Tristan could call his sword, he was knocked senseless by the axe-wielding warrior behind him.

Galahad, calm anguish on his face, moved swiftly, called his sword and in a heartbeat killed both his captor and the guard who had knocked out Tristan. He twisted around to face Cai who was still standing pathetically in front of Cromh Du.

'Why?' he spat and when Cai didn't answer, he rushed forward, screaming, before thrusting his sword into Cai's chest, both of them dropping to their knees.

Galahad was about to ask again when one, then two, then three arrows from the Dark Mistresses bit deep into his body, his eyes opening wide in shock and pain. Cai stood slowly, never taking his eyes from Galahad, his face also in pain, and calmly pulled the sword from his body, dropping it to the floor. 'Please forgive me Gal.'

Galahad stared at the man he'd counted a brother. 'No,' he said and tumbled to his side and died.

Cromh Du's smile faltered. Arthur's death was meant to change everything, to give him his power back, but he still felt that threat, he still felt like everything was temporary. He roared in anger, and the crowd, taking it as a victory scream, added their voices. Maybe they all had to die for him to live? In an effortless single movement, he swung the spear, the flaming tip cutting through the neck of an unexpecting Cai. As the body hit the floor, Cromh Du kicked the body gently, throwing his spear to the ground. 'Weak fool,' he said before turning to a barely conscious Tristan and a dumbstruck Caratacus, still holding the little girl.

He felt the power and exhilaration of killing Cai run through him, but it still wasn't enough. Time for this to end. He gestured to his guards, 'Kill them.'

Tristan, still stunned, struggled to rise but slumped to the ground. Caratacus had been frozen through fear since Olivia had come into his arms but it wasn't terror he was feeling now; it was anger. He felt a furnace deep in the centre of his soul. 'Kill them,' he heard, and his eyes blazed white with power.

'No,' was all he said.

He went rigid, his head back and mouth open in a silent scream. A wave of power flew out from him and Olivia, knocking everyone around off their feet.

Caratacus recovered quickly, looked around and seeing the path was clear to the fort, pushed Olivia towards it, 'Run!' He shouted.

Olivia seemed to wake from a sleep, her eyes growing large, before breaking and running. The fort's gate was already open, her mother amongst a group of the defenders screaming her name until she was safe in her arms.

Tristan finally got to his feet. His sword called and groggily he moved in front of Caratacus.

The Dark that faced them, drew, or called their weapons and slowly approached the last two warriors of Arthur.

Behind his people, Cromh Du struggled to his feet, aware that the cameras had caught him hitting the floor.

'Hold!' Cromh Du bellowed. He was surrounded by his children, the leaders of his armies and his religion, and an army of thousands; he could feel their confusion, their doubt and their fear. Would the hundreds of thousands watching on screens feel the same way? He could feel hope emanate from the fort, the saving of that girl and the scene of these final two facing him was creating something that tore at him. He had to do something to reassure the Dark.

He looked into the camera, his voice echoing out from the speakers, 'These are the last two warriors of Arthur. Once they are dead, we will have the Worlds in our grasp. I am giving you what I promised. Too long we have hidden, but no more! Let the powerful reign. The time of Arthur is over!' he bellowed to his worshippers, a giant sword appearing in his right hand.

Caratacus was standing up next to Tristan. 'We are about to move!' he heard Bellerophon shout to them from the battlements.

Cromh Du strode forward, smiling and twirling his battle sword. The chants of 'Cromh Du' started again and he started to prowl, buoyed by the support.

'Call Excalibur,' Tristan shouted to Caratacus as he edged forward.

He hadn't even considered it. He remembered his words, felt the markings on his hand and the mighty Excalibur appeared in his hand. He needed it immediately as the Dark god back-handed Tristan to the ground and aimed his sword at Caratacus's head. He looked like a child at play as he barely parried it away. The feeling in his stomach moved again and Cromh Du shifted back as if punched. His eyes widened. 'Who are you, boy?'

'No one,' Caratacus spat as Cromh Du moved to block the blow that had come from a recovered Tristan. He did so with ease and quickly stabbed at the side of Tristan and watched the young-looking warrior fall to the floor.

'NO!' Shouted Caratacus and another blow flew from him as his eyes again blazed white. Cromh Du didn't fall this time, but he felt shaken, and he felt weaker. He paused, trying to gain his breath.

It was pause enough for Caratacus to get down on one knee before Tristan. Blood bubbled from his mouth, but when looked up he saw his friend and smiled. 'Cati,' he coughed, 'I don't think we are going to make it, but we have to stall him long enough.'

'Don't die.'

'I don't want to,' he winced before staring at the approaching Cromh Du. 'Time to fight Cati.'

'Time to die,' Cromh du smiled and swung.

It was nearly over. Throughout this tale I have talked of moments, of friendship, of worry, of hope and this was a moment. As the Dark One's sword came down in a massive arc, Caratacus swung Excalibur up. He did it with all the righteous anger that one might expect after he'd witnesses the deaths of people he had grown to love.

The blades met.

The noise was a crack; one that could split time itself. Every face watching turned away and when they looked back it was to see a shocked Cromh Du, broken sword in hand, standing over Caratacus who lay on his back on the floor, Excalibur in two pieces beside him.

There was no smiling from the Dark God, he was panting, and he was in pain. How could that be? Was this no one the Chosen One? He tossed away his broken weapon with a snarl and fell to his knees on top of Arthur's final warrior putting his hands around his throat.

Let the fort go, all that mattered was the death of this one and the return of his power.

Caratacus felt the giant hands of Cromh Du grip his neck, he was going to die and in panic and anger and in desperation he shouted at the universe, 'No!'

And everything stopped.

Cromh Du's growl of anger ceased though his look of hatred remained, and the noise of thousands of warriors down the hill and on the walls of the fort disappeared.

The silence was shattered by the flapping of wings and, out of the corner of his eye, a crow landed by the side of his head and gently tapped him with its beak.

'Badb? Help me!' he croaked.

'That's why we are here, my Darling,' said Dannan lying on her belly, her face inches from his on other side from Badb.

'We have frozen time to speak to you.' Ceridwen's head peeked over Cromh Du's shoulder.

'Then why am I feeling his fingers getting tighter?' Caratacus squeaked, struggling again to break free.

Dannan gently brushed his cheek. 'He's a god, we cannot stop time for him, but we can slow him down a little.'

As if he was listening Caratacus saw Cromh Du's eyes very slowly closed in a blink while his fingers continued to tighten, 'Help me!' Caratacus pleaded again.

'We are here to help the Chosen One,' said Dannan before daintily touching his nose. 'You,' she added.

'You,' Badb tapped his head.

Ceridwen moved away and out of his line of sight, but he could still hear her rasping voice. 'Those who were interested took the prophecy to mean that only Arthur could stop the victory of Cromh Du, but they didn't hear the prophecy, didn't feel it. It said that after Arthur was dead, no one could kill Cromh Du. And it's true. You can. You're no one.'

'Really? Now?' He said sarcastically, despite slowly losing consciousness. Cromh Du was listening as well, his face slowly changing, the start of a snarling smile slowly beginning to appear, and his fingers still tightened.

'Hel…p…' Caratacus' vision began to swim as his breathing shortened, feeling Cromh Du's knees press down on his arms.

'Your prize my love,' Dannan said.

'Call it,' squawked Badb.

'What?' Cried Caratacus.

'You defeated the Grey Knight, Caratacus ap Neb. You have the prize. Now feel your Magick and say the words,' urged Ceridwen as realisation hit Caratacus. Pilkas!

'Now, with that, and your skill, you could beat anyone.'

'Call it!' This time the Morrigu spoke as one, but it was tinged with panic and that spurred on Caratacus as his vision swam. The pressure on his windpipe increased and Cromh Du's grin had formed, malicious and full of glee. He felt the Magick expand in his stomach, and he spoke the words told to him by Pilkas days ago.

'Goodbye, Caratacus ap Neb,' The Morrigu said, as the final word tumbled from his mouth and time began to move.

There was limited space for the pool cue to appear but appear it did, ramming up through the chin, grin, and brain of Cromh Du. No time for shock, for alarm, for fear or even a pithy comment just fast and all obliterating death. The body of Cromh Du, his eyes wide, died.

And, as it should at the end of a god, the skies darkened, the ground moved, the earth split.

Caratacus shoved the body of Cromh Du away from him and managed to stand. He stood, breathing heavily, shaking uncontrollably, and covered from the neck down in the blood of a Dark god.

In that moment, it was as if a cup of understanding had been poured into him. He was the son of prophecy; he was the one that was to stop the Dark, and he had. And now he was going to die. He stood above a groaning Tristan and before him stood 3 remaining malevolent demi-Gods and thousands of warriors who, at that moment were staring in shock at a TV picture of a man who had killed their father.

'Shit,' he said.

The Three couldn't believe what they had seen. It was meant to be their final victory but instead they watched their dead father hit the ground, 'NO!' screamed Cate.

From the fort Caratacus heard the voice of Bellerophon, 'Run!' And just as he was about to, the earth shook again knocking all before the tent to the floor. The dark clouds fizzed with power. Small lightning strikes peppered the area around the body of Cromh du scattering people in acts of self-preservation.

It gave Caratacus the chance he needed, and he began to drag Tristan to safety until he realised that dragging a person was really hard. 'Can you walk at all?' he asked in exasperation.

Even here, at the end, Tristan laughed, 'I'll try my best.'

The ground continued to shake. A crack in the earth formed outwards from the body of Cromh Du, the wooden stage that held the gallows collapsed, cameras and screens fell, warriors panicked.

Killian was the first on his feet. He ran to a spear, dropped in the chaos, and aimed it at the retreating back of Caratacus. He knew it was paltry revenge, but he had to do something. But before he could loose his vengeance, an arrow smacked into his chest, dropping him to his knees, his hands weakly fumbling to remove it. Just before losing consciousness, he looked up to see Cassie Newton throw down a bow.

The fort was beginning to fade as Caratacus fell through the doors with Tristan on his shoulders. He felt the shudder and the fort moved.

THE BEGINNING

Darkness. Strange how it sounds, but this was familiar darkness. Maybe it was the smell or maybe it was that cold feeling on his back.

Arthur was back in the cave.

He recognised the groans and exclamations of his warriors as realisation hit them.

Arthur, already feeling his youth sat up on his slab, swinging his legs off the side. He wiped his face. 'So, it wasn't our last life?' he said to himself.

A voice close by, echoed in that dark.

'No,' said Merlin. 'This one is.'

ACKNOWLEDGEMENTS

Fishguard, Caerleon, Trefdraeth and Urbania are the places that produce the people that built and continue to build the foundations of me and the story. It's been written in various establishments and thanks goes to the team in Coffiology, Beavo's gang at the Village Bakery, and especially Alessandro and all of the staff, past and present at the Snug in Caerleon, Cresswell's Café in Fishguard, the Coopers of Cnapan in Trefdraeth and not forgetting Pistolas and Lila Cafe in Urbania. Huge thanks to Pip and Andrew in Gales winebar, Llangollen (the oldest in Wales), for drink, food, bed, new people and their friendship.

Dunc, Jen, Mitch, Lloydy, and Elin, who were the first to enter This and That world and it wouldn't be as good without you.

More? Cer for the belief, Smiley for the push to do it and Nick for always talking about when the novel would be finished not if, and for always being my back up.

Alwyn Talbot for the cover, look at it, it's bloody great.

Alis Hawkins has been more than a mentor and a brilliant friend, she has shaped this story, the way I write and has cut the F word from it by a 1000. Read her books they're as amazing as she is.

And finally my family, Mam, Dad, my clan be they Mathias, Davies, Wias, Frost, Hughes, Coop, Griffiths, Brancorsini, Dalton, Hansen, real or unofficial Godchildren or mighty LC.

WHAT DID YOU THINK OF
THE ONCE AND FUTURE, NOW

A big thank you for purchasing this book. It means a lot that you chose this book specifically from such a wide range on offer. I do hope you enjoyed it.

Book reviews are incredibly important for an author. All feedback helps them improve their writing for future projects and for developing this edition. If you are able to spare a few minutes to post a review on Amazon, that would be much appreciated.

Printed in Great Britain
by Amazon